STAR TREK®

BOLDLY GO

written by
Mike Johnson

issues #7-9 written with
Ryan Parrott

issues #7-8 & 11-12 art by
Megan Levens

issues #9-10 art by
Tony Shasteen

Special thanks to Risa Kessler and John Van Citters of CBS Consumer Products for their invaluable assistance.

For international rights, contact licensing@idwpublishing.com

ISBN: 978-1-68405-103-8

21 20 19 18 1 2 3 4

IDW®
www.IDWPUBLISHING.com

Ted Adams, CEO & Publisher • **Greg Goldstein**, President & COO • **Robbie Robbins**, EVP/Sr. Graphic Artist • **Chris Ryall,** Chief Creative Officer • **David Hedgecock**, Editor-in-Chief • **Laurie Windrow**, Senior Vice President of Sales & Marketing • **Matthew Ruzicka**, CPA, Chief Financial Officer • **Lorelei Bunjes**, VP of Digital Services • **Jerry Bennington**, VP of New Product Development

Facebook: **facebook.com/idwpublishing** • Twitter: **@idwpublishing** • YouTube: **youtube.com/idwpublishing**
Tumblr: **tumblr.idwpublishing.com** • Instagram: **instagram.com/idwpublishing**

Originally published as STAR TREK: BOLDLY GO issues #7–12.

issues #7-8 colors by
Sarah Stern

issues #11-12 colors by
Marissa Louise

issues #9-10 colors by
J.D. Mettler

letters by
AndWorld Design

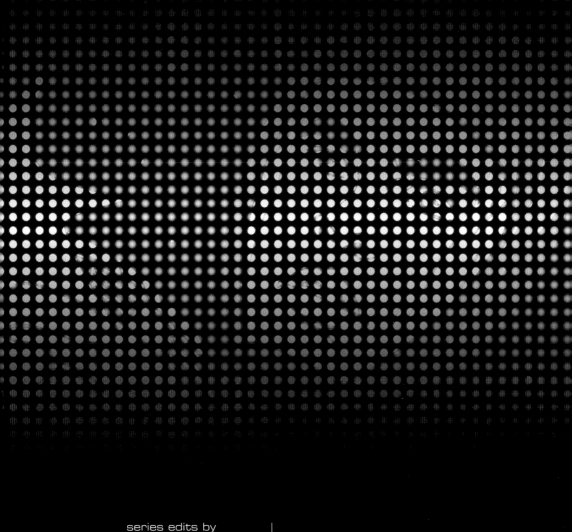

series edits by
Sarah Gaydos

cover by
George Caltsoudas

series assistant edits by
Chase Marotz

collection edits by
**Justin Eisinger
& Alonzo Simon**

publisher
Ted Adams

collection design by
Shawn Lee

star trek created by
Gene Roddenberry

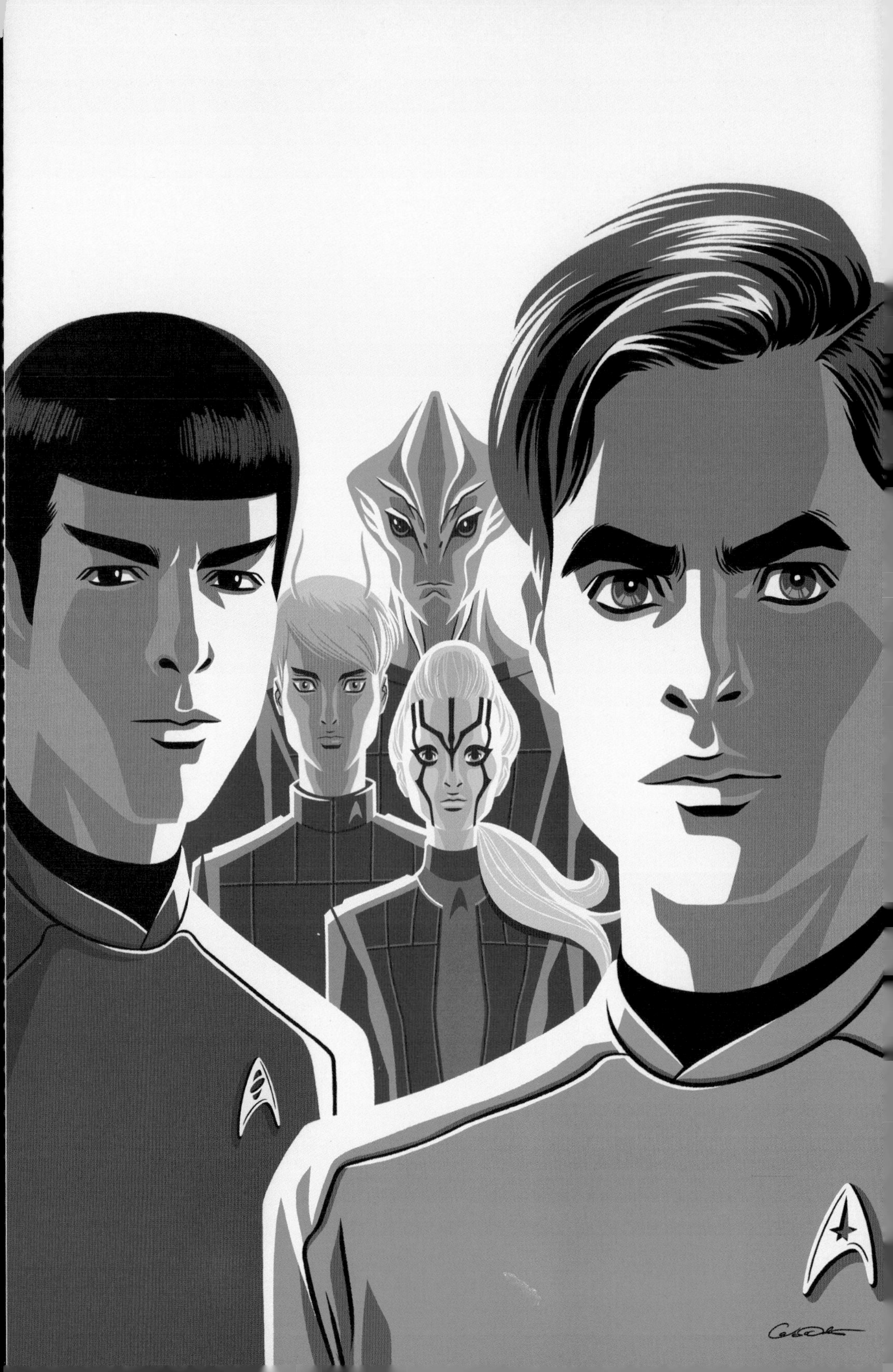

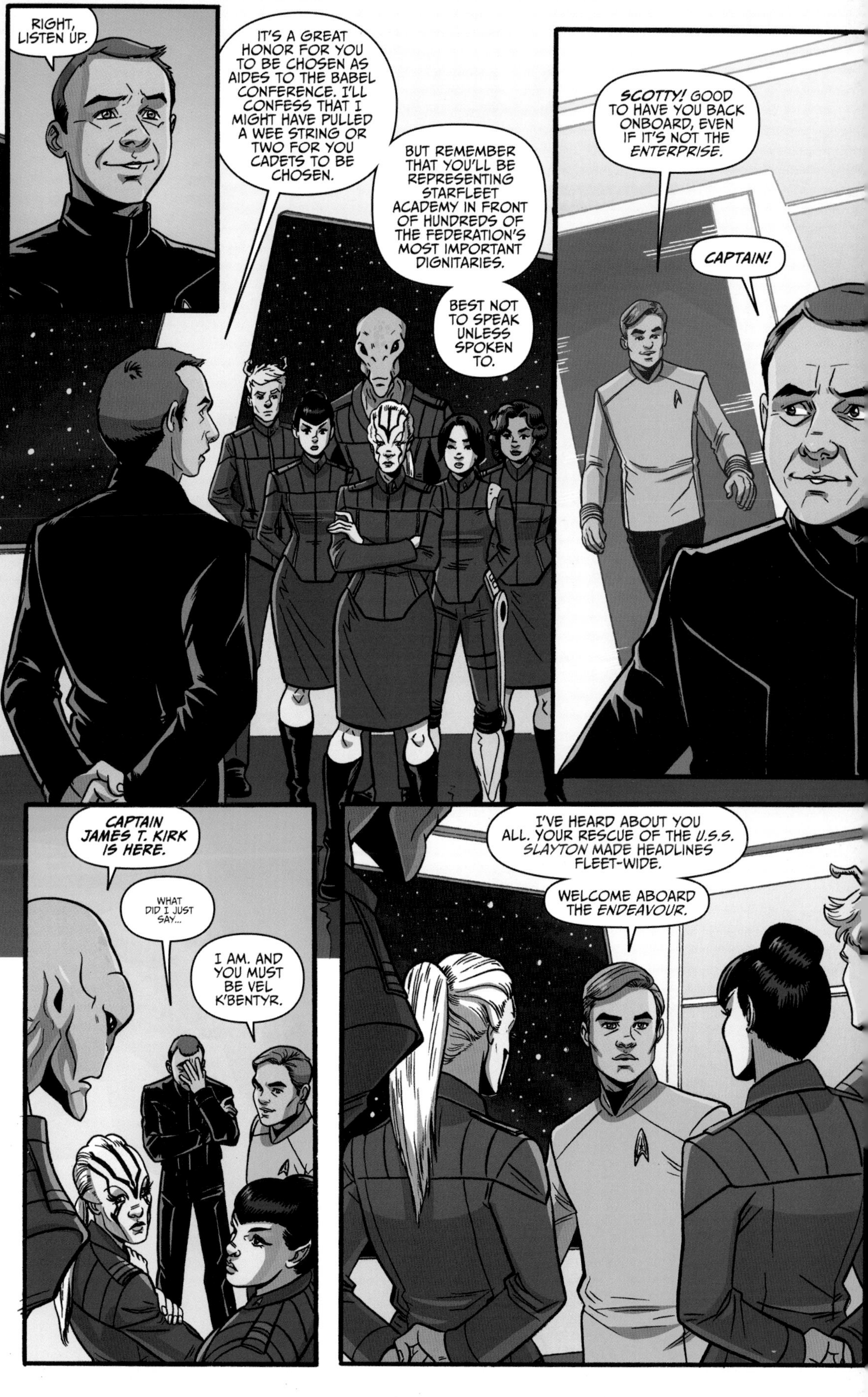
RIGHT, LISTEN UP.
IT'S A GREAT HONOR FOR YOU TO BE CHOSEN AS AIDES TO THE BABEL CONFERENCE. I'LL CONFESS THAT I MIGHT HAVE PULLED A WEE STRING OR TWO FOR YOU CADETS TO BE CHOSEN.
BUT REMEMBER THAT YOU'LL BE REPRESENTING STARFLEET ACADEMY IN FRONT OF HUNDREDS OF THE FEDERATION'S MOST IMPORTANT DIGNITARIES.
BEST NOT TO SPEAK UNLESS SPOKEN TO.
SCOTTY! GOOD TO HAVE YOU BACK ONBOARD, EVEN IF IT'S NOT THE ENTERPRISE.
CAPTAIN!
CAPTAIN JAMES T. KIRK IS HERE.
WHAT DID I JUST SAY...
I AM. AND YOU MUST BE VEL K'BENTYR.
I'VE HEARD ABOUT YOU ALL. YOUR RESCUE OF THE U.S.S. SLAYTON MADE HEADLINES FLEET-WIDE.
WELCOME ABOARD THE ENDEAVOUR.

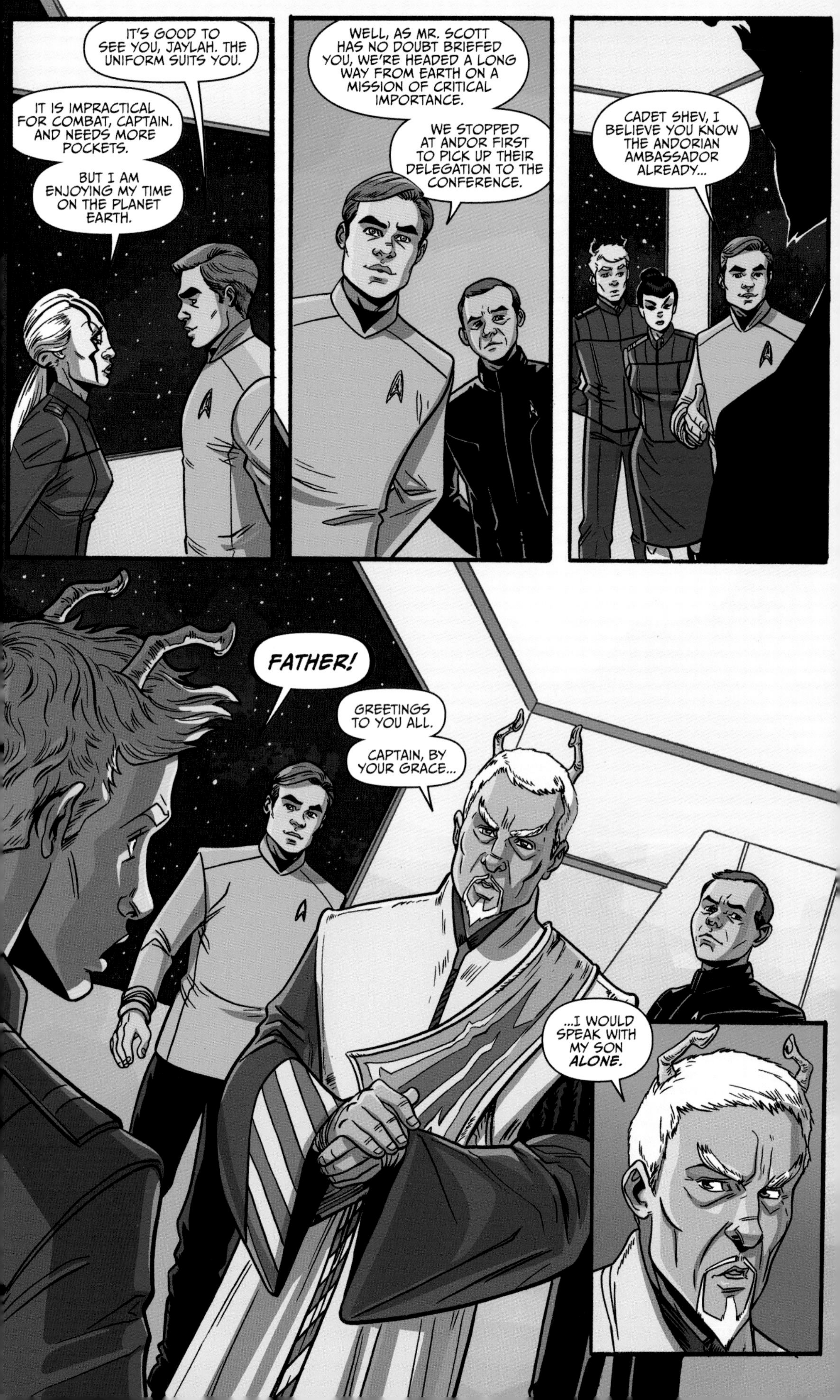
IT'S GOOD TO SEE YOU, JAYLAH. THE UNIFORM SUITS YOU.
IT IS IMPRACTICAL FOR COMBAT, CAPTAIN. AND NEEDS MORE POCKETS.
BUT I AM ENJOYING MY TIME ON THE PLANET EARTH.
WELL, AS MR. SCOTT HAS NO DOUBT BRIEFED YOU, WE'RE HEADED A LONG WAY FROM EARTH ON A MISSION OF CRITICAL IMPORTANCE.
WE STOPPED AT ANDOR FIRST TO PICK UP THEIR DELEGATION TO THE CONFERENCE.
CADET SHEV, I BELIEVE YOU KNOW THE ANDORIAN AMBASSADOR ALREADY...
FATHER!
GREETINGS TO YOU ALL.
CAPTAIN, BY YOUR GRACE...
...I WOULD SPEAK WITH MY SON ALONE.

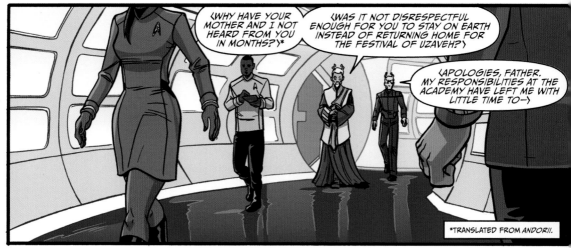

⟨WHY HAVE YOUR MOTHER AND I NOT HEARD FROM YOU IN MONTHS?⟩*

⟨WAS IT NOT DISRESPECTFUL ENOUGH FOR YOU TO STAY ON EARTH INSTEAD OF RETURNING HOME FOR THE FESTIVAL OF UZAVEH?⟩

⟨APOLOGIES, FATHER. MY RESPONSIBILITIES AT THE ACADEMY HAVE LEFT ME WITH LITTLE TIME TO—⟩

*TRANSLATED FROM ANDORII.

⟨"RESPONSIBILITIES"?⟩

⟨YOU HAVE ONLY **ONE** RESPONSIBILITY IN YOUR LIFE.⟩

⟨TO REPRESENT OUR FAMILY AND OUR RACE—TO REPRESENT **ME**—WITH DEVOTION AND DIGNITY.⟩

⟨DON'T FORGET THAT YOU ARE ANDORIAN **FIRST**, AND A MEMBER OF THE FEDERATION **SECOND**.⟩

⟨AND FAR BEHIND EITHER OF THOSE IS YOUR POSITION AT STARFLEET ACADEMY.⟩

⟨IF YOU EMBARRASS ME IN ANY WAY AT THE BABEL CONFERENCE, I WILL REVOKE YOUR PLACE AT THE HUMANS' SCHOOL AND BRING YOU HOME TO BE **CORRECTED** IN YOUR WAYS.⟩

⟨OR YOU CAN RESIST MY WISHES AND BE CUT OFF FROM YOUR FAMILY ALTOGETHER.⟩

⟨DO NOT INDULGE IN THE ILLUSION THAT YOU ACTUALLY HAVE A **CHOICE**.⟩

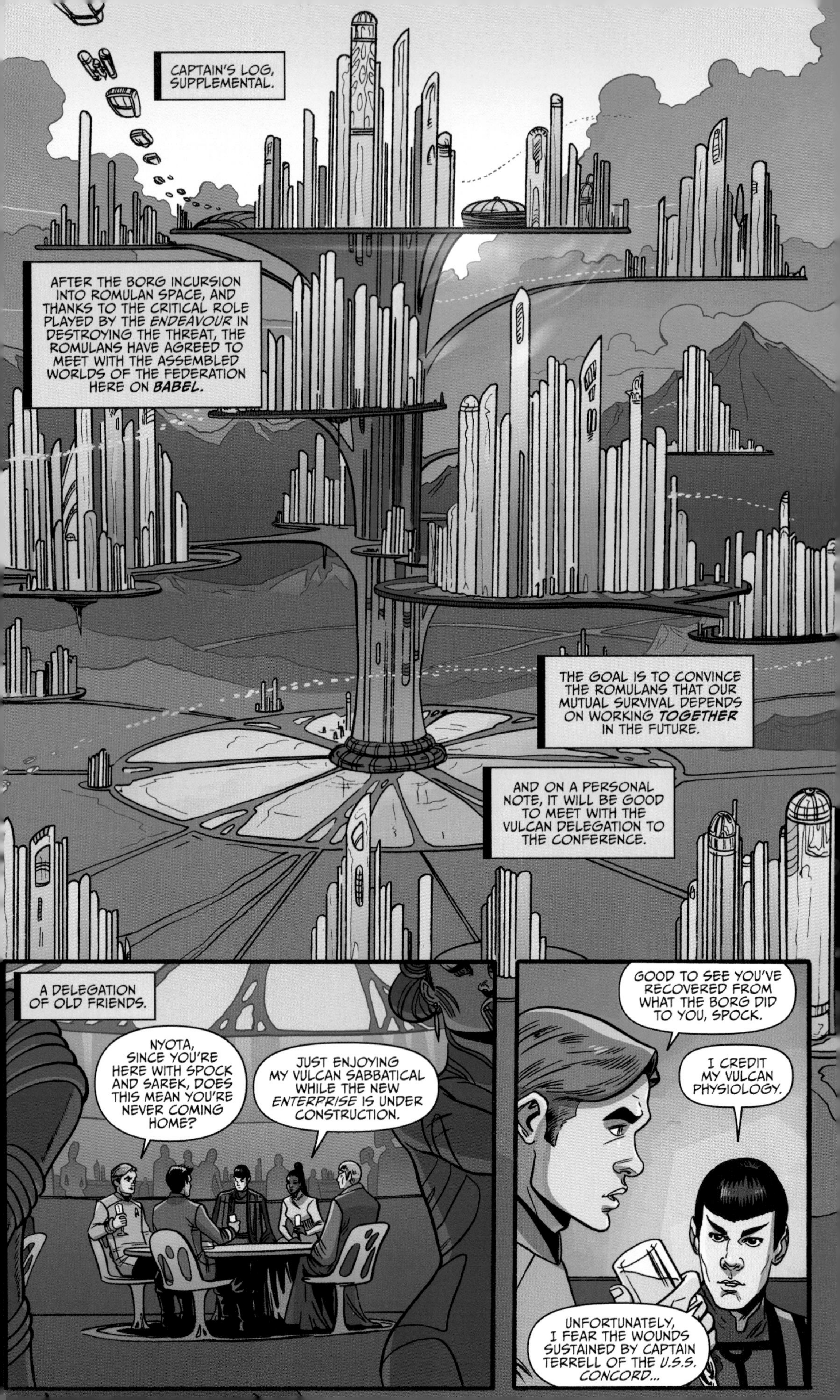
CAPTAIN'S LOG, SUPPLEMENTAL.
AFTER THE BORG INCURSION INTO ROMULAN SPACE, AND THANKS TO THE CRITICAL ROLE PLAYED BY THE *ENDEAVOUR* IN DESTROYING THE THREAT, THE ROMULANS HAVE AGREED TO MEET WITH THE ASSEMBLED WORLDS OF THE FEDERATION HERE ON ***BABEL.***
THE GOAL IS TO CONVINCE THE ROMULANS THAT OUR MUTUAL SURVIVAL DEPENDS ON WORKING ***TOGETHER*** IN THE FUTURE.
AND ON A PERSONAL NOTE, IT WILL BE GOOD TO MEET WITH THE VULCAN DELEGATION TO THE CONFERENCE.
A DELEGATION OF OLD FRIENDS.
NYOTA, SINCE YOU'RE HERE WITH SPOCK AND SAREK, DOES THIS MEAN YOU'RE NEVER COMING HOME?
JUST ENJOYING MY VULCAN SABBATICAL WHILE THE NEW *ENTERPRISE* IS UNDER CONSTRUCTION.
GOOD TO SEE YOU'VE RECOVERED FROM WHAT THE BORG DID TO YOU, SPOCK.
I CREDIT MY VULCAN PHYSIOLOGY.
UNFORTUNATELY, I FEAR THE WOUNDS SUSTAINED BY CAPTAIN TERRELL OF THE *U.S.S. CONCORD*...

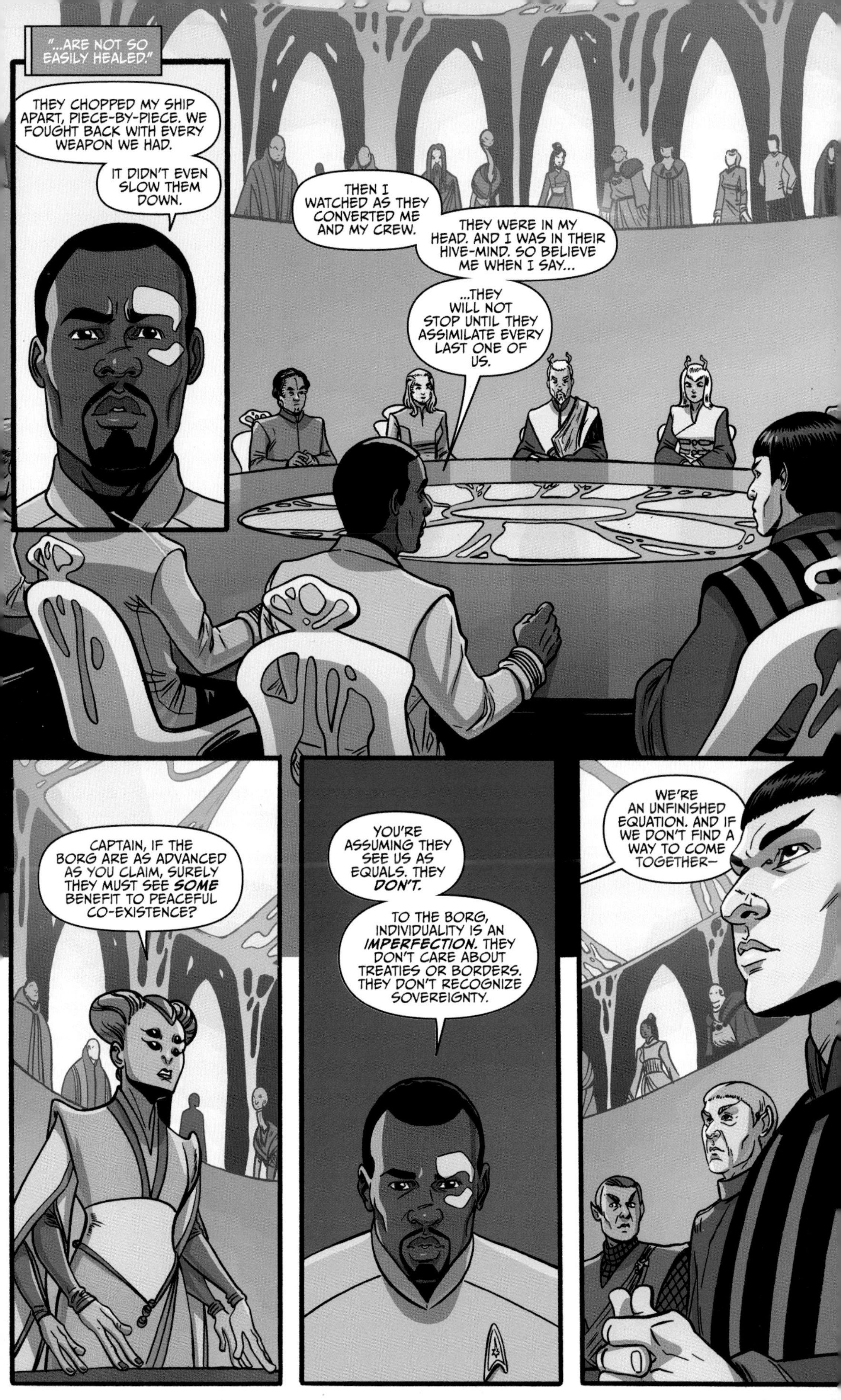
"...ARE NOT SO EASILY HEALED."
THEY CHOPPED MY SHIP APART, PIECE-BY-PIECE. WE FOUGHT BACK WITH EVERY WEAPON WE HAD.
IT DIDN'T EVEN SLOW THEM DOWN.
THEN I WATCHED AS THEY CONVERTED ME AND MY CREW.
THEY WERE IN MY HEAD. AND I WAS IN THEIR HIVE-MIND. SO BELIEVE ME WHEN I SAY...
...THEY WILL NOT STOP UNTIL THEY ASSIMILATE EVERY LAST ONE OF US.
CAPTAIN, IF THE BORG ARE AS ADVANCED AS YOU CLAIM, SURELY THEY MUST SEE *SOME* BENEFIT TO PEACEFUL CO-EXISTENCE?
YOU'RE ASSUMING THEY SEE US AS EQUALS. THEY *DON'T.*
TO THE BORG, INDIVIDUALITY IS AN *IMPERFECTION.* THEY DON'T CARE ABOUT TREATIES OR BORDERS. THEY DON'T RECOGNIZE SOVEREIGNTY.
WE'RE AN UNFINISHED EQUATION. AND IF WE DON'T FIND A WAY TO COME TOGETHER—

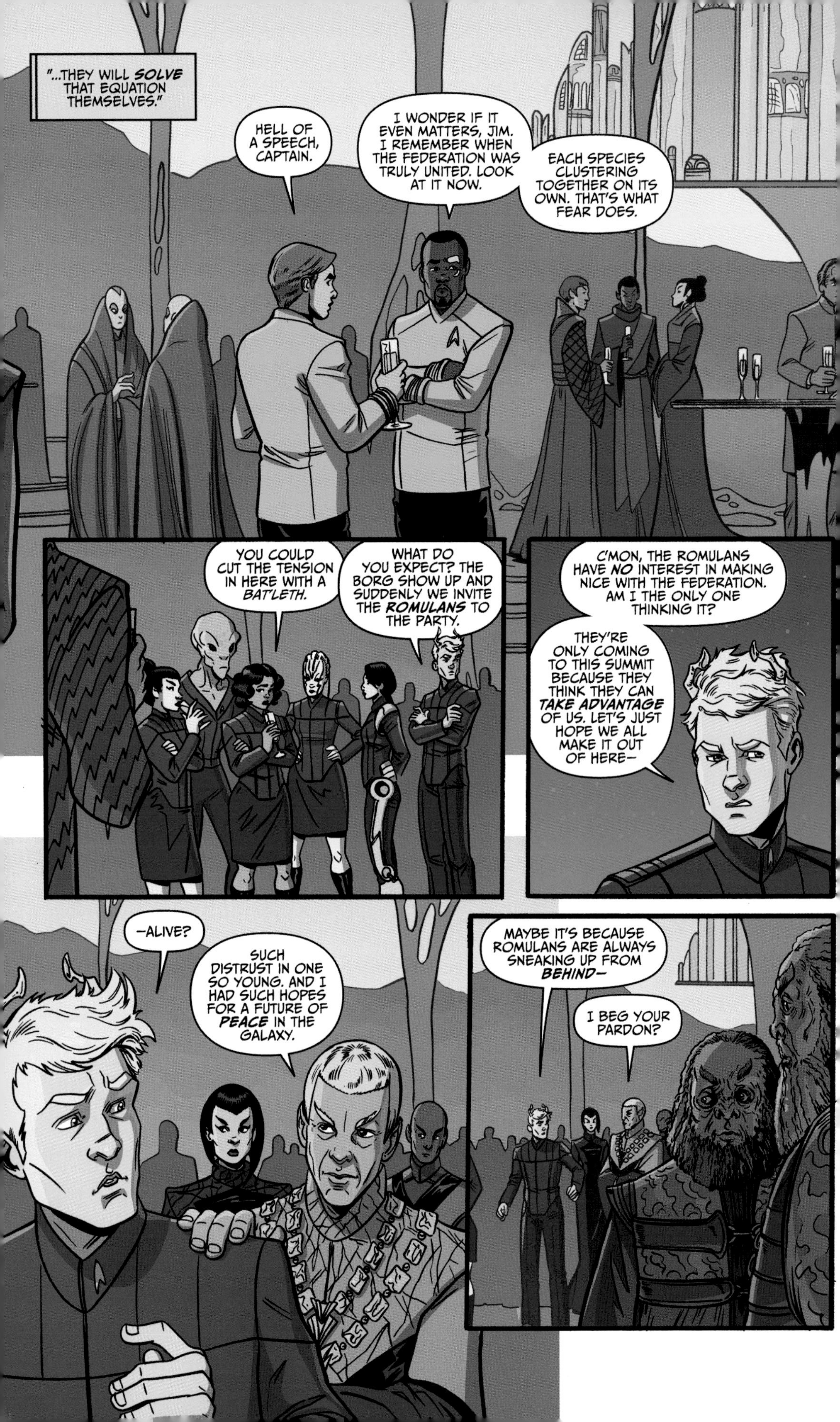
"...THEY WILL *SOLVE* THAT EQUATION THEMSELVES."
HELL OF A SPEECH, CAPTAIN.
I WONDER IF IT EVEN MATTERS, JIM. I REMEMBER WHEN THE FEDERATION WAS TRULY UNITED. LOOK AT IT NOW.
EACH SPECIES CLUSTERING TOGETHER ON ITS OWN. THAT'S WHAT FEAR DOES.
YOU COULD CUT THE TENSION IN HERE WITH A *BAT'LETH.*
WHAT DO YOU EXPECT? THE BORG SHOW UP AND SUDDENLY WE INVITE THE ***ROMULANS*** TO THE PARTY.
C'MON, THE ROMULANS HAVE ***NO*** INTEREST IN MAKING NICE WITH THE FEDERATION. AM I THE ONLY ONE THINKING IT?
THEY'RE ONLY COMING TO THIS SUMMIT BECAUSE THEY THINK THEY CAN ***TAKE ADVANTAGE*** OF US. LET'S JUST HOPE WE ALL MAKE IT OUT OF HERE–
–ALIVE?
SUCH DISTRUST IN ONE SO YOUNG. AND I HAD SUCH HOPES FOR A FUTURE OF ***PEACE*** IN THE GALAXY.
MAYBE IT'S BECAUSE ROMULANS ARE ALWAYS SNEAKING UP FROM ***BEHIND***–
I BEG YOUR PARDON?

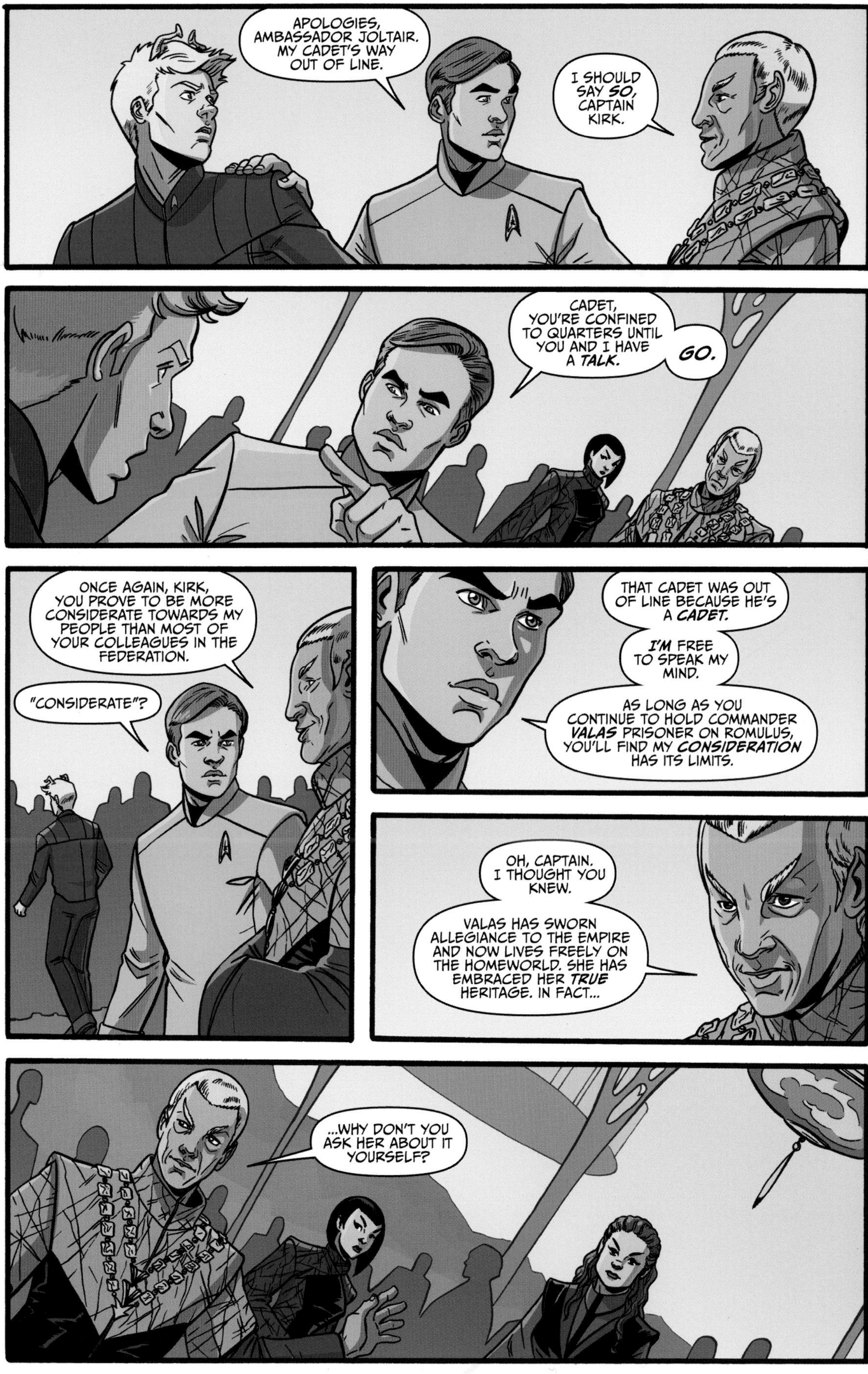

APOLOGIES, AMBASSADOR JOLTAIR. MY CADET'S WAY OUT OF LINE.
I SHOULD SAY *SO,* CAPTAIN KIRK.
CADET, YOU'RE CONFINED TO QUARTERS UNTIL YOU AND I HAVE A *TALK.*
GO.
ONCE AGAIN, KIRK, YOU PROVE TO BE MORE CONSIDERATE TOWARDS MY PEOPLE THAN MOST OF YOUR COLLEAGUES IN THE FEDERATION.
"CONSIDERATE"?
THAT CADET WAS OUT OF LINE BECAUSE HE'S A *CADET.*
I'M FREE TO SPEAK MY MIND.
AS LONG AS YOU CONTINUE TO HOLD COMMANDER *VALAS* PRISONER ON ROMULUS, YOU'LL FIND MY *CONSIDERATION* HAS ITS LIMITS.
OH, CAPTAIN. I THOUGHT YOU KNEW.
VALAS HAS SWORN ALLEGIANCE TO THE EMPIRE AND NOW LIVES FREELY ON THE HOMEWORLD. SHE HAS EMBRACED HER *TRUE* HERITAGE. IN FACT...
...WHY DON'T YOU ASK HER ABOUT IT YOURSELF?

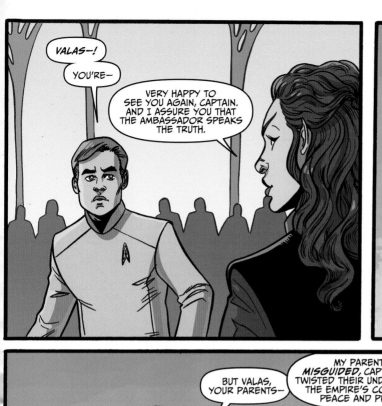

VALAS—!

YOU'RE—

VERY HAPPY TO SEE YOU AGAIN, CAPTAIN. AND I ASSURE YOU THAT THE AMBASSADOR SPEAKS THE TRUTH.

GROWING UP ON EARTH, I YEARNED TO VISIT THE HOME OF MY FAMILY. TO KNOW WHAT IT WAS TO BE TRULY *ROMULAN*.

I HAVE COME HERE TO FORMALLY SUBMIT MY *RESIGNATION* FROM STARFLEET.

BUT VALAS, YOUR PARENTS—

MY PARENTS WERE *MISGUIDED*, CAPTAIN. FEAR HAD TWISTED THEIR UNDERSTANDING OF THE EMPIRE'S COMMITMENT TO PEACE AND PROSPERITY.

I AM SO GLAD THAT THIS SUMMIT HAS BROUGHT OUR TWO SIDES TOGETHER TO ENSURE THAT PROMISE FOR *ALL WORLDS*.

"YOUR MISTRUST IS NOT MISGUIDED."

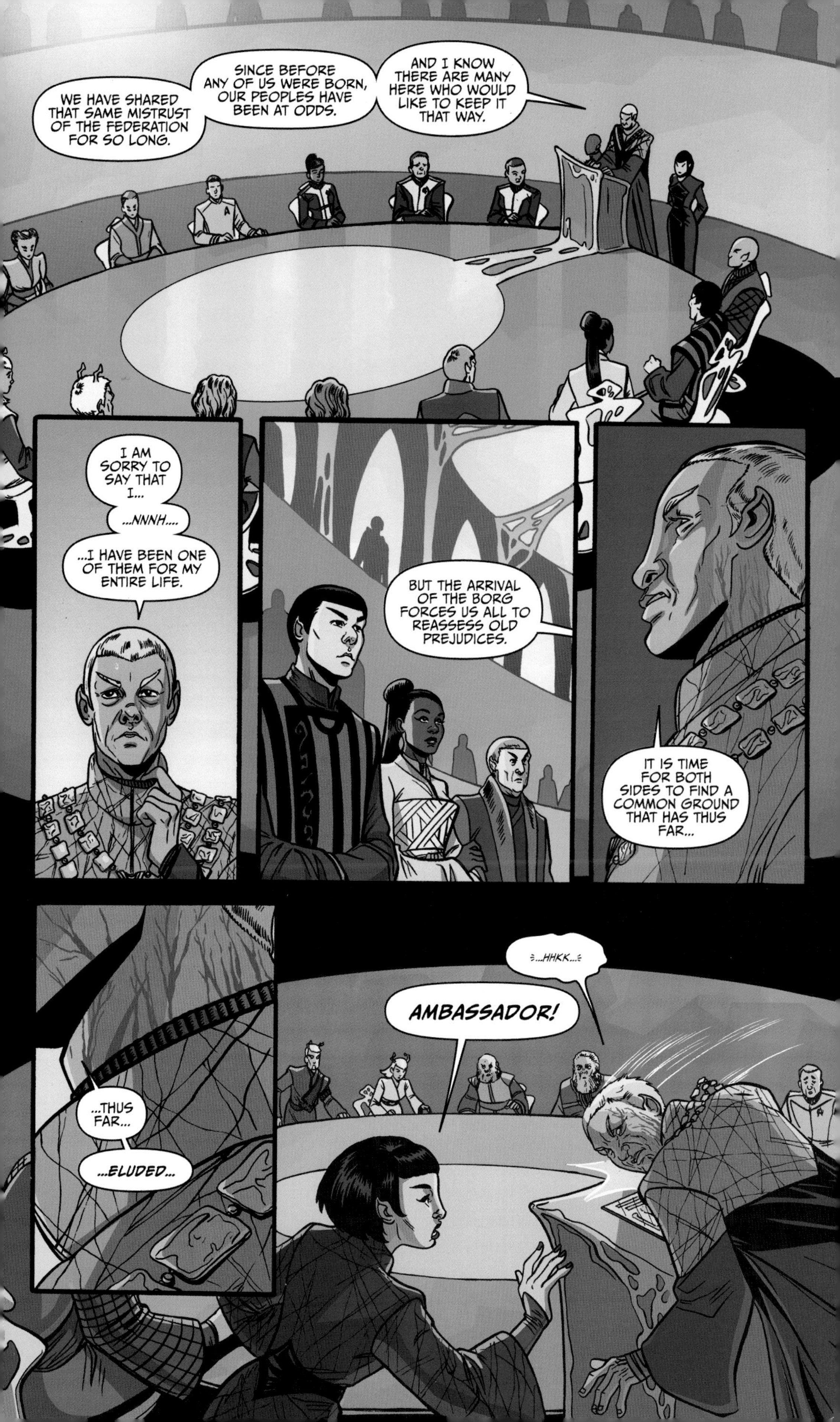
WE HAVE SHARED THAT SAME MISTRUST OF THE FEDERATION FOR SO LONG.
SINCE BEFORE ANY OF US WERE BORN, OUR PEOPLES HAVE BEEN AT ODDS.
AND I KNOW THERE ARE MANY HERE WHO WOULD LIKE TO KEEP IT THAT WAY.
I AM SORRY TO SAY THAT I...
...NNNH....
...I HAVE BEEN ONE OF THEM FOR MY ENTIRE LIFE.
BUT THE ARRIVAL OF THE BORG FORCES US ALL TO REASSESS OLD PREJUDICES.
IT IS TIME FOR BOTH SIDES TO FIND A COMMON GROUND THAT HAS THUS FAR...
...THUS FAR...
...ELUDED...
...HHKK...
AMBASSADOR!

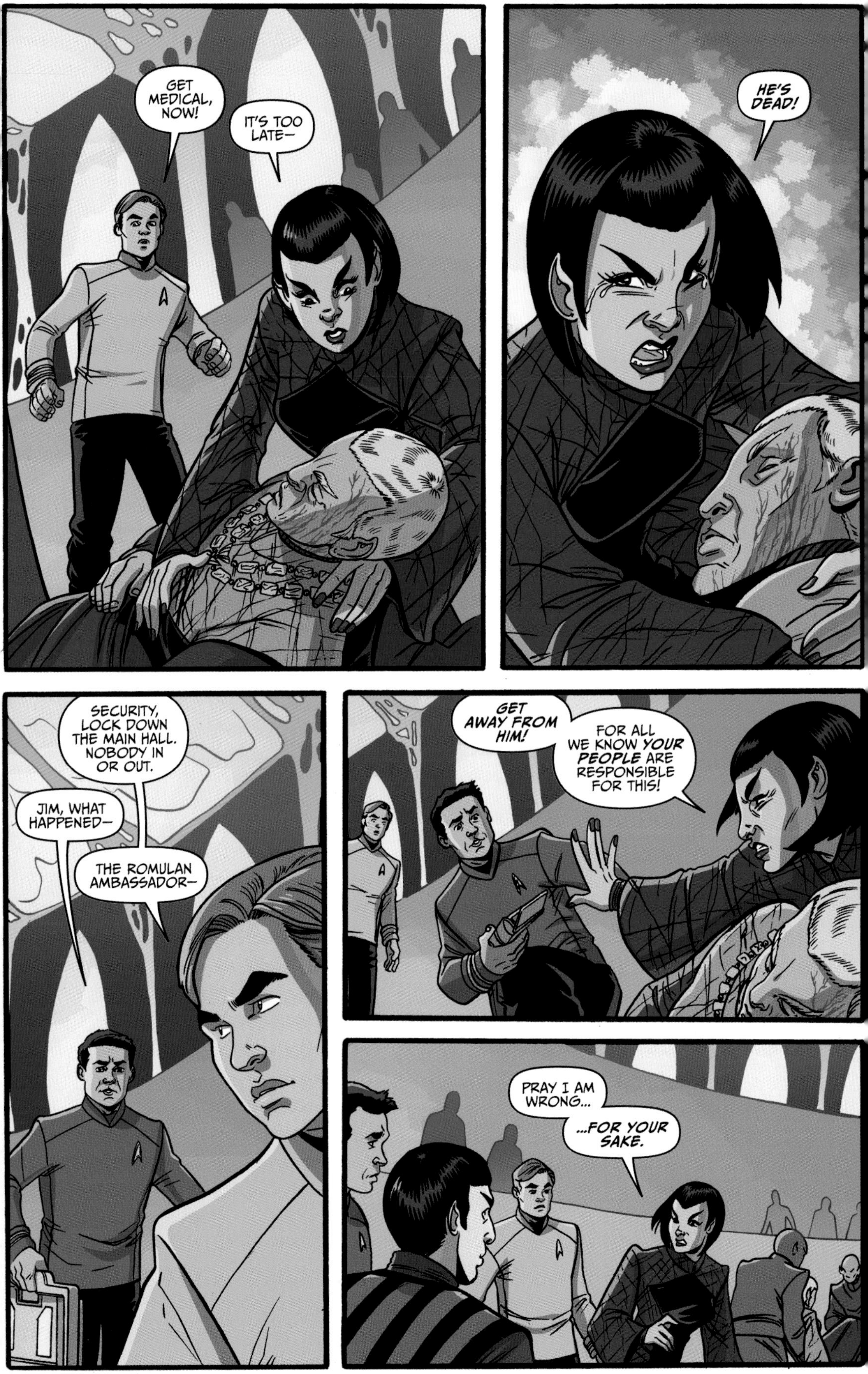
GET MEDICAL, NOW!
IT'S TOO LATE—
HE'S DEAD!
SECURITY, LOCK DOWN THE MAIN HALL. NOBODY IN OR OUT.
JIM, WHAT HAPPENED—
THE ROMULAN AMBASSADOR—
GET AWAY FROM HIM!
FOR ALL WE KNOW YOUR PEOPLE ARE RESPONSIBLE FOR THIS!
PRAY I AM WRONG...
...FOR YOUR SAKE.

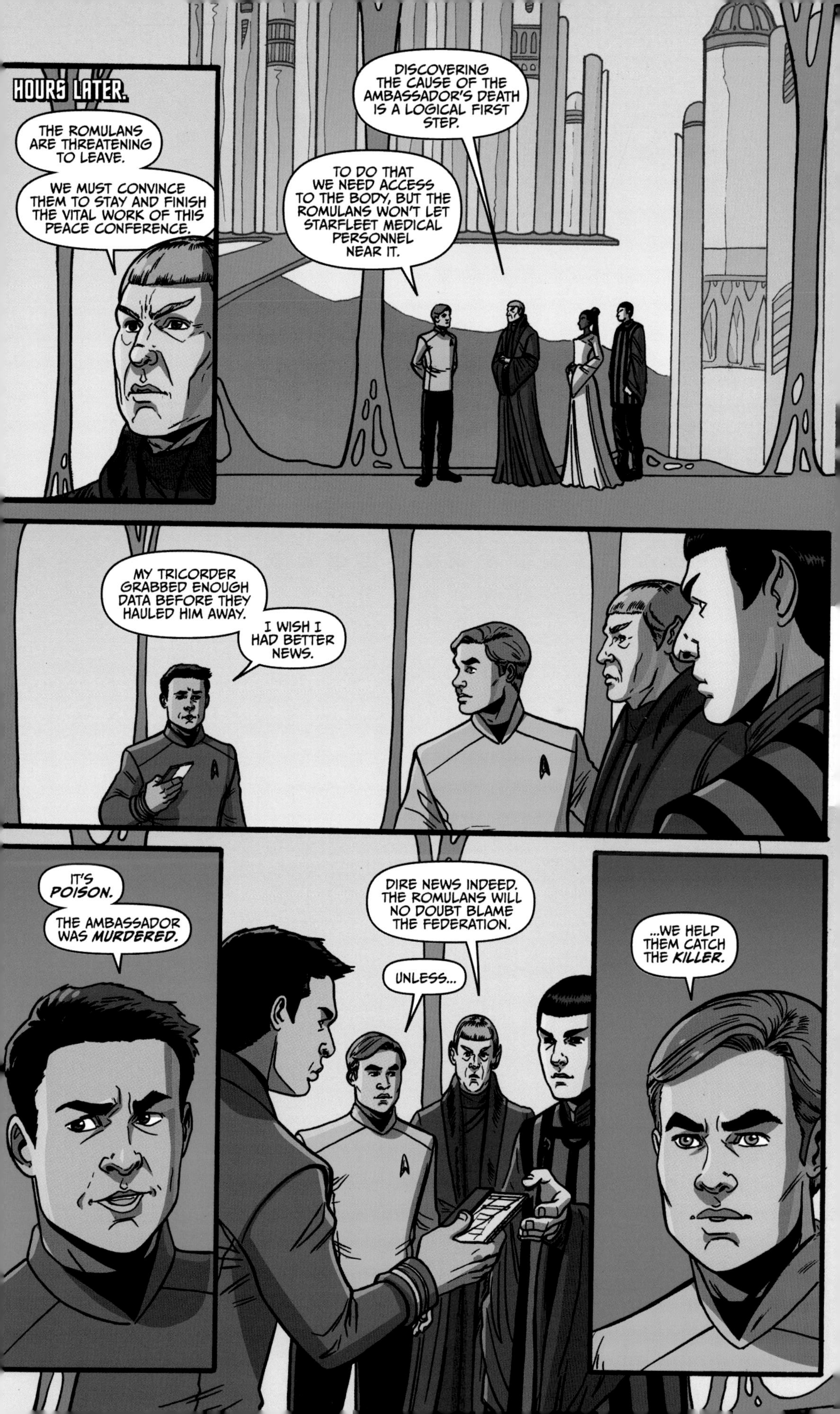
HOURS LATER.
THE ROMULANS ARE THREATENING TO LEAVE.
WE MUST CONVINCE THEM TO STAY AND FINISH THE VITAL WORK OF THIS PEACE CONFERENCE.
DISCOVERING THE CAUSE OF THE AMBASSADOR'S DEATH IS A LOGICAL FIRST STEP.
TO DO THAT WE NEED ACCESS TO THE BODY, BUT THE ROMULANS WON'T LET STARFLEET MEDICAL PERSONNEL NEAR IT.
MY TRICORDER GRABBED ENOUGH DATA BEFORE THEY HAULED HIM AWAY.
I WISH I HAD BETTER NEWS.
IT'S *POISON.*
THE AMBASSADOR WAS *MURDERED.*
DIRE NEWS INDEED. THE ROMULANS WILL NO DOUBT BLAME THE FEDERATION.
UNLESS...
...WE HELP THEM CATCH THE *KILLER.*

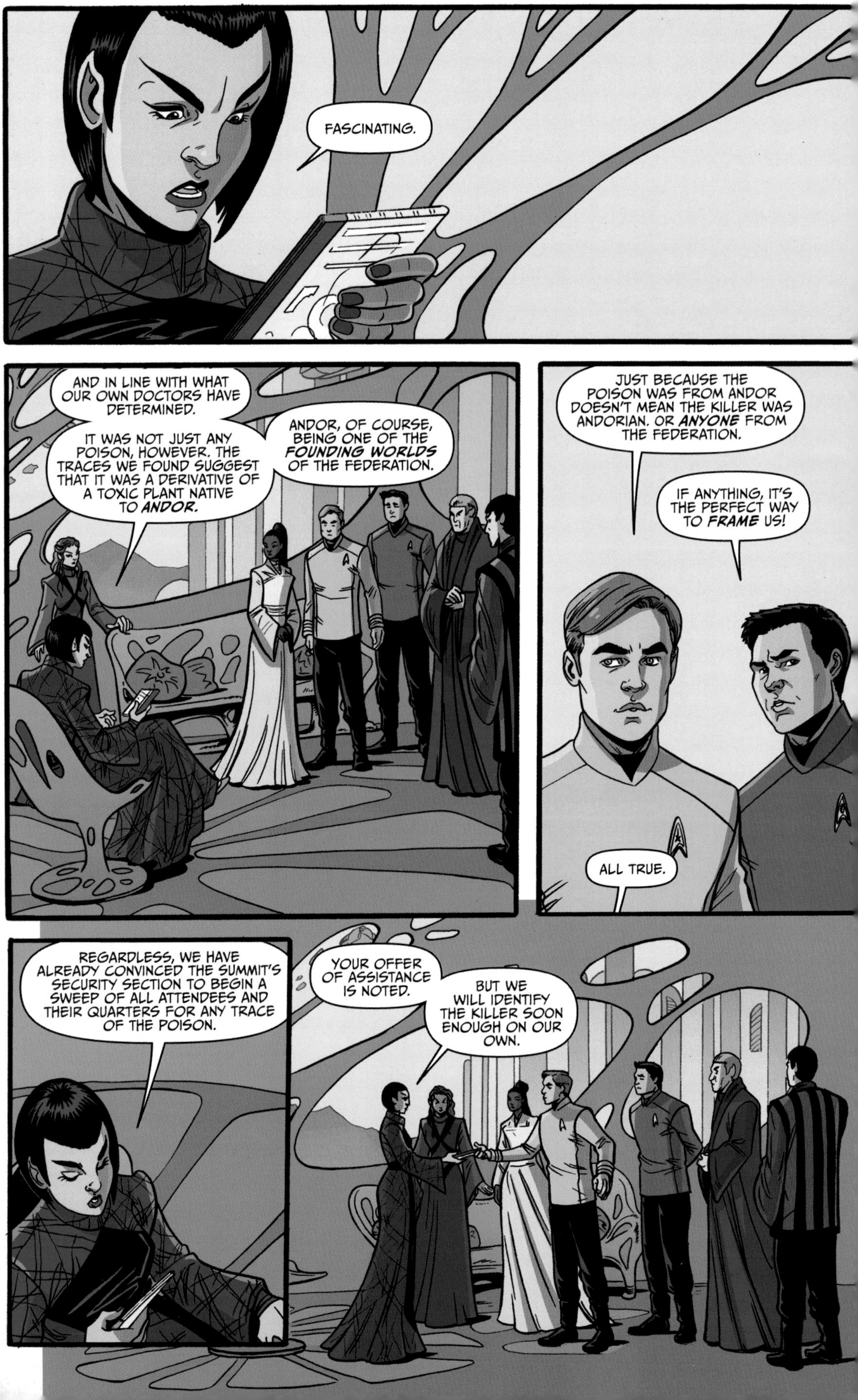
FASCINATING.
AND IN LINE WITH WHAT OUR OWN DOCTORS HAVE DETERMINED.
IT WAS NOT JUST ANY POISON, HOWEVER. THE TRACES WE FOUND SUGGEST THAT IT WAS A DERIVATIVE OF A TOXIC PLANT NATIVE TO ANDOR.
ANDOR, OF COURSE, BEING ONE OF THE FOUNDING WORLDS OF THE FEDERATION.
JUST BECAUSE THE POISON WAS FROM ANDOR DOESN'T MEAN THE KILLER WAS ANDORIAN. OR ANYONE FROM THE FEDERATION.
IF ANYTHING, IT'S THE PERFECT WAY TO FRAME US!
ALL TRUE.
REGARDLESS, WE HAVE ALREADY CONVINCED THE SUMMIT'S SECURITY SECTION TO BEGIN A SWEEP OF ALL ATTENDEES AND THEIR QUARTERS FOR ANY TRACE OF THE POISON.
YOUR OFFER OF ASSISTANCE IS NOTED.
BUT WE WILL IDENTIFY THE KILLER SOON ENOUGH ON OUR OWN.

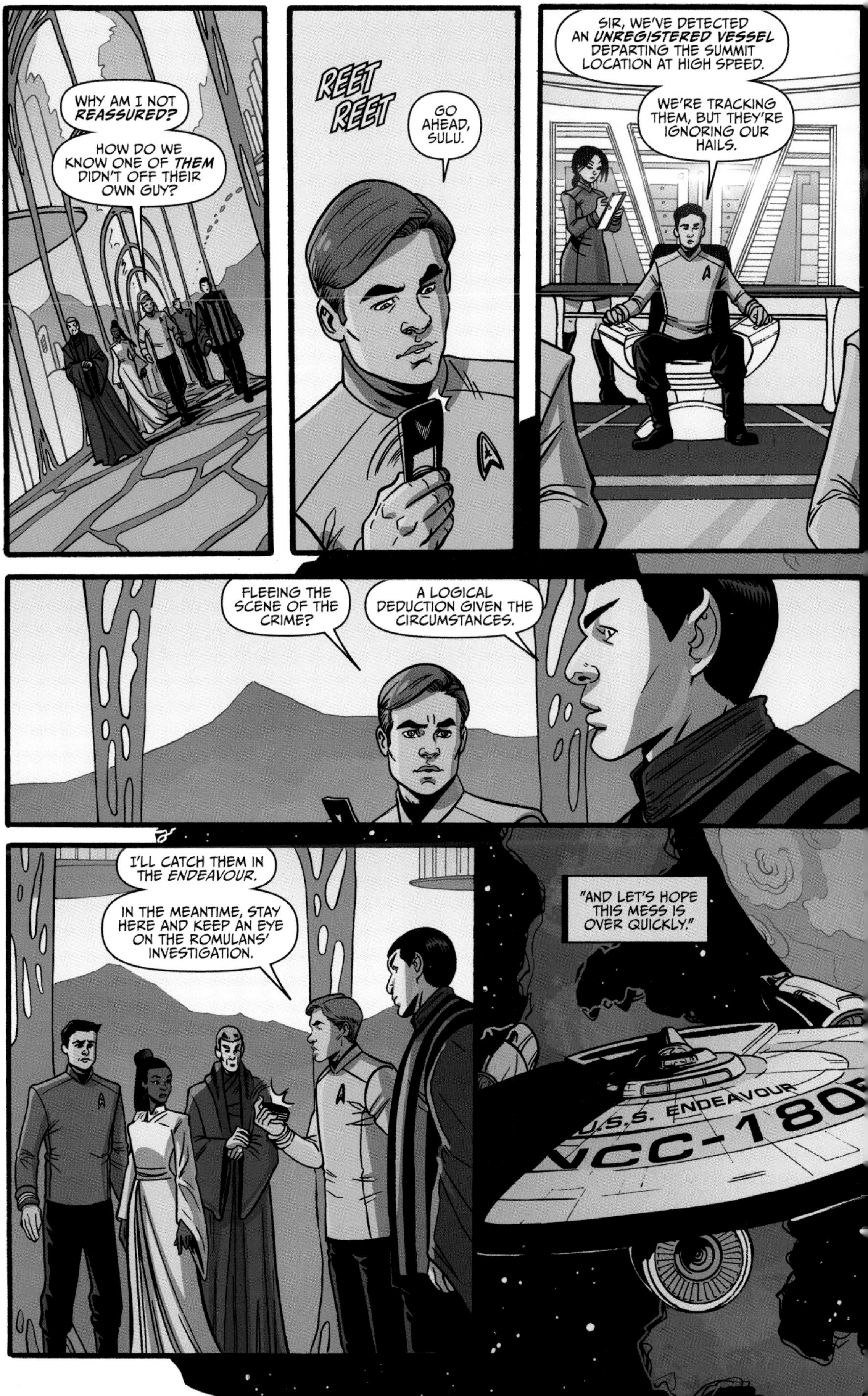
WHY AM I NOT REASSURED?
HOW DO WE KNOW ONE OF THEM DIDN'T OFF THEIR OWN GUY?
REET REET
GO AHEAD, SULU.
SIR, WE'VE DETECTED AN UNREGISTERED VESSEL DEPARTING THE SUMMIT LOCATION AT HIGH SPEED.
WE'RE TRACKING THEM, BUT THEY'RE IGNORING OUR HAILS.
FLEEING THE SCENE OF THE CRIME?
A LOGICAL DEDUCTION GIVEN THE CIRCUMSTANCES.
I'LL CATCH THEM IN THE ENDEAVOUR.
IN THE MEANTIME, STAY HERE AND KEEP AN EYE ON THE ROMULANS' INVESTIGATION.
"AND LET'S HOPE THIS MESS IS OVER QUICKLY."
U.S.S. ENDEAVOUR
NCC-180

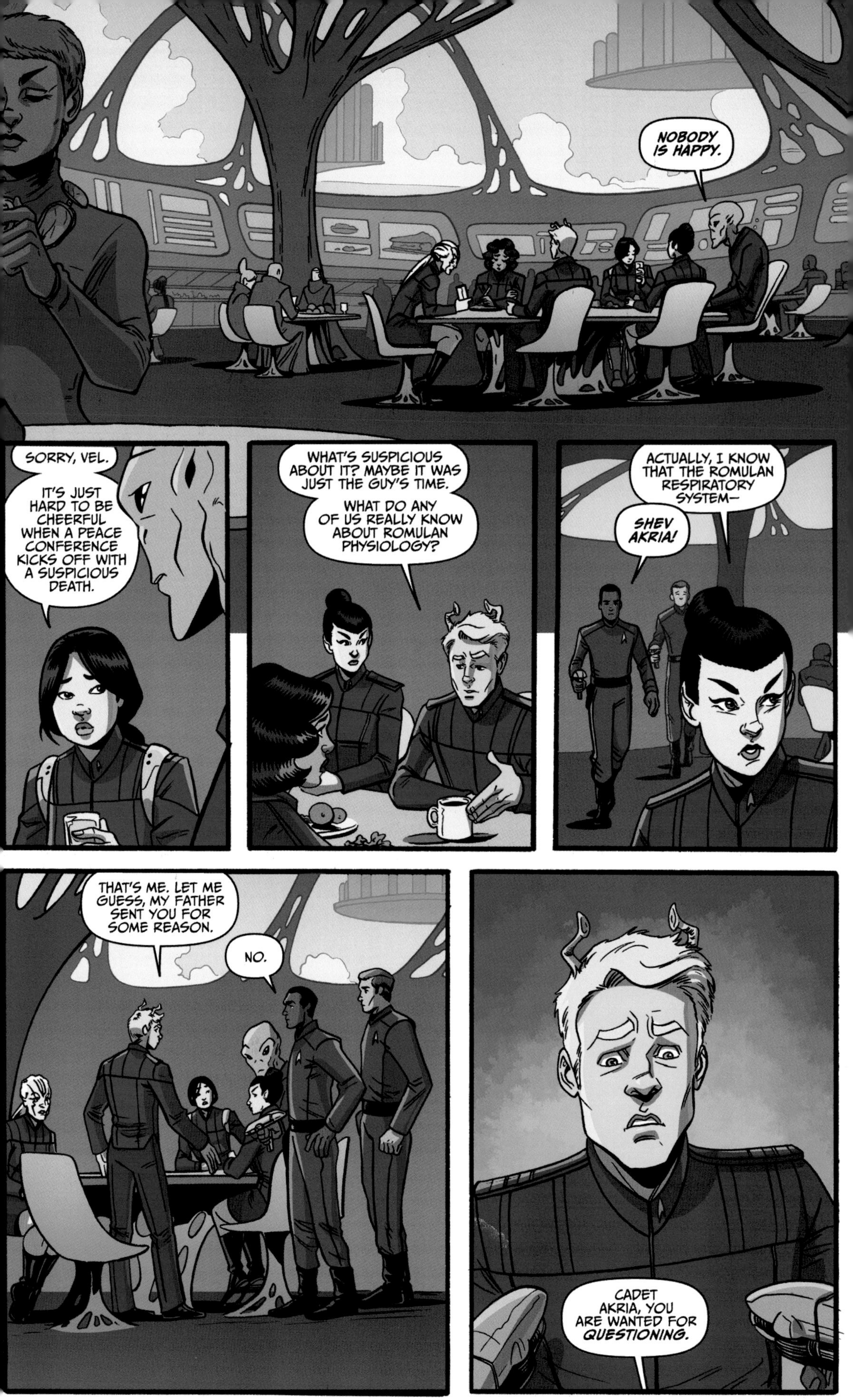
NOBODY IS HAPPY.
SORRY, VEL.
IT'S JUST HARD TO BE CHEERFUL WHEN A PEACE CONFERENCE KICKS OFF WITH A SUSPICIOUS DEATH.
WHAT'S SUSPICIOUS ABOUT IT? MAYBE IT WAS JUST THE GUY'S TIME.
WHAT DO ANY OF US REALLY KNOW ABOUT ROMULAN PHYSIOLOGY?
ACTUALLY, I KNOW THAT THE ROMULAN RESPIRATORY SYSTEM—
SHEV AKRIA!
THAT'S ME. LET ME GUESS, MY FATHER SENT YOU FOR SOME REASON.
NO.
CADET AKRIA, YOU ARE WANTED FOR QUESTIONING.

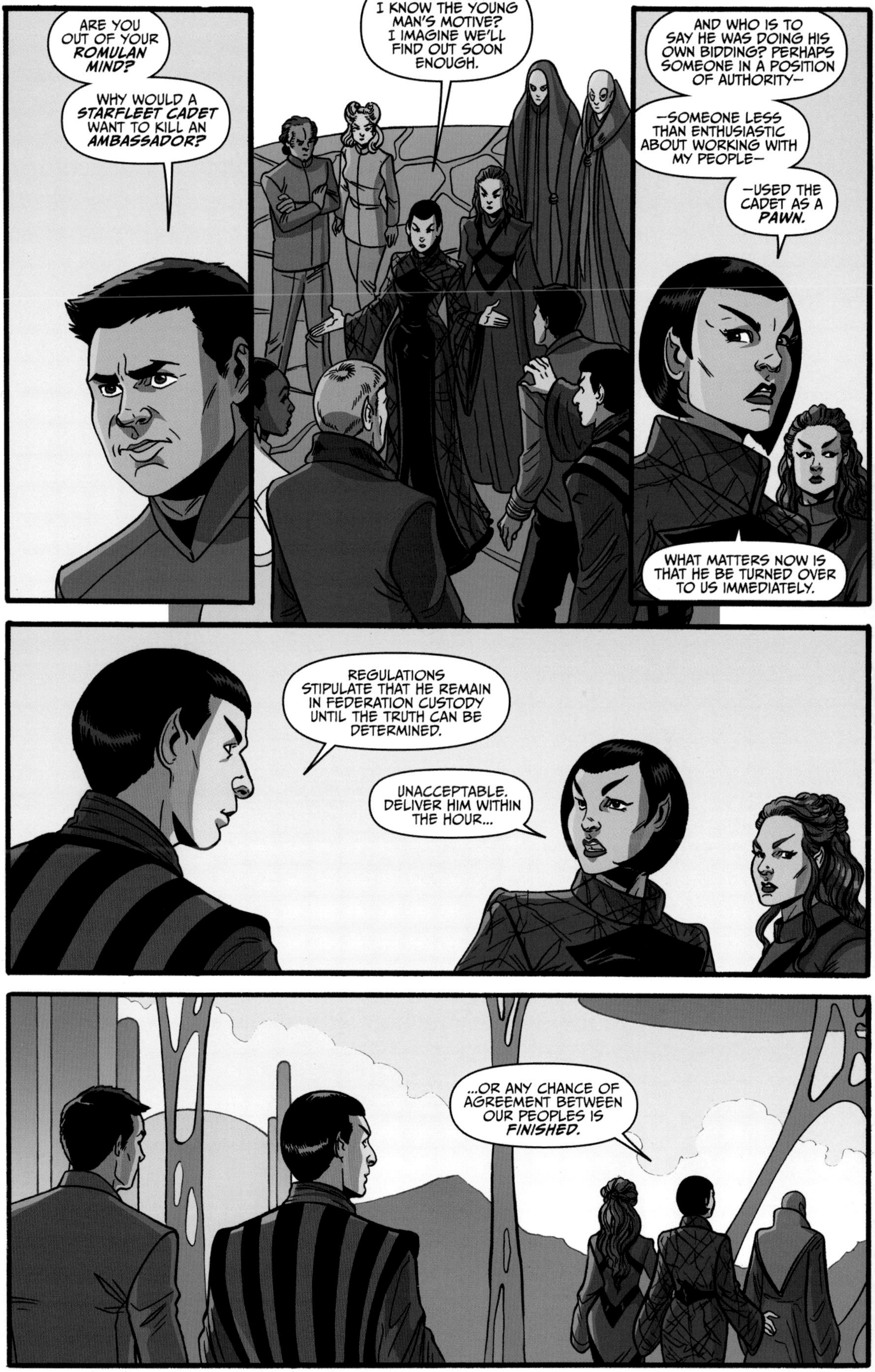
ARE YOU OUT OF YOUR *ROMULAN MIND?*
WHY WOULD A *STARFLEET CADET* WANT TO KILL AN *AMBASSADOR?*
HOW WOULD I KNOW THE YOUNG MAN'S MOTIVE? I IMAGINE WE'LL FIND OUT SOON ENOUGH.
AND WHO IS TO SAY HE WAS DOING HIS OWN BIDDING? PERHAPS SOMEONE IN A POSITION OF AUTHORITY—
—SOMEONE LESS THAN ENTHUSIASTIC ABOUT WORKING WITH MY PEOPLE—
—USED THE CADET AS A *PAWN.*
WHAT MATTERS NOW IS THAT HE BE TURNED OVER TO US IMMEDIATELY.
REGULATIONS STIPULATE THAT HE REMAIN IN FEDERATION CUSTODY UNTIL THE TRUTH CAN BE DETERMINED.
UNACCEPTABLE. DELIVER HIM WITHIN THE HOUR...
...OR ANY CHANCE OF AGREEMENT BETWEEN OUR PEOPLES IS *FINISHED.*

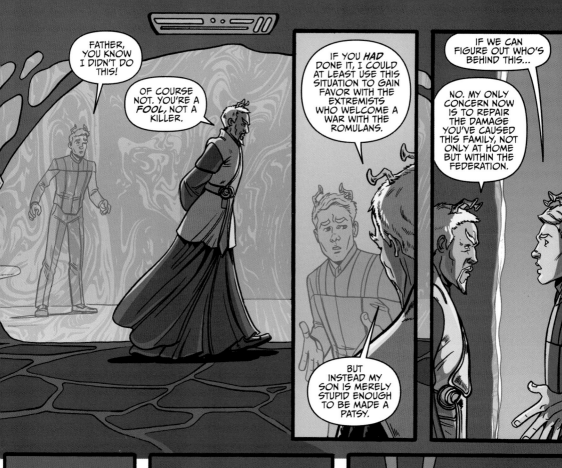

FATHER, YOU KNOW I DIDN'T DO THIS!

OF COURSE NOT. YOU'RE A *FOOL*, NOT A KILLER.

IF YOU *HAD* DONE IT, I COULD AT LEAST USE THIS SITUATION TO GAIN FAVOR WITH THE EXTREMISTS WHO WELCOME A WAR WITH THE ROMULANS.

BUT INSTEAD MY SON IS MERELY STUPID ENOUGH TO BE MADE A PATSY.

IF WE CAN FIGURE OUT WHO'S BEHIND THIS...

NO. MY ONLY CONCERN NOW IS TO REPAIR THE DAMAGE YOU'VE CAUSED THIS FAMILY, NOT ONLY AT HOME BUT WITHIN THE FEDERATION.

PLEASE. I NEED YOUR HELP.

I WAS MISGUIDED IN PLACING ANY AMOUNT OF FAITH IN YOU.

THAT IS A MISTAKE I WILL *NEVER* MAKE AGAIN.

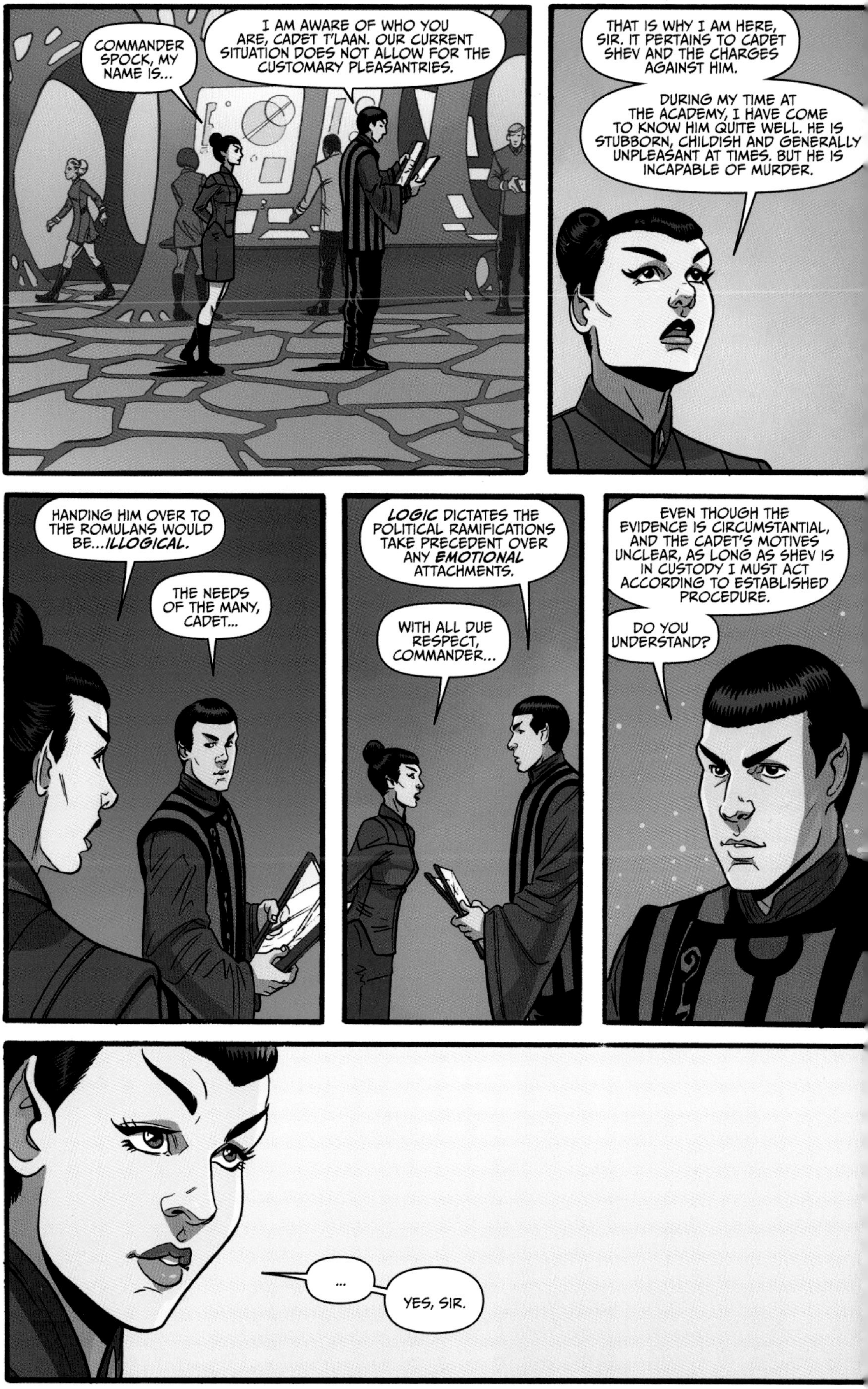

COMMANDER SPOCK, MY NAME IS...
I AM AWARE OF WHO YOU ARE, CADET T'LAAN. OUR CURRENT SITUATION DOES NOT ALLOW FOR THE CUSTOMARY PLEASANTRIES.
THAT IS WHY I AM HERE, SIR. IT PERTAINS TO CADET SHEV AND THE CHARGES AGAINST HIM.
DURING MY TIME AT THE ACADEMY, I HAVE COME TO KNOW HIM QUITE WELL. HE IS STUBBORN, CHILDISH AND GENERALLY UNPLEASANT AT TIMES. BUT HE IS INCAPABLE OF MURDER.
HANDING HIM OVER TO THE ROMULANS WOULD BE...*ILLOGICAL.*
THE NEEDS OF THE MANY, CADET...
LOGIC DICTATES THE POLITICAL RAMIFICATIONS TAKE PRECEDENT OVER ANY *EMOTIONAL* ATTACHMENTS.
WITH ALL DUE RESPECT, COMMANDER...
EVEN THOUGH THE EVIDENCE IS CIRCUMSTANTIAL, AND THE CADET'S MOTIVES UNCLEAR, AS LONG AS SHEV IS IN CUSTODY I MUST ACT ACCORDING TO ESTABLISHED PROCEDURE.
DO YOU UNDERSTAND?
...
YES, SIR.

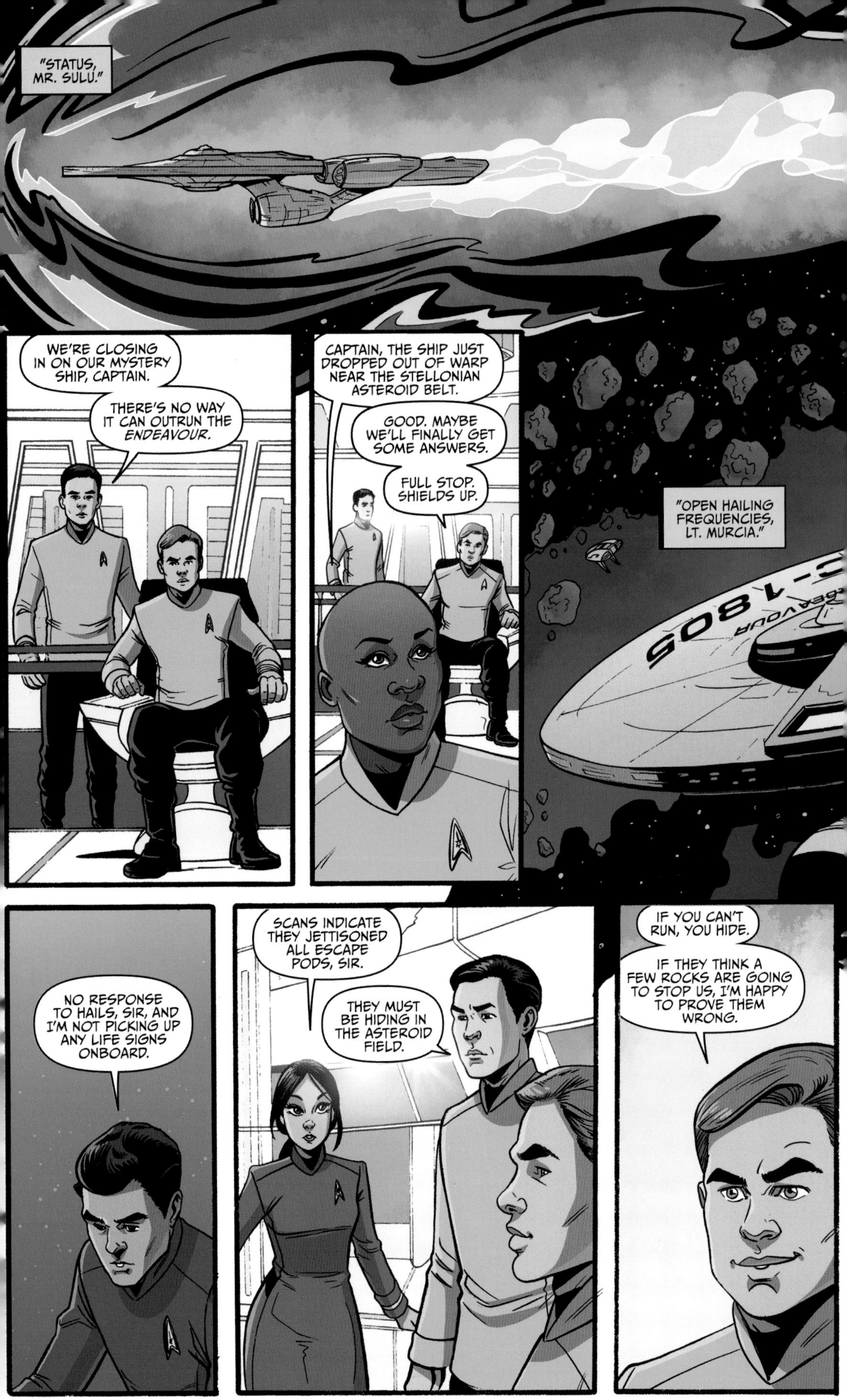
"STATUS, MR. SULU."
WE'RE CLOSING IN ON OUR MYSTERY SHIP, CAPTAIN.
THERE'S NO WAY IT CAN OUTRUN THE *ENDEAVOUR.*
CAPTAIN, THE SHIP JUST DROPPED OUT OF WARP NEAR THE STELLONIAN ASTEROID BELT.
GOOD. MAYBE WE'LL FINALLY GET SOME ANSWERS.
FULL STOP. SHIELDS UP.
"OPEN HAILING FREQUENCIES, LT. MURCIA."
1805
NO RESPONSE TO HAILS, SIR, AND I'M NOT PICKING UP ANY LIFE SIGNS ONBOARD.
SCANS INDICATE THEY JETTISONED ALL ESCAPE PODS, SIR.
THEY MUST BE HIDING IN THE ASTEROID FIELD.
IF YOU CAN'T RUN, YOU HIDE.
IF THEY THINK A FEW ROCKS ARE GOING TO STOP US, I'M HAPPY TO PROVE THEM WRONG.

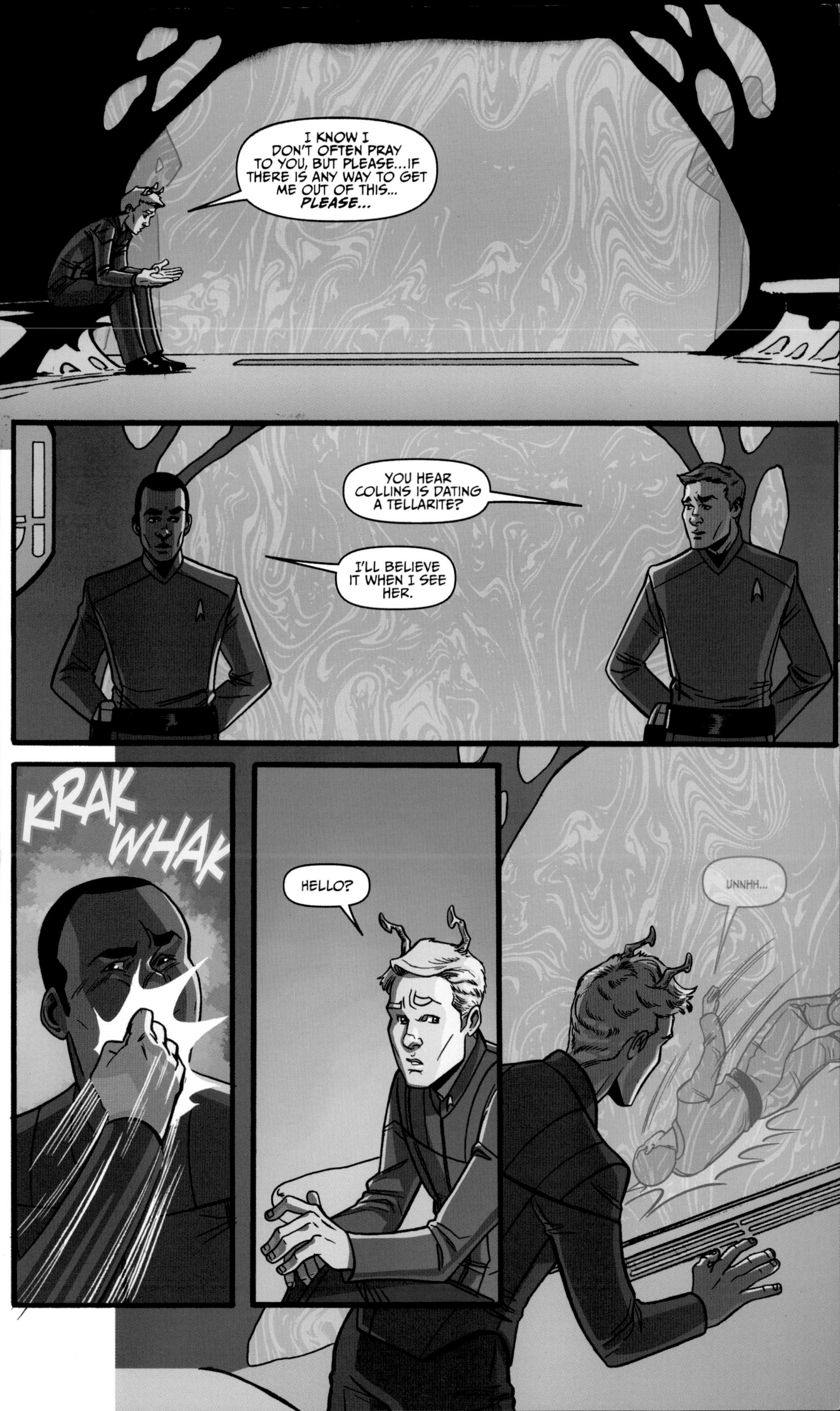
I KNOW I DON'T OFTEN PRAY TO YOU, BUT PLEASE...IF THERE IS ANY WAY TO GET ME OUT OF THIS... *PLEASE...*
YOU HEAR COLLINS IS DATING A TELLARITE?
I'LL BELIEVE IT WHEN I SEE HER.
KRAK
WHAK
HELLO?
UNNHH...

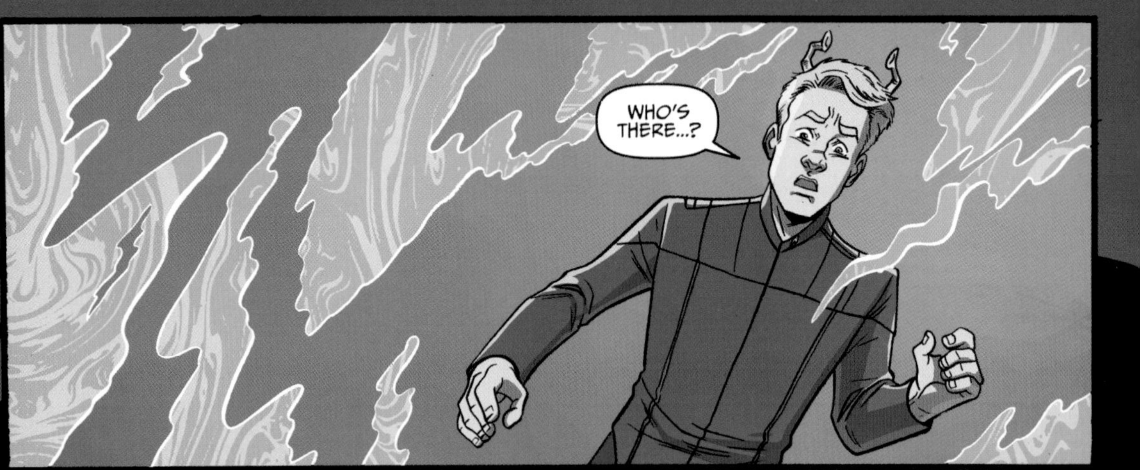
WHO'S THERE...?

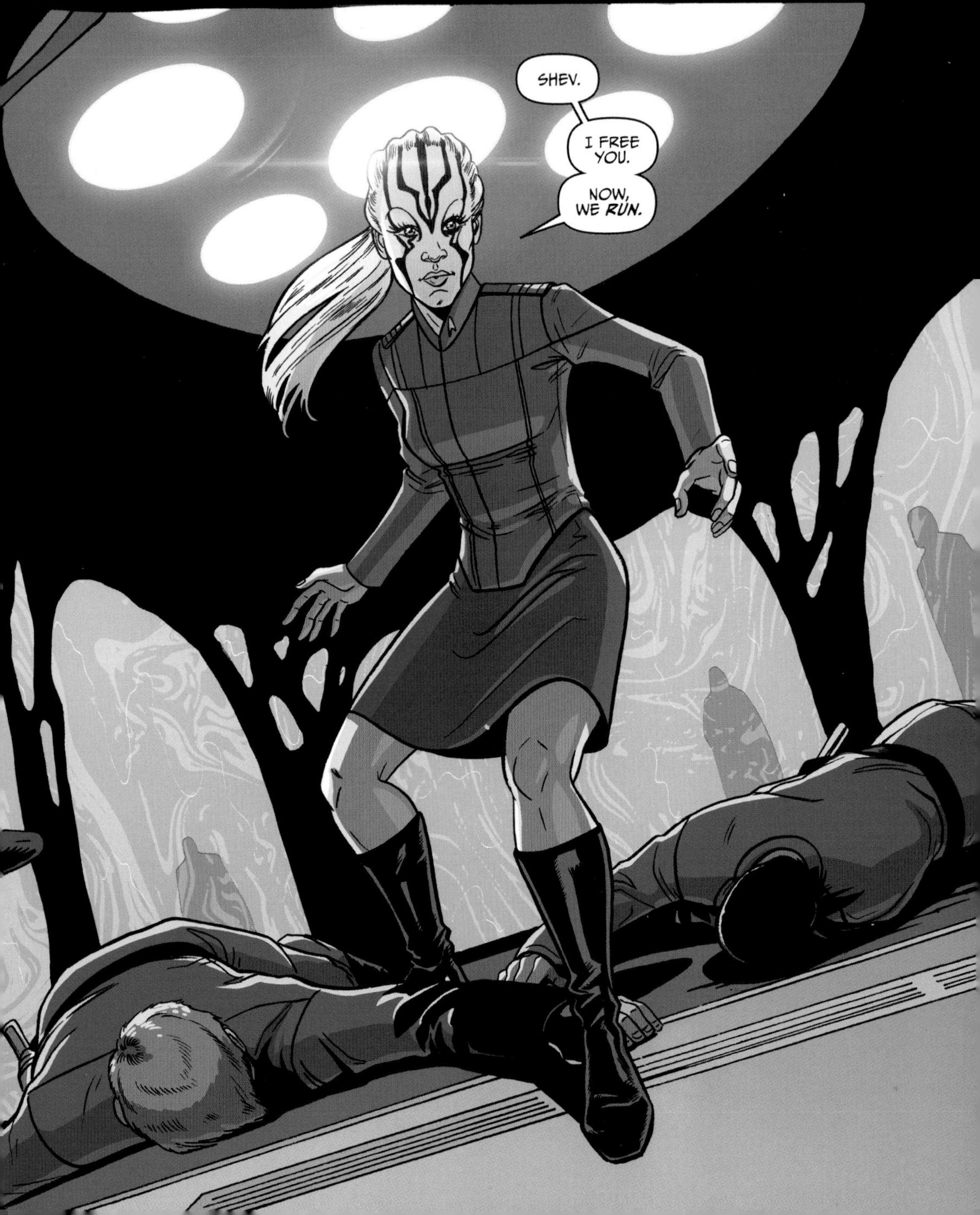
SHEV.
I FREE YOU.
NOW, WE *RUN.*

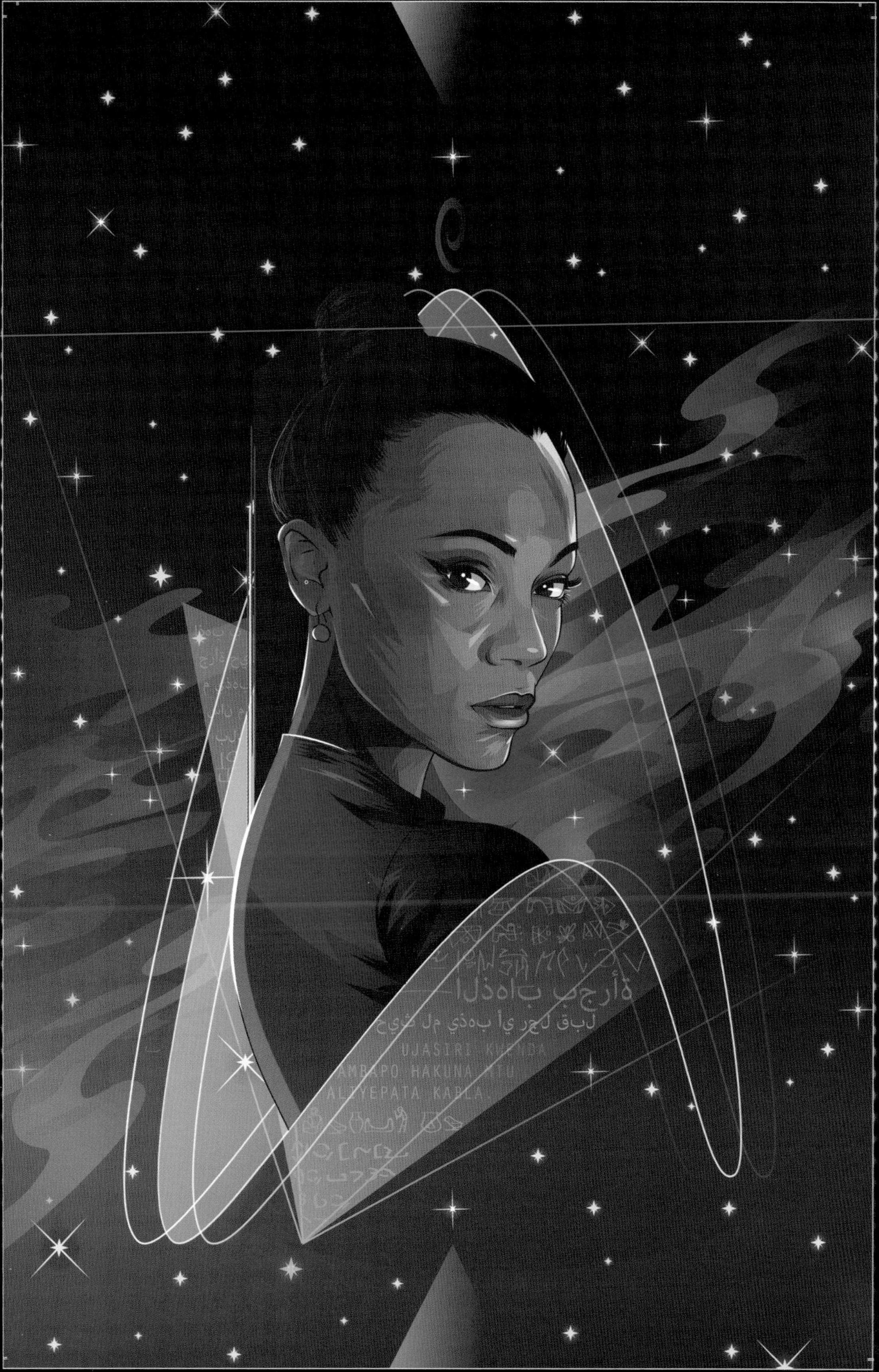

UJASIRI
AMBAPO HAKUNA MTU
ALIYEPATA KABLA

art by

Cryssy Cheung

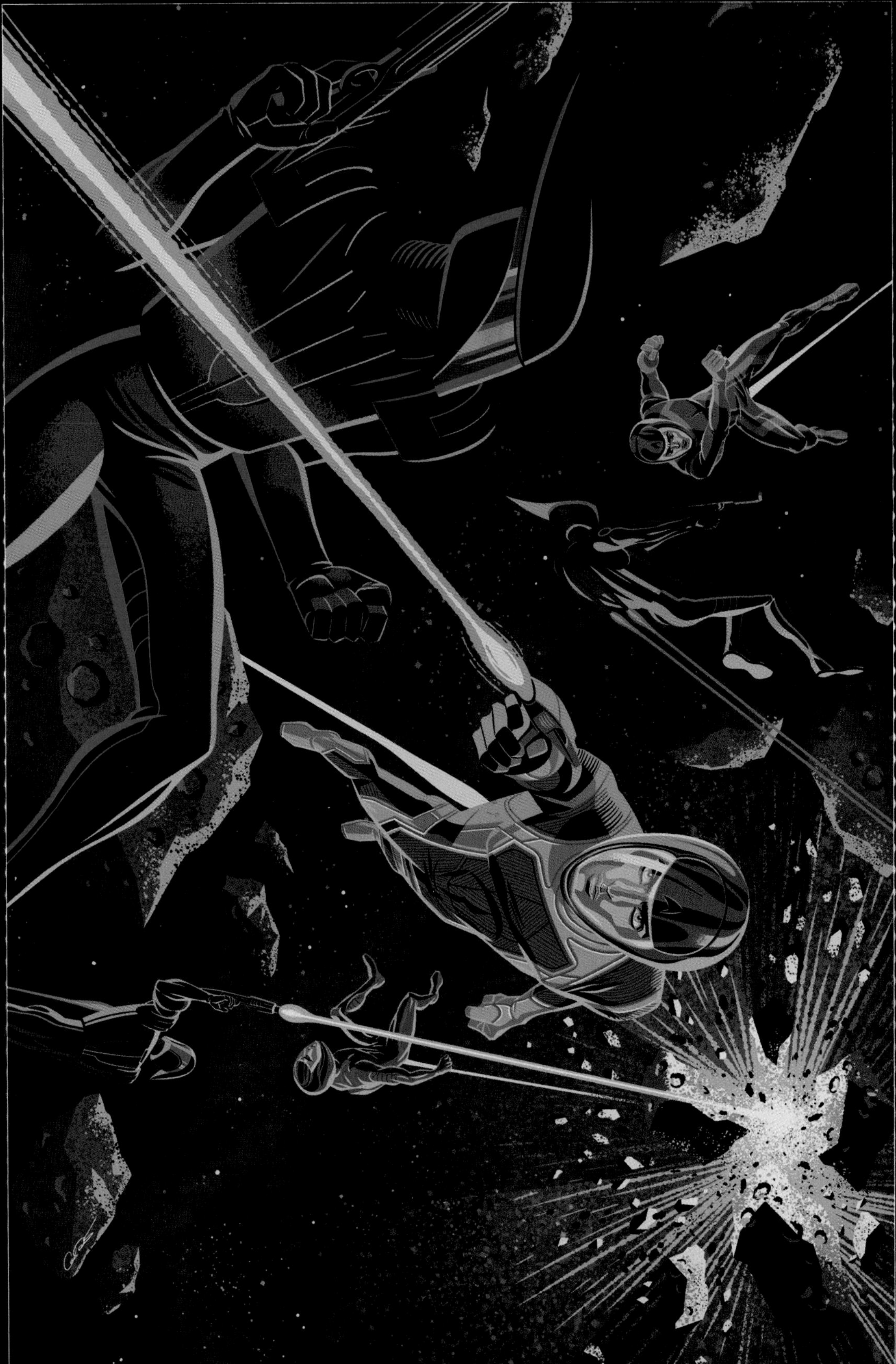

art by
George Caltsoudas

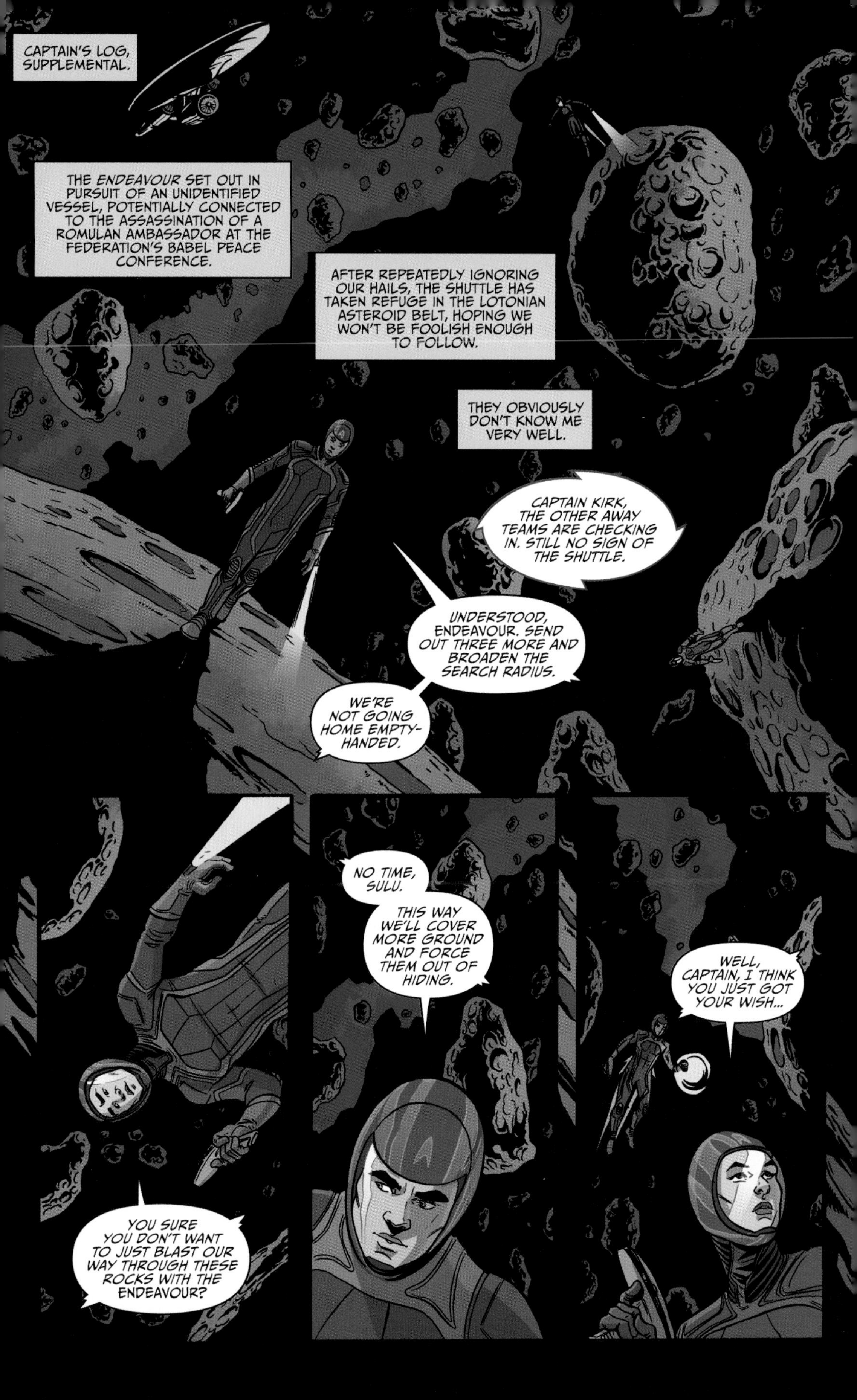
CAPTAIN'S LOG, SUPPLEMENTAL.
THE *ENDEAVOUR* SET OUT IN PURSUIT OF AN UNIDENTIFIED VESSEL, POTENTIALLY CONNECTED TO THE ASSASSINATION OF A ROMULAN AMBASSADOR AT THE FEDERATION'S BABEL PEACE CONFERENCE.
AFTER REPEATEDLY IGNORING OUR HAILS, THE SHUTTLE HAS TAKEN REFUGE IN THE LOTONIAN ASTEROID BELT, HOPING WE WON'T BE FOOLISH ENOUGH TO FOLLOW.
THEY OBVIOUSLY DON'T KNOW ME VERY WELL.
CAPTAIN KIRK, THE OTHER AWAY TEAMS ARE CHECKING IN. STILL NO SIGN OF THE SHUTTLE.
UNDERSTOOD, ENDEAVOUR. SEND OUT THREE MORE AND BROADEN THE SEARCH RADIUS.
WE'RE NOT GOING HOME EMPTY-HANDED.
YOU SURE YOU DON'T WANT TO JUST BLAST OUR WAY THROUGH THESE ROCKS WITH THE ENDEAVOUR?
NO TIME, SULU.
THIS WAY WE'LL COVER MORE GROUND AND FORCE THEM OUT OF HIDING.
WELL, CAPTAIN, I THINK YOU JUST GOT YOUR WISH...

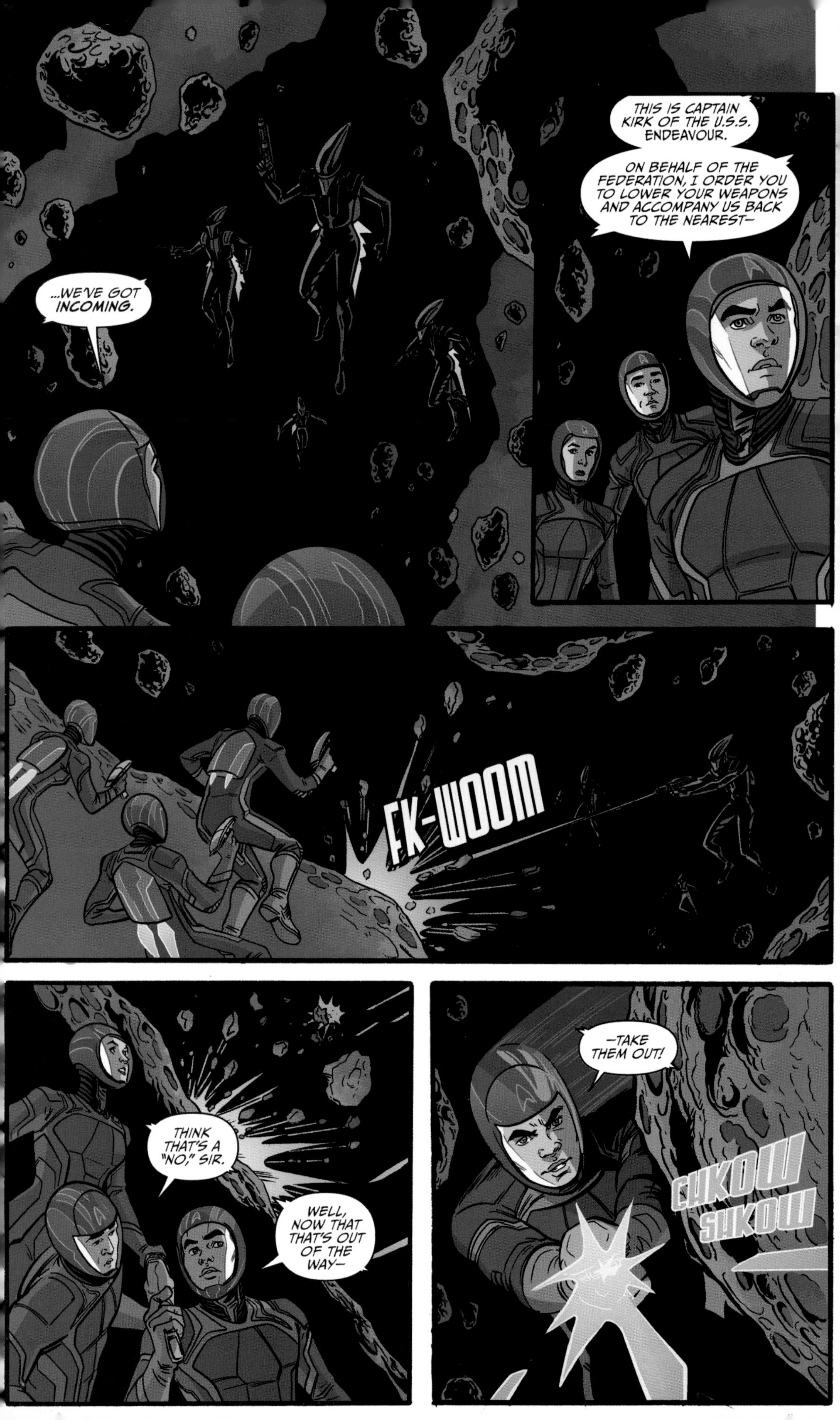
...WE'VE GOT INCOMING.
THIS IS CAPTAIN KIRK OF THE U.S.S. ENDEAVOUR.
ON BEHALF OF THE FEDERATION, I ORDER YOU TO LOWER YOUR WEAPONS AND ACCOMPANY US BACK TO THE NEAREST—
FK-WOOM
THINK THAT'S A "NO," SIR.
WELL, NOW THAT THAT'S OUT OF THE WAY—
—TAKE THEM OUT!
CHKOW
SHKOW

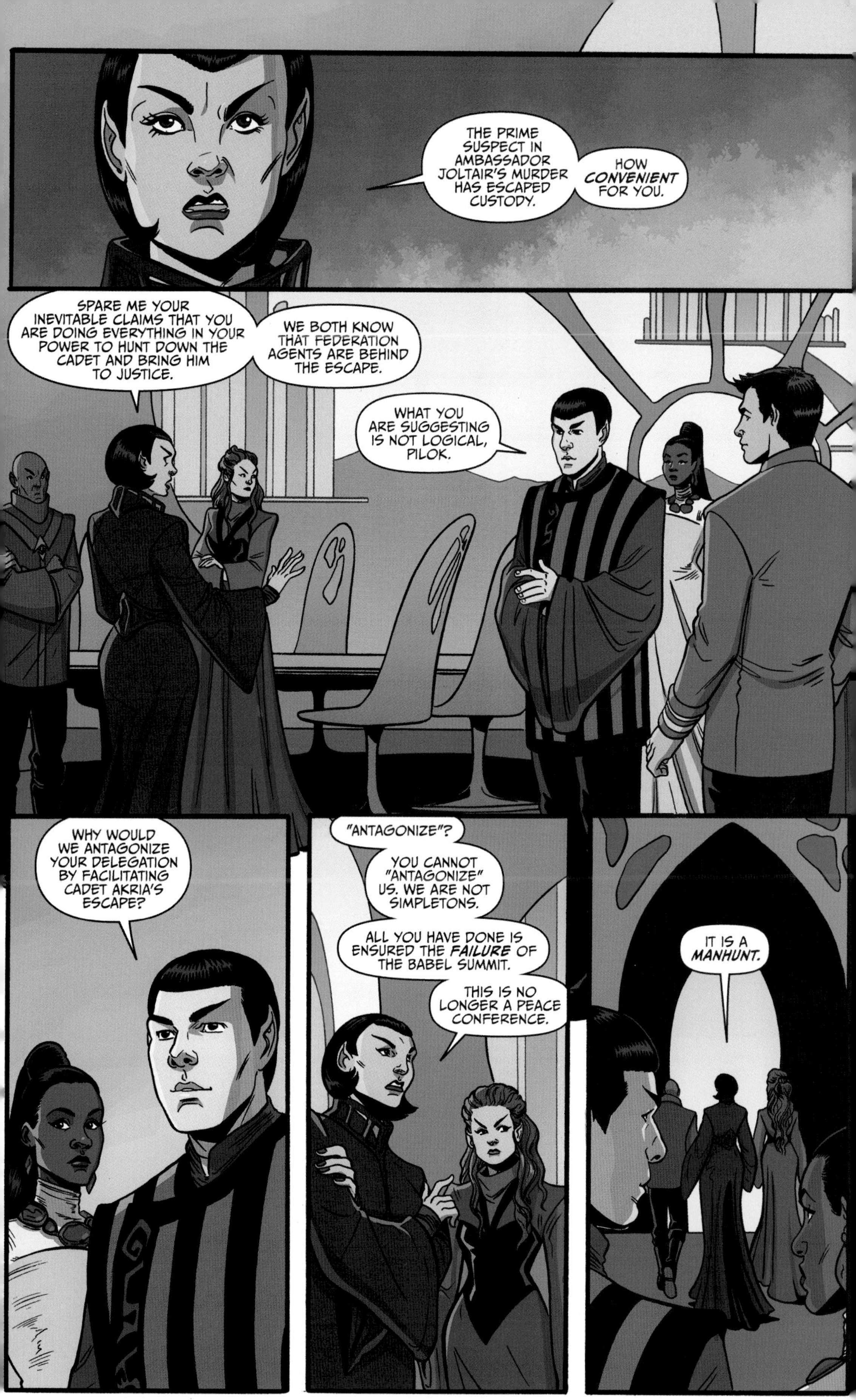
THE PRIME SUSPECT IN AMBASSADOR JOLTAIR'S MURDER HAS ESCAPED CUSTODY.
HOW *CONVENIENT* FOR YOU.
SPARE ME YOUR INEVITABLE CLAIMS THAT YOU ARE DOING EVERYTHING IN YOUR POWER TO HUNT DOWN THE CADET AND BRING HIM TO JUSTICE.
WE BOTH KNOW THAT FEDERATION AGENTS ARE BEHIND THE ESCAPE.
WHAT YOU ARE SUGGESTING IS NOT LOGICAL, PILOK.
WHY WOULD WE ANTAGONIZE YOUR DELEGATION BY FACILITATING CADET AKRIA'S ESCAPE?
"ANTAGONIZE"?
YOU CANNOT "ANTAGONIZE" US. WE ARE NOT SIMPLETONS.
ALL YOU HAVE DONE IS ENSURED THE *FAILURE* OF THE BABEL SUMMIT.
THIS IS NO LONGER A PEACE CONFERENCE.
IT IS A *MANHUNT.*

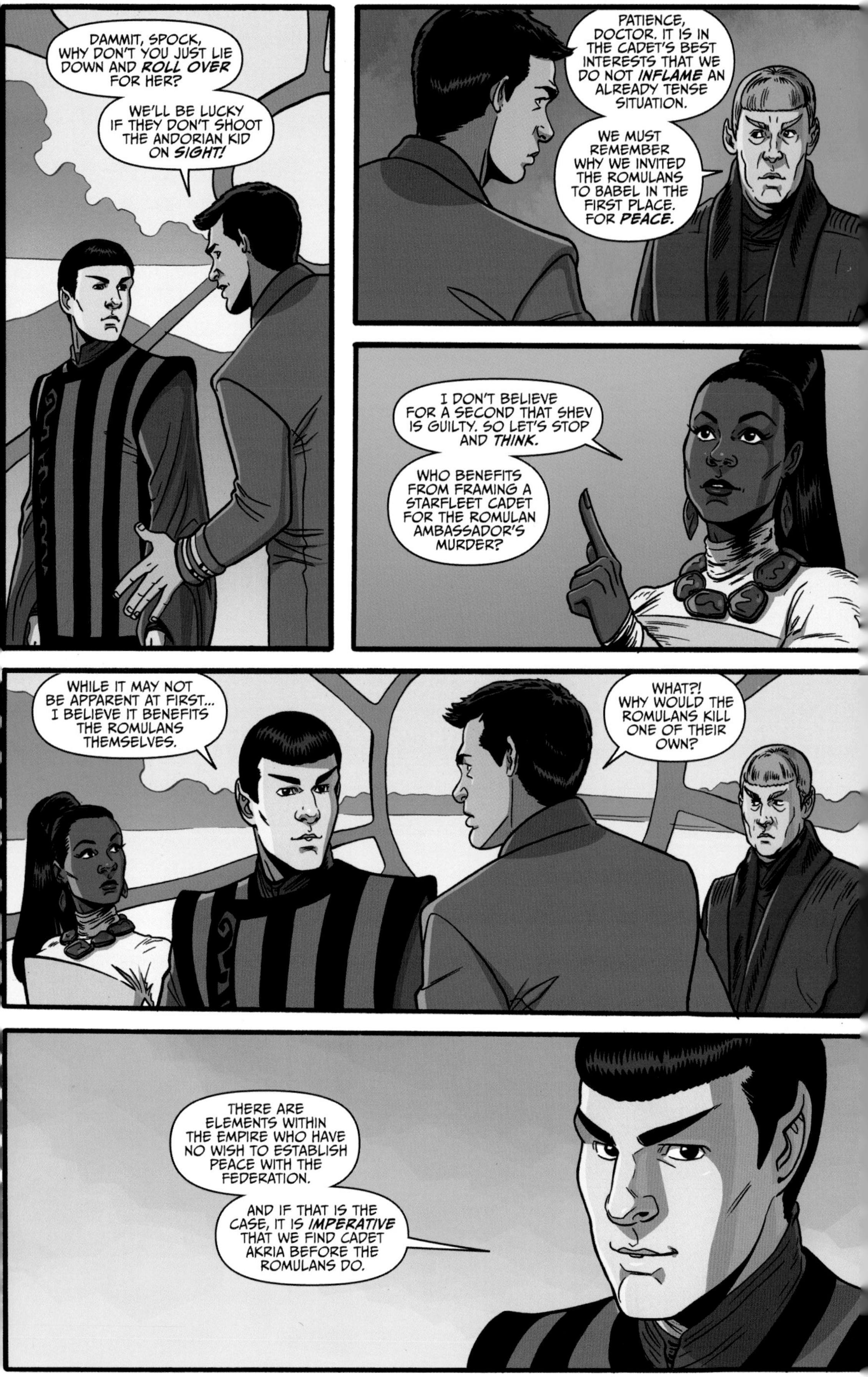
DAMMIT, SPOCK, WHY DON'T YOU JUST LIE DOWN AND ***ROLL OVER*** FOR HER?
WE'LL BE LUCKY IF THEY DON'T SHOOT THE ANDORIAN KID ON ***SIGHT!***
PATIENCE, DOCTOR. IT IS IN THE CADET'S BEST INTERESTS THAT WE DO NOT ***INFLAME*** AN ALREADY TENSE SITUATION.
WE MUST REMEMBER WHY WE INVITED THE ROMULANS TO BABEL IN THE FIRST PLACE. FOR ***PEACE.***
I DON'T BELIEVE FOR A SECOND THAT SHEV IS GUILTY. SO LET'S STOP AND ***THINK.***
WHO BENEFITS FROM FRAMING A STARFLEET CADET FOR THE ROMULAN AMBASSADOR'S MURDER?
WHILE IT MAY NOT BE APPARENT AT FIRST... I BELIEVE IT BENEFITS THE ROMULANS THEMSELVES.
WHAT?! WHY WOULD THE ROMULANS KILL ONE OF THEIR OWN?
THERE ARE ELEMENTS WITHIN THE EMPIRE WHO HAVE NO WISH TO ESTABLISH PEACE WITH THE FEDERATION.
AND IF THAT IS THE CASE, IT IS ***IMPERATIVE*** THAT WE FIND CADET AKRIA BEFORE THE ROMULANS DO.

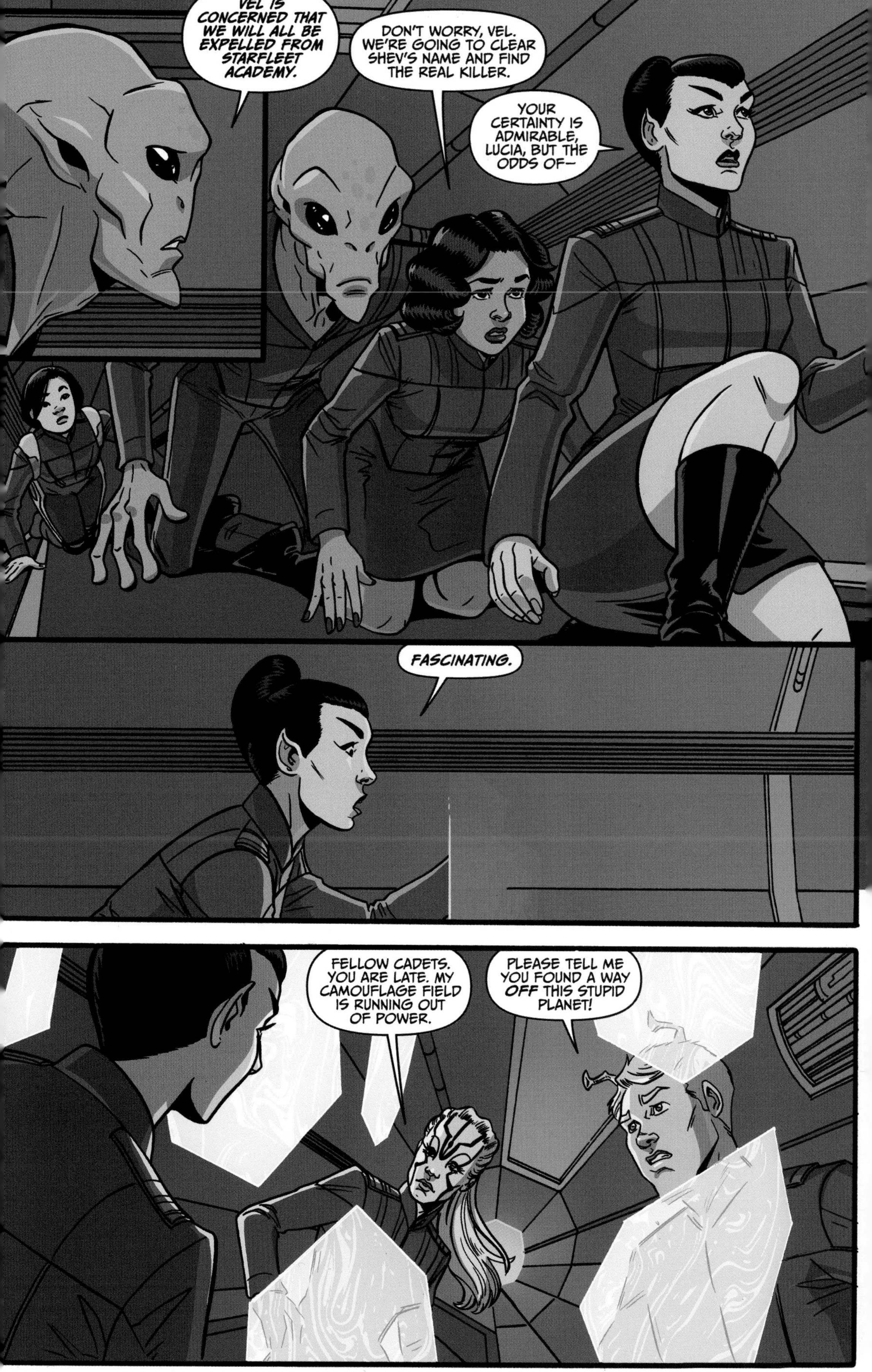
VEL IS CONCERNED THAT WE WILL ALL BE EXPELLED FROM STARFLEET ACADEMY.
DON'T WORRY, VEL. WE'RE GOING TO CLEAR SHEV'S NAME AND FIND THE REAL KILLER.
YOUR CERTAINTY IS ADMIRABLE, LUCIA, BUT THE ODDS OF—
FASCINATING.
FELLOW CADETS. YOU ARE LATE. MY CAMOUFLAGE FIELD IS RUNNING OUT OF POWER.
PLEASE TELL ME YOU FOUND A WAY OFF THIS STUPID PLANET!

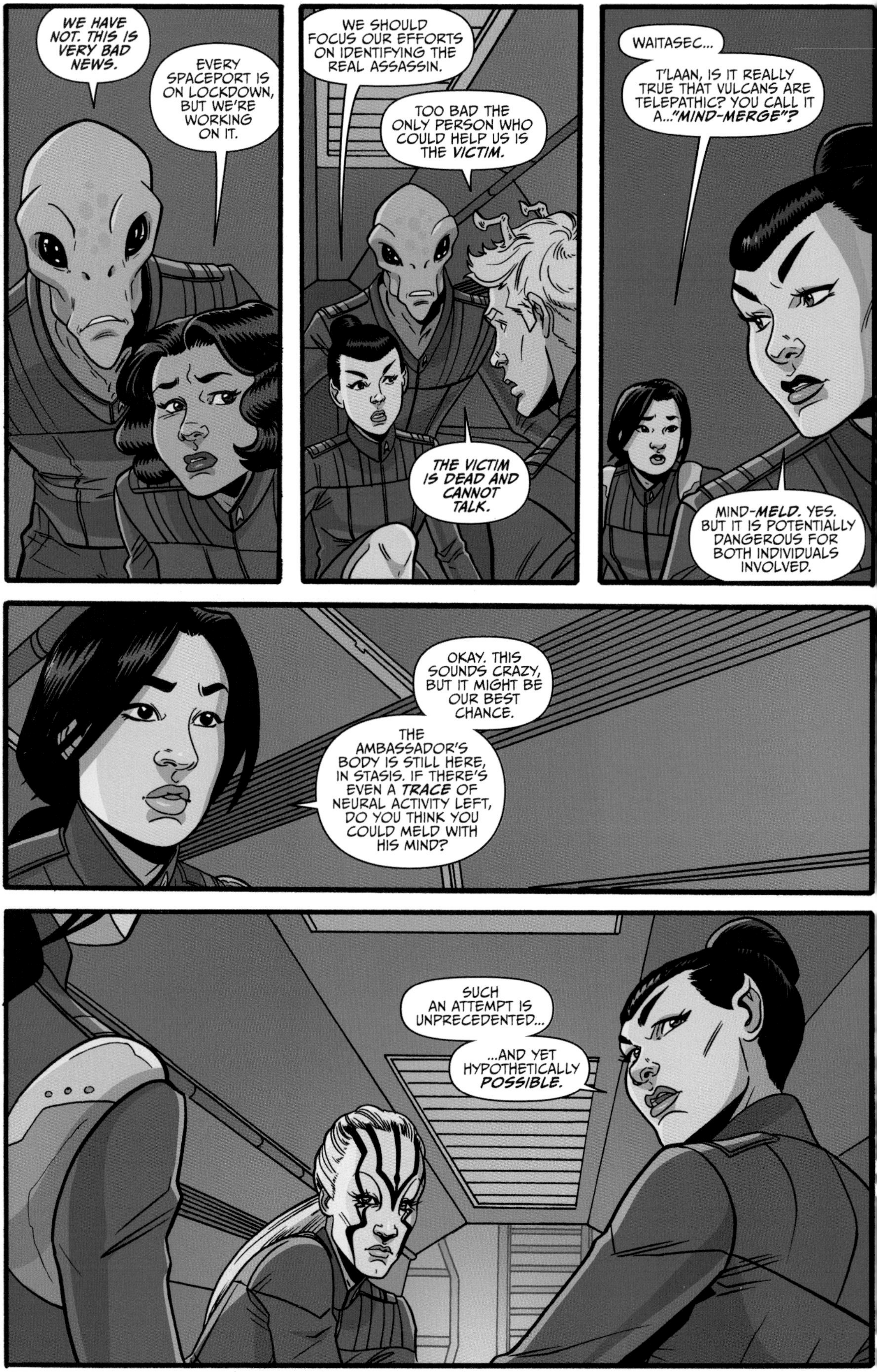
WE HAVE NOT. THIS IS VERY BAD NEWS.
EVERY SPACEPORT IS ON LOCKDOWN, BUT WE'RE WORKING ON IT.
WE SHOULD FOCUS OUR EFFORTS ON IDENTIFYING THE REAL ASSASSIN.
TOO BAD THE ONLY PERSON WHO COULD HELP US IS THE VICTIM.
THE VICTIM IS DEAD AND CANNOT TALK.
WAITASEC...
T'LAAN, IS IT REALLY TRUE THAT VULCANS ARE TELEPATHIC? YOU CALL IT A..."MIND-MERGE"?
MIND-MELD. YES. BUT IT IS POTENTIALLY DANGEROUS FOR BOTH INDIVIDUALS INVOLVED.
OKAY. THIS SOUNDS CRAZY, BUT IT MIGHT BE OUR BEST CHANCE.
THE AMBASSADOR'S BODY IS STILL HERE, IN STASIS. IF THERE'S EVEN A TRACE OF NEURAL ACTIVITY LEFT, DO YOU THINK YOU COULD MELD WITH HIS MIND?
SUCH AN ATTEMPT IS UNPRECEDENTED...
...AND YET HYPOTHETICALLY POSSIBLE.

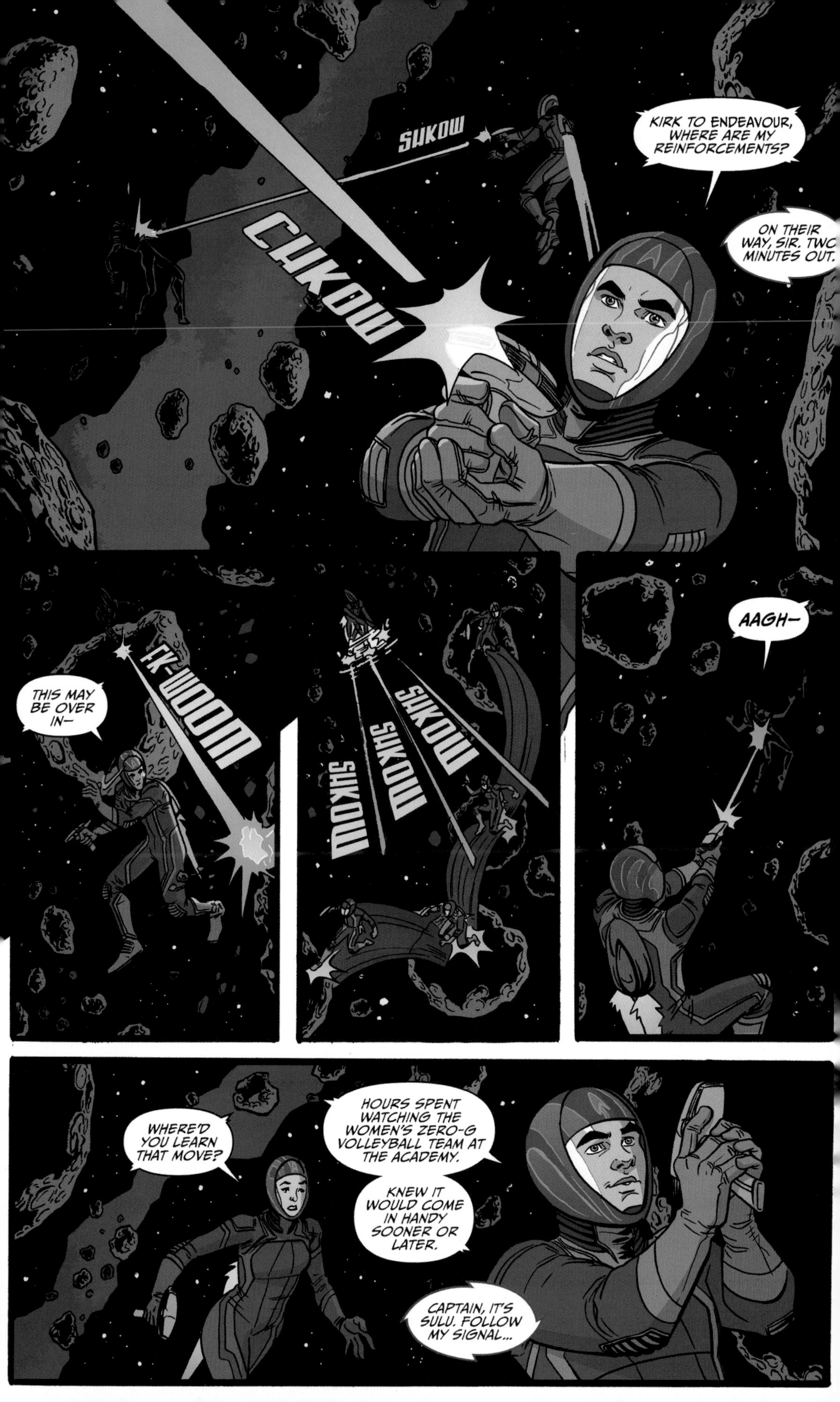
SUKOW
CUKOW
KIRK TO ENDEAVOUR, WHERE ARE MY REINFORCEMENTS?
ON THEIR WAY, SIR. TWO MINUTES OUT.
THIS MAY BE OVER IN—
FK-WOOM
SUKOW
SUKOW
SUKOW
AAGH—
WHERE'D YOU LEARN THAT MOVE?
HOURS SPENT WATCHING THE WOMEN'S ZERO-G VOLLEYBALL TEAM AT THE ACADEMY.
KNEW IT WOULD COME IN HANDY SOONER OR LATER.
CAPTAIN, IT'S SULU. FOLLOW MY SIGNAL...

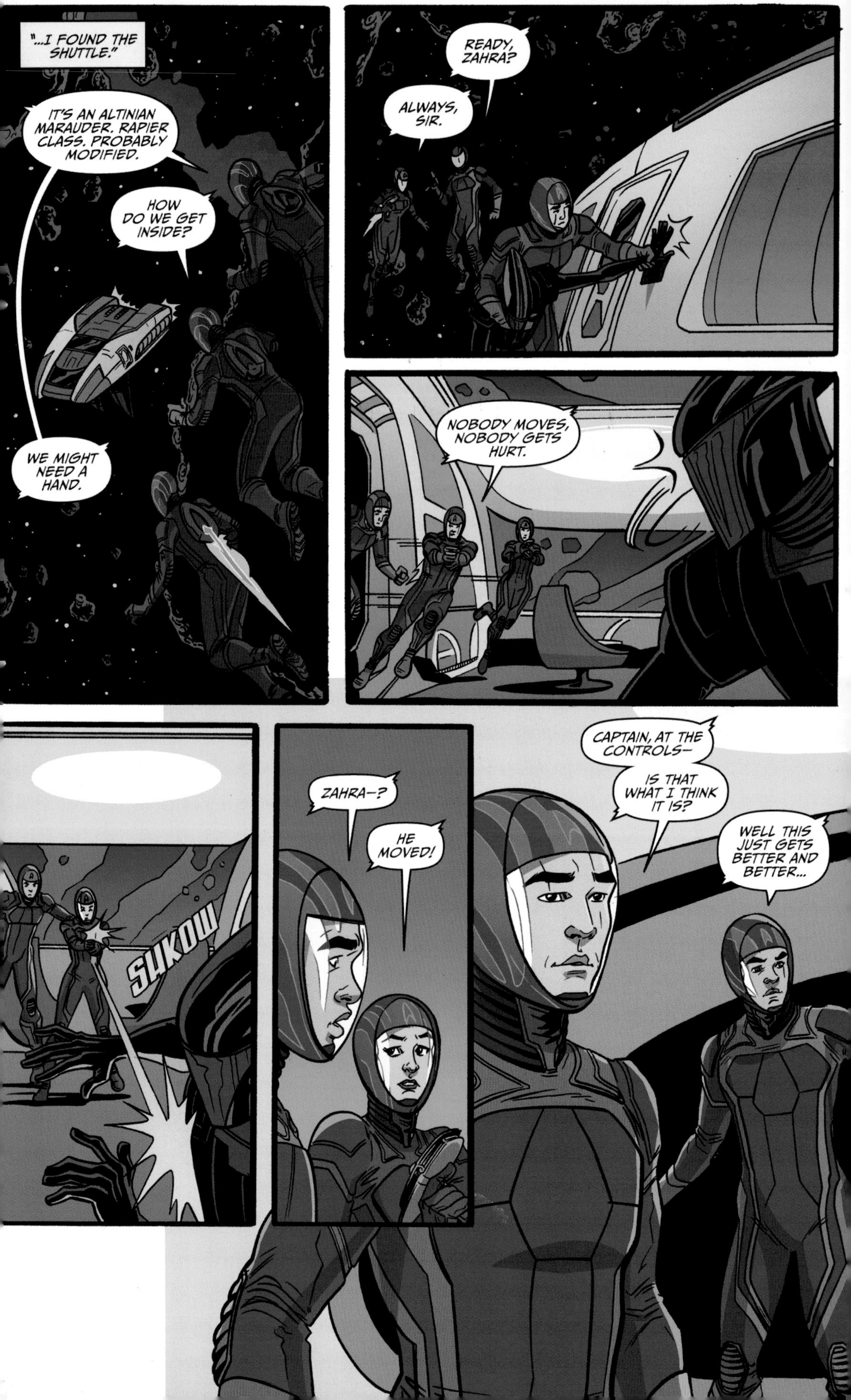
"...I FOUND THE SHUTTLE."
IT'S AN ALTINIAN MARAUDER. RAPIER CLASS. PROBABLY MODIFIED.
HOW DO WE GET INSIDE?
WE MIGHT NEED A HAND.
READY, ZAHRA?
ALWAYS, SIR.
NOBODY MOVES, NOBODY GETS HURT.
SUKOW
ZAHRA--?
HE MOVED!
CAPTAIN, AT THE CONTROLS--
IS THAT WHAT I THINK IT IS?
WELL THIS JUST GETS BETTER AND BETTER...

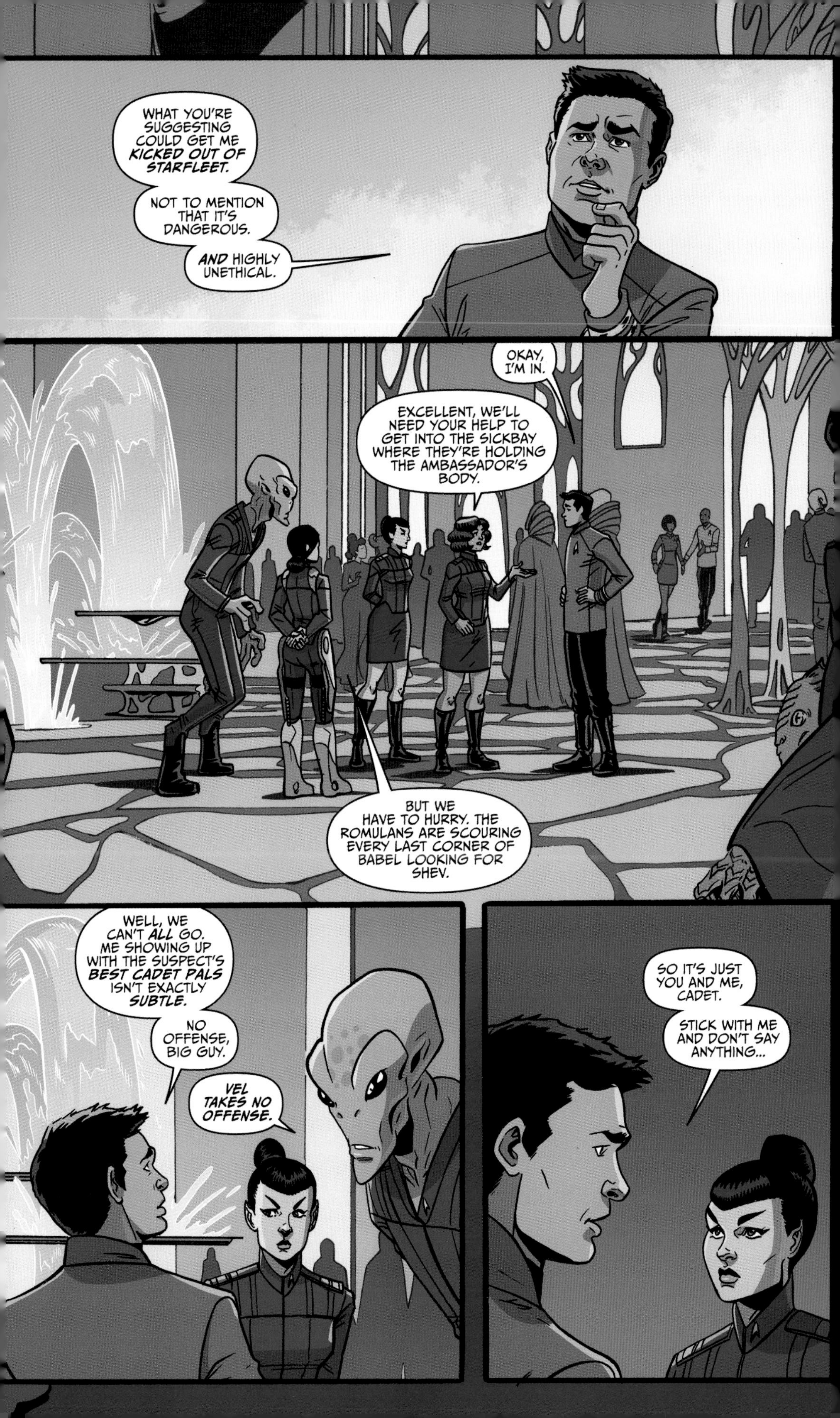

WHAT YOU'RE SUGGESTING COULD GET ME *KICKED OUT OF STARFLEET.*
NOT TO MENTION THAT IT'S DANGEROUS.
AND HIGHLY UNETHICAL.
OKAY, I'M IN.
EXCELLENT, WE'LL NEED YOUR HELP TO GET INTO THE SICKBAY WHERE THEY'RE HOLDING THE AMBASSADOR'S BODY.
BUT WE HAVE TO HURRY. THE ROMULANS ARE SCOURING EVERY LAST CORNER OF BABEL LOOKING FOR SHEV.
WELL, WE CAN'T *ALL* GO. ME SHOWING UP WITH THE SUSPECT'S *BEST CADET PALS* ISN'T EXACTLY *SUBTLE.*
NO OFFENSE, BIG GUY.
VEL TAKES NO OFFENSE.
SO IT'S JUST YOU AND ME, CADET.
STICK WITH ME AND DON'T SAY ANYTHING...

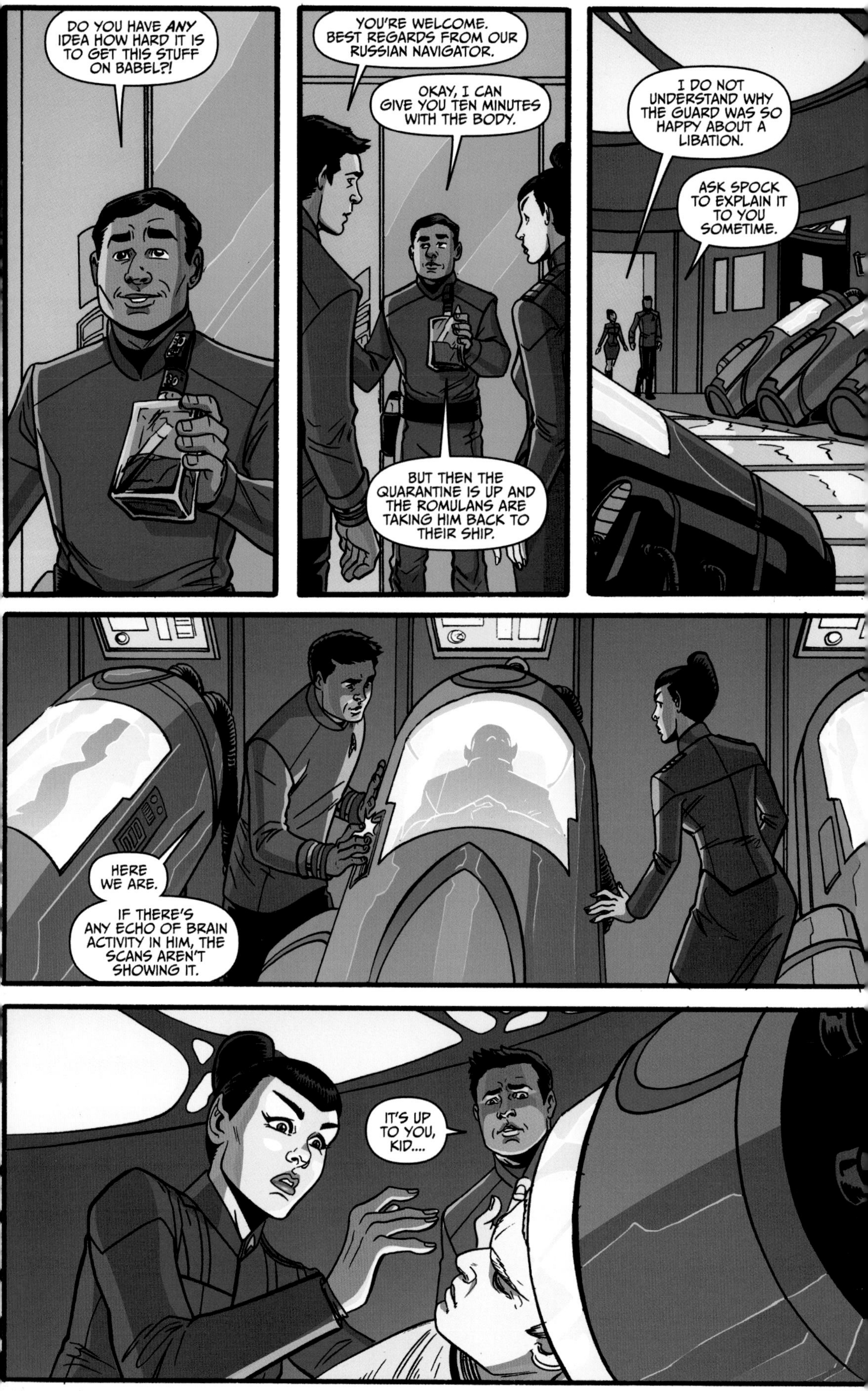
DO YOU HAVE ANY IDEA HOW HARD IT IS TO GET THIS STUFF ON BABEL?!
YOU'RE WELCOME. BEST REGARDS FROM OUR RUSSIAN NAVIGATOR.
OKAY, I CAN GIVE YOU TEN MINUTES WITH THE BODY.
BUT THEN THE QUARANTINE IS UP AND THE ROMULANS ARE TAKING HIM BACK TO THEIR SHIP.
I DO NOT UNDERSTAND WHY THE GUARD WAS SO HAPPY ABOUT A LIBATION.
ASK SPOCK TO EXPLAIN IT TO YOU SOMETIME.
HERE WE ARE.
IF THERE'S ANY ECHO OF BRAIN ACTIVITY IN HIM, THE SCANS AREN'T SHOWING IT.
IT'S UP TO YOU, KID....

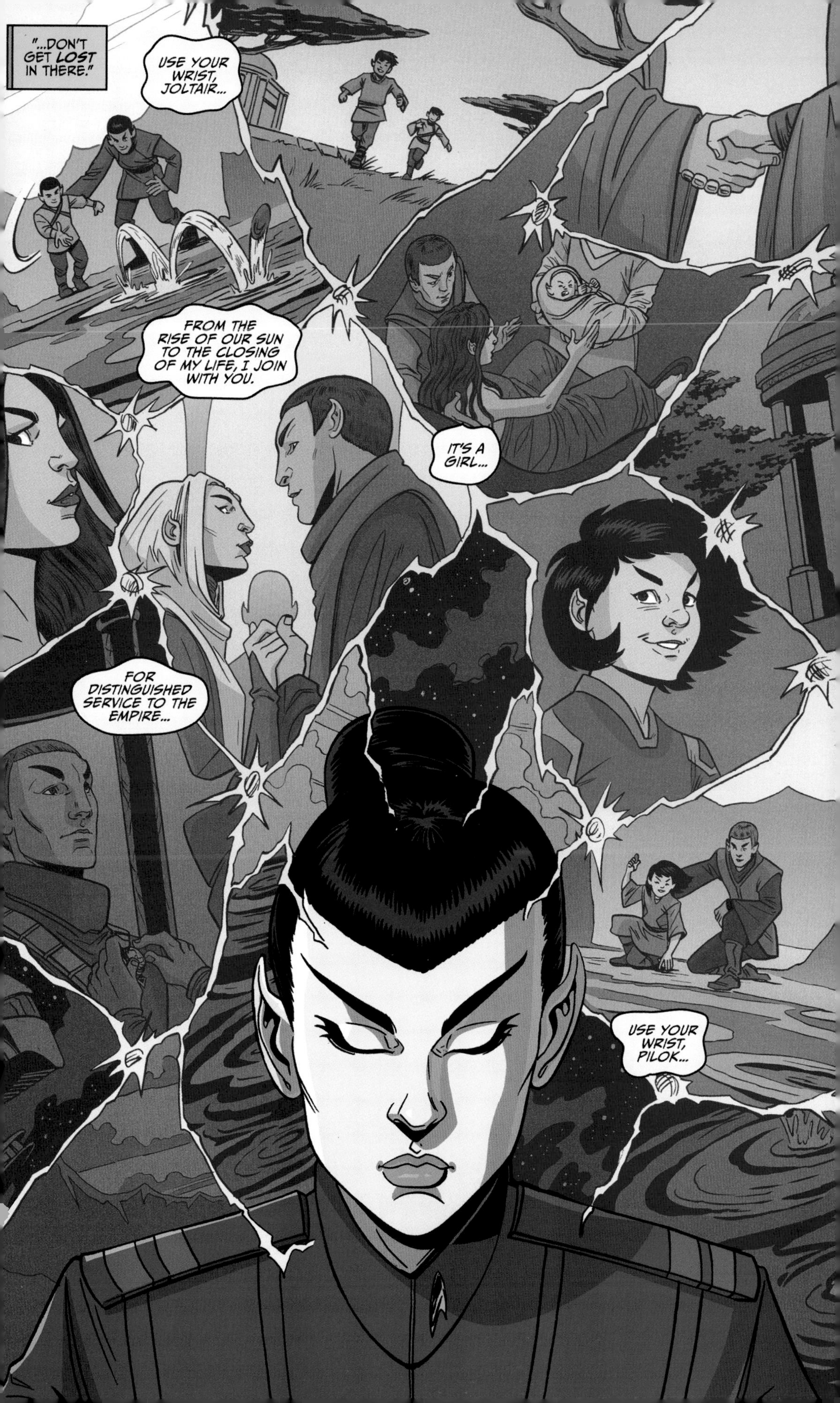

"...DON'T GET LOST IN THERE."
USE YOUR WRIST, JOLTAIR...
FROM THE RISE OF OUR SUN TO THE CLOSING OF MY LIFE, I JOIN WITH YOU.
IT'S A GIRL...
FOR DISTINGUISHED SERVICE TO THE EMPIRE...
USE YOUR WRIST, PILOK...

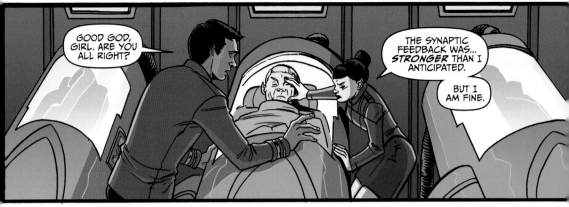

GOOD GOD, GIRL. ARE YOU ALL RIGHT?

THE SYNAPTIC FEEDBACK WAS... *STRONGER* THAN I ANTICIPATED.

BUT I AM FINE.

I AM SEARCHING THE AMBASSADOR'S LAST CONSCIOUS MOMENTS, BUT THE CONNECTION IS ALREADY FADING.

"WHILE SPEAKING WITH THE COUNCIL, HE FELT THE SICKNESS COME OVER HIM.

"HE WAS TERRIFIED.

HE KNEW HE WAS DYING BUT...

BUT WANTED TO FORGE A PEACE BEFORE...

"THE LAST SUBSTANCE THE AMBASSADOR INGESTED WAS GIVEN TO HIM BY SOMEONE ELSE."

THE MELD IS BROKEN. THE LAST TRACE OF HIS MIND IS GONE.

BUT WE HAVE A *NEW* SUSPECT.

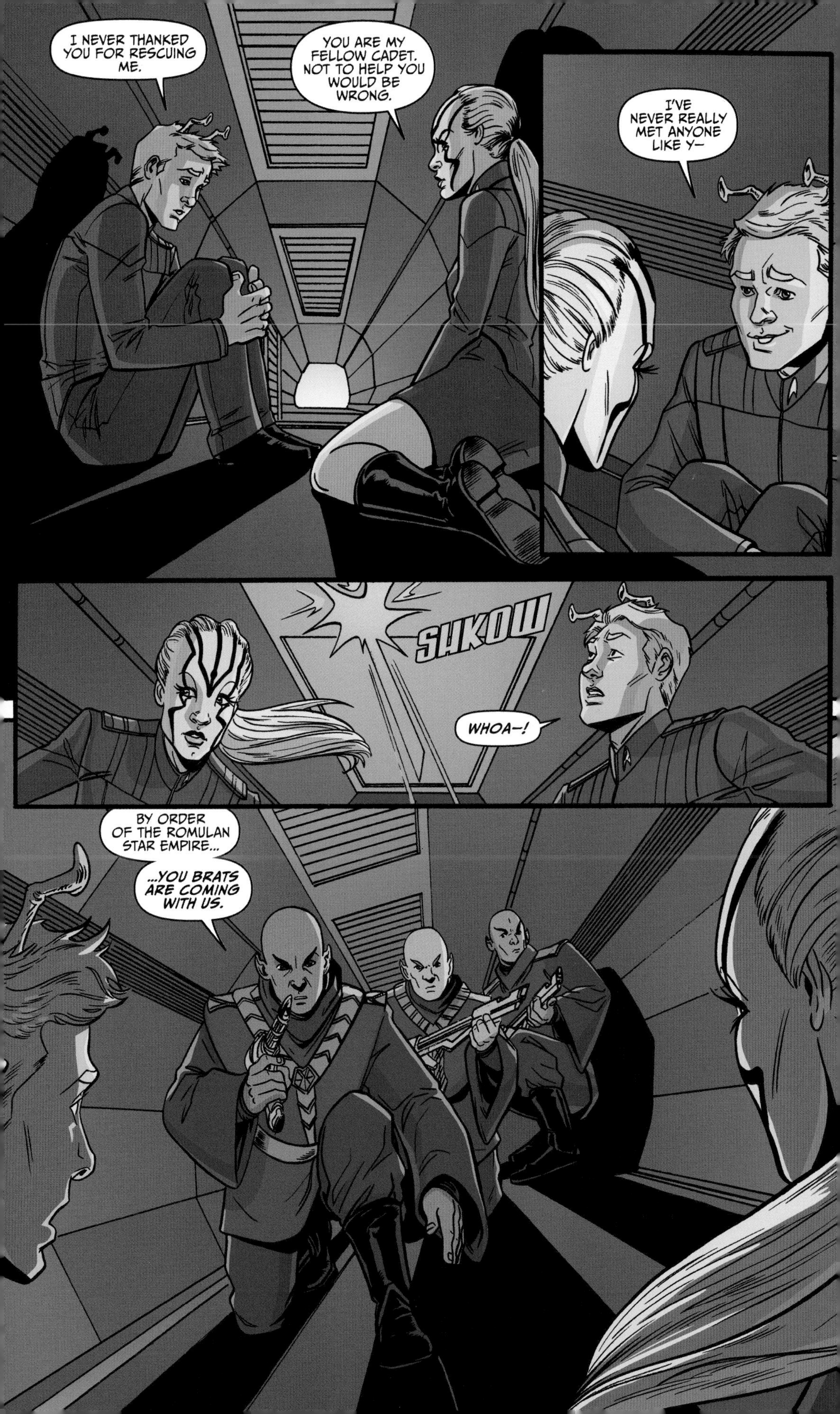
I NEVER THANKED YOU FOR RESCUING ME.
YOU ARE MY FELLOW CADET. NOT TO HELP YOU WOULD BE WRONG.
I'VE NEVER REALLY MET ANYONE LIKE Y–
SHKOW
WHOA–!
BY ORDER OF THE ROMULAN STAR EMPIRE...
...YOU BRATS ARE COMING WITH US.

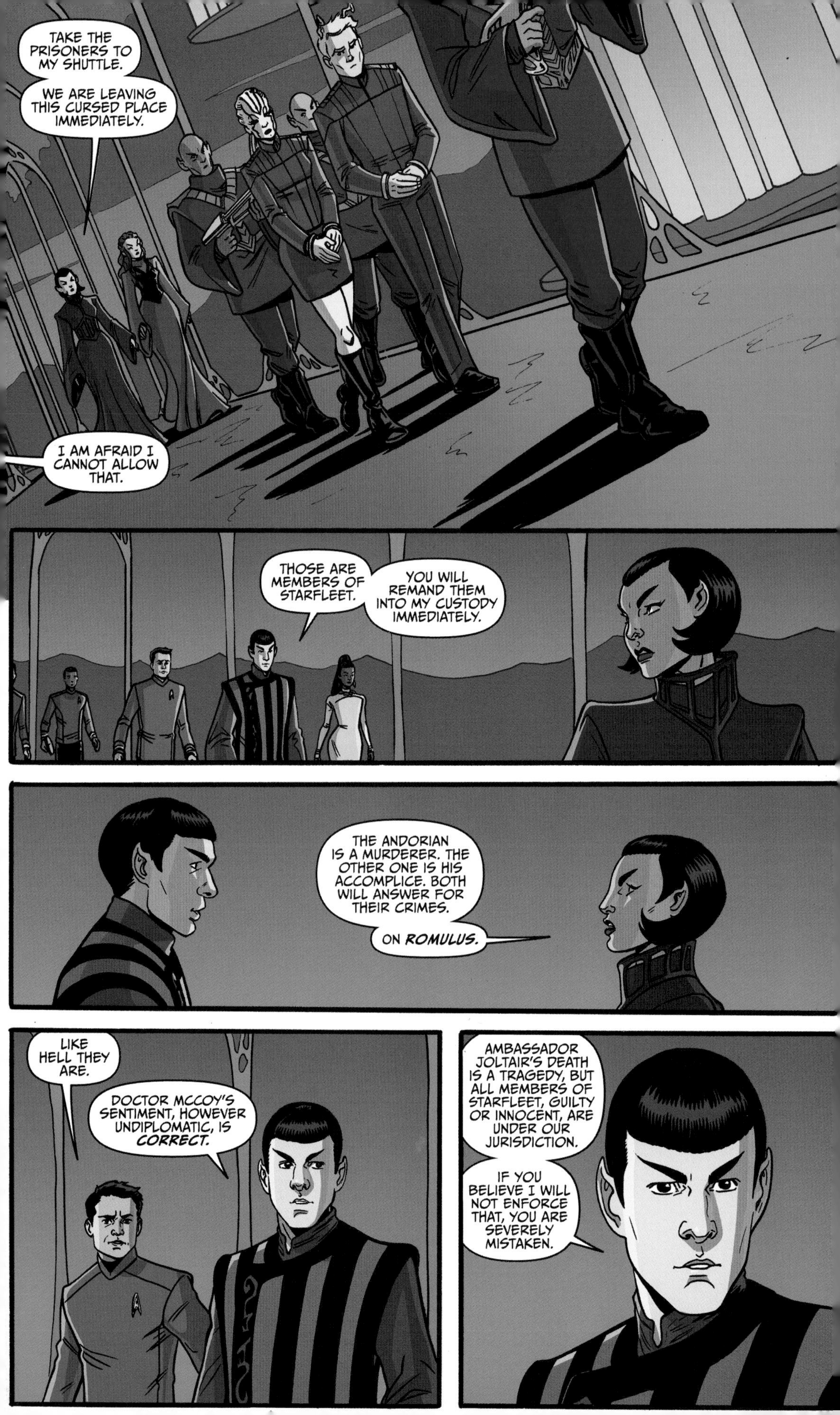

TAKE THE PRISONERS TO MY SHUTTLE.
WE ARE LEAVING THIS CURSED PLACE IMMEDIATELY.
I AM AFRAID I CANNOT ALLOW THAT.
THOSE ARE MEMBERS OF STARFLEET.
YOU WILL REMAND THEM INTO MY CUSTODY IMMEDIATELY.
THE ANDORIAN IS A MURDERER. THE OTHER ONE IS HIS ACCOMPLICE. BOTH WILL ANSWER FOR THEIR CRIMES.
ON ***ROMULUS.***
LIKE HELL THEY ARE.
DOCTOR MCCOY'S SENTIMENT, HOWEVER UNDIPLOMATIC, IS ***CORRECT.***
AMBASSADOR JOLTAIR'S DEATH IS A TRAGEDY, BUT ALL MEMBERS OF STARFLEET, GUILTY OR INNOCENT, ARE UNDER OUR JURISDICTION.
IF YOU BELIEVE I WILL NOT ENFORCE THAT, YOU ARE SEVERELY MISTAKEN.

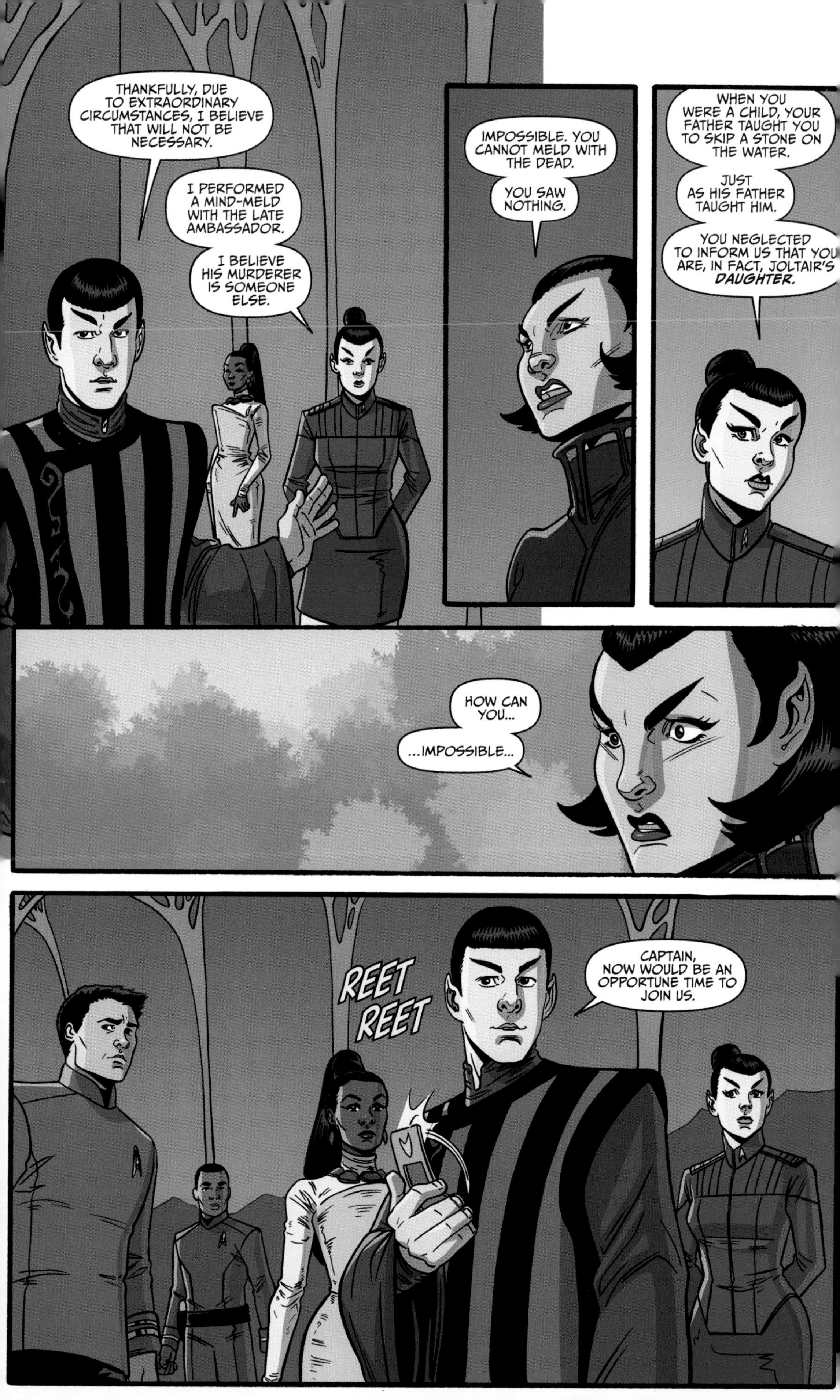

THANKFULLY, DUE TO EXTRAORDINARY CIRCUMSTANCES, I BELIEVE THAT WILL NOT BE NECESSARY.
I PERFORMED A MIND-MELD WITH THE LATE AMBASSADOR.
I BELIEVE HIS MURDERER IS SOMEONE ELSE.
IMPOSSIBLE. YOU CANNOT MELD WITH THE DEAD.
YOU SAW NOTHING.
WHEN YOU WERE A CHILD, YOUR FATHER TAUGHT YOU TO SKIP A STONE ON THE WATER.
JUST AS HIS FATHER TAUGHT HIM.
YOU NEGLECTED TO INFORM US THAT YOU ARE, IN FACT, JOLTAIR'S ***DAUGHTER.***
HOW CAN YOU...
...IMPOSSIBLE...
REET REET
CAPTAIN, NOW WOULD BE AN OPPORTUNE TIME TO JOIN US.

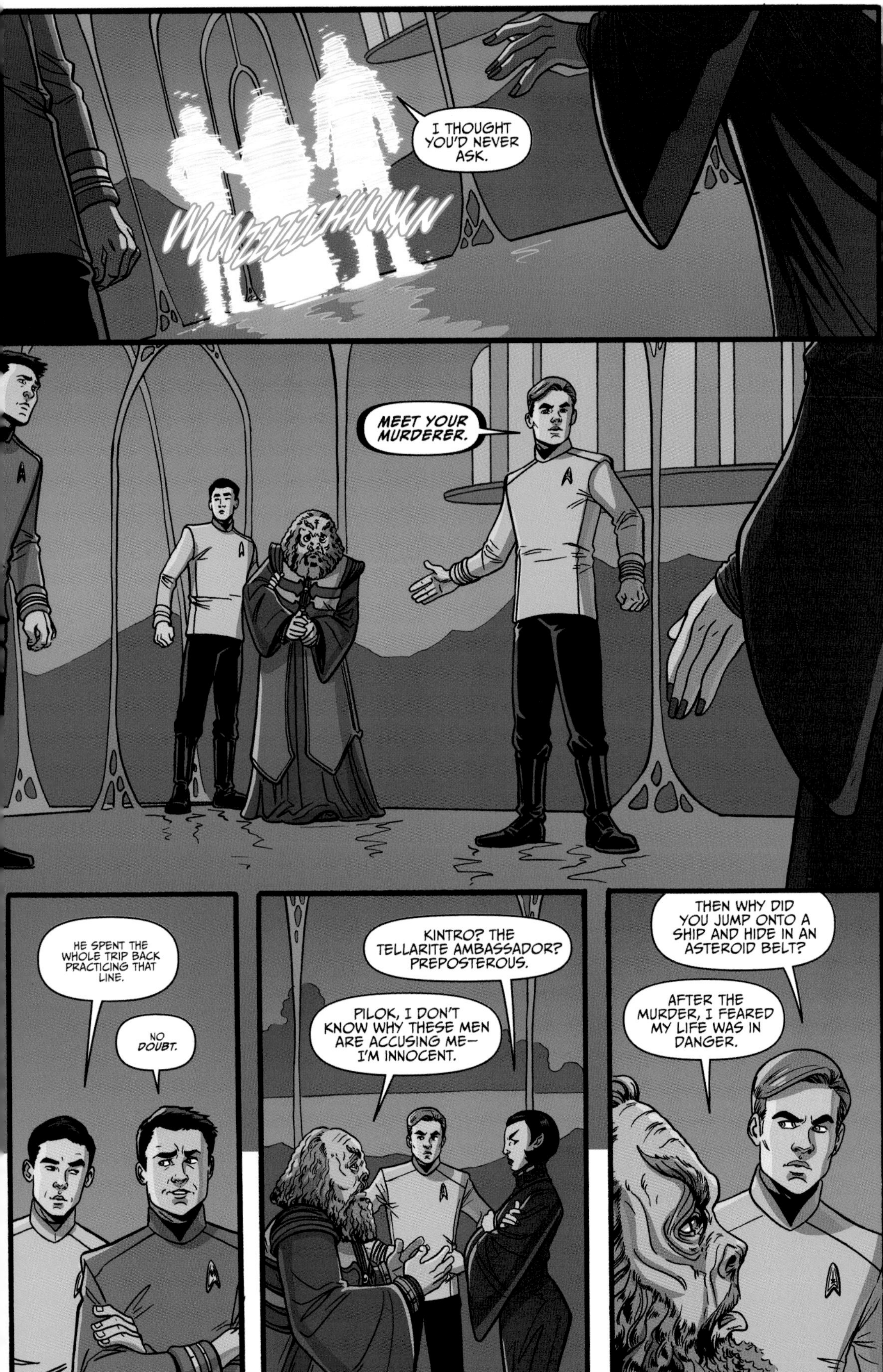
I THOUGHT YOU'D NEVER ASK.
VVVVVZZZZZHHNNNN
MEET YOUR MURDERER.
HE SPENT THE WHOLE TRIP BACK PRACTICING THAT LINE.
NO DOUBT.
KINTRO? THE TELLARITE AMBASSADOR? PREPOSTEROUS.
PILOK, I DON'T KNOW WHY THESE MEN ARE ACCUSING ME— I'M INNOCENT.
THEN WHY DID YOU JUMP ONTO A SHIP AND HIDE IN AN ASTEROID BELT?
AFTER THE MURDER, I FEARED MY LIFE WAS IN DANGER.

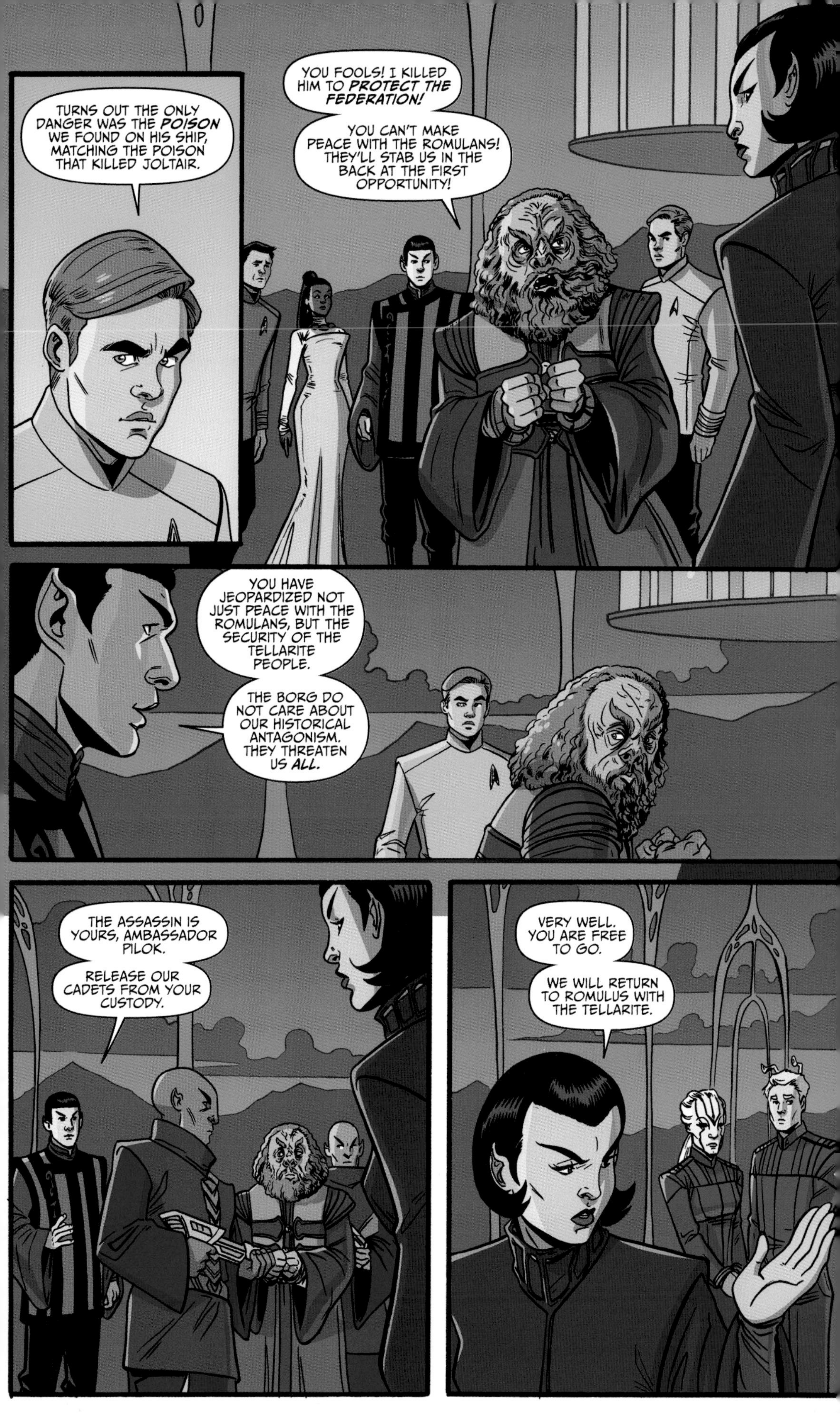
TURNS OUT THE ONLY DANGER WAS THE *POISON* WE FOUND ON HIS SHIP, MATCHING THE POISON THAT KILLED JOLTAIR.
YOU FOOLS! I KILLED HIM TO *PROTECT THE FEDERATION!*
YOU CAN'T MAKE PEACE WITH THE ROMULANS! THEY'LL STAB US IN THE BACK AT THE FIRST OPPORTUNITY!
YOU HAVE JEOPARDIZED NOT JUST PEACE WITH THE ROMULANS, BUT THE SECURITY OF THE TELLARITE PEOPLE.
THE BORG DO NOT CARE ABOUT OUR HISTORICAL ANTAGONISM. THEY THREATEN US *ALL.*
THE ASSASSIN IS YOURS, AMBASSADOR PILOK.
RELEASE OUR CADETS FROM YOUR CUSTODY.
VERY WELL. YOU ARE FREE TO GO.
WE WILL RETURN TO ROMULUS WITH THE TELLARITE.

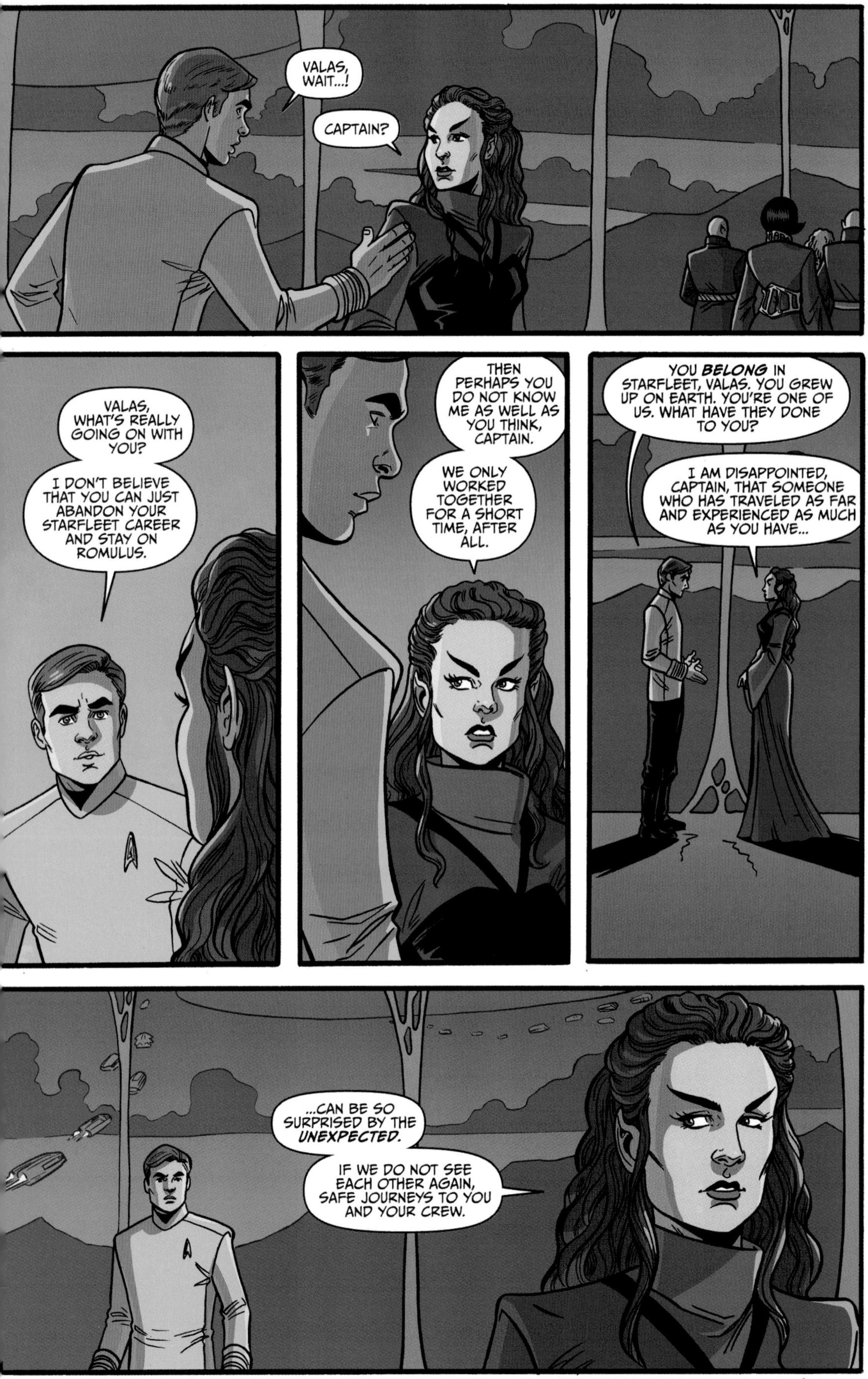
VALAS, WAIT...!
CAPTAIN?
VALAS, WHAT'S REALLY GOING ON WITH YOU?
I DON'T BELIEVE THAT YOU CAN JUST ABANDON YOUR STARFLEET CAREER AND STAY ON ROMULUS.
THEN PERHAPS YOU DO NOT KNOW ME AS WELL AS YOU THINK, CAPTAIN.
WE ONLY WORKED TOGETHER FOR A SHORT TIME, AFTER ALL.
YOU ***BELONG*** IN STARFLEET, VALAS. YOU GREW UP ON EARTH. YOU'RE ONE OF US. WHAT HAVE THEY DONE TO YOU?
I AM DISAPPOINTED, CAPTAIN, THAT SOMEONE WHO HAS TRAVELED AS FAR AND EXPERIENCED AS MUCH AS YOU HAVE...
...CAN BE SO SURPRISED BY THE ***UNEXPECTED.***
IF WE DO NOT SEE EACH OTHER AGAIN, SAFE JOURNEYS TO YOU AND YOUR CREW.

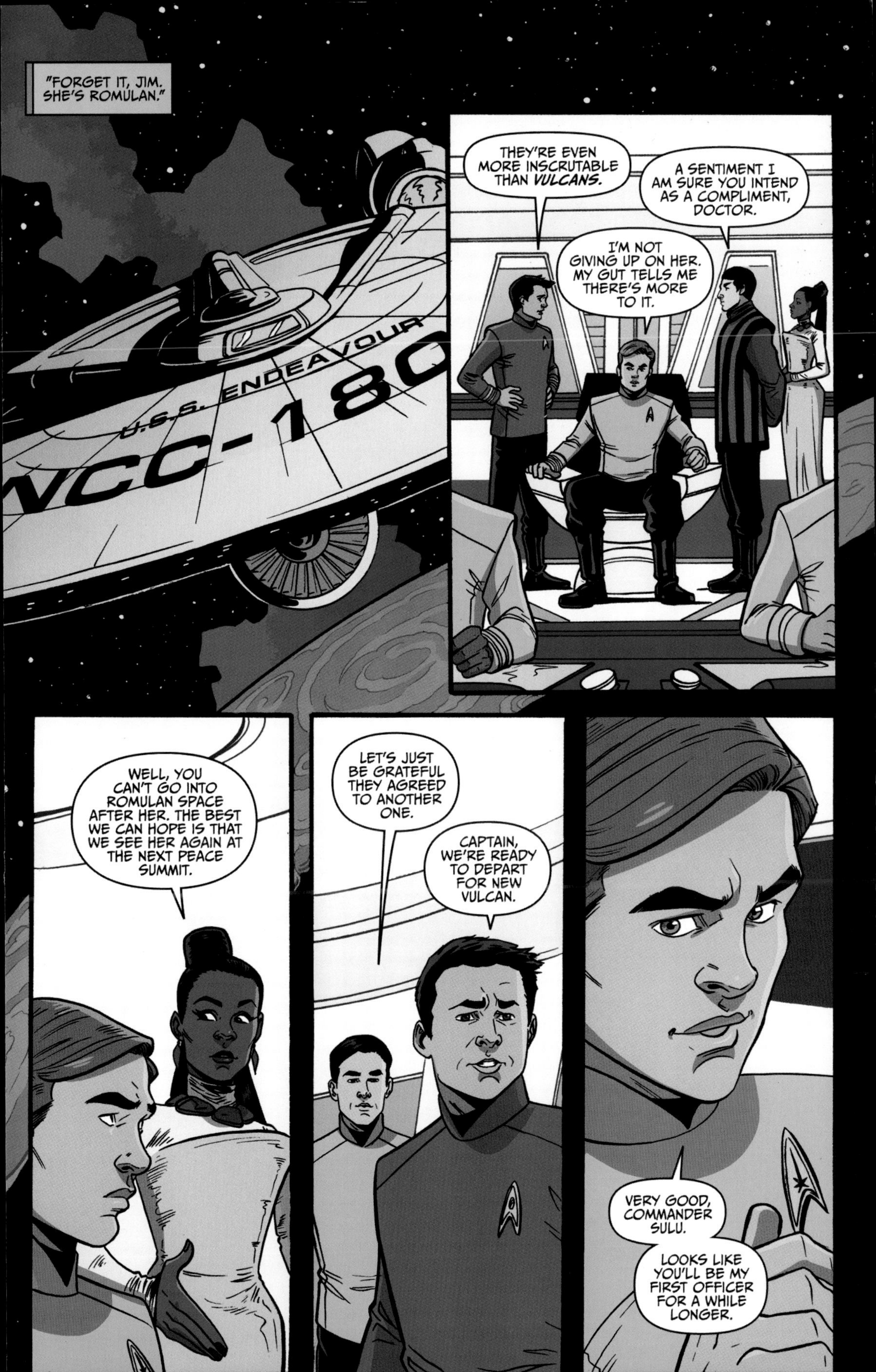
"FORGET IT, JIM. SHE'S ROMULAN."
U.S.S. ENDEAVOUR
NCC-180
THEY'RE EVEN MORE INSCRUTABLE THAN VULCANS.
A SENTIMENT I AM SURE YOU INTEND AS A COMPLIMENT, DOCTOR.
I'M NOT GIVING UP ON HER. MY GUT TELLS ME THERE'S MORE TO IT.
WELL, YOU CAN'T GO INTO ROMULAN SPACE AFTER HER. THE BEST WE CAN HOPE IS THAT WE SEE HER AGAIN AT THE NEXT PEACE SUMMIT.
LET'S JUST BE GRATEFUL THEY AGREED TO ANOTHER ONE.
CAPTAIN, WE'RE READY TO DEPART FOR NEW VULCAN.
VERY GOOD, COMMANDER SULU.
LOOKS LIKE YOU'LL BE MY FIRST OFFICER FOR A WHILE LONGER.

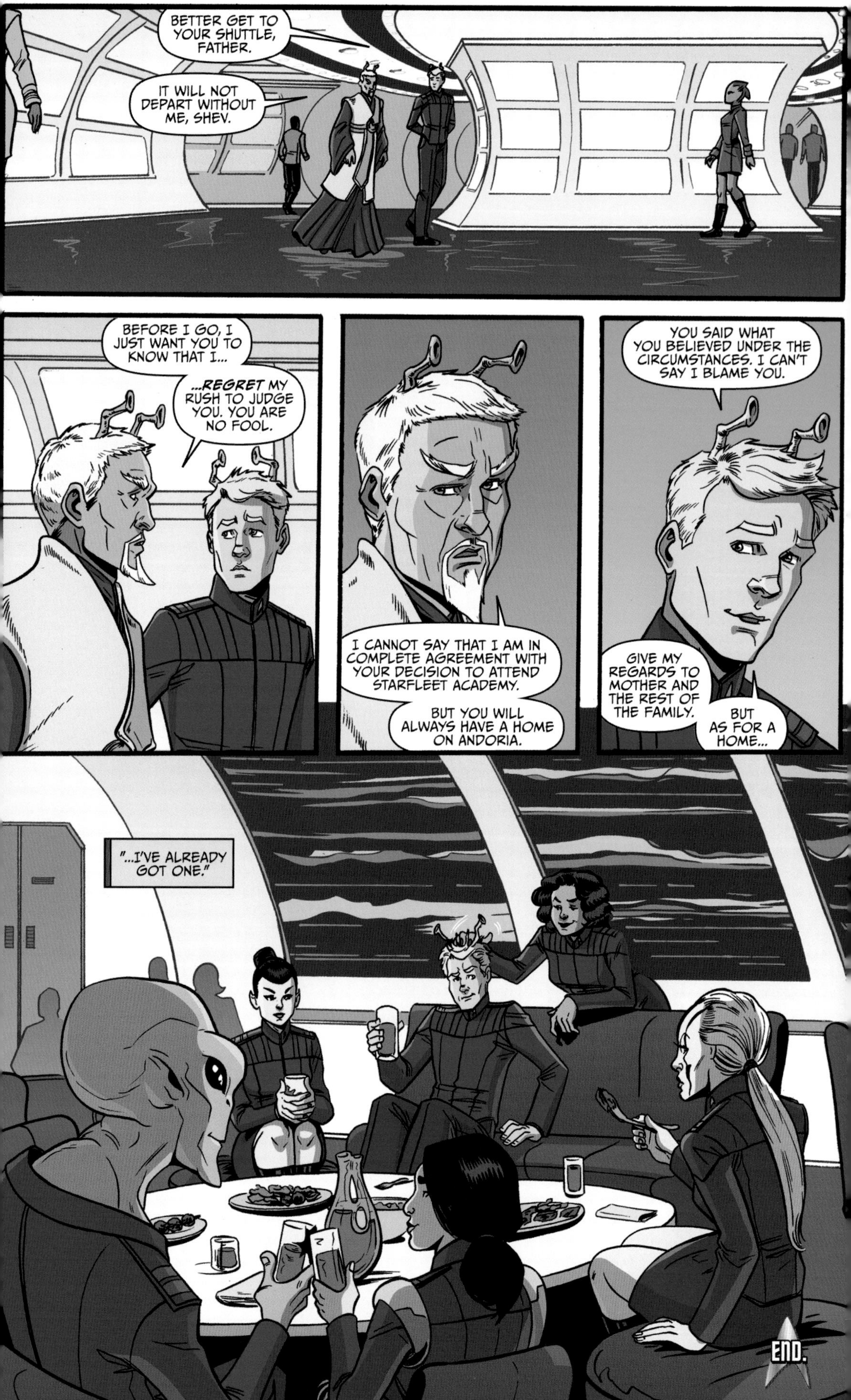

BETTER GET TO YOUR SHUTTLE, FATHER.
IT WILL NOT DEPART WITHOUT ME, SHEV.
BEFORE I GO, I JUST WANT YOU TO KNOW THAT I...
...REGRET MY RUSH TO JUDGE YOU. YOU ARE NO FOOL.
I CANNOT SAY THAT I AM IN COMPLETE AGREEMENT WITH YOUR DECISION TO ATTEND STARFLEET ACADEMY.
BUT YOU WILL ALWAYS HAVE A HOME ON ANDORIA.
YOU SAID WHAT YOU BELIEVED UNDER THE CIRCUMSTANCES. I CAN'T SAY I BLAME YOU.
GIVE MY REGARDS TO MOTHER AND THE REST OF THE FAMILY.
BUT AS FOR A HOME...
"...I'VE ALREADY GOT ONE."
END.

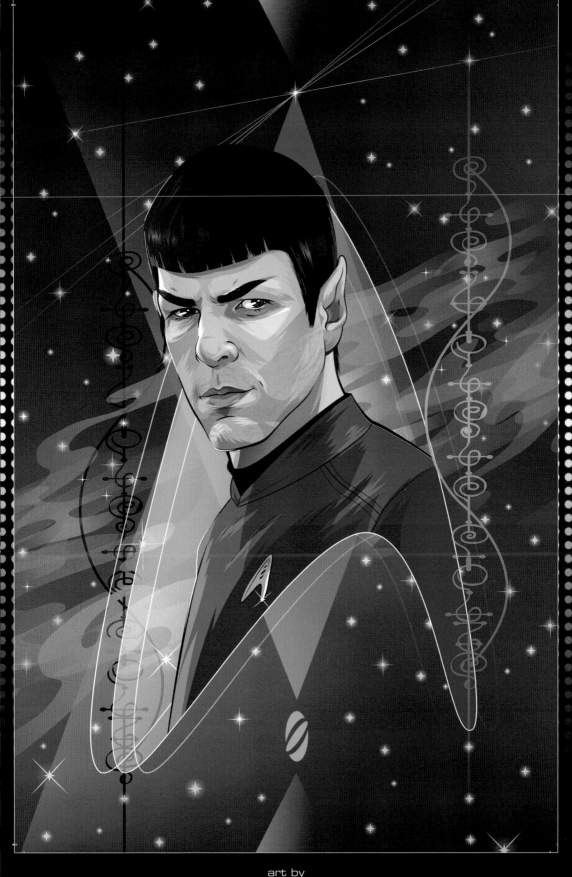

art by
Cryssy Cheung

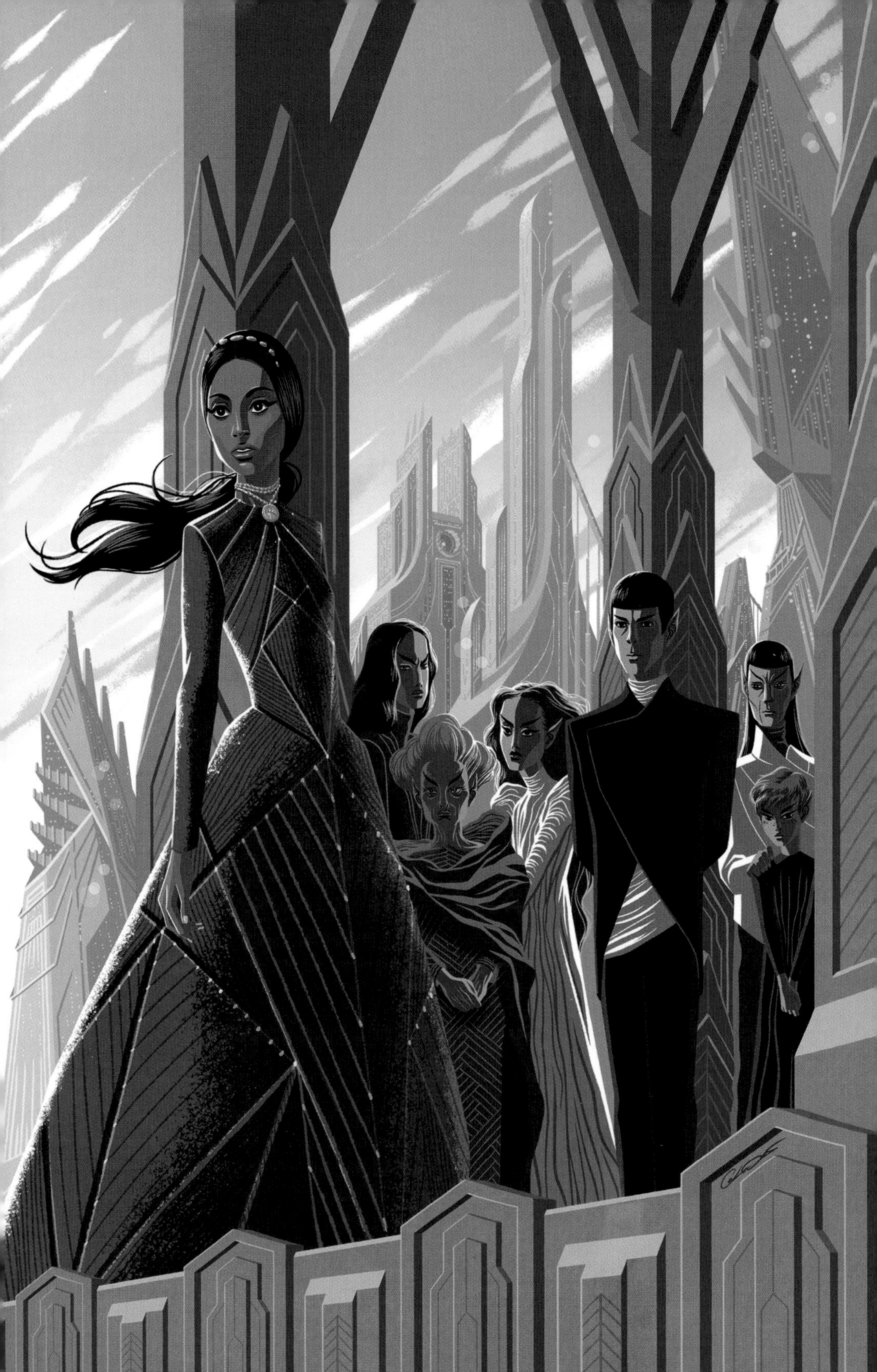

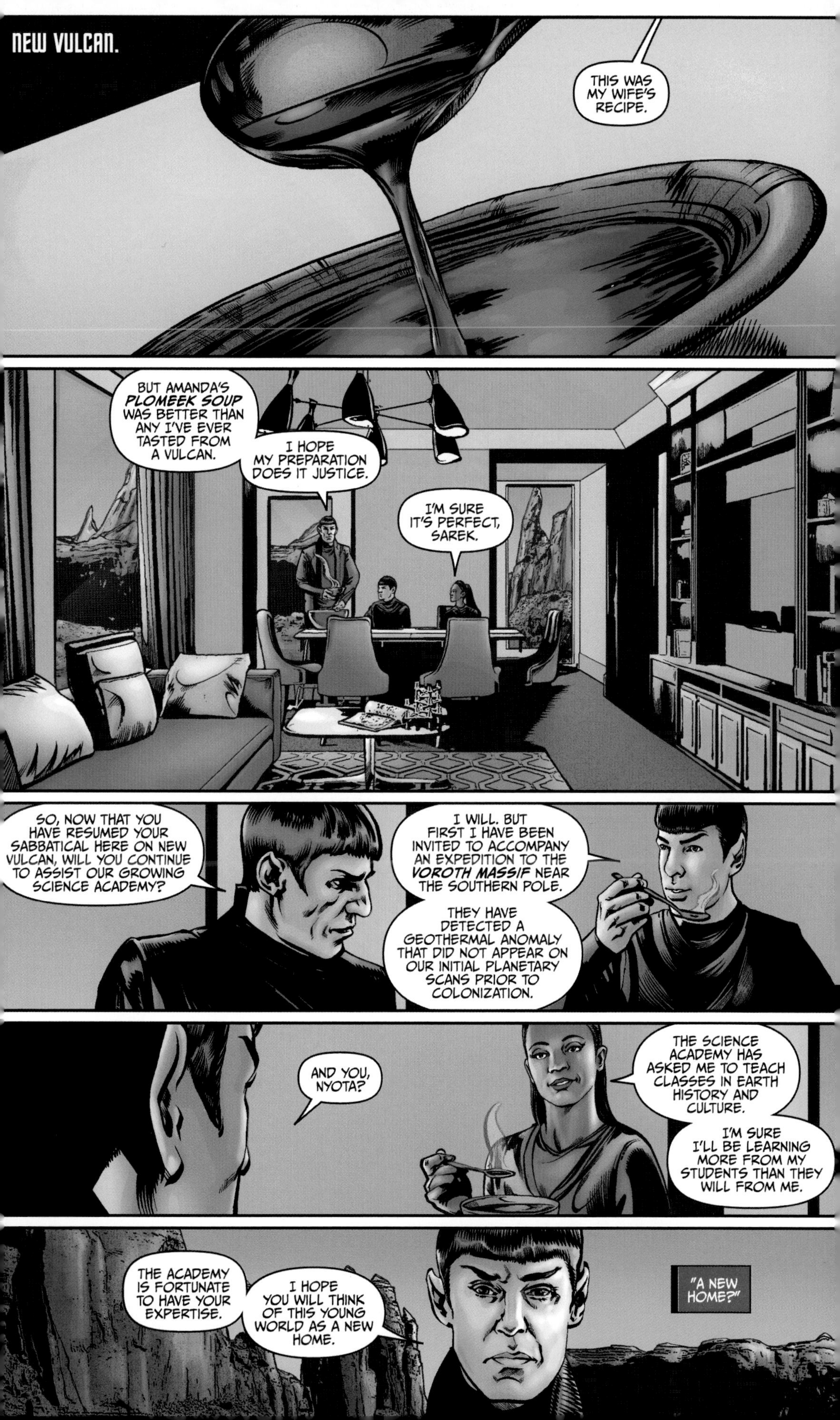
NEW VULCAN.
THIS WAS MY WIFE'S RECIPE.
BUT AMANDA'S PLOMEEK SOUP WAS BETTER THAN ANY I'VE EVER TASTED FROM A VULCAN.
I HOPE MY PREPARATION DOES IT JUSTICE.
I'M SURE IT'S PERFECT, SAREK.
SO, NOW THAT YOU HAVE RESUMED YOUR SABBATICAL HERE ON NEW VULCAN, WILL YOU CONTINUE TO ASSIST OUR GROWING SCIENCE ACADEMY?
I WILL. BUT FIRST I HAVE BEEN INVITED TO ACCOMPANY AN EXPEDITION TO THE VOROTH MASSIF NEAR THE SOUTHERN POLE.
THEY HAVE DETECTED A GEOTHERMAL ANOMALY THAT DID NOT APPEAR ON OUR INITIAL PLANETARY SCANS PRIOR TO COLONIZATION.
AND YOU, NYOTA?
THE SCIENCE ACADEMY HAS ASKED ME TO TEACH CLASSES IN EARTH HISTORY AND CULTURE.
I'M SURE I'LL BE LEARNING MORE FROM MY STUDENTS THAN THEY WILL FROM ME.
THE ACADEMY IS FORTUNATE TO HAVE YOUR EXPERTISE.
I HOPE YOU WILL THINK OF THIS YOUNG WORLD AS A NEW HOME.
"A NEW HOME?"

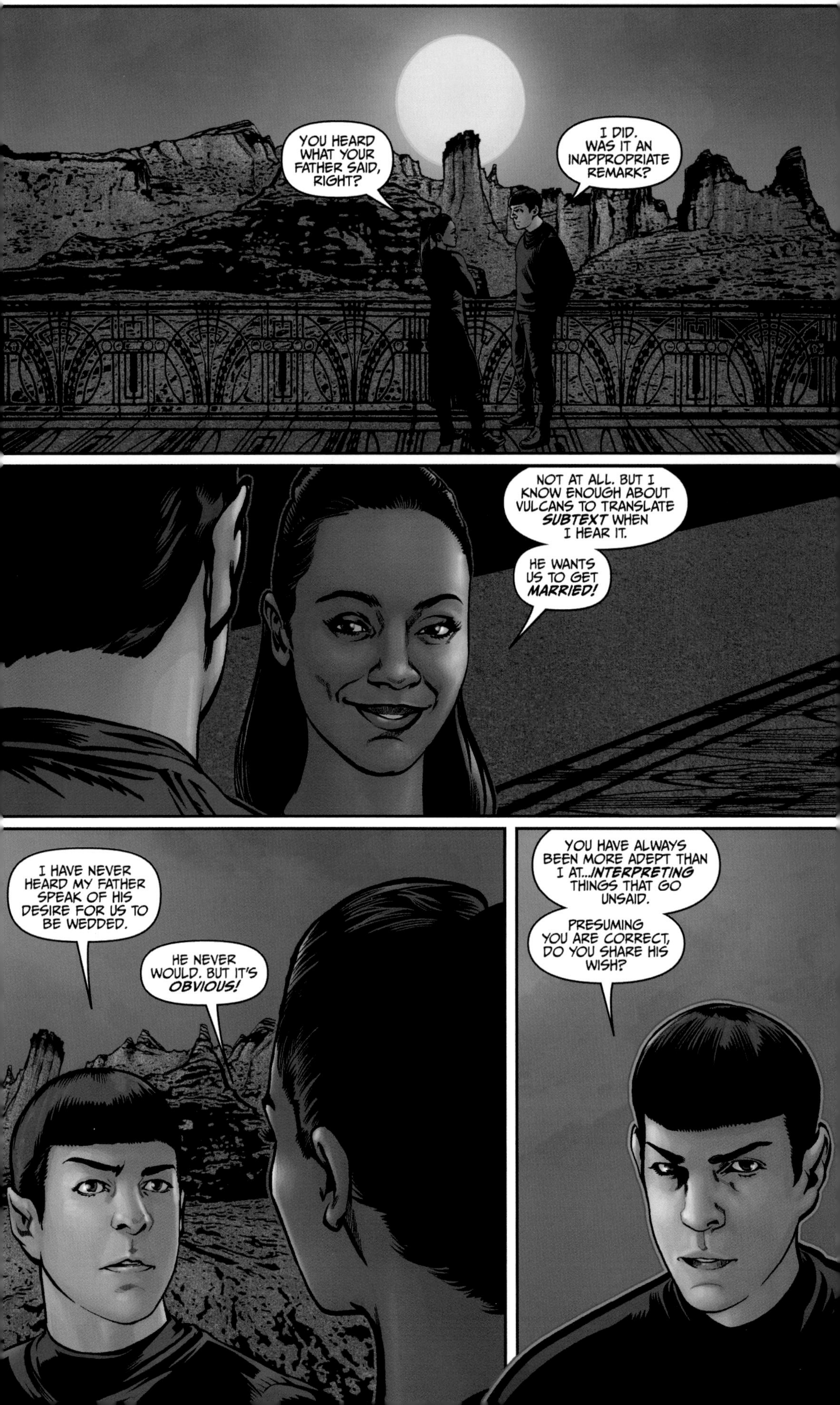
YOU HEARD WHAT YOUR FATHER SAID, RIGHT?
I DID. WAS IT AN INAPPROPRIATE REMARK?
NOT AT ALL. BUT I KNOW ENOUGH ABOUT VULCANS TO TRANSLATE SUBTEXT WHEN I HEAR IT.
HE WANTS US TO GET MARRIED!
I HAVE NEVER HEARD MY FATHER SPEAK OF HIS DESIRE FOR US TO BE WEDDED.
HE NEVER WOULD. BUT IT'S OBVIOUS!
YOU HAVE ALWAYS BEEN MORE ADEPT THAN I AT...INTERPRETING THINGS THAT GO UNSAID.
PRESUMING YOU ARE CORRECT, DO YOU SHARE HIS WISH?

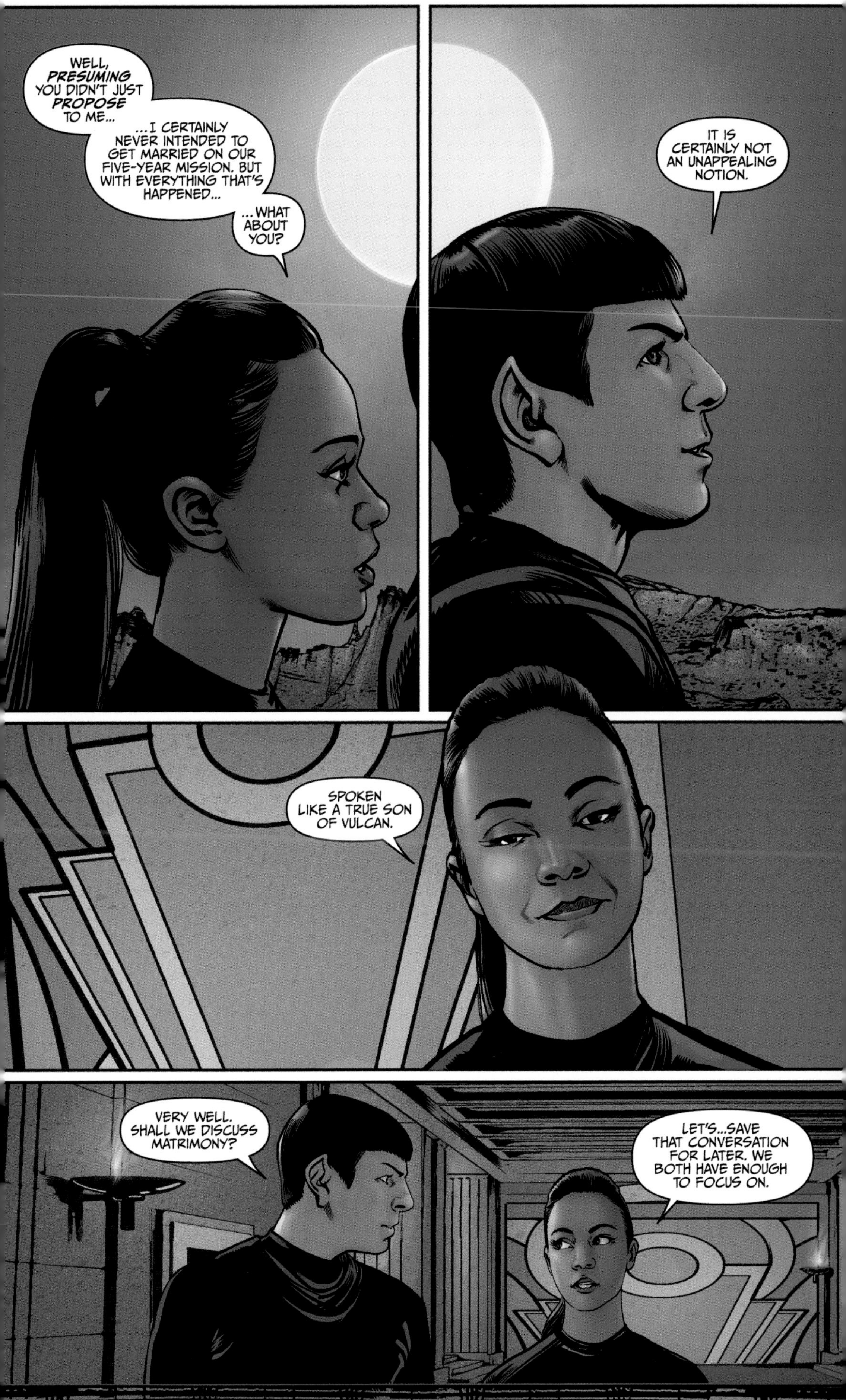
WELL, PRESUMING YOU DIDN'T JUST PROPOSE TO ME...
...I CERTAINLY NEVER INTENDED TO GET MARRIED ON OUR FIVE-YEAR MISSION. BUT WITH EVERYTHING THAT'S HAPPENED...
...WHAT ABOUT YOU?
IT IS CERTAINLY NOT AN UNAPPEALING NOTION.
SPOKEN LIKE A TRUE SON OF VULCAN.
VERY WELL. SHALL WE DISCUSS MATRIMONY?
LET'S...SAVE THAT CONVERSATION FOR LATER. WE BOTH HAVE ENOUGH TO FOCUS ON.

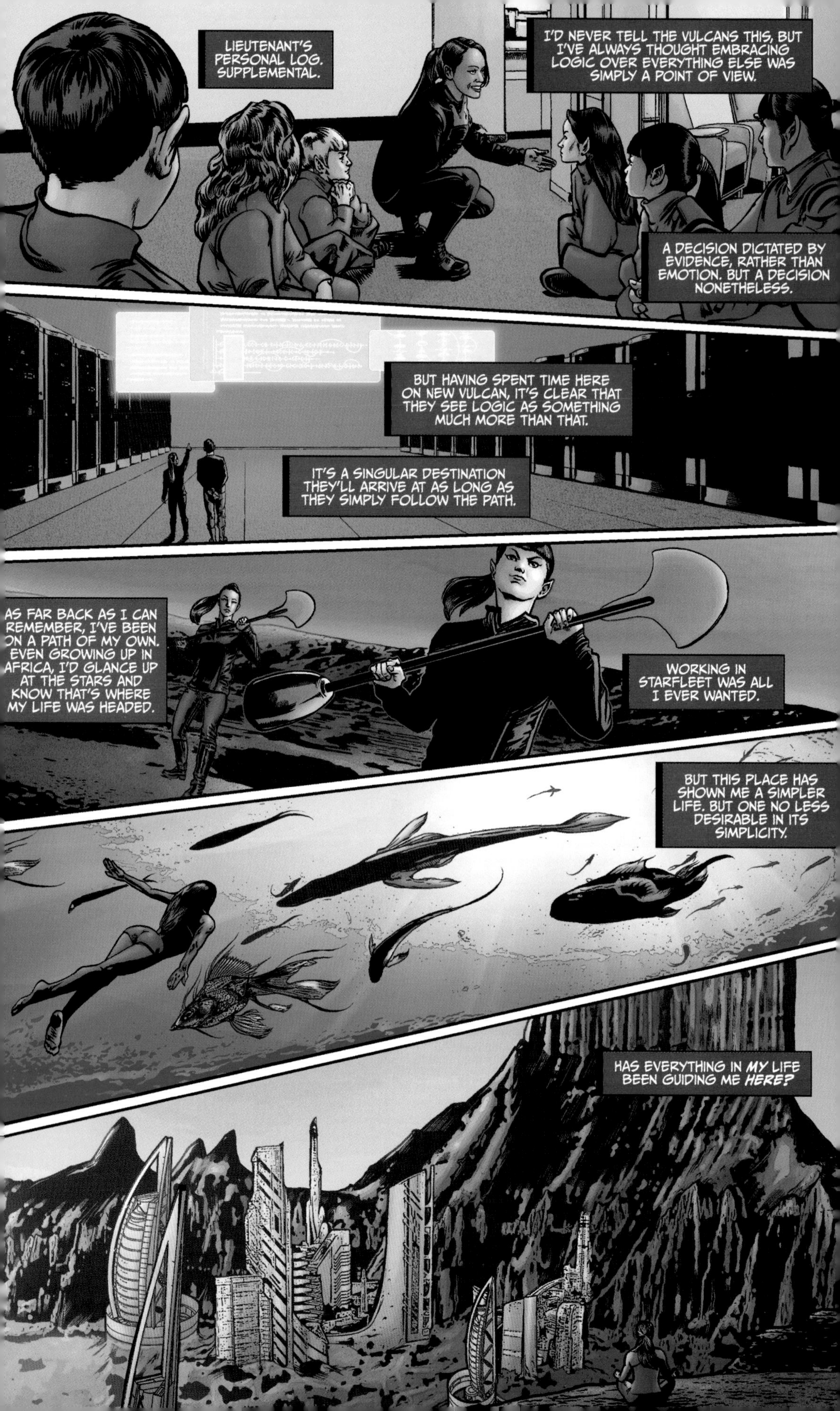
LIEUTENANT'S PERSONAL LOG. SUPPLEMENTAL.
I'D NEVER TELL THE VULCANS THIS, BUT I'VE ALWAYS THOUGHT EMBRACING LOGIC OVER EVERYTHING ELSE WAS SIMPLY A POINT OF VIEW.
A DECISION DICTATED BY EVIDENCE, RATHER THAN EMOTION. BUT A DECISION NONETHELESS.
BUT HAVING SPENT TIME HERE ON NEW VULCAN, IT'S CLEAR THAT THEY SEE LOGIC AS SOMETHING MUCH MORE THAN THAT.
IT'S A SINGULAR DESTINATION THEY'LL ARRIVE AT AS LONG AS THEY SIMPLY FOLLOW THE PATH.
AS FAR BACK AS I CAN REMEMBER, I'VE BEEN ON A PATH OF MY OWN. EVEN GROWING UP IN AFRICA, I'D GLANCE UP AT THE STARS AND KNOW THAT'S WHERE MY LIFE WAS HEADED.
WORKING IN STARFLEET WAS ALL I EVER WANTED.
BUT THIS PLACE HAS SHOWN ME A SIMPLER LIFE. BUT ONE NO LESS DESIRABLE IN ITS SIMPLICITY.
HAS EVERYTHING IN *MY* LIFE BEEN GUIDING ME *HERE?*

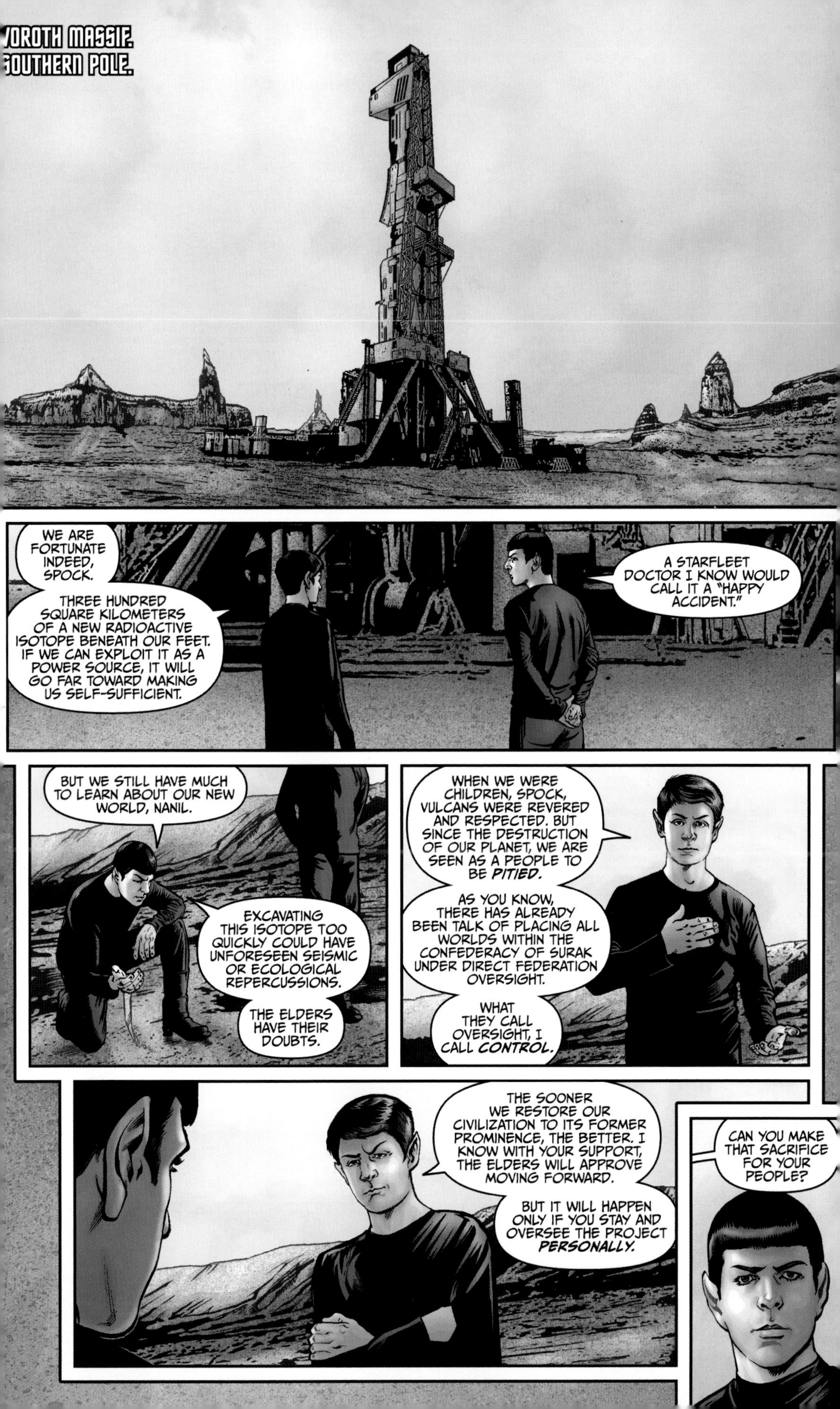
VOROTH MASSIF.
SOUTHERN POLE.
WE ARE FORTUNATE INDEED, SPOCK.
THREE HUNDRED SQUARE KILOMETERS OF A NEW RADIOACTIVE ISOTOPE BENEATH OUR FEET. IF WE CAN EXPLOIT IT AS A POWER SOURCE, IT WILL GO FAR TOWARD MAKING US SELF-SUFFICIENT.
A STARFLEET DOCTOR I KNOW WOULD CALL IT A "HAPPY ACCIDENT."
BUT WE STILL HAVE MUCH TO LEARN ABOUT OUR NEW WORLD, NANIL.
EXCAVATING THIS ISOTOPE TOO QUICKLY COULD HAVE UNFORESEEN SEISMIC OR ECOLOGICAL REPERCUSSIONS.
THE ELDERS HAVE THEIR DOUBTS.
WHEN WE WERE CHILDREN, SPOCK, VULCANS WERE REVERED AND RESPECTED. BUT SINCE THE DESTRUCTION OF OUR PLANET, WE ARE SEEN AS A PEOPLE TO BE *PITIED.*
AS YOU KNOW, THERE HAS ALREADY BEEN TALK OF PLACING ALL WORLDS WITHIN THE CONFEDERACY OF SURAK UNDER DIRECT FEDERATION OVERSIGHT.
WHAT THEY CALL OVERSIGHT, I CALL *CONTROL.*
THE SOONER WE RESTORE OUR CIVILIZATION TO ITS FORMER PROMINENCE, THE BETTER. I KNOW WITH YOUR SUPPORT, THE ELDERS WILL APPROVE MOVING FORWARD.
BUT IT WILL HAPPEN ONLY IF YOU STAY AND OVERSEE THE PROJECT *PERSONALLY.*
CAN YOU MAKE THAT SACRIFICE FOR YOUR PEOPLE?

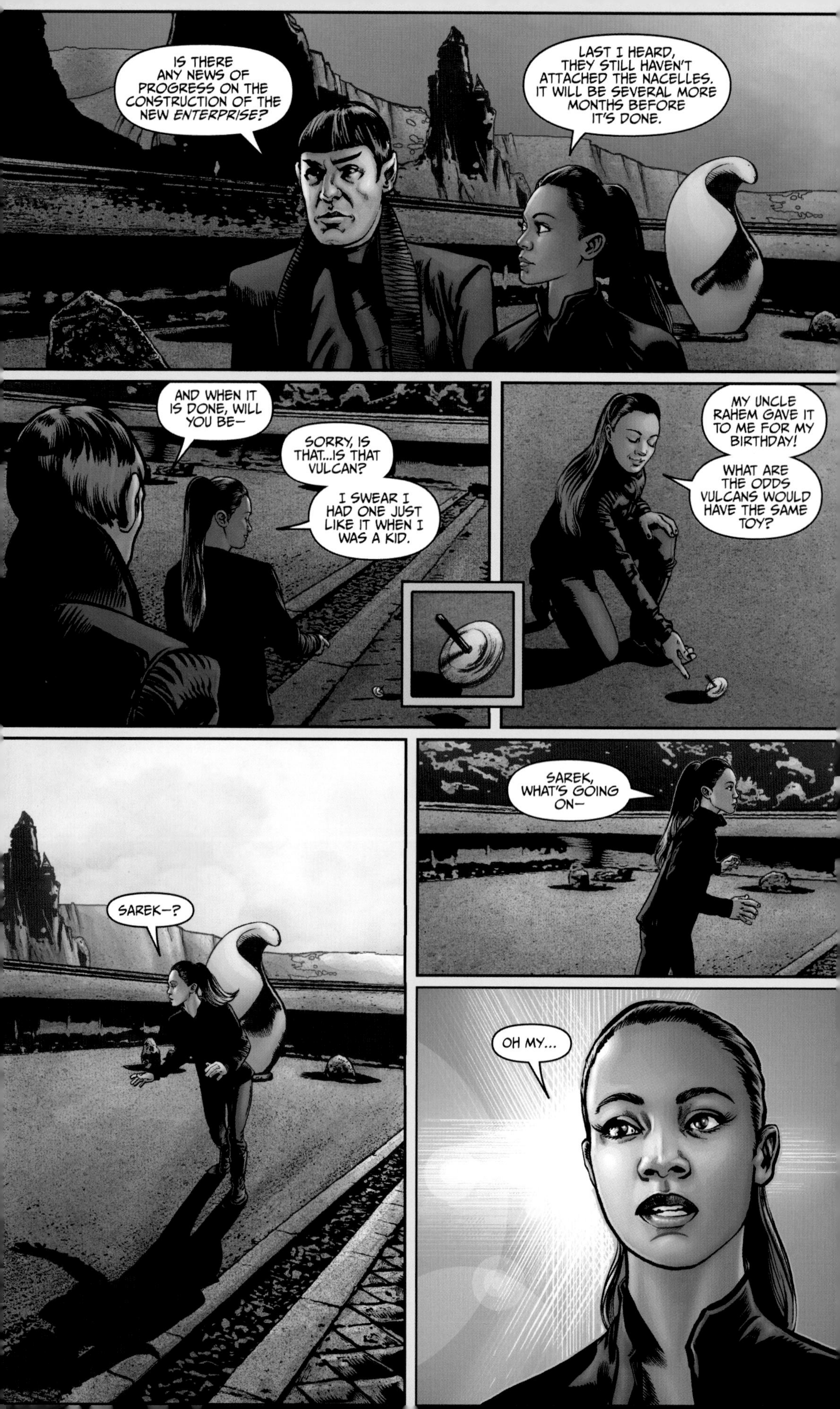
IS THERE ANY NEWS OF PROGRESS ON THE CONSTRUCTION OF THE NEW *ENTERPRISE?*
LAST I HEARD, THEY STILL HAVEN'T ATTACHED THE NACELLES. IT WILL BE SEVERAL MORE MONTHS BEFORE IT'S DONE.
AND WHEN IT IS DONE, WILL YOU BE—
SORRY, IS THAT...IS THAT VULCAN?
I SWEAR I HAD ONE JUST LIKE IT WHEN I WAS A KID.
MY UNCLE RAHEM GAVE IT TO ME FOR MY BIRTHDAY!
WHAT ARE THE ODDS VULCANS WOULD HAVE THE SAME TOY?
SAREK—?
SAREK, WHAT'S GOING ON—
OH MY...

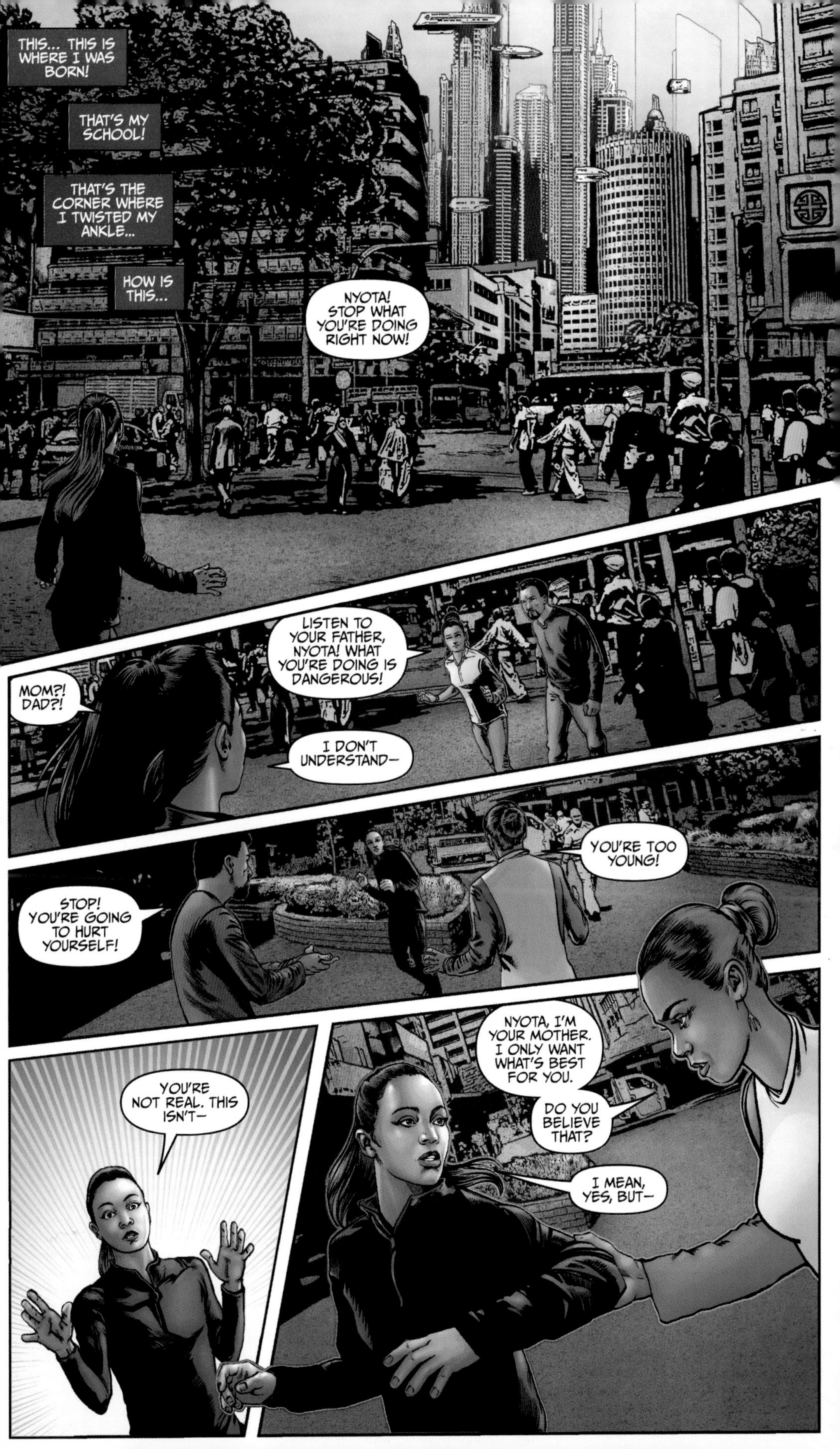
THIS... THIS IS WHERE I WAS BORN!
THAT'S MY SCHOOL!
THAT'S THE CORNER WHERE I TWISTED MY ANKLE...
HOW IS THIS...
NYOTA! STOP WHAT YOU'RE DOING RIGHT NOW!
MOM?! DAD?!
LISTEN TO YOUR FATHER, NYOTA! WHAT YOU'RE DOING IS DANGEROUS!
I DON'T UNDERSTAND—
STOP! YOU'RE GOING TO HURT YOURSELF!
YOU'RE TOO YOUNG!
YOU'RE NOT REAL. THIS ISN'T—
NYOTA, I'M YOUR MOTHER. I ONLY WANT WHAT'S BEST FOR YOU.
DO YOU BELIEVE THAT?
I MEAN, YES, BUT—

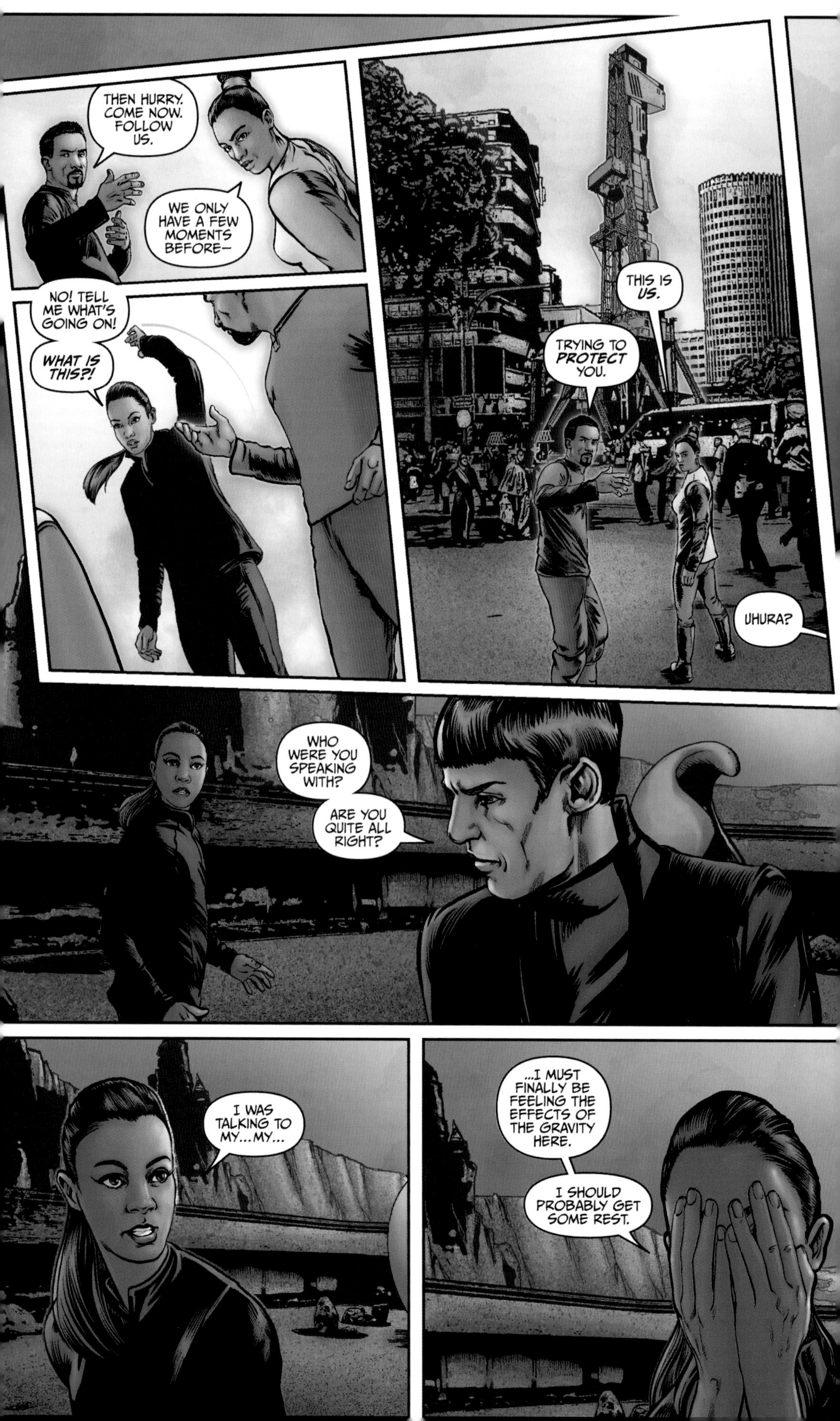
THEN HURRY. COME NOW. FOLLOW US.
WE ONLY HAVE A FEW MOMENTS BEFORE—
NO! TELL ME WHAT'S GOING ON!
WHAT IS THIS?!
THIS IS US.
TRYING TO PROTECT YOU.
UHURA?
WHO WERE YOU SPEAKING WITH?
ARE YOU QUITE ALL RIGHT?
I WAS TALKING TO MY...MY...
...I MUST FINALLY BE FEELING THE EFFECTS OF THE GRAVITY HERE.
I SHOULD PROBABLY GET SOME REST.

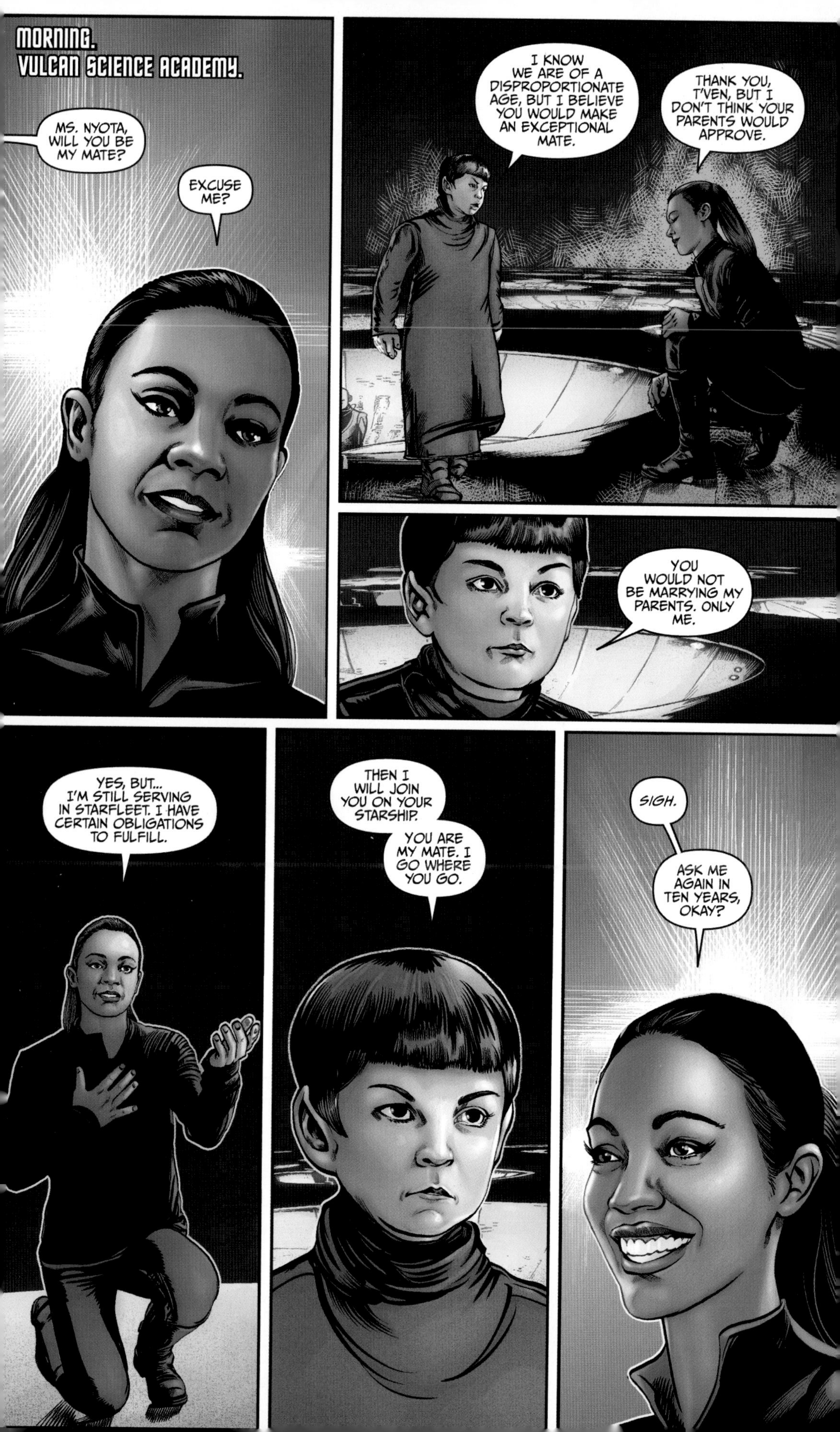
MORNING.
VULCAN SCIENCE ACADEMY.
MS. NYOTA, WILL YOU BE MY MATE?
EXCUSE ME?
I KNOW WE ARE OF A DISPROPORTIONATE AGE, BUT I BELIEVE YOU WOULD MAKE AN EXCEPTIONAL MATE.
THANK YOU, T'VEN, BUT I DON'T THINK YOUR PARENTS WOULD APPROVE.
YOU WOULD NOT BE MARRYING MY PARENTS. ONLY ME.
YES, BUT... I'M STILL SERVING IN STARFLEET. I HAVE CERTAIN OBLIGATIONS TO FULFILL.
THEN I WILL JOIN YOU ON YOUR STARSHIP.
YOU ARE MY MATE. I GO WHERE YOU GO.
SIGH.
ASK ME AGAIN IN TEN YEARS, OKAY?

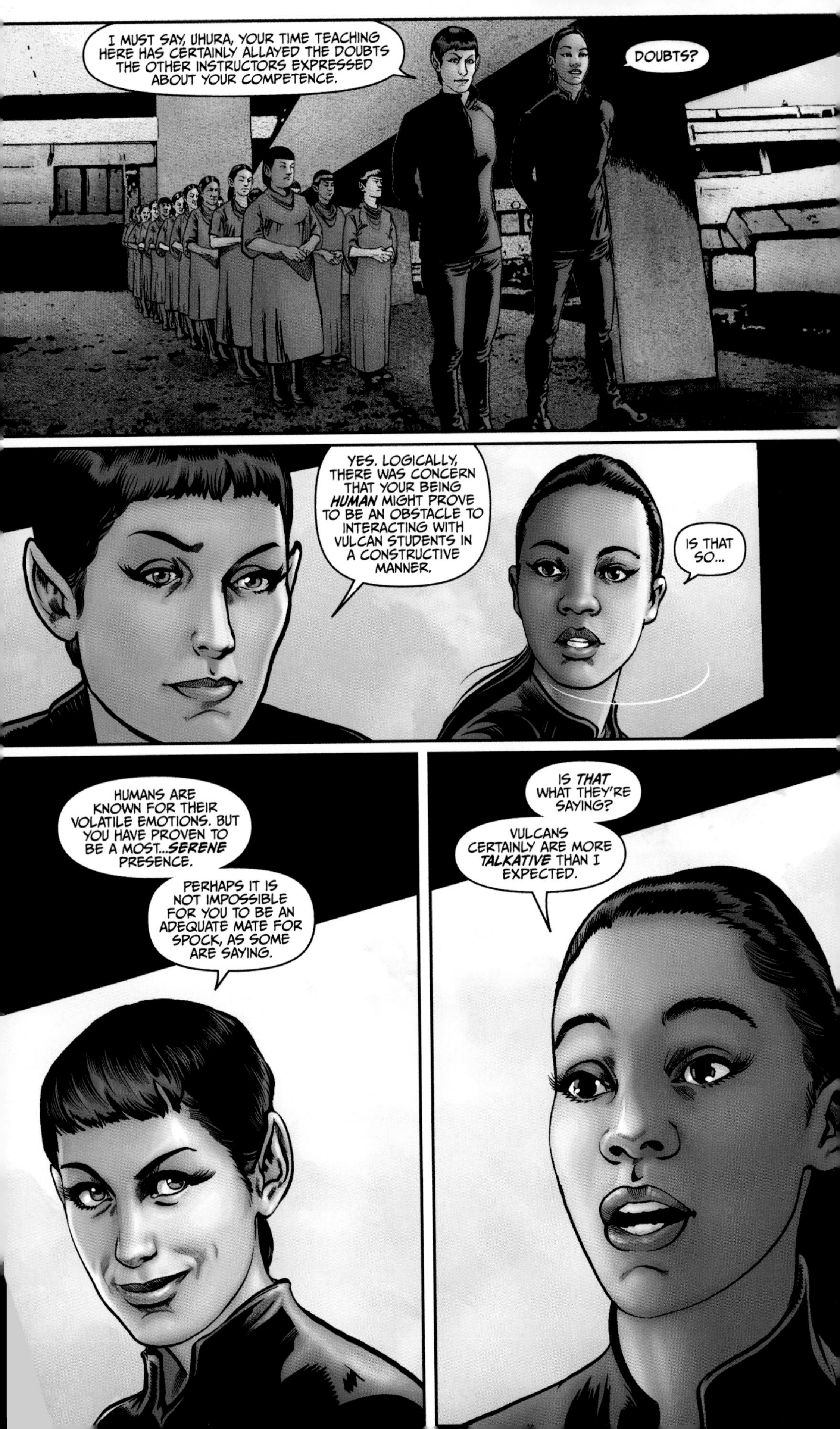
I MUST SAY, UHURA, YOUR TIME TEACHING HERE HAS CERTAINLY ALLAYED THE DOUBTS THE OTHER INSTRUCTORS EXPRESSED ABOUT YOUR COMPETENCE.
DOUBTS?
YES. LOGICALLY, THERE WAS CONCERN THAT YOUR BEING *HUMAN* MIGHT PROVE TO BE AN OBSTACLE TO INTERACTING WITH VULCAN STUDENTS IN A CONSTRUCTIVE MANNER.
IS THAT SO...
HUMANS ARE KNOWN FOR THEIR VOLATILE EMOTIONS. BUT YOU HAVE PROVEN TO BE A MOST...*SERENE* PRESENCE.
PERHAPS IT IS NOT IMPOSSIBLE FOR YOU TO BE AN ADEQUATE MATE FOR SPOCK, AS SOME ARE SAYING.
IS *THAT* WHAT THEY'RE SAYING?
VULCANS CERTAINLY ARE MORE *TALKATIVE* THAN I EXPECTED.

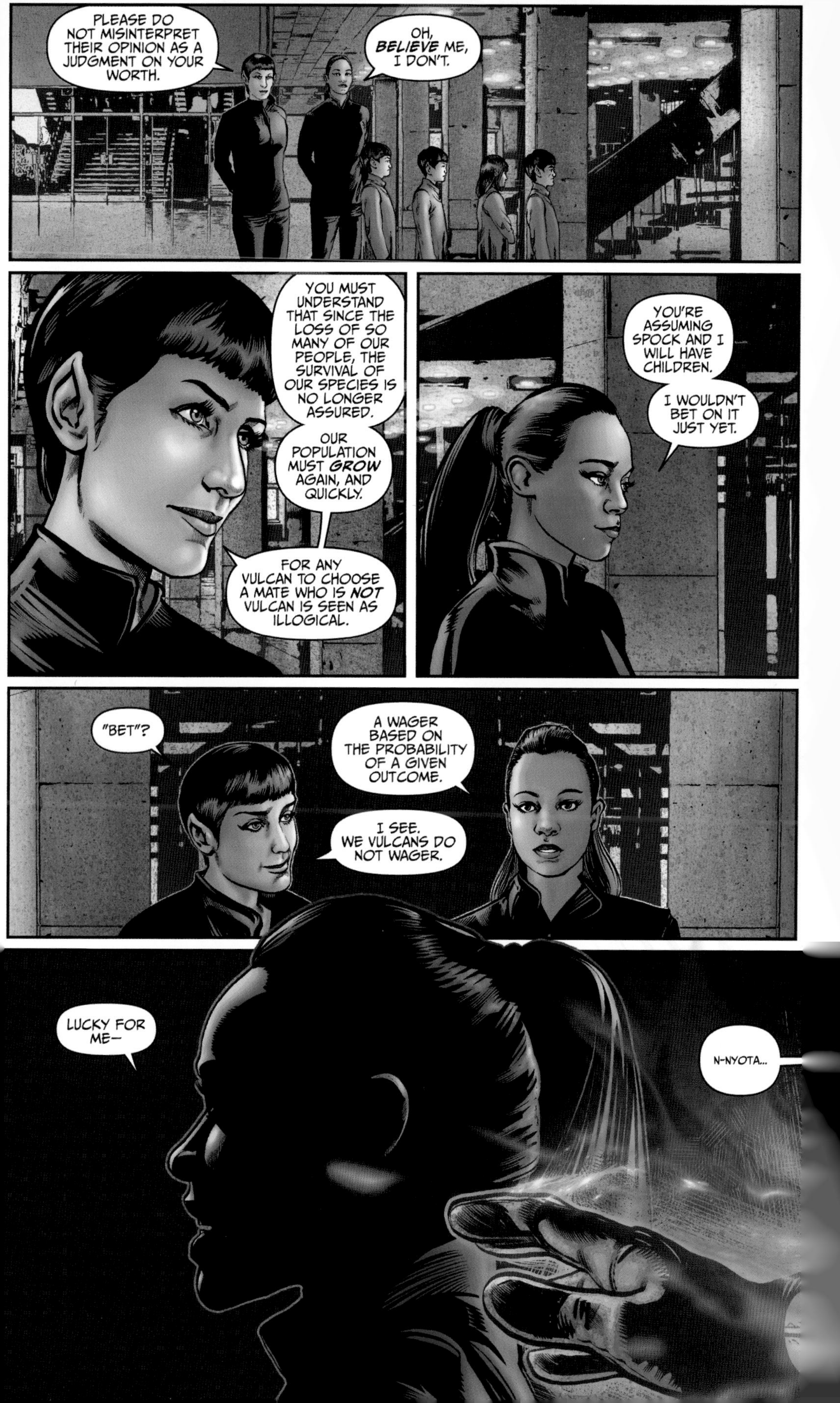

PLEASE DO NOT MISINTERPRET THEIR OPINION AS A JUDGMENT ON YOUR WORTH.
OH, *BELIEVE* ME, I DON'T.
YOU MUST UNDERSTAND THAT SINCE THE LOSS OF SO MANY OF OUR PEOPLE, THE SURVIVAL OF OUR SPECIES IS NO LONGER ASSURED.
OUR POPULATION MUST *GROW* AGAIN, AND QUICKLY.
FOR ANY VULCAN TO CHOOSE A MATE WHO IS *NOT* VULCAN IS SEEN AS ILLOGICAL.
YOU'RE ASSUMING SPOCK AND I WILL HAVE CHILDREN.
I WOULDN'T BET ON IT JUST YET.
"BET"?
A WAGER BASED ON THE PROBABILITY OF A GIVEN OUTCOME.
I SEE. WE VULCANS DO NOT WAGER.
LUCKY FOR ME—
N-NYOTA...

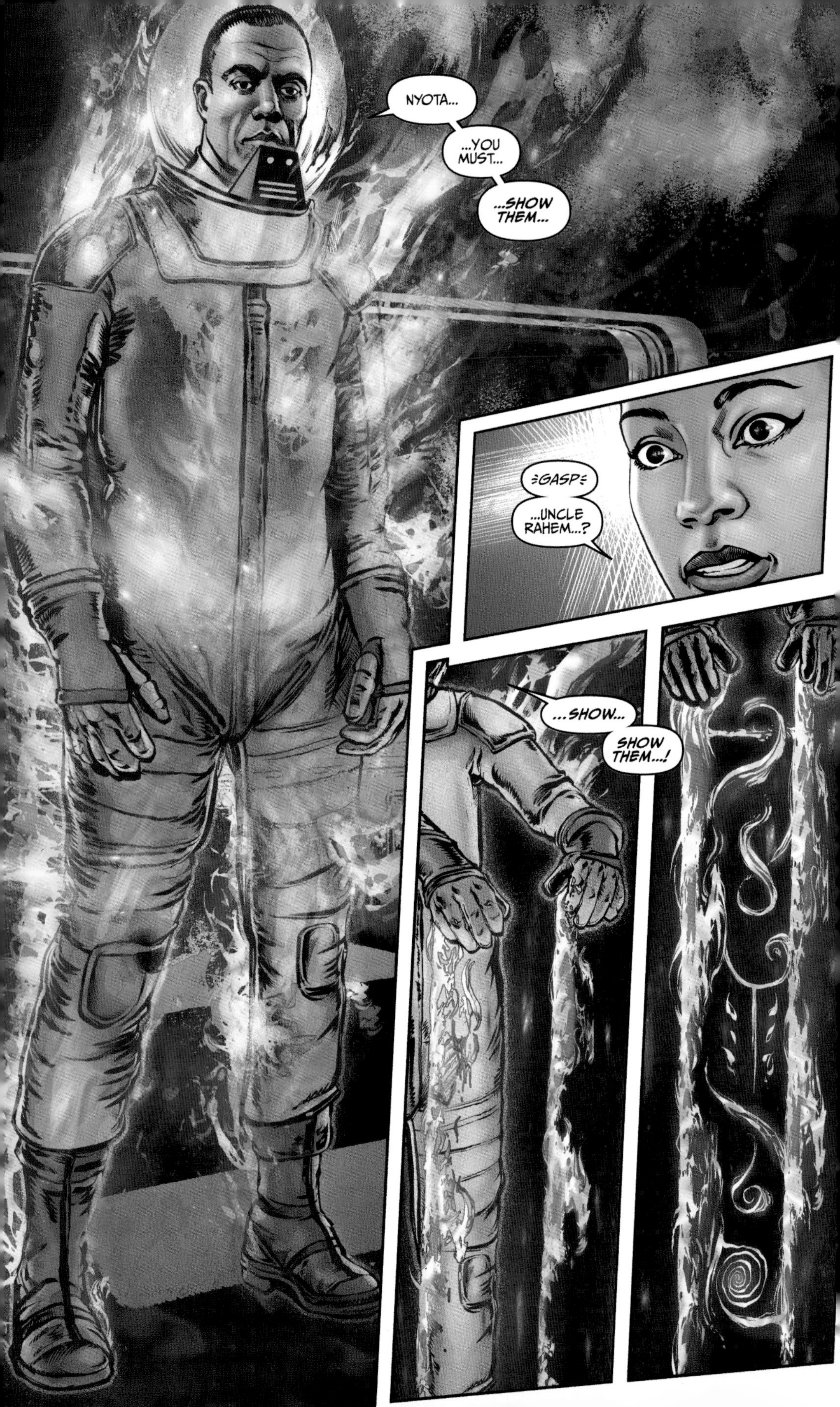
NYOTA...
...YOU MUST...
...SHOW THEM...
GASP
...UNCLE RAHEM...?
...SHOW...
SHOW THEM...!

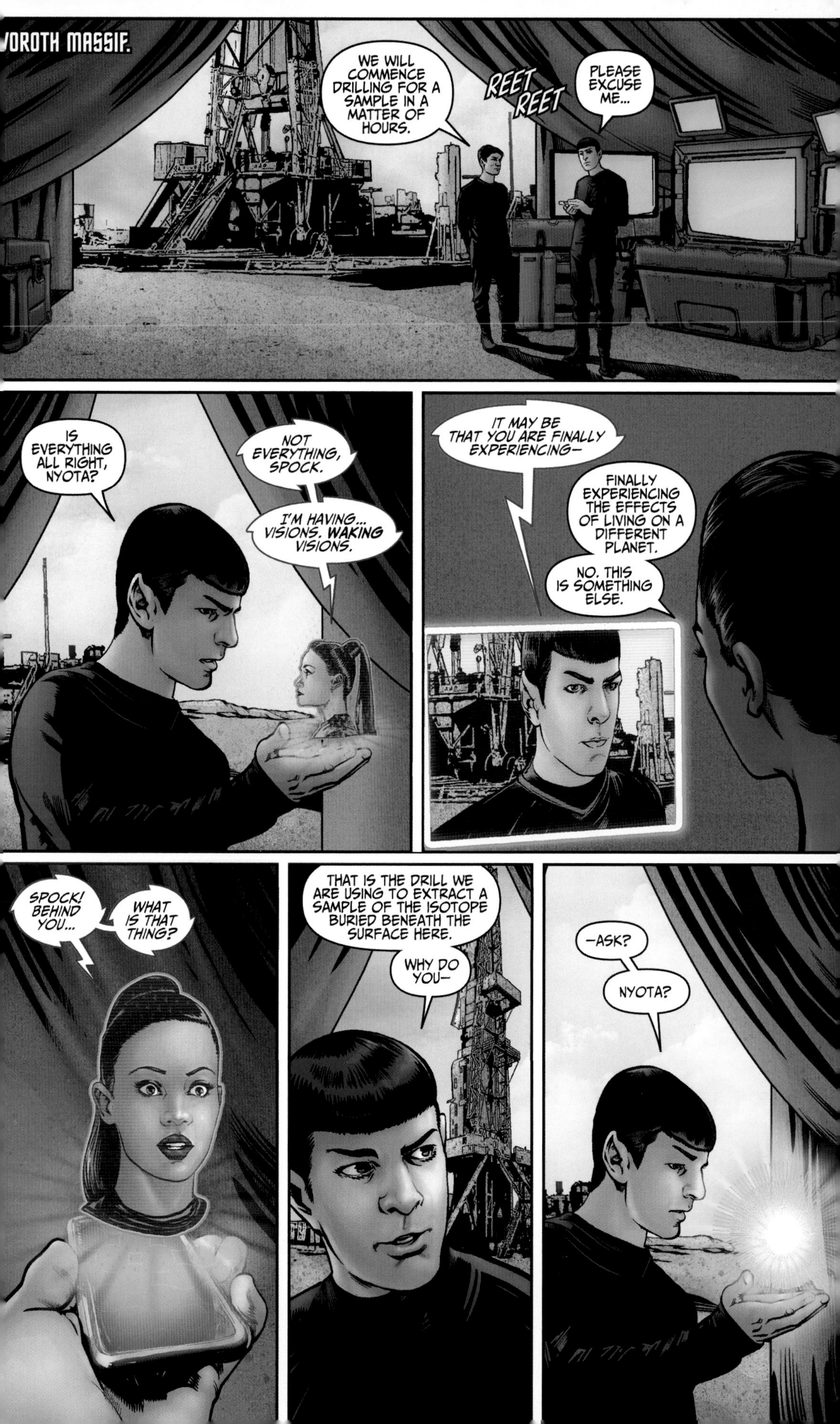

VOROTH MASSIF.
WE WILL COMMENCE DRILLING FOR A SAMPLE IN A MATTER OF HOURS.
REET REET
PLEASE EXCUSE ME...
IS EVERYTHING ALL RIGHT, NYOTA?
NOT EVERYTHING, SPOCK.
I'M HAVING... VISIONS. WAKING VISIONS.
IT MAY BE THAT YOU ARE FINALLY EXPERIENCING—
FINALLY EXPERIENCING THE EFFECTS OF LIVING ON A DIFFERENT PLANET.
NO. THIS IS SOMETHING ELSE.
SPOCK! BEHIND YOU...
WHAT IS THAT THING?
THAT IS THE DRILL WE ARE USING TO EXTRACT A SAMPLE OF THE ISOTOPE BURIED BENEATH THE SURFACE HERE.
WHY DO YOU—
—ASK?
NYOTA?

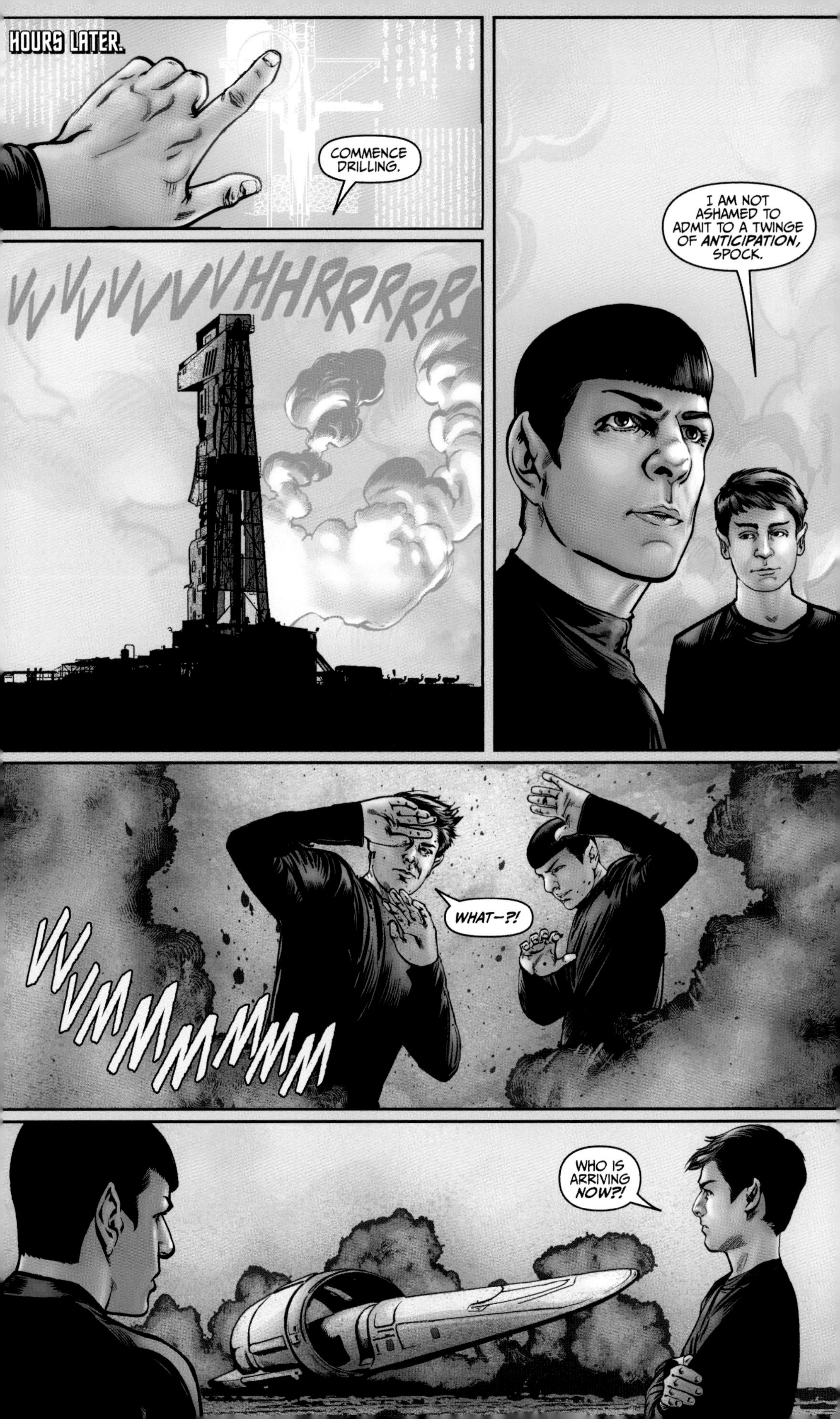
HOURS LATER.
COMMENCE DRILLING.
VVVVVVVVHHRRRRR
I AM NOT ASHAMED TO ADMIT TO A TWINGE OF *ANTICIPATION,* SPOCK.
WHAT—?!
VVMMMMMMMM
WHO IS ARRIVING *NOW?!*

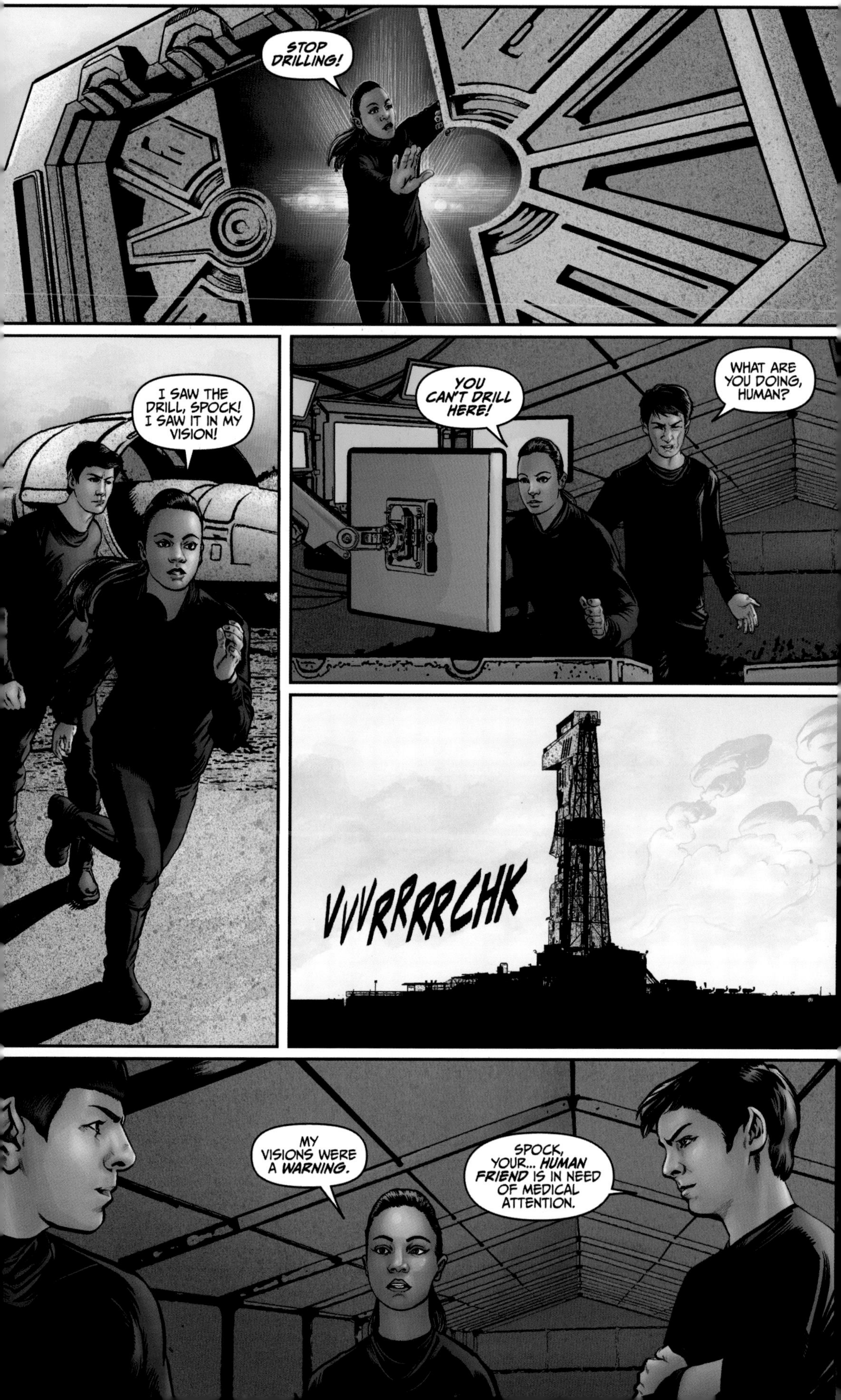
STOP DRILLING!
I SAW THE DRILL, SPOCK! I SAW IT IN MY VISION!
YOU CAN'T DRILL HERE!
WHAT ARE YOU DOING, HUMAN?
VVVRRRRCHK
MY VISIONS WERE A WARNING.
SPOCK, YOUR... HUMAN FRIEND IS IN NEED OF MEDICAL ATTENTION.

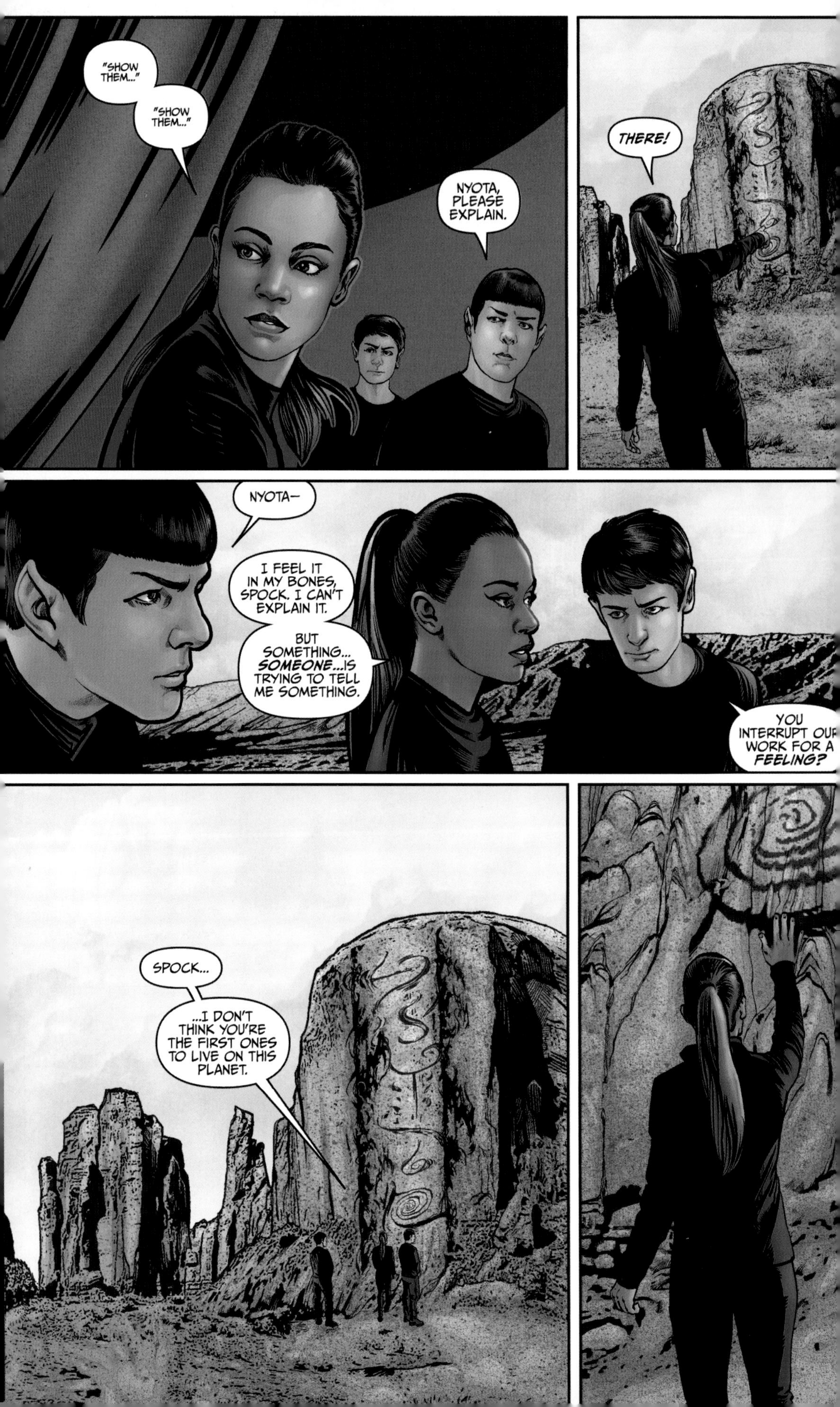

"SHOW THEM..."
"SHOW THEM..."
NYOTA, PLEASE EXPLAIN.
THERE!
NYOTA—
I FEEL IT IN MY BONES, SPOCK. I CAN'T EXPLAIN IT.
BUT SOMETHING... SOMEONE...IS TRYING TO TELL ME SOMETHING.
YOU INTERRUPT OUR WORK FOR A FEELING?
SPOCK...
...I DON'T THINK YOU'RE THE FIRST ONES TO LIVE ON THIS PLANET.

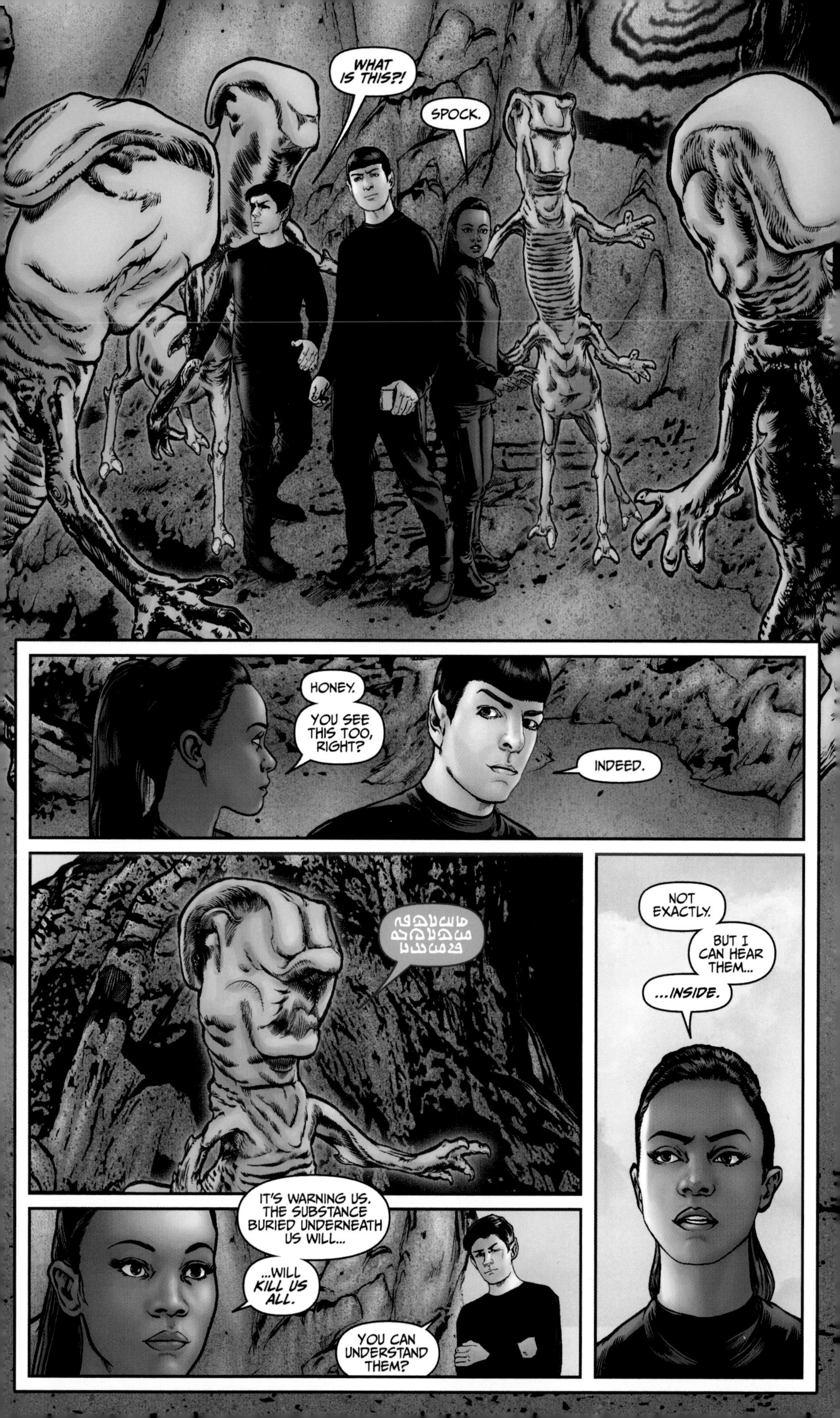
WHAT IS THIS?!
SPOCK.
HONEY.
YOU SEE THIS TOO, RIGHT?
INDEED.
NOT EXACTLY.
BUT I CAN HEAR THEM...
...INSIDE.
IT'S WARNING US. THE SUBSTANCE BURIED UNDERNEATH US WILL...
...WILL KILL US ALL.
YOU CAN UNDERSTAND THEM?

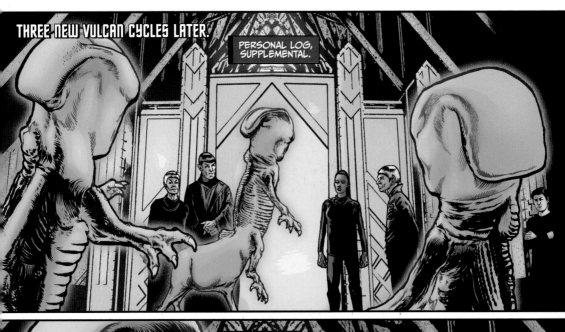

THREE NEW VULCAN CYCLES LATER.
PERSONAL LOG, SUPPLEMENTAL.
NOTHING ABOUT IT WAS LOGICAL.
THESE NATIVE INHABITANTS ARE NOT ALIVE, NOT IN ANY TRADITIONAL SENSE.
SPOCK'S BEST HYPOTHESIS IS THAT THEY ARE *PSYCHIC ECHOES* OF THE LAST SURVIVORS.
BY THEIR TELLING, THEY ARE THE LAST OF A SPECIES WIPED OUT BY A CATACLYSM THAT RESULTED FROM THEIR USE OF THE ISOTOPE THE VULCANS DISCOVERED.
IT ONCE EXISTED IN ABUNDANCE, POWERING THEIR CIVILIZATION.
IT DESTROYED THE ONCE FERTILE ECOSYSTEM, LEAVING THIS ARID WORLD.
THEY MARKED WHAT REMAINED OF THE ISOTOPE WITH A WARNING.
A WARNING ONLY *I* COULD HEAR.

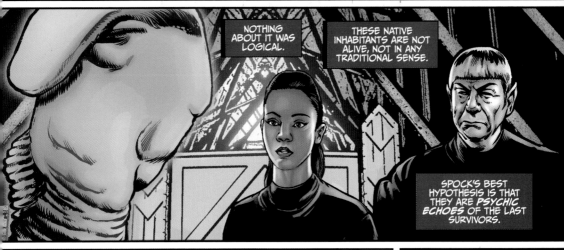

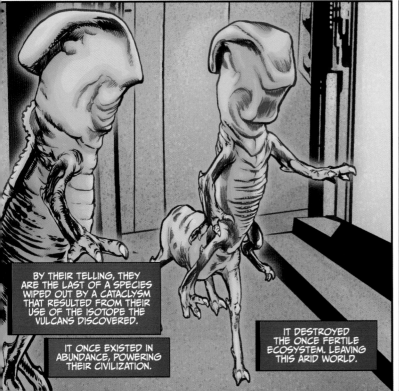

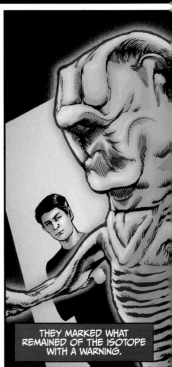

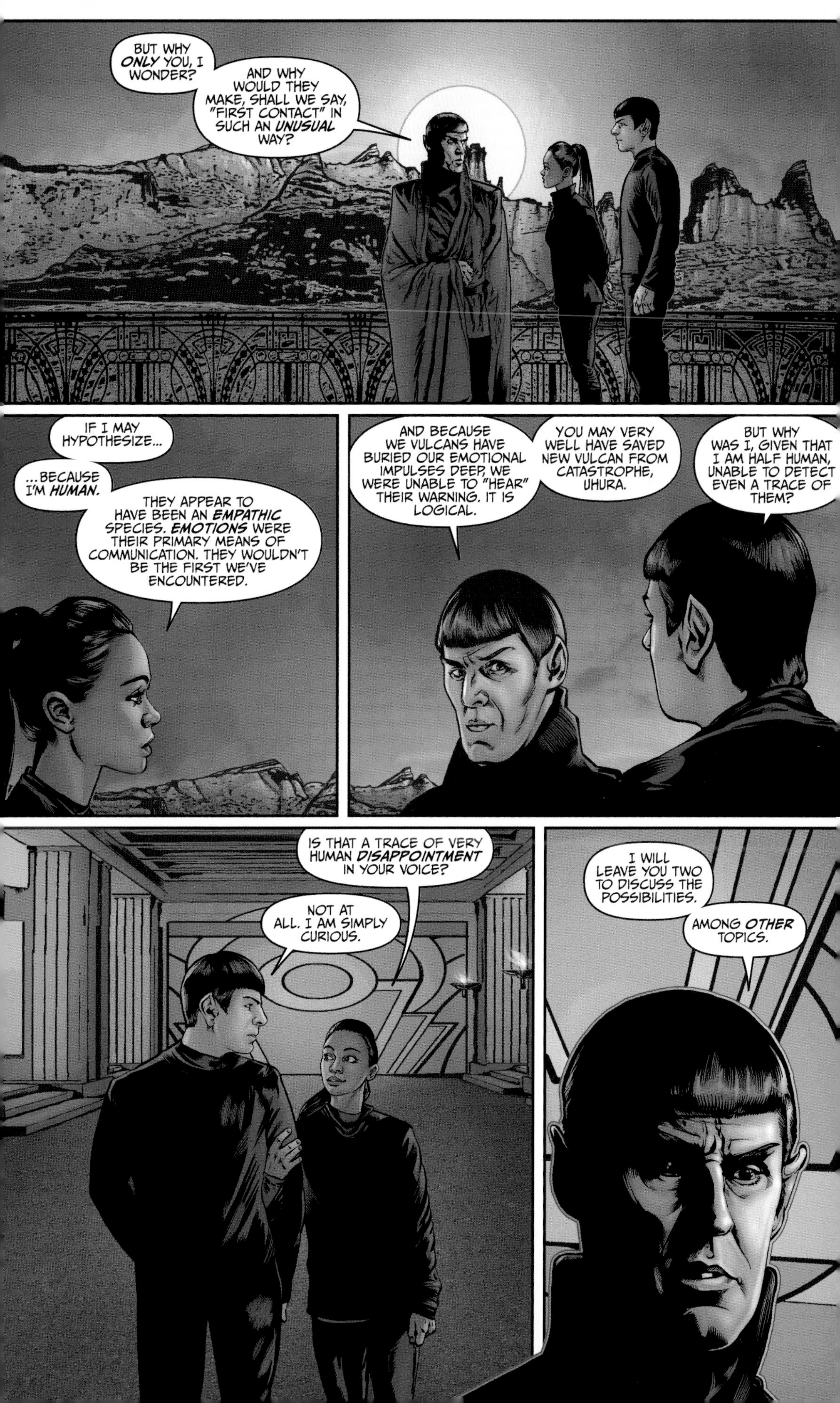

BUT WHY ONLY YOU, I WONDER?
AND WHY WOULD THEY MAKE, SHALL WE SAY, "FIRST CONTACT" IN SUCH AN UNUSUAL WAY?
IF I MAY HYPOTHESIZE...
...BECAUSE I'M HUMAN.
THEY APPEAR TO HAVE BEEN AN EMPATHIC SPECIES. EMOTIONS WERE THEIR PRIMARY MEANS OF COMMUNICATION. THEY WOULDN'T BE THE FIRST WE'VE ENCOUNTERED.
AND BECAUSE WE VULCANS HAVE BURIED OUR EMOTIONAL IMPULSES DEEP, WE WERE UNABLE TO "HEAR" THEIR WARNING. IT IS LOGICAL.
YOU MAY VERY WELL HAVE SAVED NEW VULCAN FROM CATASTROPHE, UHURA.
BUT WHY WAS I, GIVEN THAT I AM HALF HUMAN, UNABLE TO DETECT EVEN A TRACE OF THEM?
IS THAT A TRACE OF VERY HUMAN DISAPPOINTMENT IN YOUR VOICE?
NOT AT ALL. I AM SIMPLY CURIOUS.
I WILL LEAVE YOU TWO TO DISCUSS THE POSSIBILITIES.
AMONG OTHER TOPICS.

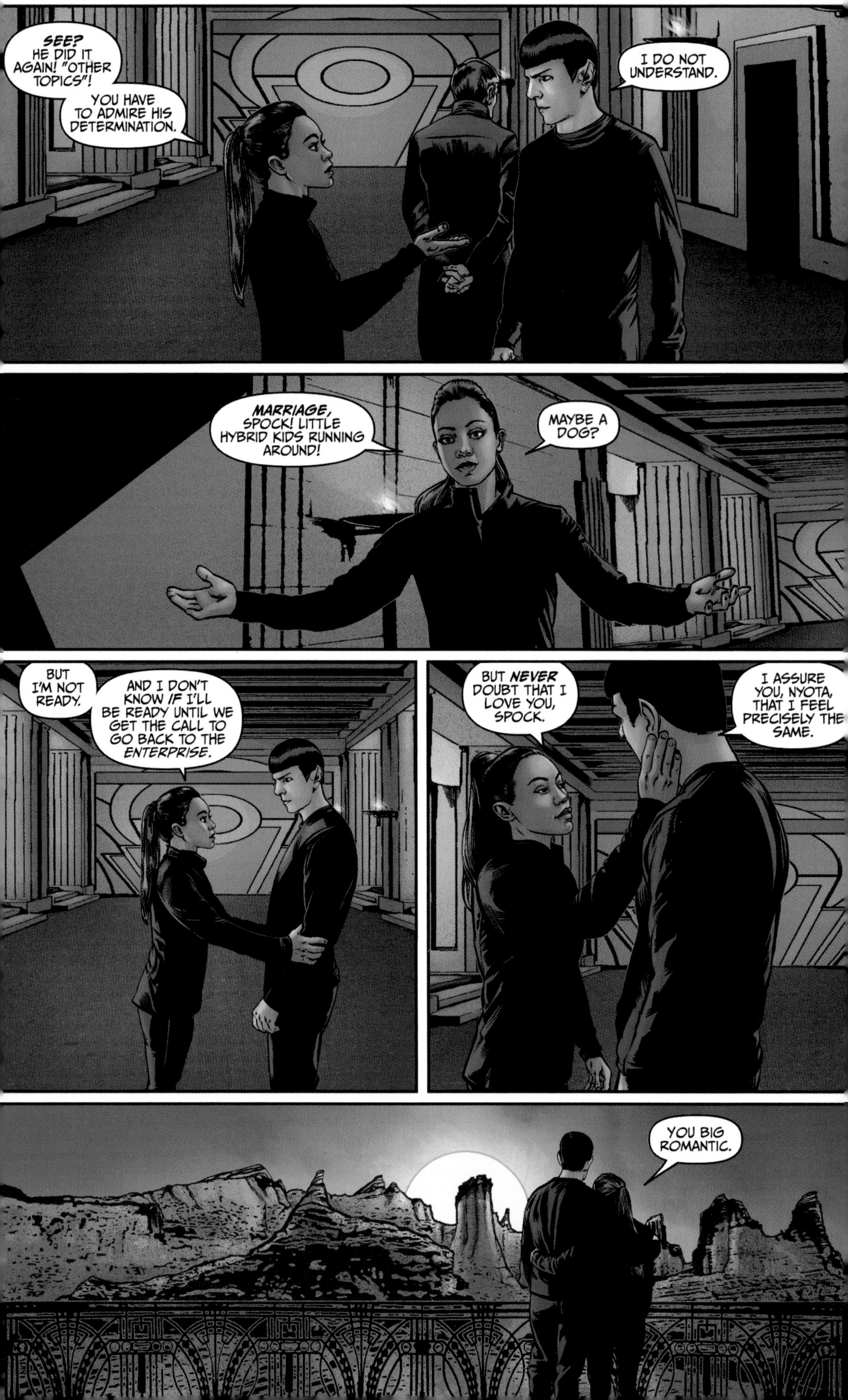
SEE? HE DID IT AGAIN! "OTHER TOPICS"!
YOU HAVE TO ADMIRE HIS DETERMINATION.
I DO NOT UNDERSTAND.
MARRIAGE, SPOCK! LITTLE HYBRID KIDS RUNNING AROUND!
MAYBE A DOG?
BUT I'M NOT READY.
AND I DON'T KNOW IF I'LL BE READY UNTIL WE GET THE CALL TO GO BACK TO THE ENTERPRISE.
BUT NEVER DOUBT THAT I LOVE YOU, SPOCK.
I ASSURE YOU, NYOTA, THAT I FEEL PRECISELY THE SAME.
YOU BIG ROMANTIC.

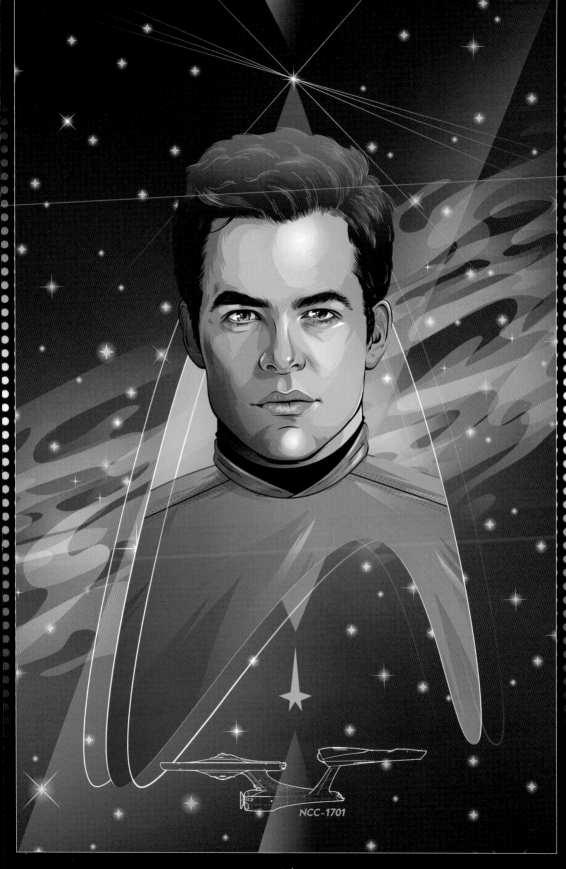

NCC-1701

art by
Cryssy Cheung

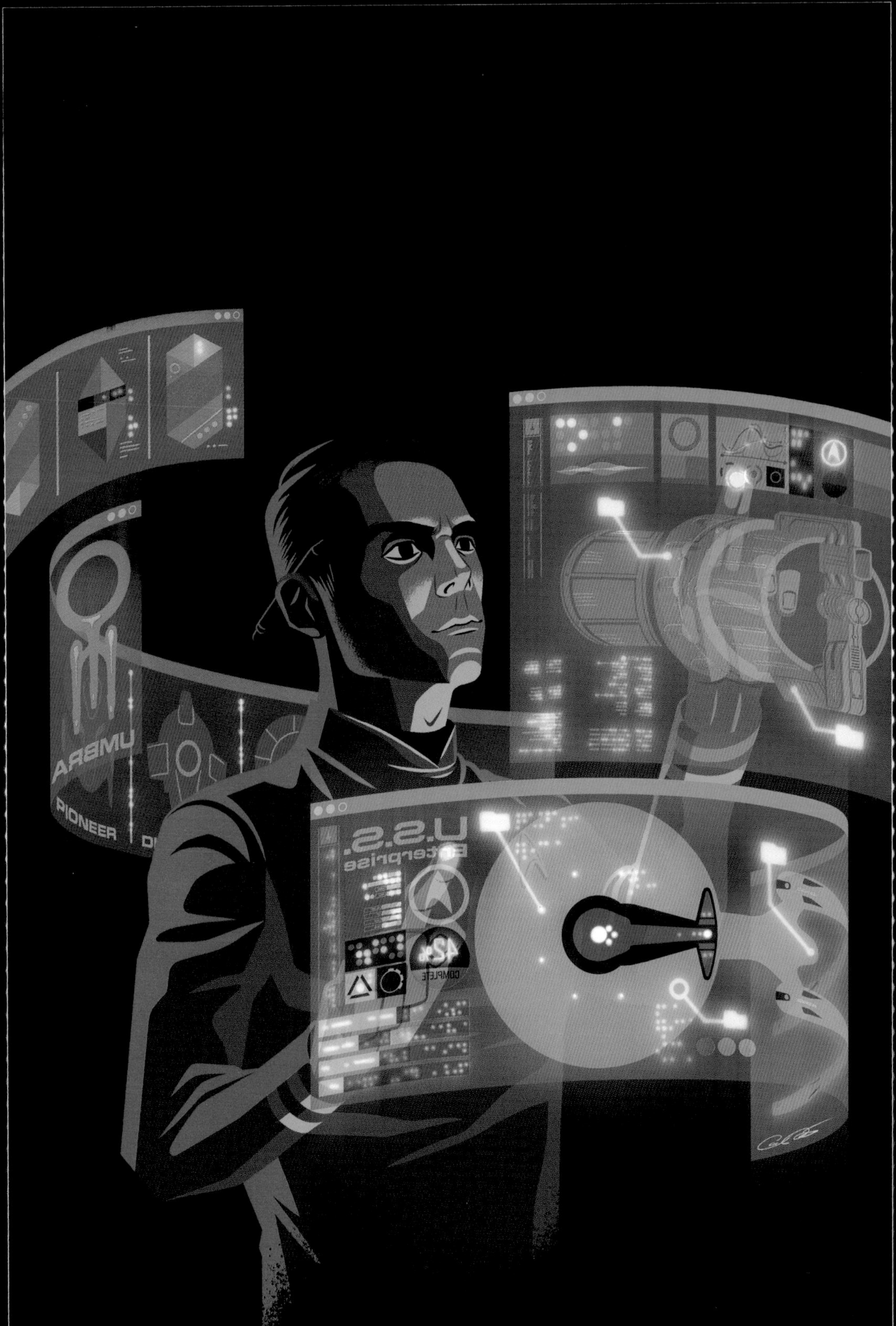
U.S.S. Enterprise
PIONEER

art by
George Caltsoudas

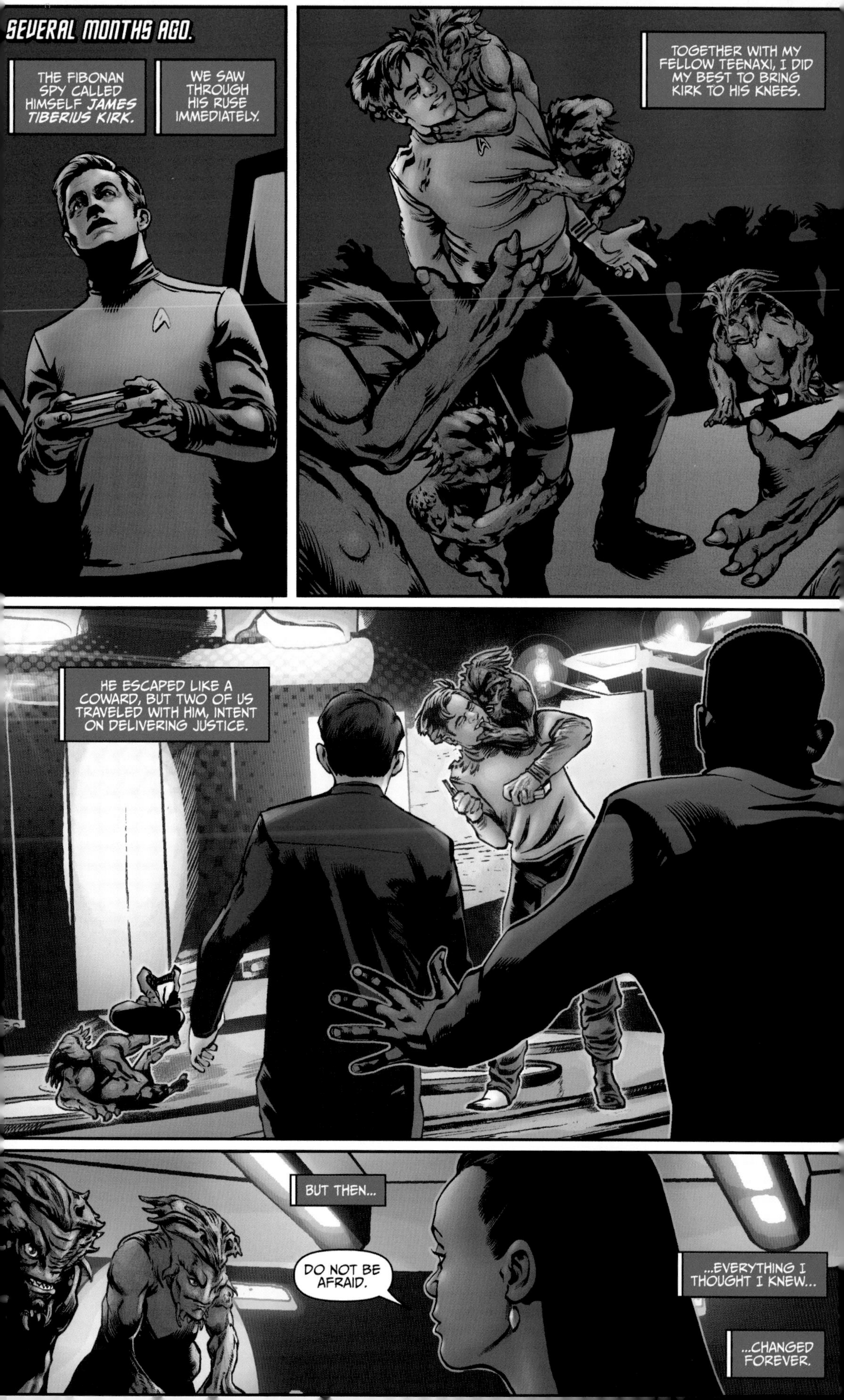
SEVERAL MONTHS AGO.
THE FIBONAN SPY CALLED HIMSELF *JAMES TIBERIUS KIRK.*
WE SAW THROUGH HIS RUSE IMMEDIATELY.
TOGETHER WITH MY FELLOW TEENAXI, I DID MY BEST TO BRING KIRK TO HIS KNEES.
HE ESCAPED LIKE A COWARD, BUT TWO OF US TRAVELED WITH HIM, INTENT ON DELIVERING JUSTICE.
BUT THEN...
DO NOT BE AFRAID.
...EVERYTHING I THOUGHT I KNEW...
...CHANGED FOREVER.

I CHOSE TO STAY AMONG KIRK'S PEOPLE.

MY NAME IS UNPRONOUNCEABLE IN THEIR LANGUAGE. THE CLOSEST TRANSLATION IS...

...KEVIN.

MY SUSPICIONS ABOUT KIRK PROVED UNFOUNDED.

INSTEAD, I HAVE COME TO APPRECIATE THE PEACEFUL AND VIBRANT SOCIETY THEY CALL THE FEDERATION.

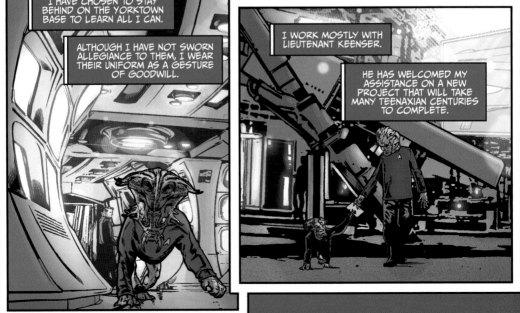

I HAVE CHOSEN TO STAY BEHIND ON THE YORKTOWN BASE TO LEARN ALL I CAN.

ALTHOUGH I HAVE NOT SWORN ALLEGIANCE TO THEM, I WEAR THEIR UNIFORM AS A GESTURE OF GOODWILL.

I WORK MOSTLY WITH LIEUTENANT KEENSER.

HE HAS WELCOMED MY ASSISTANCE ON A NEW PROJECT THAT WILL TAKE MANY TEENAXIAN CENTURIES TO COMPLETE.

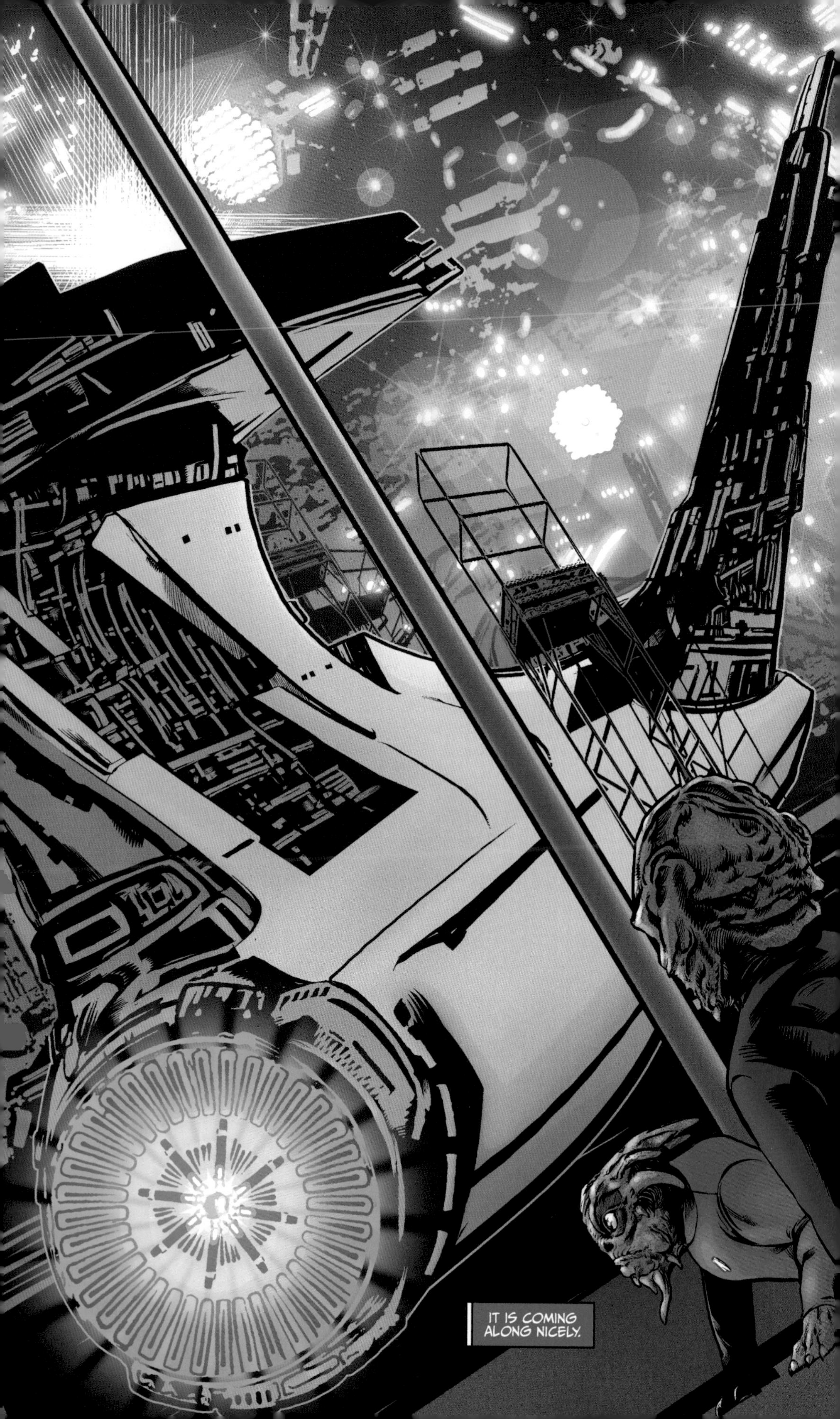
IT IS COMING ALONG NICELY.

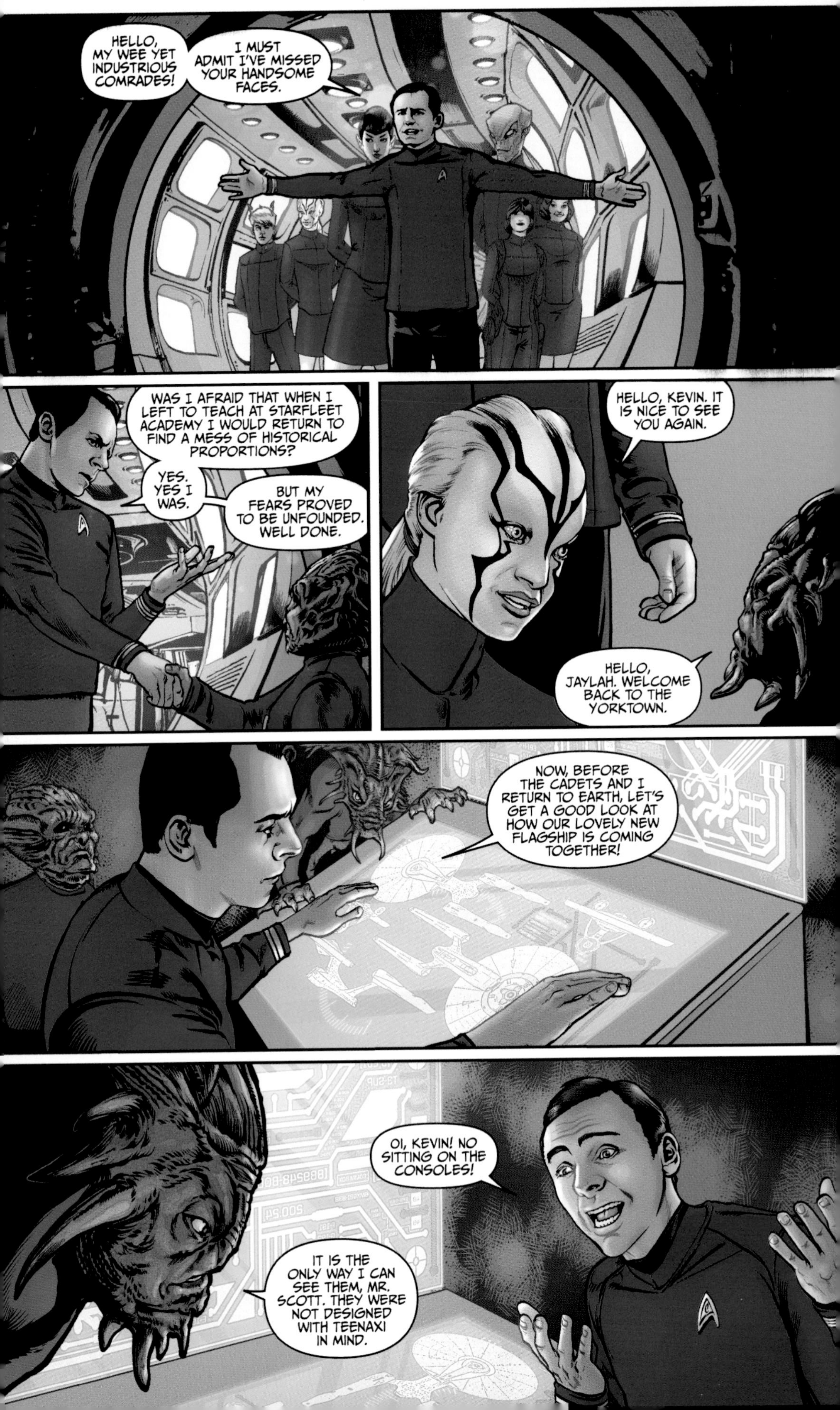
HELLO, MY WEE YET INDUSTRIOUS COMRADES!
I MUST ADMIT I'VE MISSED YOUR HANDSOME FACES.
WAS I AFRAID THAT WHEN I LEFT TO TEACH AT STARFLEET ACADEMY I WOULD RETURN TO FIND A MESS OF HISTORICAL PROPORTIONS?
YES. YES I WAS.
BUT MY FEARS PROVED TO BE UNFOUNDED. WELL DONE.
HELLO, KEVIN. IT IS NICE TO SEE YOU AGAIN.
HELLO, JAYLAH. WELCOME BACK TO THE YORKTOWN.
NOW, BEFORE THE CADETS AND I RETURN TO EARTH, LET'S GET A GOOD LOOK AT HOW OUR LOVELY NEW FLAGSHIP IS COMING TOGETHER!
OI, KEVIN! NO SITTING ON THE CONSOLES!
IT IS THE ONLY WAY I CAN SEE THEM, MR. SCOTT. THEY WERE NOT DESIGNED WITH TEENAXI IN MIND.

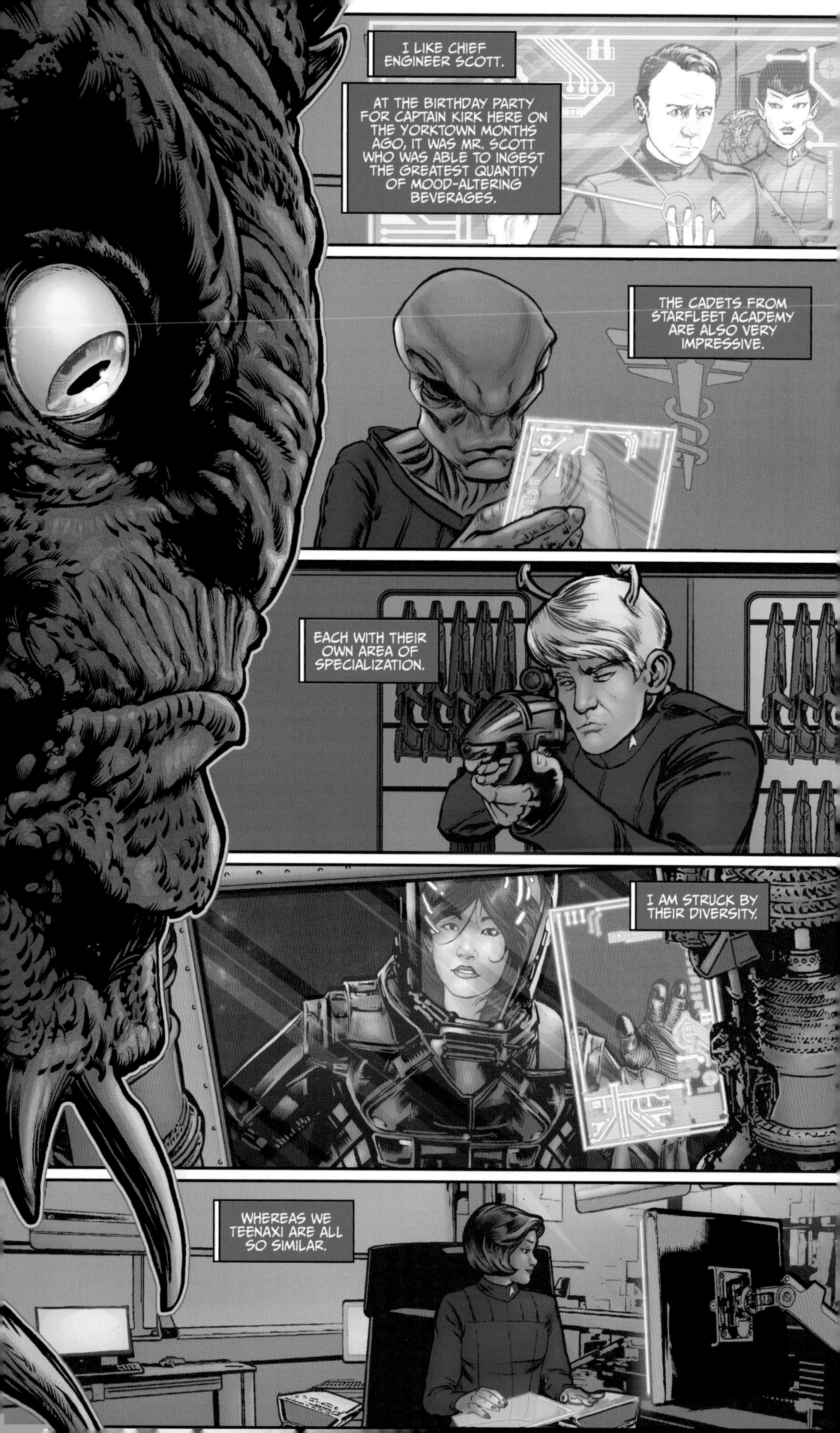

I LIKE CHIEF ENGINEER SCOTT.
AT THE BIRTHDAY PARTY FOR CAPTAIN KIRK HERE ON THE YORKTOWN MONTHS AGO, IT WAS MR. SCOTT WHO WAS ABLE TO INGEST THE GREATEST QUANTITY OF MOOD-ALTERING BEVERAGES.
THE CADETS FROM STARFLEET ACADEMY ARE ALSO VERY IMPRESSIVE.
EACH WITH THEIR OWN AREA OF SPECIALIZATION.
I AM STRUCK BY THEIR DIVERSITY.
WHEREAS WE TEENAXI ARE ALL SO SIMILAR.

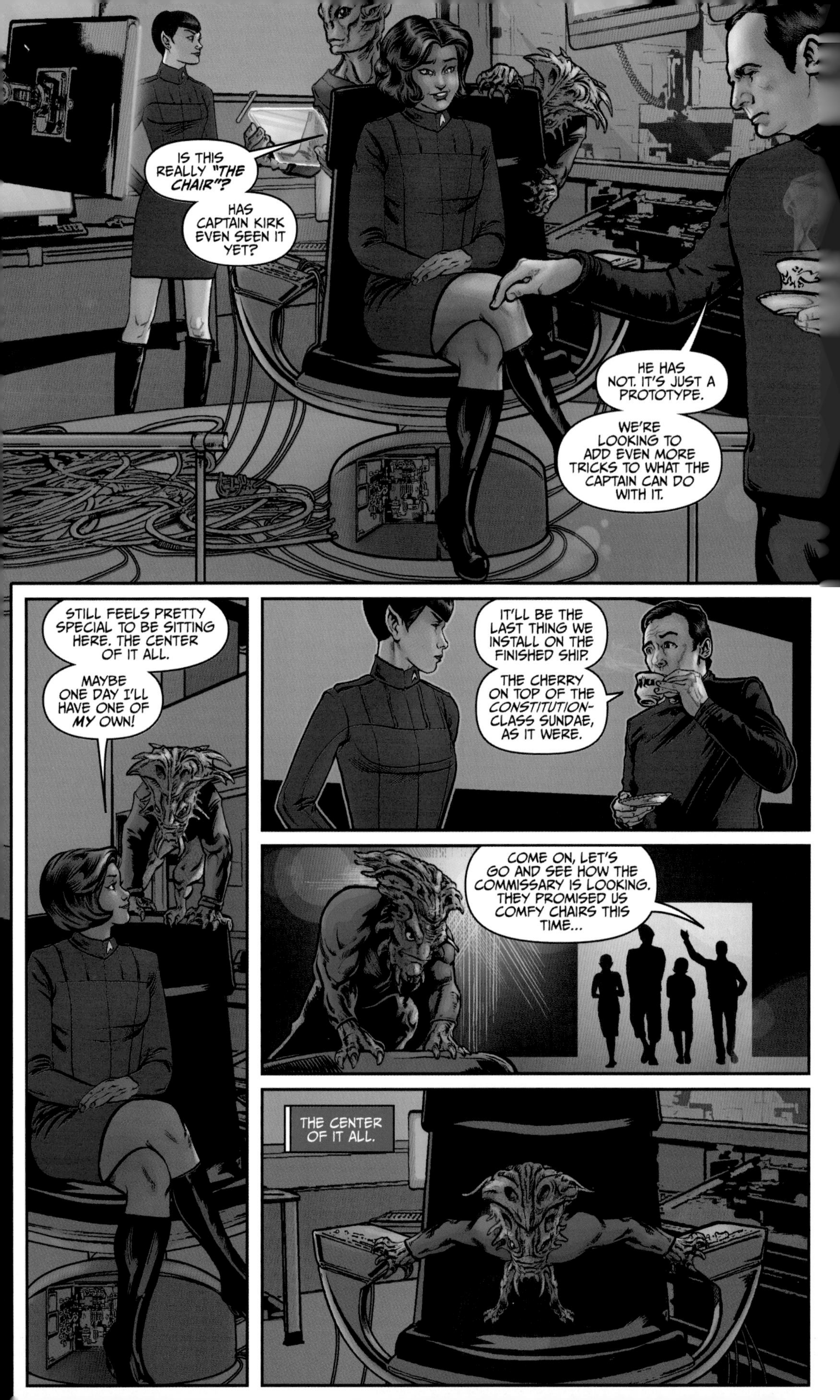
IS THIS REALLY "THE CHAIR"?
HAS CAPTAIN KIRK EVEN SEEN IT YET?
HE HAS NOT. IT'S JUST A PROTOTYPE.
WE'RE LOOKING TO ADD EVEN MORE TRICKS TO WHAT THE CAPTAIN CAN DO WITH IT.
STILL FEELS PRETTY SPECIAL TO BE SITTING HERE. THE CENTER OF IT ALL.
MAYBE ONE DAY I'LL HAVE ONE OF MY OWN!
IT'LL BE THE LAST THING WE INSTALL ON THE FINISHED SHIP.
THE CHERRY ON TOP OF THE CONSTITUTION-CLASS SUNDAE, AS IT WERE.
COME ON, LET'S GO AND SEE HOW THE COMMISSARY IS LOOKING. THEY PROMISED US COMFY CHAIRS THIS TIME...
THE CENTER OF IT ALL.

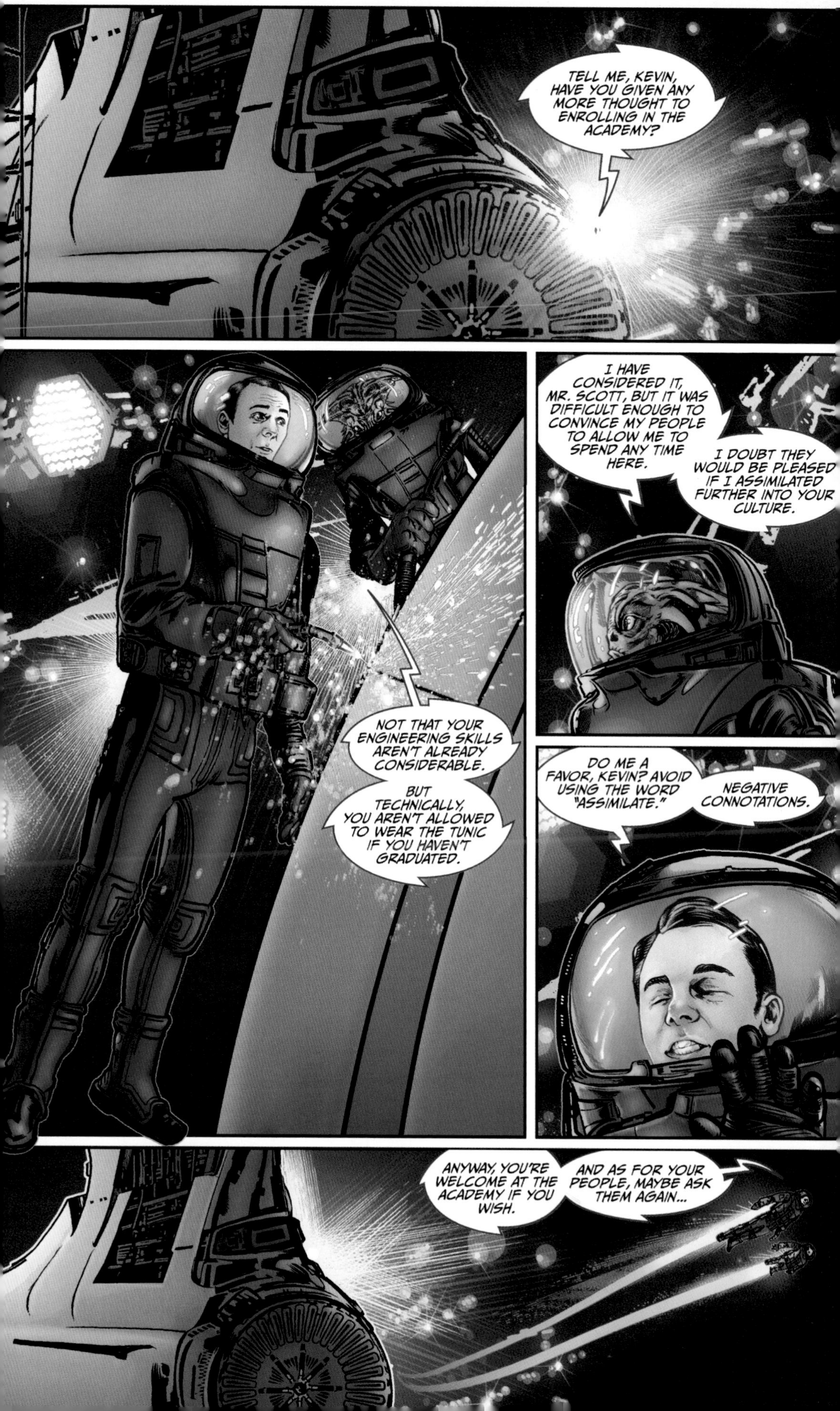
TELL ME, KEVIN, HAVE YOU GIVEN ANY MORE THOUGHT TO ENROLLING IN THE ACADEMY?
I HAVE CONSIDERED IT, MR. SCOTT, BUT IT WAS DIFFICULT ENOUGH TO CONVINCE MY PEOPLE TO ALLOW ME TO SPEND ANY TIME HERE.
I DOUBT THEY WOULD BE PLEASED IF I ASSIMILATED FURTHER INTO YOUR CULTURE.
NOT THAT YOUR ENGINEERING SKILLS AREN'T ALREADY CONSIDERABLE.
BUT TECHNICALLY, YOU AREN'T ALLOWED TO WEAR THE TUNIC IF YOU HAVEN'T GRADUATED.
DO ME A FAVOR, KEVIN? AVOID USING THE WORD "ASSIMILATE."
NEGATIVE CONNOTATIONS.
ANYWAY, YOU'RE WELCOME AT THE ACADEMY IF YOU WISH.
AND AS FOR YOUR PEOPLE, MAYBE ASK THEM AGAIN...

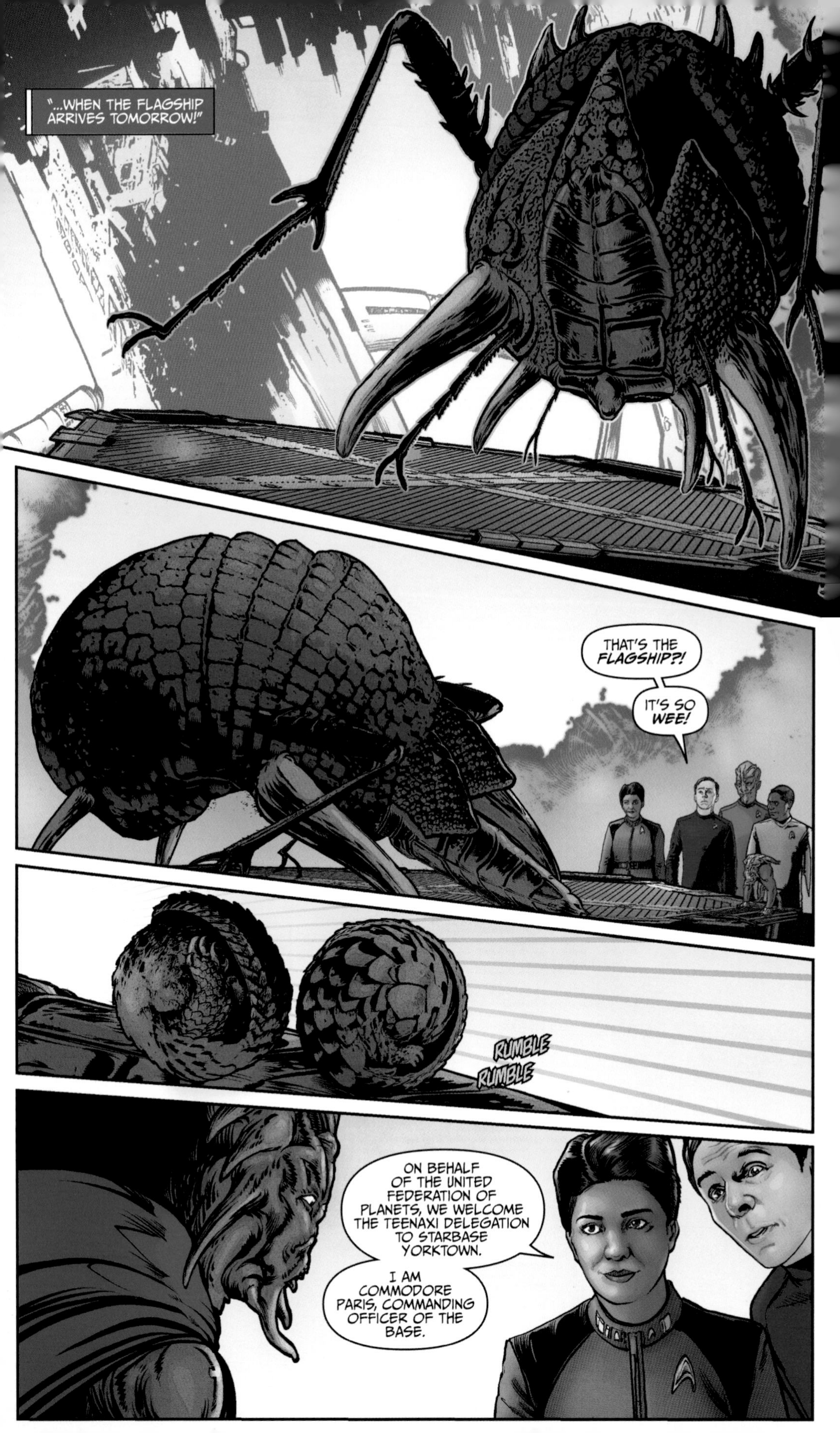
"...WHEN THE FLAGSHIP ARRIVES TOMORROW!"
THAT'S THE FLAGSHIP?!
IT'S SO WEE!
RUMBLE
RUMBLE
ON BEHALF OF THE UNITED FEDERATION OF PLANETS, WE WELCOME THE TEENAXI DELEGATION TO STARBASE YORKTOWN.
I AM COMMODORE PARIS, COMMANDING OFFICER OF THE BASE.

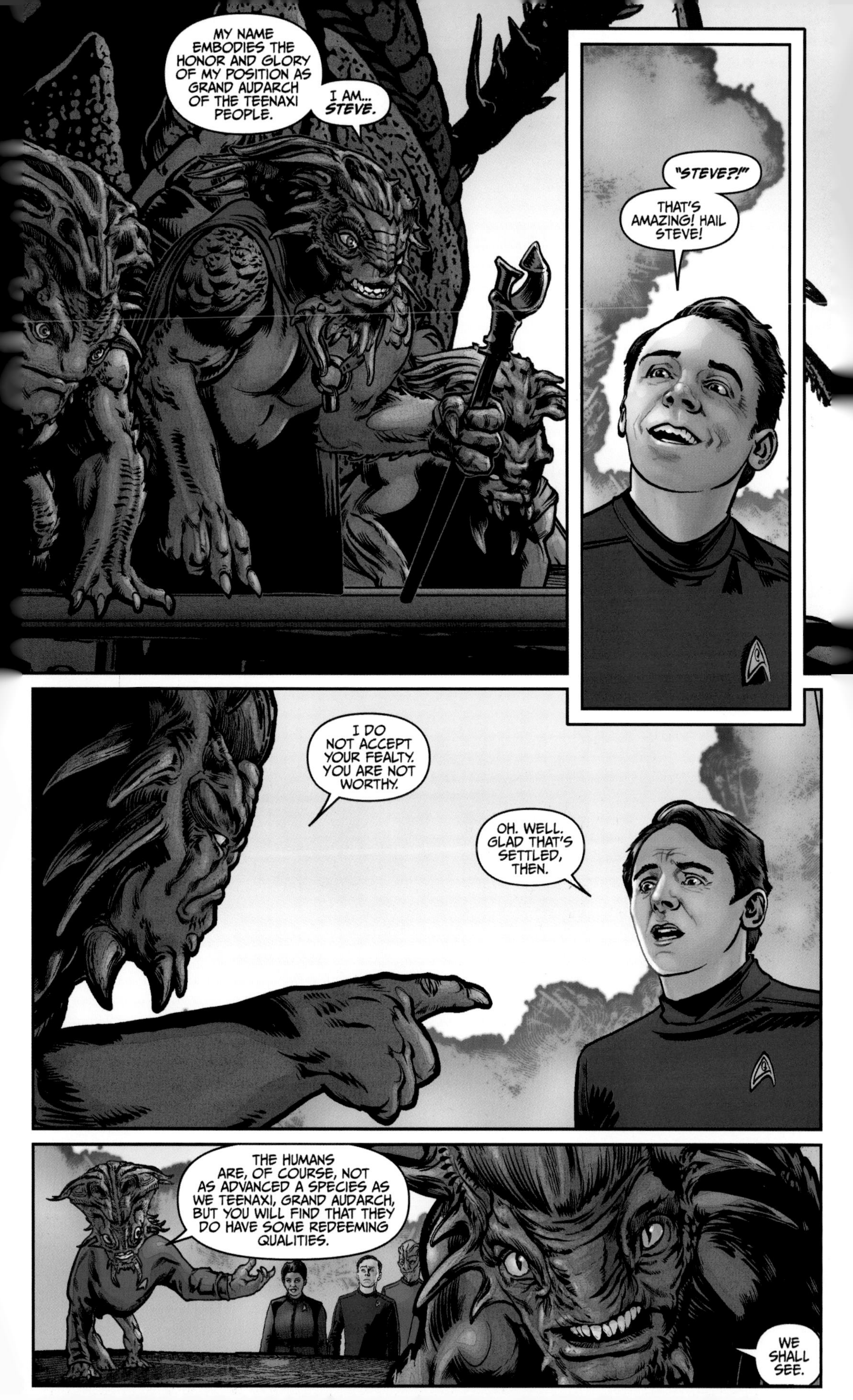
MY NAME EMBODIES THE HONOR AND GLORY OF MY POSITION AS GRAND AUDARCH OF THE TEENAXI PEOPLE.
I AM... STEVE.
"STEVE?!"
THAT'S AMAZING! HAIL STEVE!
I DO NOT ACCEPT YOUR FEALTY. YOU ARE NOT WORTHY.
OH. WELL. GLAD THAT'S SETTLED, THEN.
THE HUMANS ARE, OF COURSE, NOT AS ADVANCED A SPECIES AS WE TEENAXI, GRAND AUDARCH, BUT YOU WILL FIND THAT THEY DO HAVE SOME REDEEMING QUALITIES.
WE SHALL SEE.

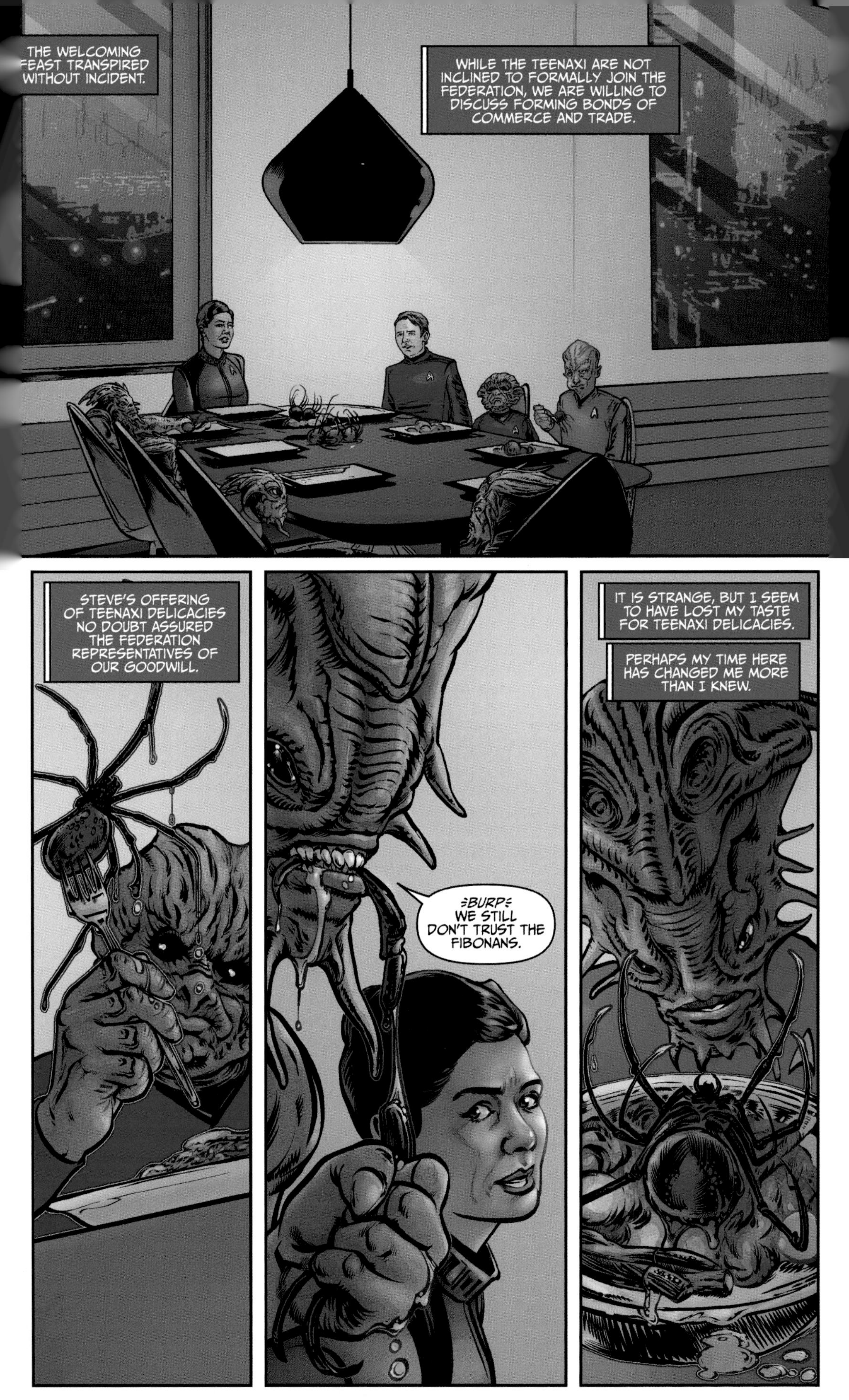
THE WELCOMING FEAST TRANSPIRED WITHOUT INCIDENT.
WHILE THE TEENAXI ARE NOT INCLINED TO FORMALLY JOIN THE FEDERATION, WE ARE WILLING TO DISCUSS FORMING BONDS OF COMMERCE AND TRADE.
STEVE'S OFFERING OF TEENAXI DELICACIES NO DOUBT ASSURED THE FEDERATION REPRESENTATIVES OF OUR GOODWILL.
BURP
WE STILL DON'T TRUST THE FIBONANS.
IT IS STRANGE, BUT I SEEM TO HAVE LOST MY TASTE FOR TEENAXI DELICACIES.
PERHAPS MY TIME HERE HAS CHANGED ME MORE THAN I KNEW.

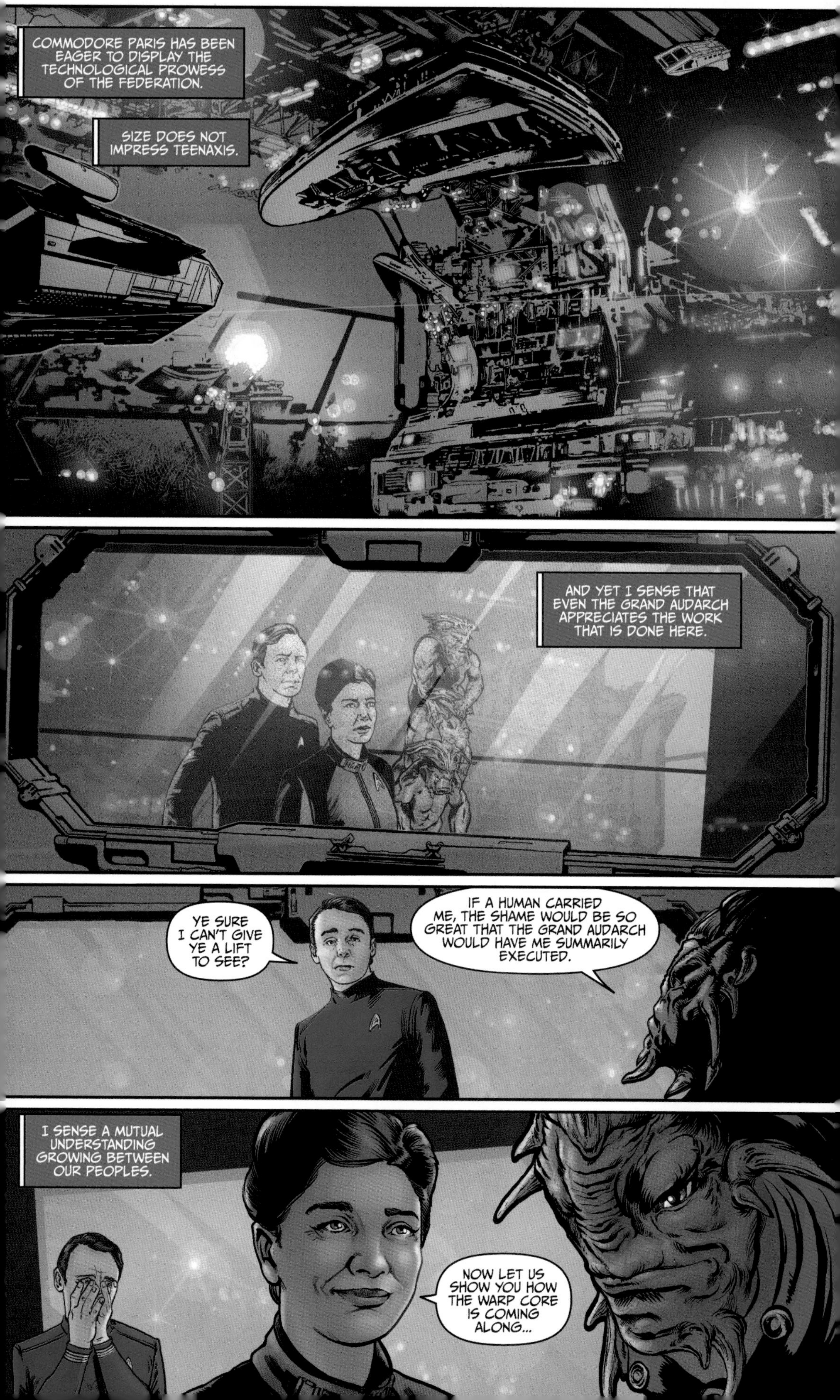
COMMODORE PARIS HAS BEEN EAGER TO DISPLAY THE TECHNOLOGICAL PROWESS OF THE FEDERATION.
SIZE DOES NOT IMPRESS TEENAXIS.
AND YET I SENSE THAT EVEN THE GRAND AUDARCH APPRECIATES THE WORK THAT IS DONE HERE.
YE SURE I CAN'T GIVE YE A LIFT TO SEE?
IF A HUMAN CARRIED ME, THE SHAME WOULD BE SO GREAT THAT THE GRAND AUDARCH WOULD HAVE ME SUMMARILY EXECUTED.
I SENSE A MUTUAL UNDERSTANDING GROWING BETWEEN OUR PEOPLES.
NOW LET US SHOW YOU HOW THE WARP CORE IS COMING ALONG...

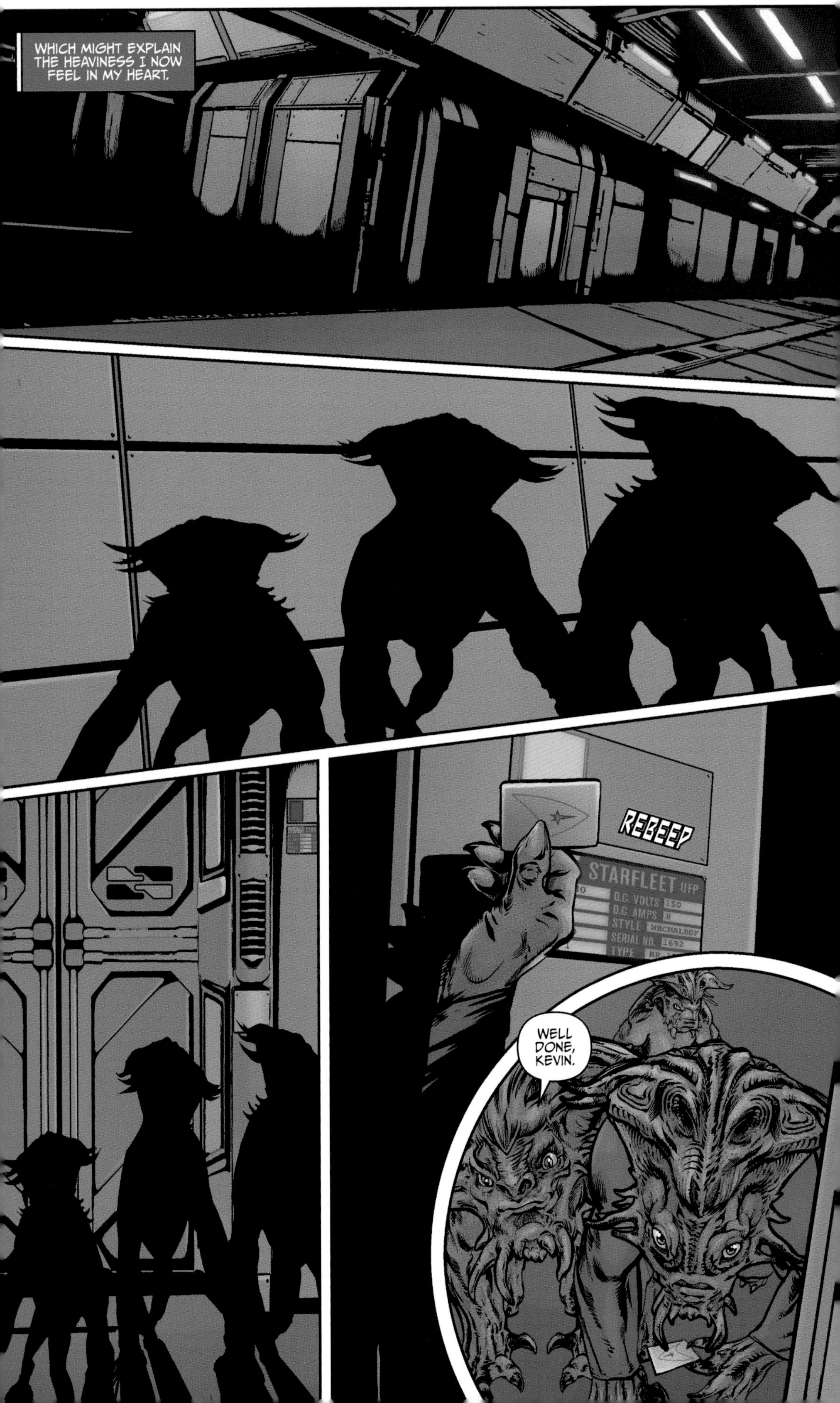
WHICH MIGHT EXPLAIN THE HEAVINESS I NOW FEEL IN MY HEART.
REBEEP
STARFLEET UFP
D.C. VOLTS 150
D.C. AMPS 8
STYLE WBCMALDDF
SERIAL NO. 1692
TYPE
WELL DONE, KEVIN.

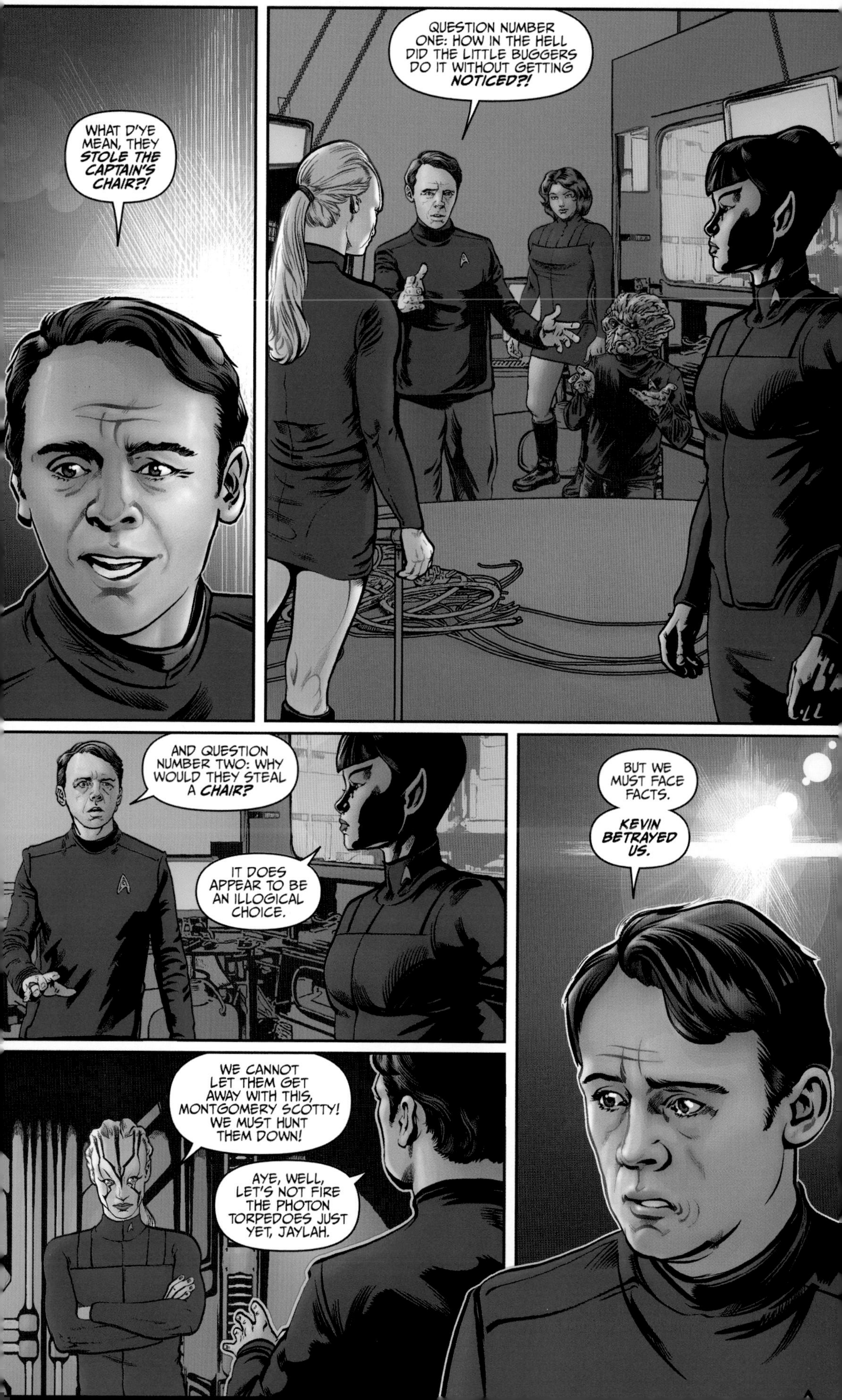
WHAT D'YE MEAN, THEY STOLE THE CAPTAIN'S CHAIR?!
QUESTION NUMBER ONE: HOW IN THE HELL DID THE LITTLE BUGGERS DO IT WITHOUT GETTING NOTICED?!
AND QUESTION NUMBER TWO: WHY WOULD THEY STEAL A CHAIR?
IT DOES APPEAR TO BE AN ILLOGICAL CHOICE.
BUT WE MUST FACE FACTS.
KEVIN BETRAYED US.
WE CANNOT LET THEM GET AWAY WITH THIS, MONTGOMERY SCOTTY! WE MUST HUNT THEM DOWN!
AYE, WELL, LET'S NOT FIRE THE PHOTON TORPEDOES JUST YET, JAYLAH.

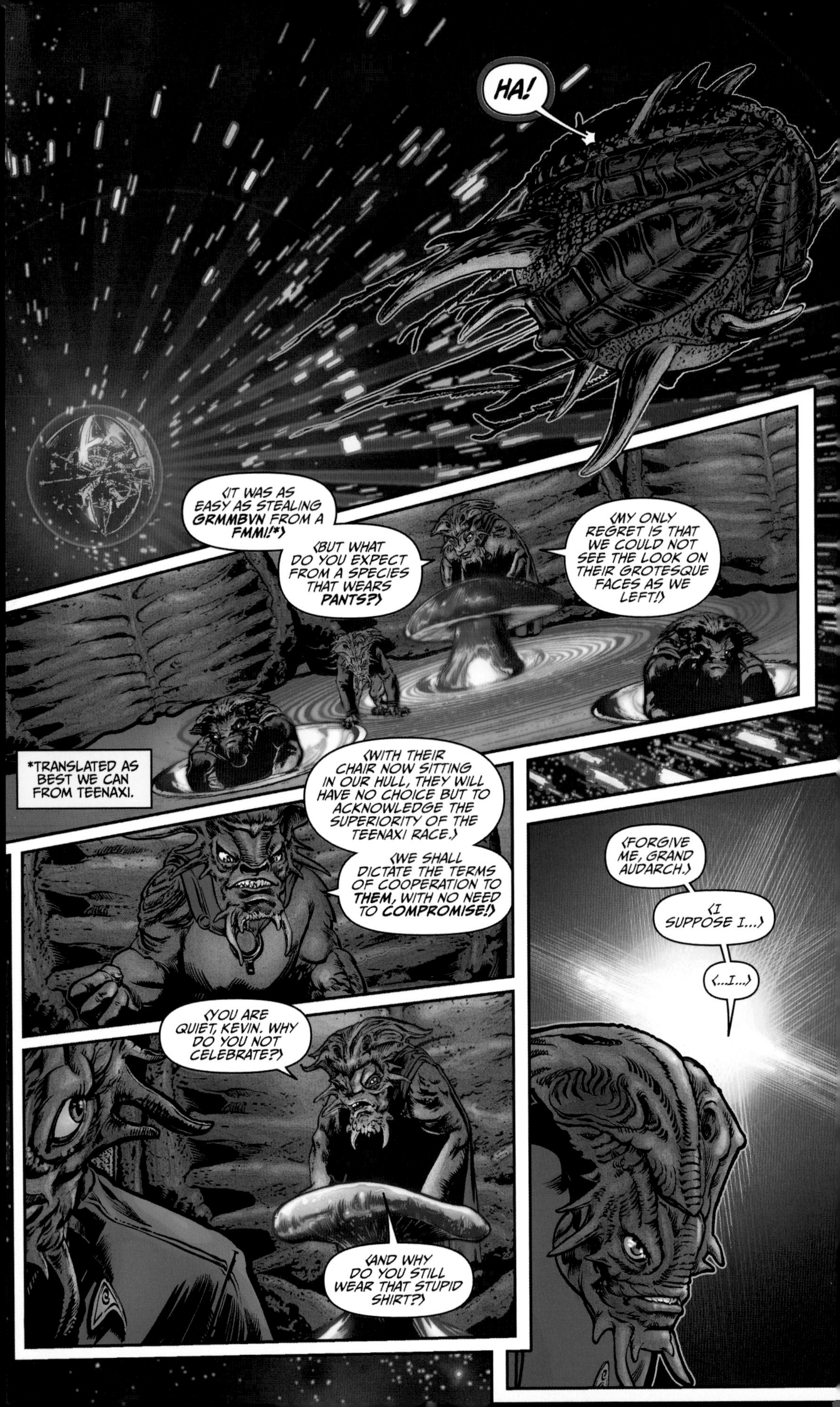
HA!
‹IT WAS AS EASY AS STEALING GRMMBVN FROM A FMMI!*›
‹BUT WHAT DO YOU EXPECT FROM A SPECIES THAT WEARS PANTS?›
‹MY ONLY REGRET IS THAT WE COULD NOT SEE THE LOOK ON THEIR GROTESQUE FACES AS WE LEFT!›
*TRANSLATED AS BEST WE CAN FROM TEENAXI.
‹WITH THEIR CHAIR NOW SITTING IN OUR HULL, THEY WILL HAVE NO CHOICE BUT TO ACKNOWLEDGE THE SUPERIORITY OF THE TEENAXI RACE.›
‹WE SHALL DICTATE THE TERMS OF COOPERATION TO THEM, WITH NO NEED TO COMPROMISE!›
‹YOU ARE QUIET, KEVIN. WHY DO YOU NOT CELEBRATE?›
‹AND WHY DO YOU STILL WEAR THAT STUPID SHIRT?›
‹FORGIVE ME, GRAND AUDARCH.›
‹I SUPPOSE I...›
‹...I...›

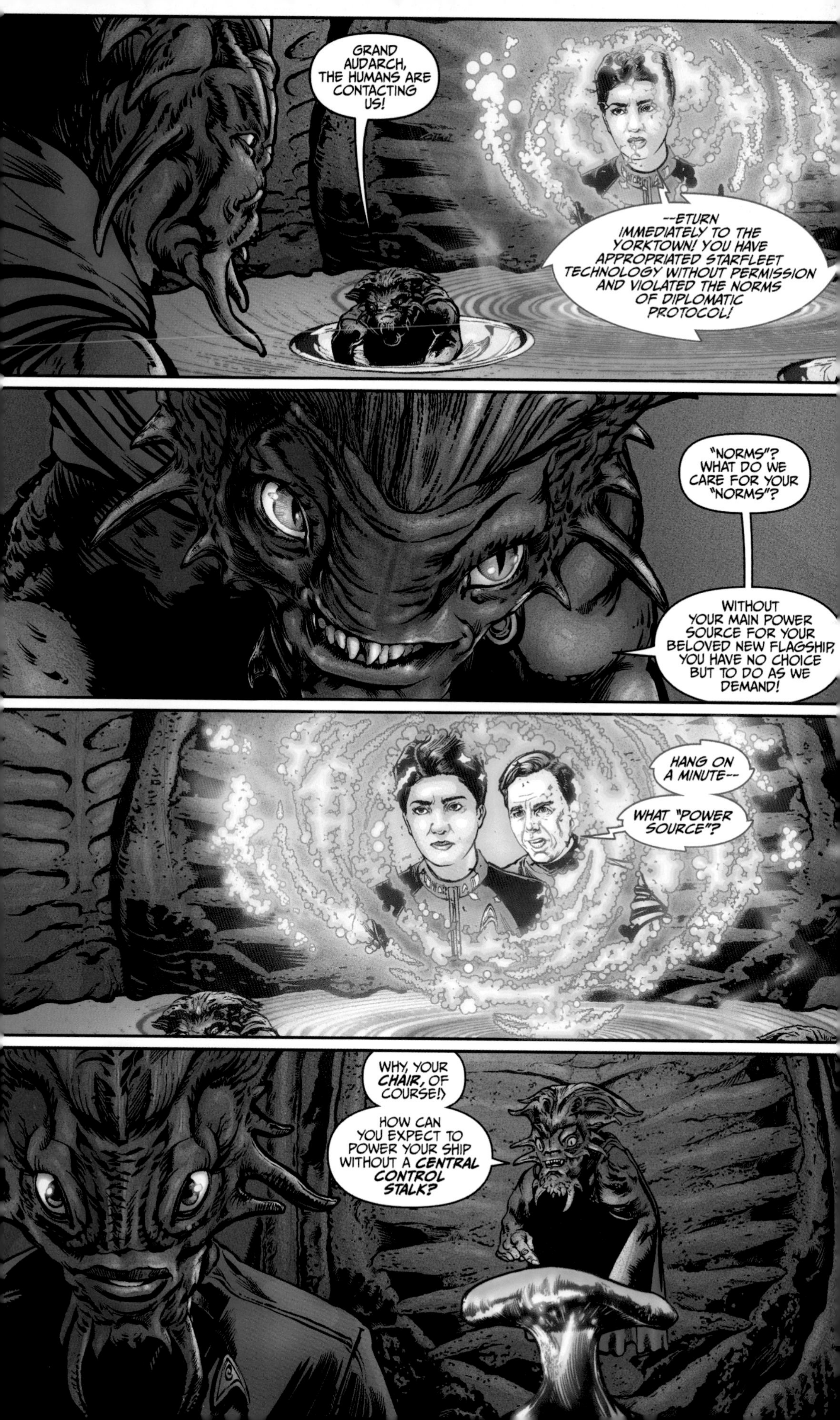
GRAND AUDARCH, THE HUMANS ARE CONTACTING US!
--ETURN IMMEDIATELY TO THE YORKTOWN! YOU HAVE APPROPRIATED STARFLEET TECHNOLOGY WITHOUT PERMISSION AND VIOLATED THE NORMS OF DIPLOMATIC PROTOCOL!
"NORMS"? WHAT DO WE CARE FOR YOUR "NORMS"?
WITHOUT YOUR MAIN POWER SOURCE FOR YOUR BELOVED NEW FLAGSHIP, YOU HAVE NO CHOICE BUT TO DO AS WE DEMAND!
HANG ON A MINUTE--
WHAT "POWER SOURCE"?
WHY, YOUR CHAIR, OF COURSE!)
HOW CAN YOU EXPECT TO POWER YOUR SHIP WITHOUT A CENTRAL CONTROL STALK?

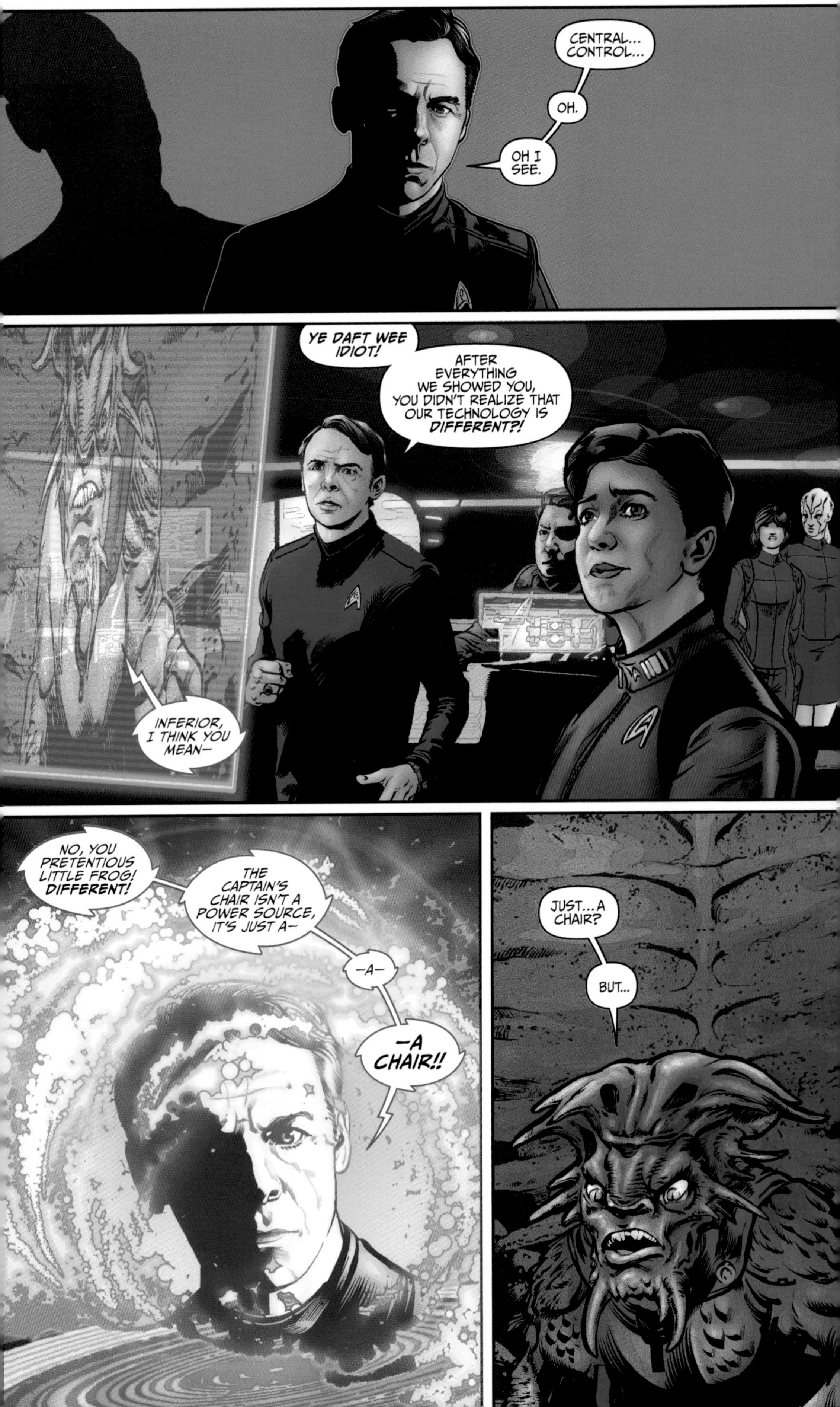
CENTRAL... CONTROL...
OH.
OH I SEE.
YE DAFT WEE IDIOT!
AFTER EVERYTHING WE SHOWED YOU, YOU DIDN'T REALIZE THAT OUR TECHNOLOGY IS DIFFERENT?!
INFERIOR, I THINK YOU MEAN—
NO, YOU PRETENTIOUS LITTLE FROG! DIFFERENT!
THE CAPTAIN'S CHAIR ISN'T A POWER SOURCE, IT'S JUST A—
—A—
—A CHAIR!!
JUST...A CHAIR?
BUT...

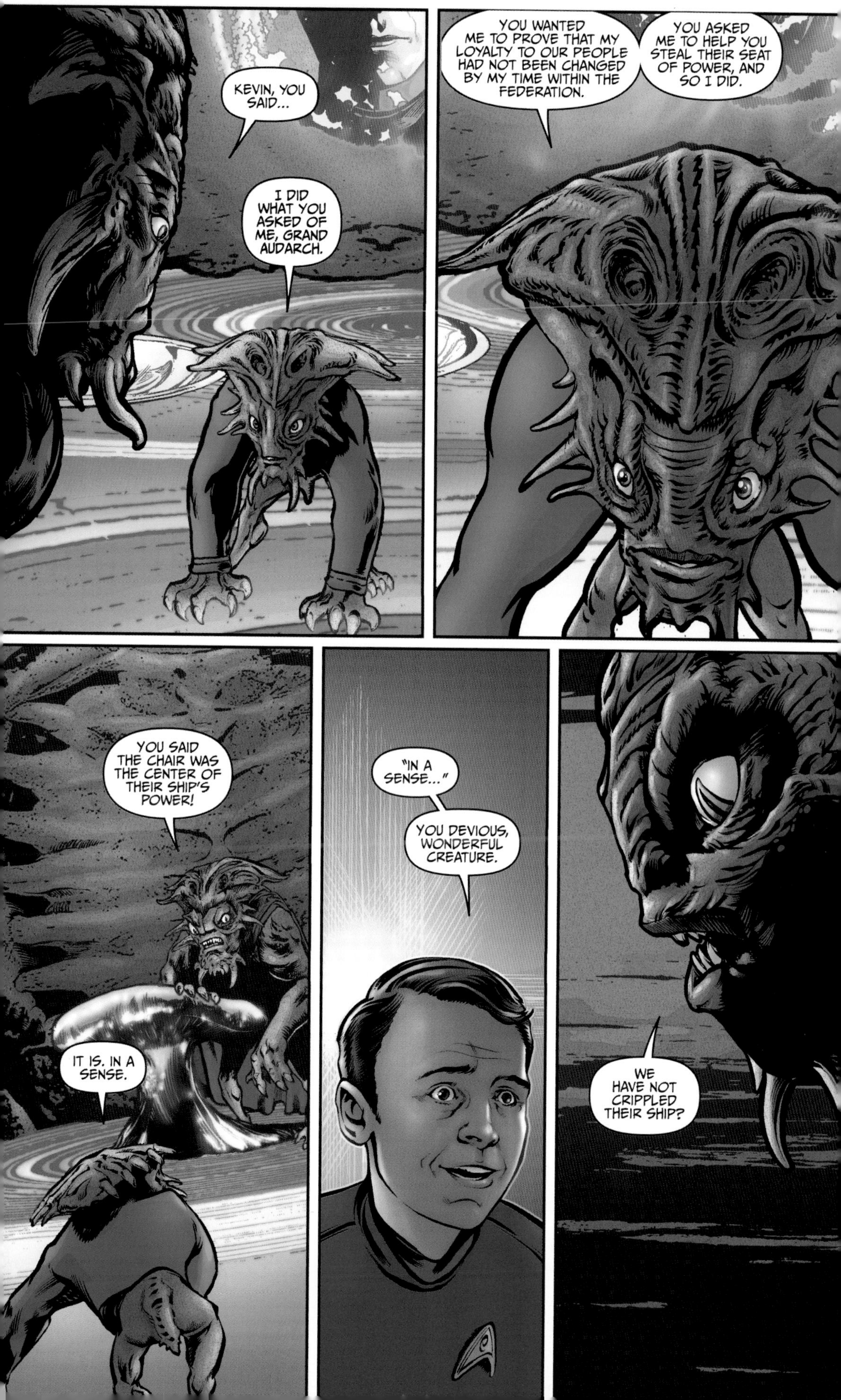
KEVIN, YOU SAID...
I DID WHAT YOU ASKED OF ME, GRAND AUDARCH.
YOU WANTED ME TO PROVE THAT MY LOYALTY TO OUR PEOPLE HAD NOT BEEN CHANGED BY MY TIME WITHIN THE FEDERATION.
YOU ASKED ME TO HELP YOU STEAL THEIR SEAT OF POWER, AND SO I DID.
YOU SAID THE CHAIR WAS THE CENTER OF THEIR SHIP'S POWER!
IT IS. IN A SENSE.
"IN A SENSE..."
YOU DEVIOUS, WONDERFUL CREATURE.
WE HAVE NOT CRIPPLED THEIR SHIP?

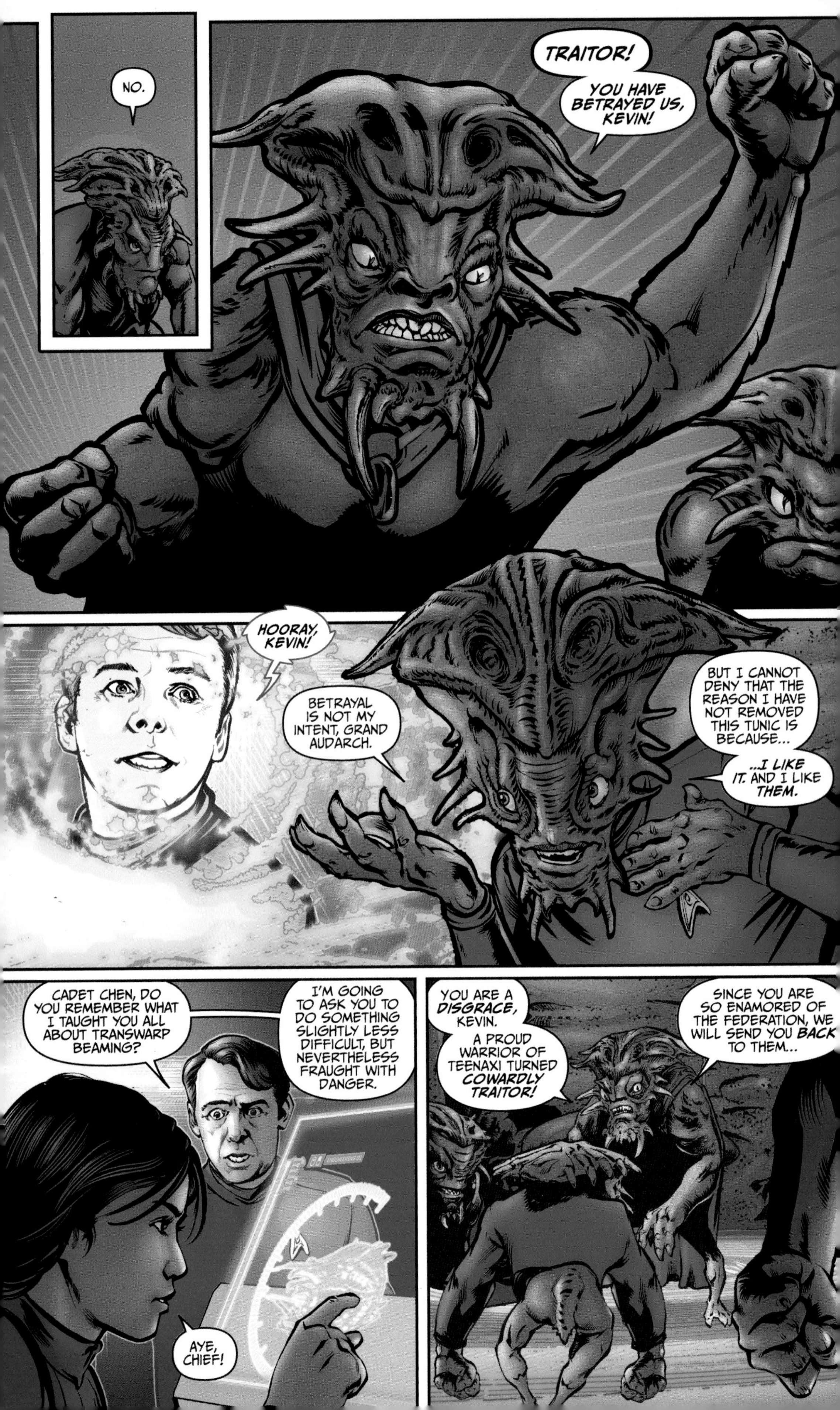
NO.
TRAITOR!
YOU HAVE BETRAYED US, KEVIN!
HOORAY, KEVIN!
BETRAYAL IS NOT MY INTENT, GRAND AUDARCH.
BUT I CANNOT DENY THAT THE REASON I HAVE NOT REMOVED THIS TUNIC IS BECAUSE...
...I LIKE IT. AND I LIKE THEM.
CADET CHEN, DO YOU REMEMBER WHAT I TAUGHT YOU ALL ABOUT TRANSWARP BEAMING?
I'M GOING TO ASK YOU TO DO SOMETHING SLIGHTLY LESS DIFFICULT, BUT NEVERTHELESS FRAUGHT WITH DANGER.
AYE, CHIEF!
YOU ARE A DISGRACE, KEVIN.
A PROUD WARRIOR OF TEENAXI TURNED COWARDLY TRAITOR!
SINCE YOU ARE SO ENAMORED OF THE FEDERATION, WE WILL SEND YOU BACK TO THEM...

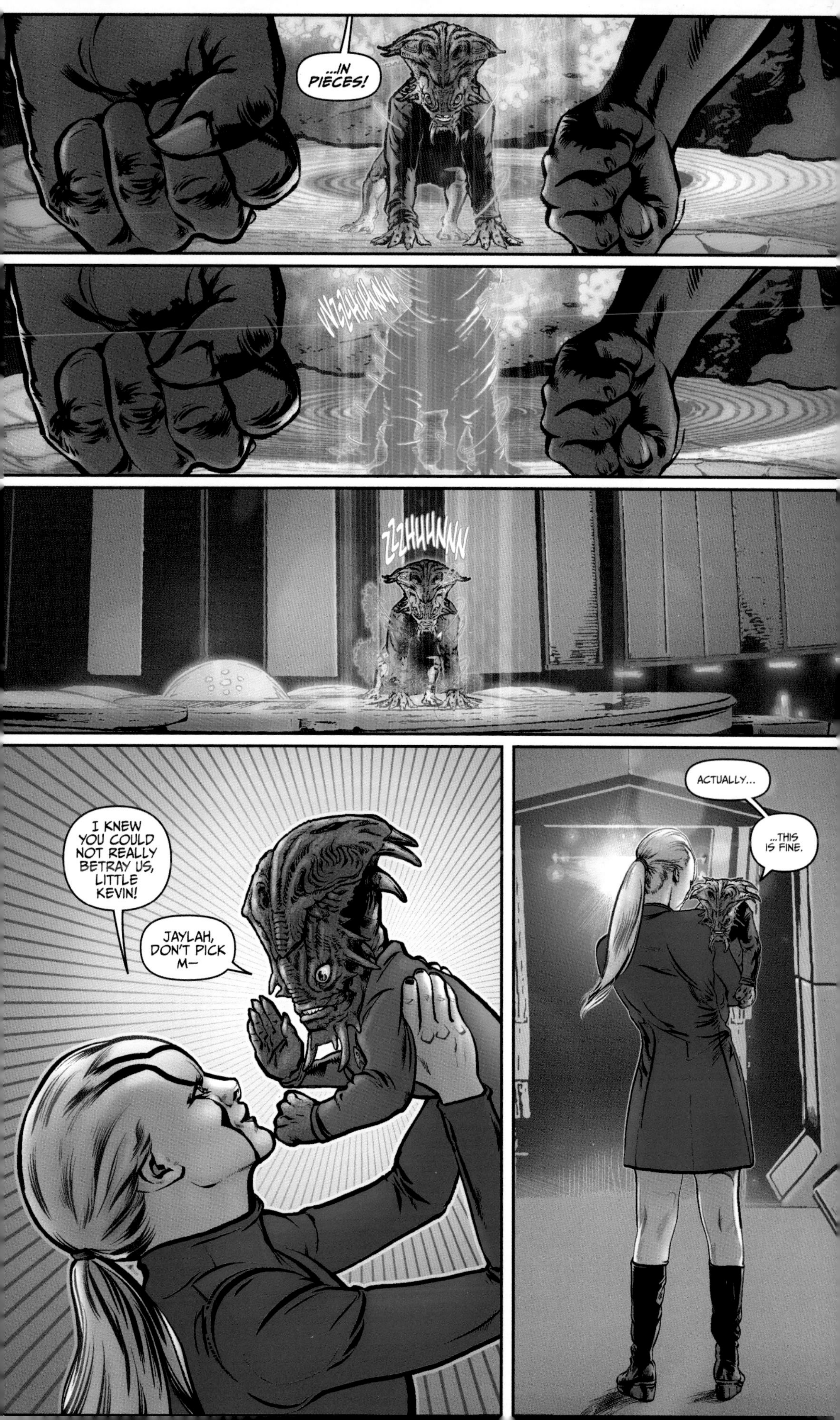

...IN PIECES!
VVZZZHHHNNN
ZZZHHHNNN
I KNEW YOU COULD NOT REALLY BETRAY US, LITTLE KEVIN!
JAYLAH, DON'T PICK M—
ACTUALLY...
...THIS IS FINE.

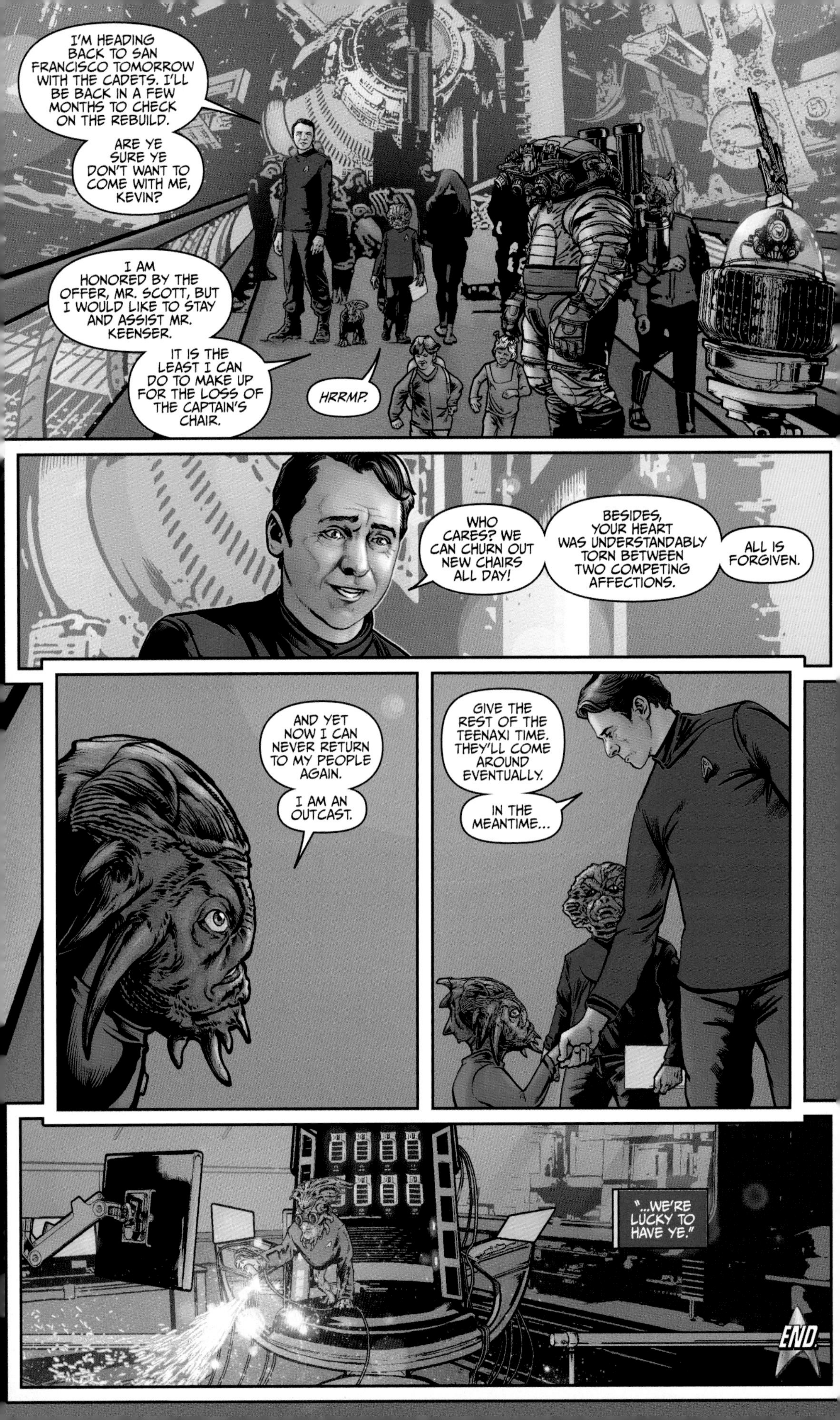
I'M HEADING BACK TO SAN FRANCISCO TOMORROW WITH THE CADETS. I'LL BE BACK IN A FEW MONTHS TO CHECK ON THE REBUILD.
ARE YE SURE YE DON'T WANT TO COME WITH ME, KEVIN?
I AM HONORED BY THE OFFER, MR. SCOTT, BUT I WOULD LIKE TO STAY AND ASSIST MR. KEENSER.
IT IS THE LEAST I CAN DO TO MAKE UP FOR THE LOSS OF THE CAPTAIN'S CHAIR.
HRRMP.
WHO CARES? WE CAN CHURN OUT NEW CHAIRS ALL DAY!
BESIDES, YOUR HEART WAS UNDERSTANDABLY TORN BETWEEN TWO COMPETING AFFECTIONS.
ALL IS FORGIVEN.
AND YET NOW I CAN NEVER RETURN TO MY PEOPLE AGAIN.
I AM AN OUTCAST.
GIVE THE REST OF THE TEENAXI TIME. THEY'LL COME AROUND EVENTUALLY.
IN THE MEANTIME...
"...WE'RE LUCKY TO HAVE YE."
END.

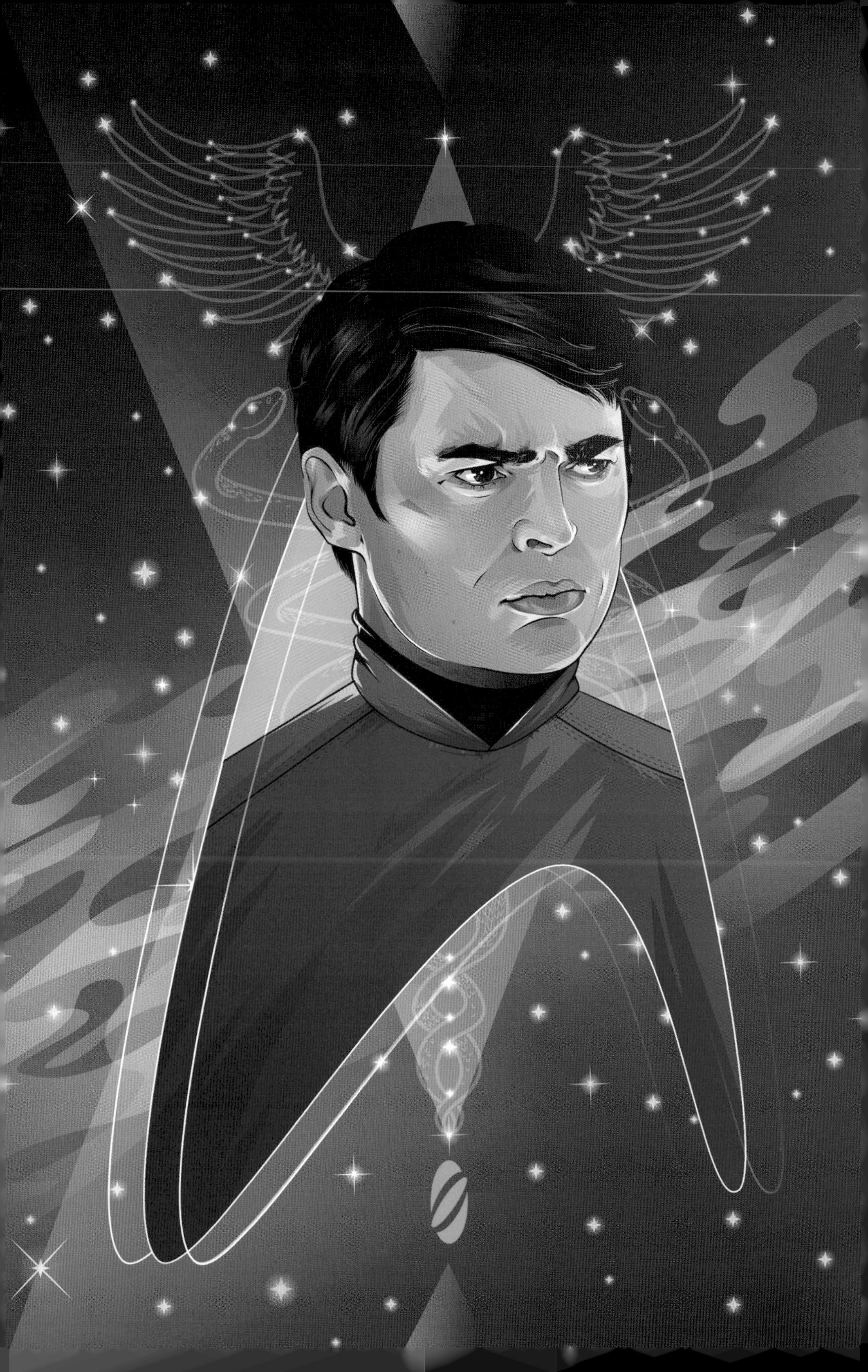

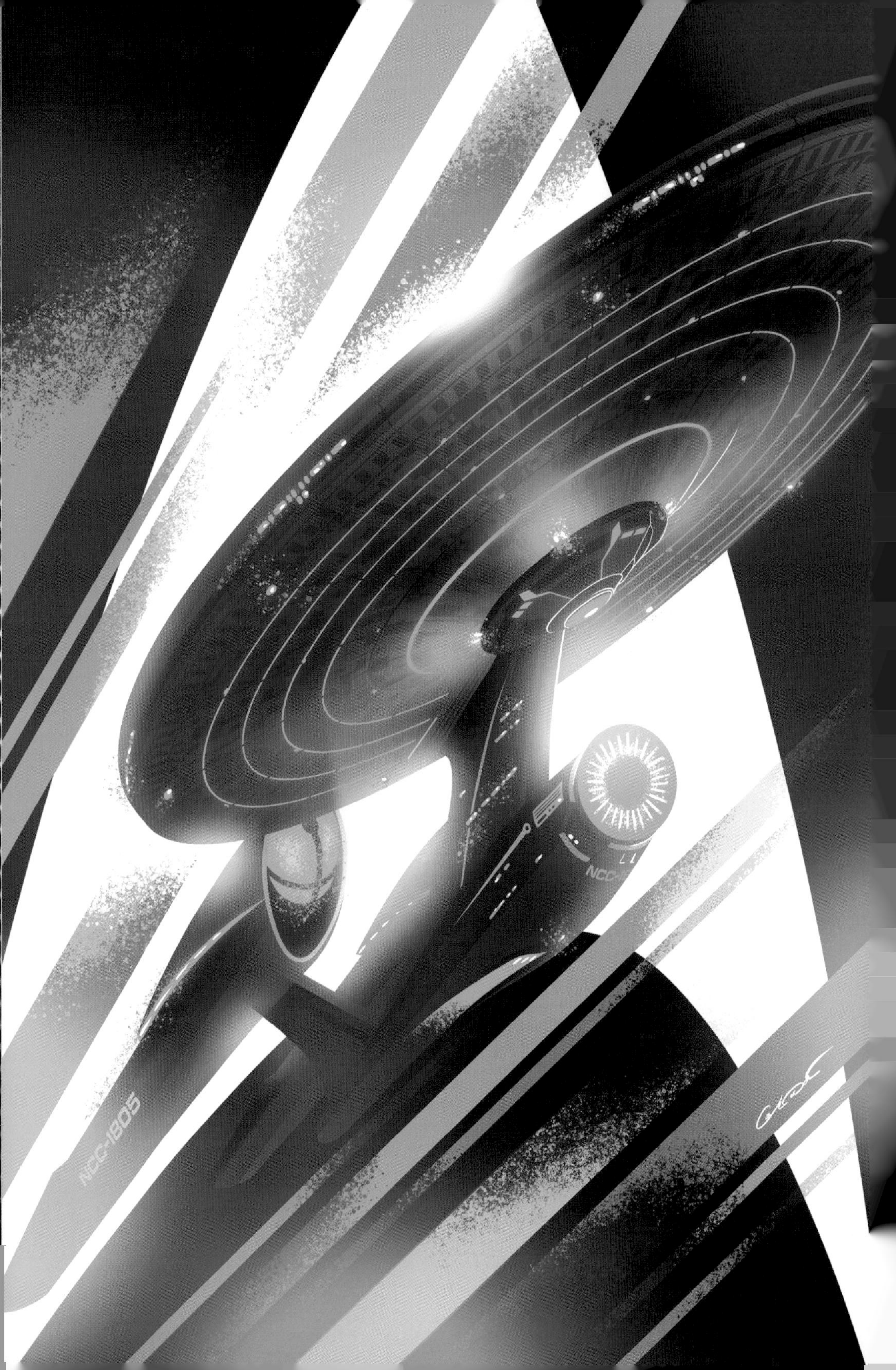
NCC-1805

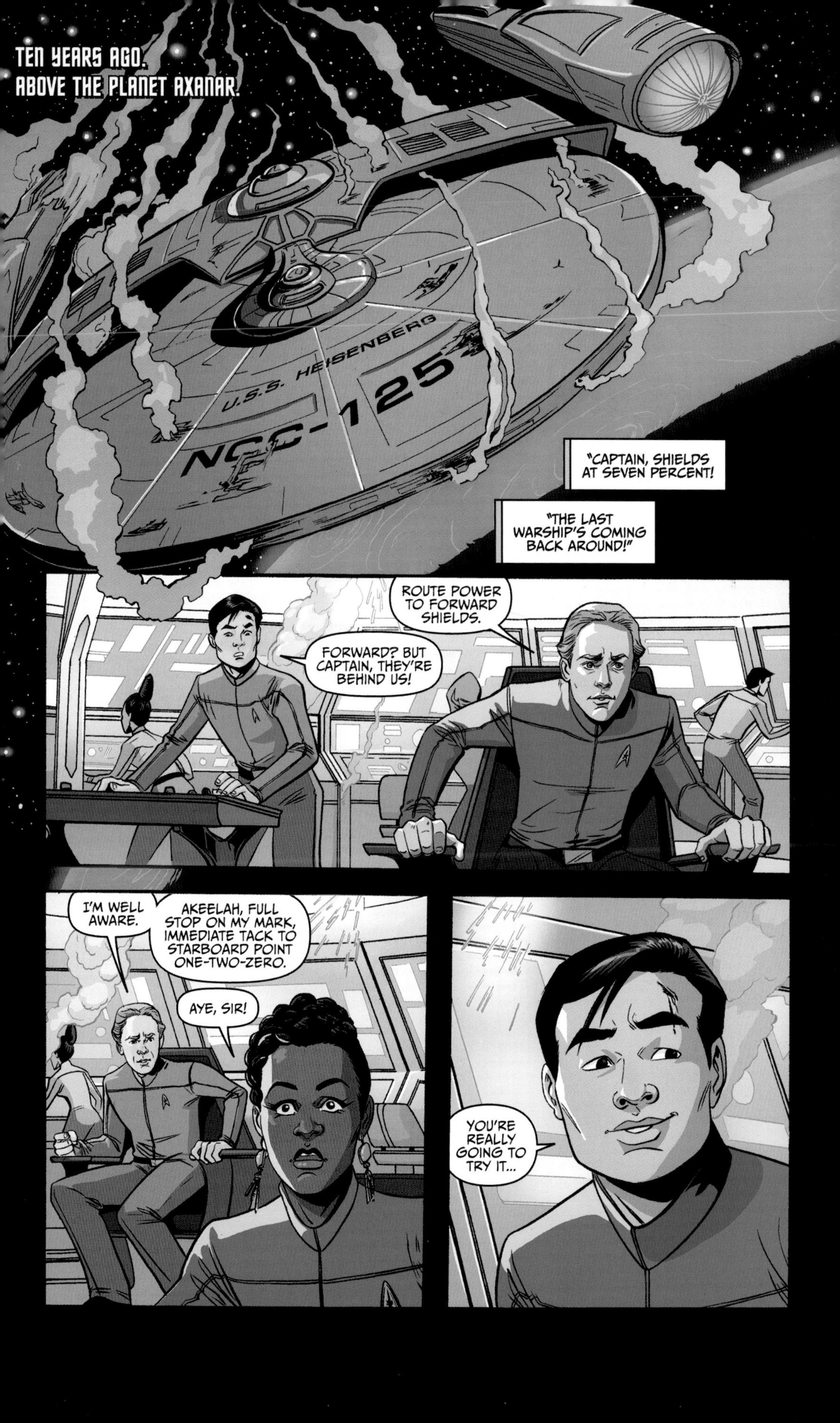
TEN YEARS AGO.
ABOVE THE PLANET AXANAR.
U.S.S. HEISENBERG
NCC-125
"CAPTAIN, SHIELDS AT SEVEN PERCENT!
"THE LAST WARSHIP'S COMING BACK AROUND!"
ROUTE POWER TO FORWARD SHIELDS.
FORWARD? BUT CAPTAIN, THEY'RE BEHIND US!
I'M WELL AWARE.
AKEELAH, FULL STOP ON MY MARK, IMMEDIATE TACK TO STARBOARD POINT ONE-TWO-ZERO.
AYE, SIR!
YOU'RE REALLY GOING TO TRY IT...

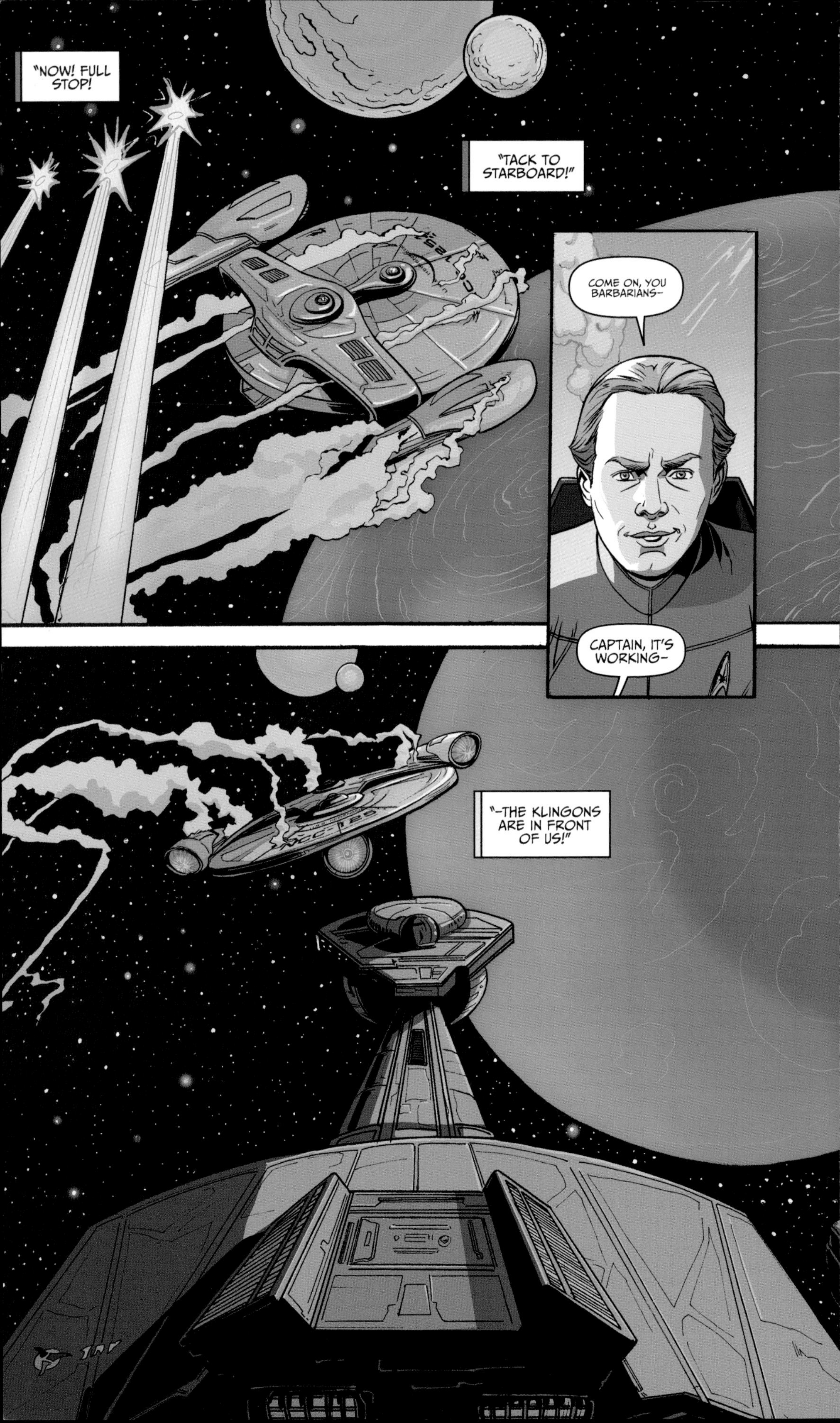
"NOW! FULL STOP!
"TACK TO STARBOARD!"
COME ON, YOU BARBARIANS–
CAPTAIN, IT'S WORKING–
"–THE KLINGONS ARE IN FRONT OF US!"

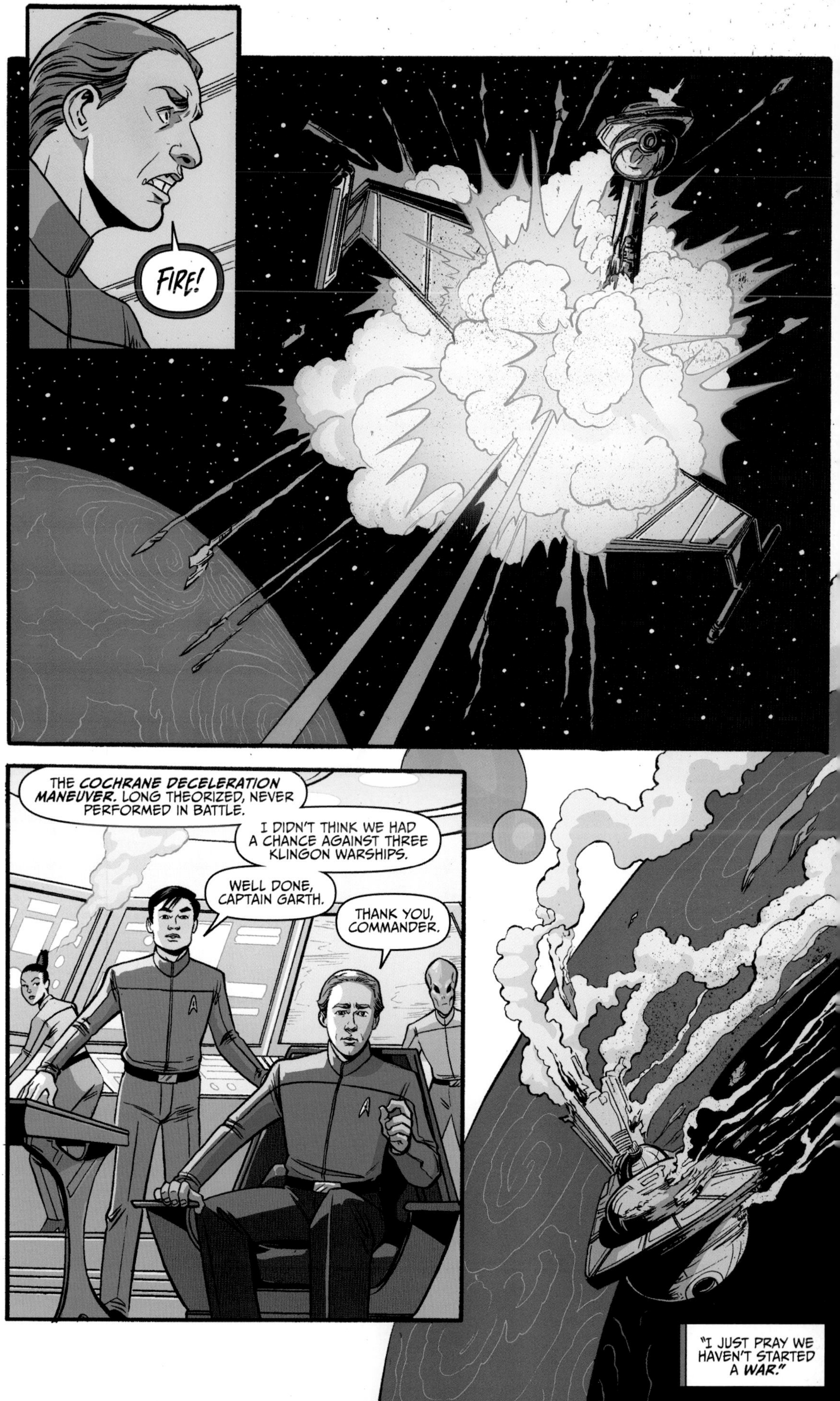
FIRE!
THE *COCHRANE DECELERATION MANEUVER.* LONG THEORIZED, NEVER PERFORMED IN BATTLE.
I DIDN'T THINK WE HAD A CHANCE AGAINST THREE KLINGON WARSHIPS.
WELL DONE, CAPTAIN GARTH.
THANK YOU, COMMANDER.
"I JUST PRAY WE HAVEN'T STARTED A *WAR.*"

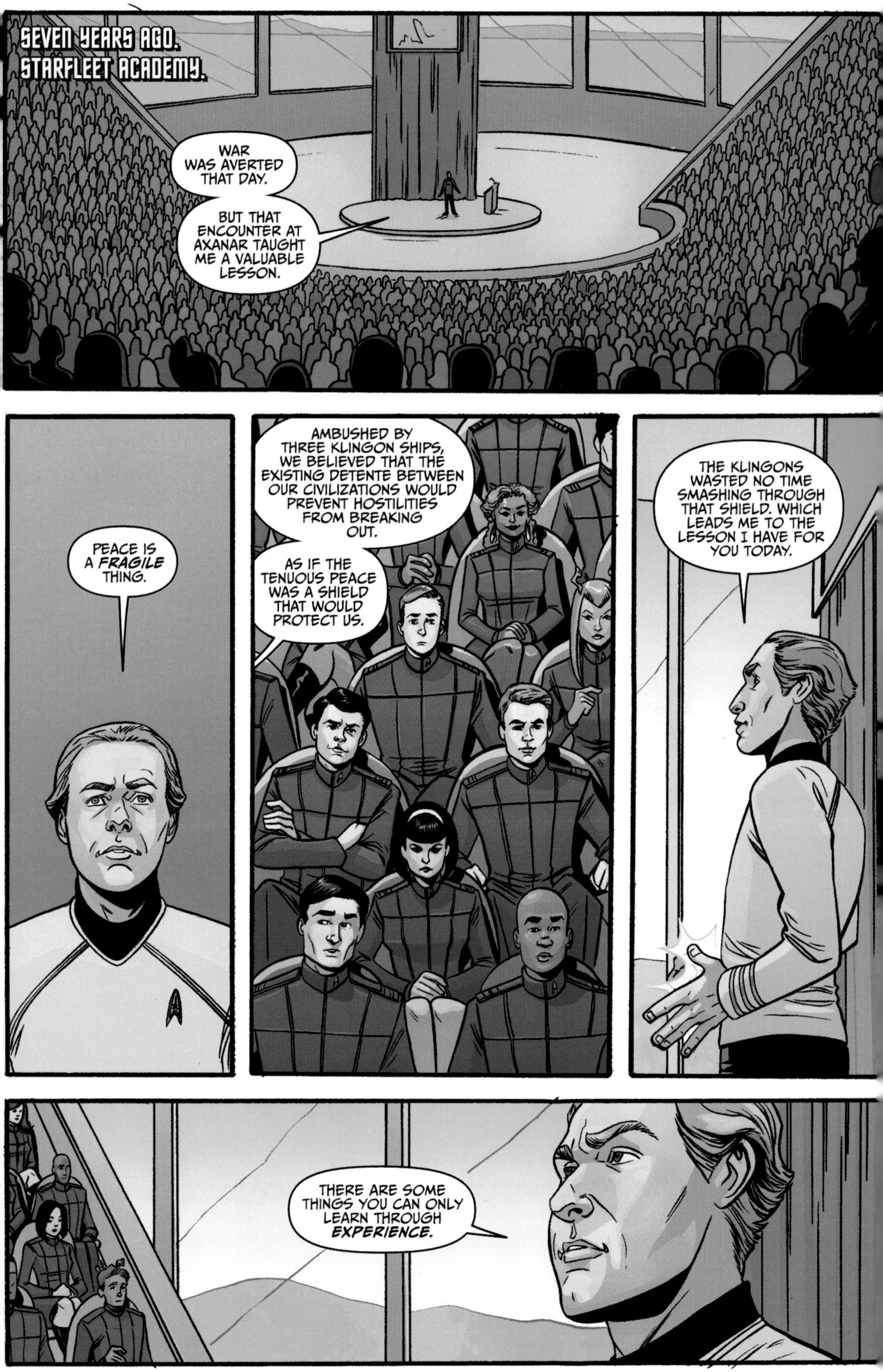
SEVEN YEARS AGO. STARFLEET ACADEMY.
WAR WAS AVERTED THAT DAY.
BUT THAT ENCOUNTER AT AXANAR TAUGHT ME A VALUABLE LESSON.
PEACE IS A *FRAGILE* THING.
AMBUSHED BY THREE KLINGON SHIPS, WE BELIEVED THAT THE EXISTING DETENTE BETWEEN OUR CIVILIZATIONS WOULD PREVENT HOSTILITIES FROM BREAKING OUT.
AS IF THE TENUOUS PEACE WAS A SHIELD THAT WOULD PROTECT US.
THE KLINGONS WASTED NO TIME SMASHING THROUGH THAT SHIELD. WHICH LEADS ME TO THE LESSON I HAVE FOR YOU TODAY.
THERE ARE SOME THINGS YOU CAN ONLY LEARN THROUGH *EXPERIENCE.*

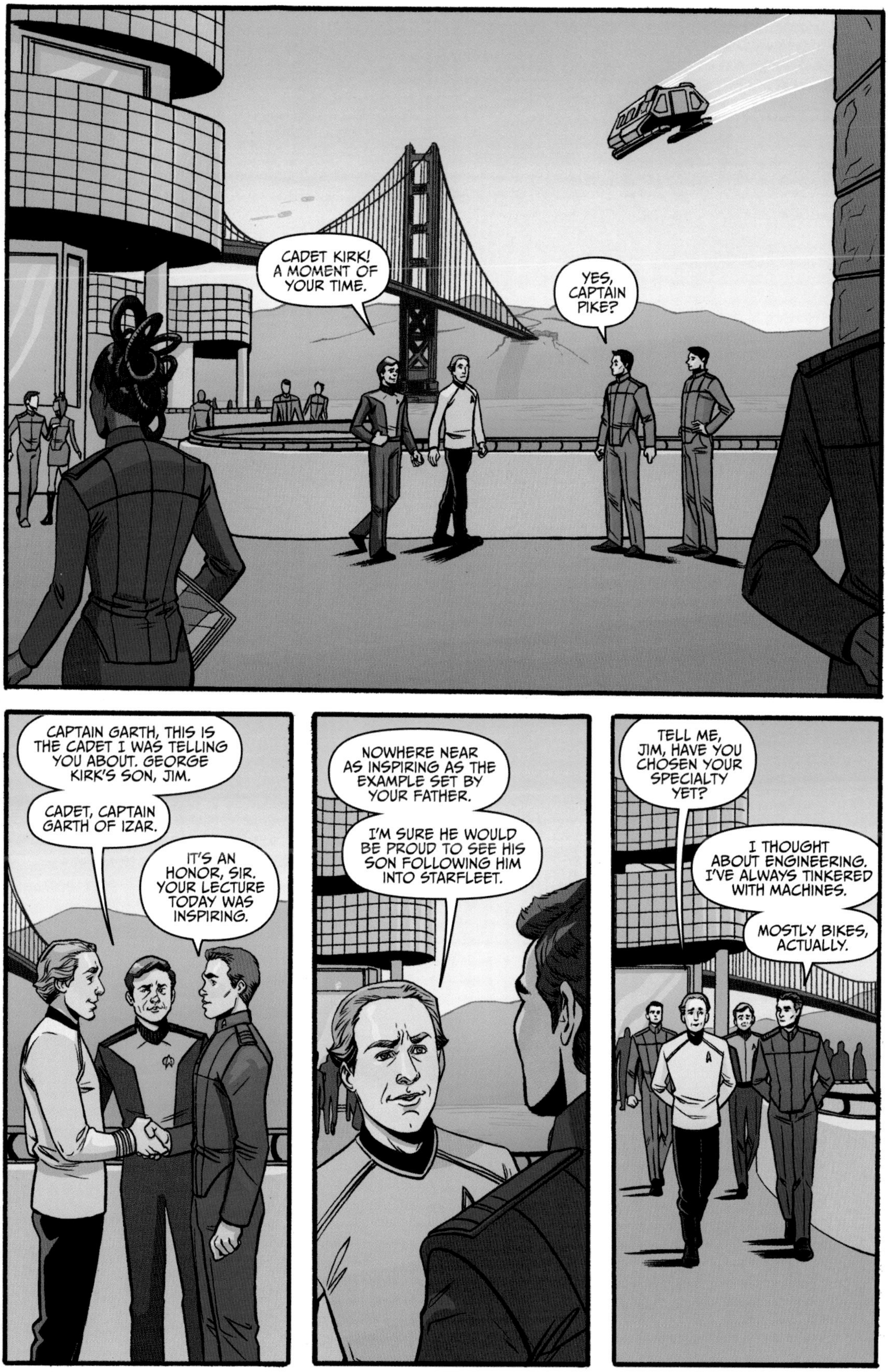
CADET KIRK! A MOMENT OF YOUR TIME.
YES, CAPTAIN PIKE?
CAPTAIN GARTH, THIS IS THE CADET I WAS TELLING YOU ABOUT. GEORGE KIRK'S SON, JIM.
CADET, CAPTAIN GARTH OF IZAR.
IT'S AN HONOR, SIR. YOUR LECTURE TODAY WAS INSPIRING.
NOWHERE NEAR AS INSPIRING AS THE EXAMPLE SET BY YOUR FATHER.
I'M SURE HE WOULD BE PROUD TO SEE HIS SON FOLLOWING HIM INTO STARFLEET.
TELL ME, JIM, HAVE YOU CHOSEN YOUR SPECIALTY YET?
I THOUGHT ABOUT ENGINEERING. I'VE ALWAYS TINKERED WITH MACHINES.
MOSTLY BIKES, ACTUALLY.

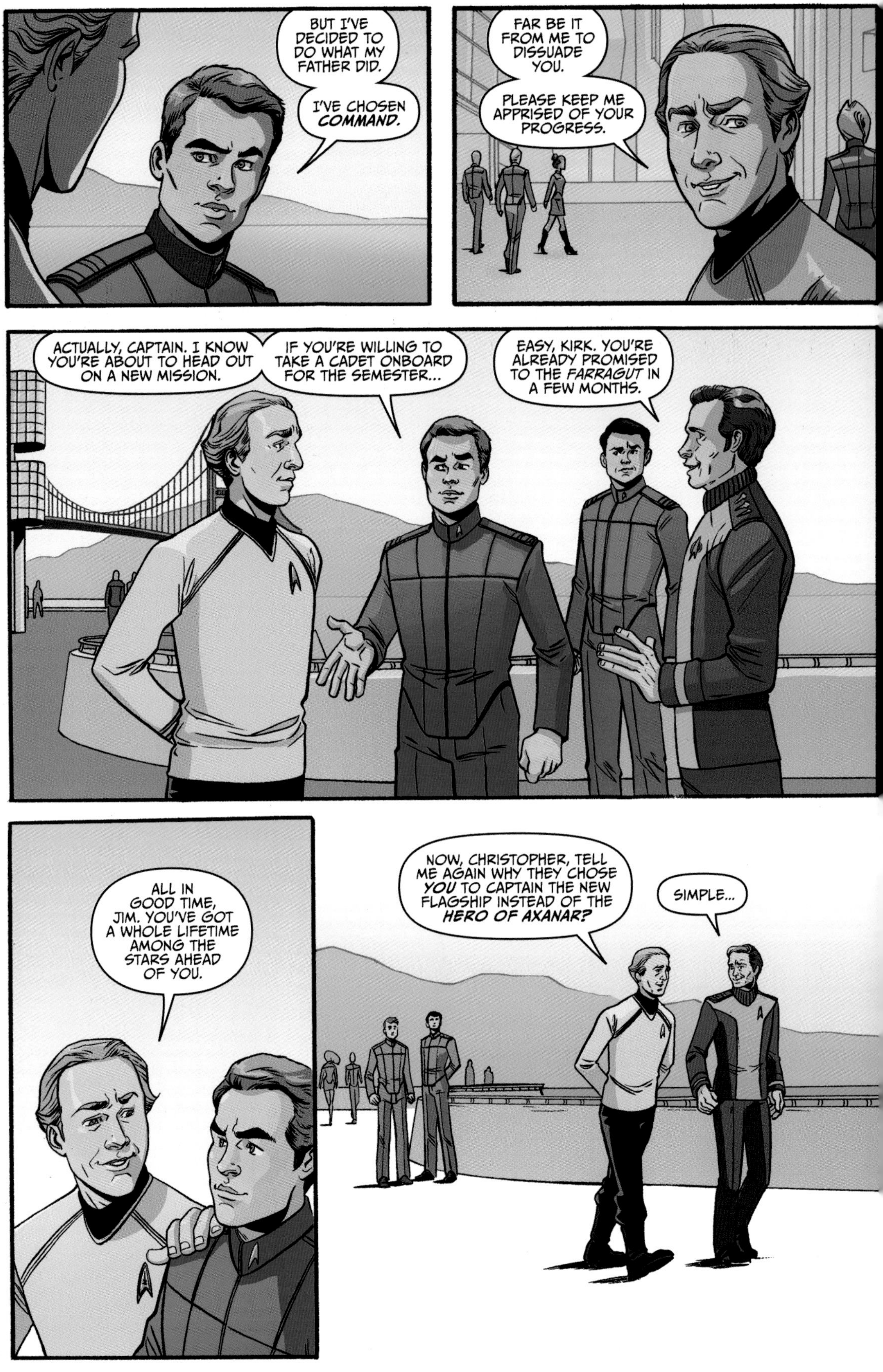
BUT I'VE DECIDED TO DO WHAT MY FATHER DID.
I'VE CHOSEN COMMAND.
FAR BE IT FROM ME TO DISSUADE YOU.
PLEASE KEEP ME APPRISED OF YOUR PROGRESS.
ACTUALLY, CAPTAIN. I KNOW YOU'RE ABOUT TO HEAD OUT ON A NEW MISSION.
IF YOU'RE WILLING TO TAKE A CADET ONBOARD FOR THE SEMESTER...
EASY, KIRK. YOU'RE ALREADY PROMISED TO THE FARRAGUT IN A FEW MONTHS.
ALL IN GOOD TIME, JIM. YOU'VE GOT A WHOLE LIFETIME AMONG THE STARS AHEAD OF YOU.
NOW, CHRISTOPHER, TELL ME AGAIN WHY THEY CHOSE YOU TO CAPTAIN THE NEW FLAGSHIP INSTEAD OF THE HERO OF AXANAR?
SIMPLE...

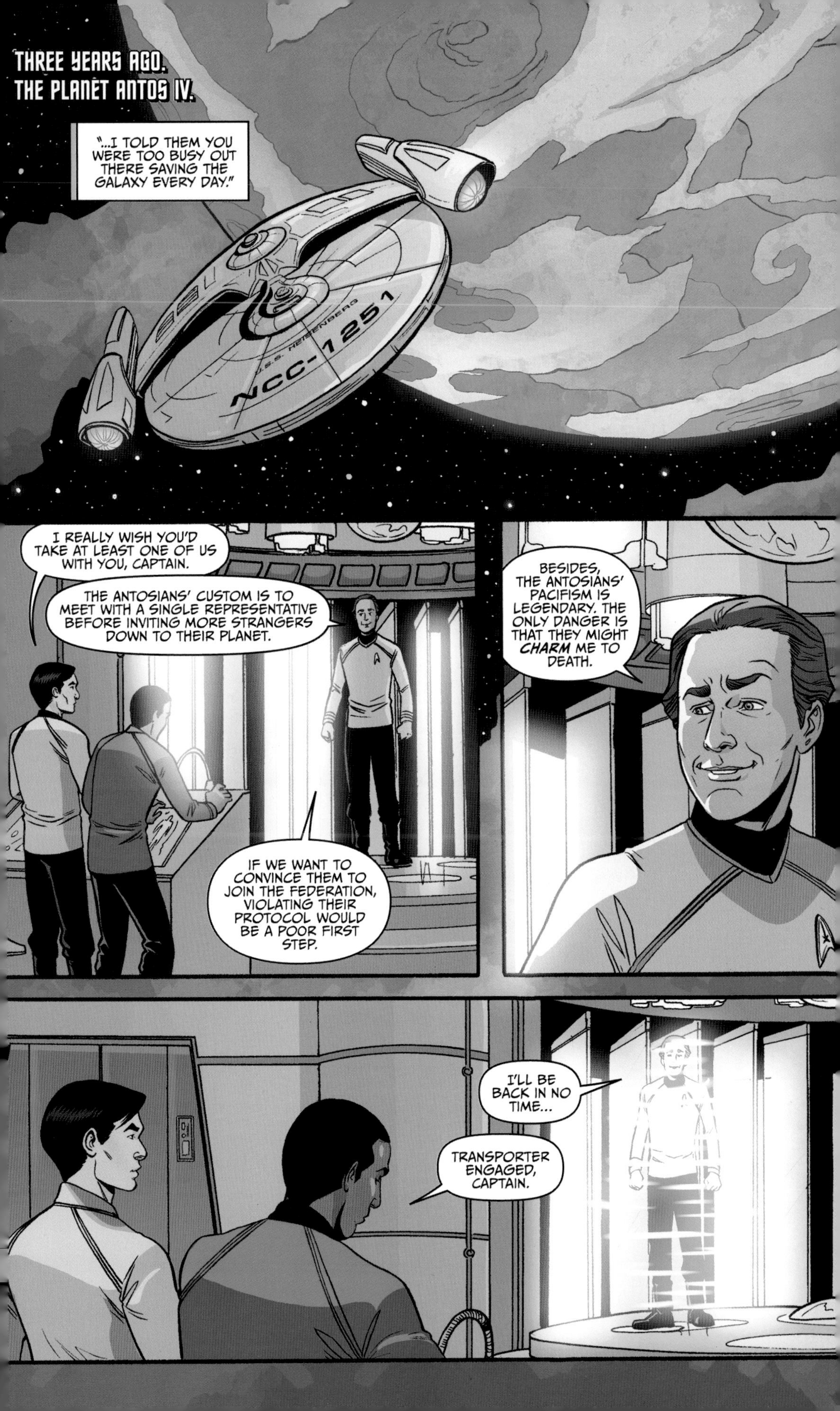
THREE YEARS AGO. THE PLANET ANTOS IV.
"...I TOLD THEM YOU WERE TOO BUSY OUT THERE SAVING THE GALAXY EVERY DAY."
U.S.S. HEISENBERG
NCC-1251
I REALLY WISH YOU'D TAKE AT LEAST ONE OF US WITH YOU, CAPTAIN.
THE ANTOSIANS' CUSTOM IS TO MEET WITH A SINGLE REPRESENTATIVE BEFORE INVITING MORE STRANGERS DOWN TO THEIR PLANET.
IF WE WANT TO CONVINCE THEM TO JOIN THE FEDERATION, VIOLATING THEIR PROTOCOL WOULD BE A POOR FIRST STEP.
BESIDES, THE ANTOSIANS' PACIFISM IS LEGENDARY. THE ONLY DANGER IS THAT THEY MIGHT *CHARM* ME TO DEATH.
I'LL BE BACK IN NO TIME...
TRANSPORTER ENGAGED, CAPTAIN.

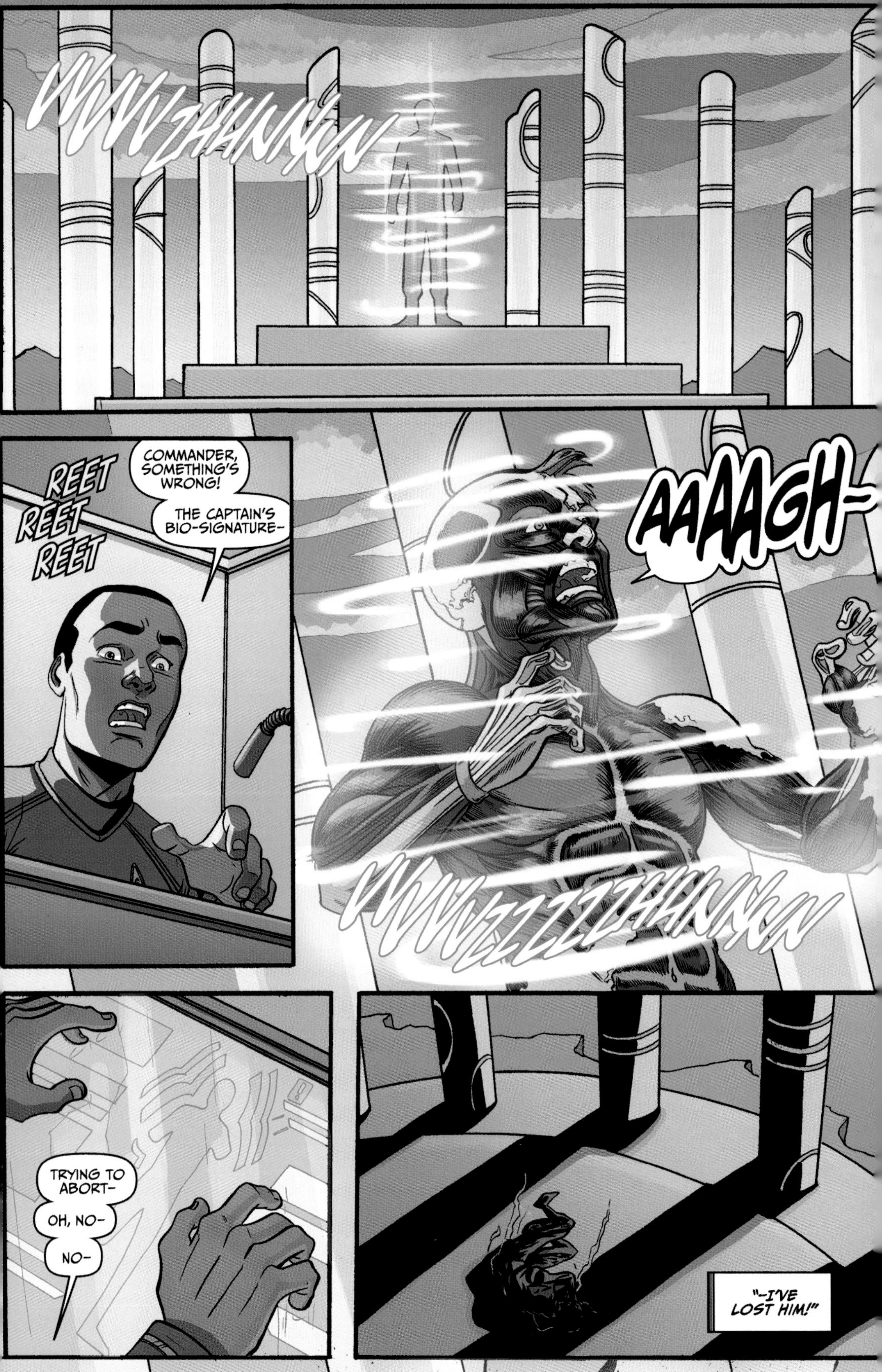
VVVVVZHHNNNN
REET REET REET
COMMANDER, SOMETHING'S WRONG!
THE CAPTAIN'S BIO-SIGNATURE-
AAAAGH-
VVVVZZZZZHHNNNN
TRYING TO ABORT-
OH, NO-
NO-
"-I'VE LOST HIM!"

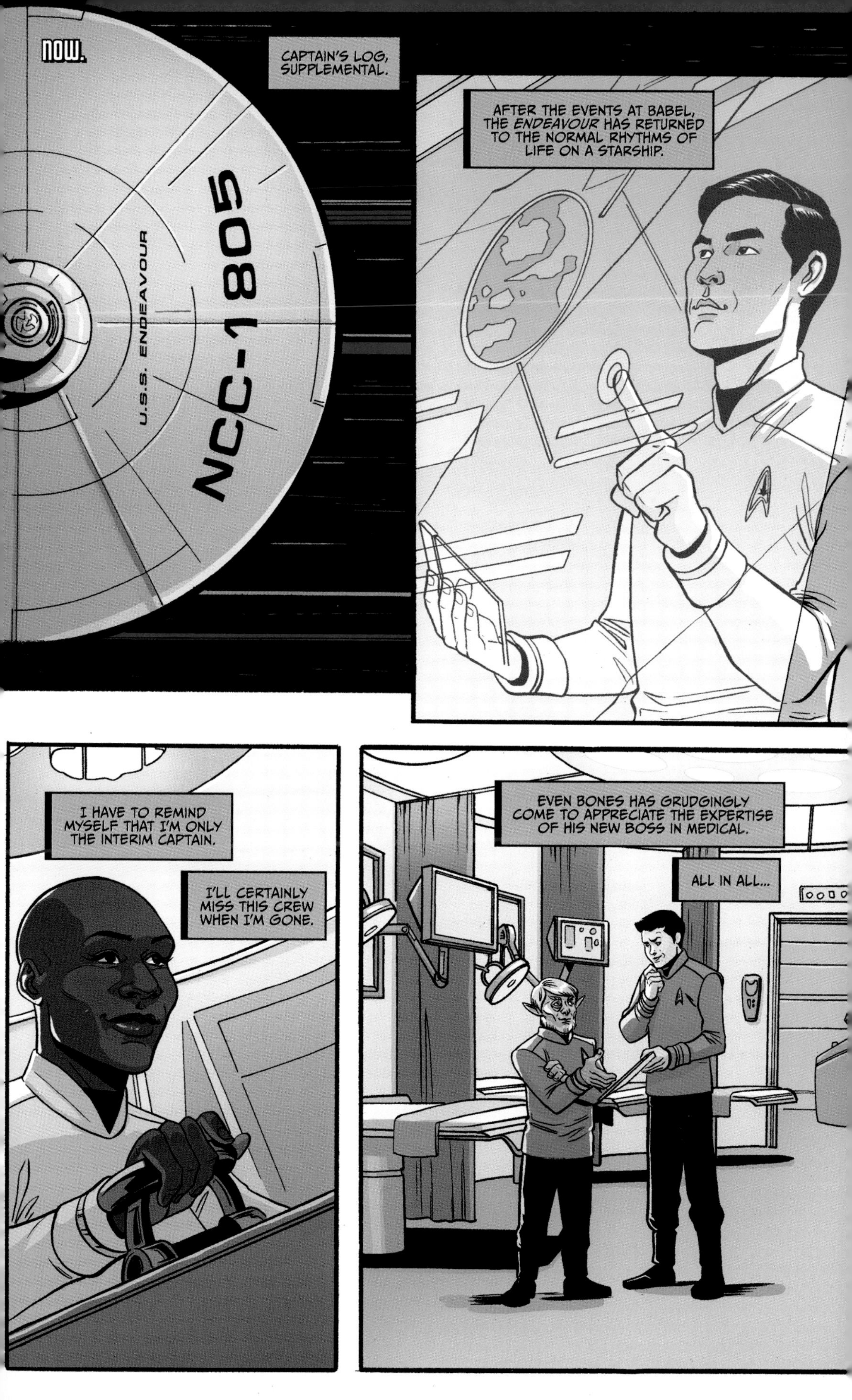
NOW.
CAPTAIN'S LOG, SUPPLEMENTAL.
U.S.S. ENDEAVOUR
NCC-1805
AFTER THE EVENTS AT BABEL, THE *ENDEAVOUR* HAS RETURNED TO THE NORMAL RHYTHMS OF LIFE ON A STARSHIP.
I HAVE TO REMIND MYSELF THAT I'M ONLY THE INTERIM CAPTAIN.
I'LL CERTAINLY MISS THIS CREW WHEN I'M GONE.
EVEN BONES HAS GRUDGINGLY COME TO APPRECIATE THE EXPERTISE OF HIS NEW BOSS IN MEDICAL.
ALL IN ALL...

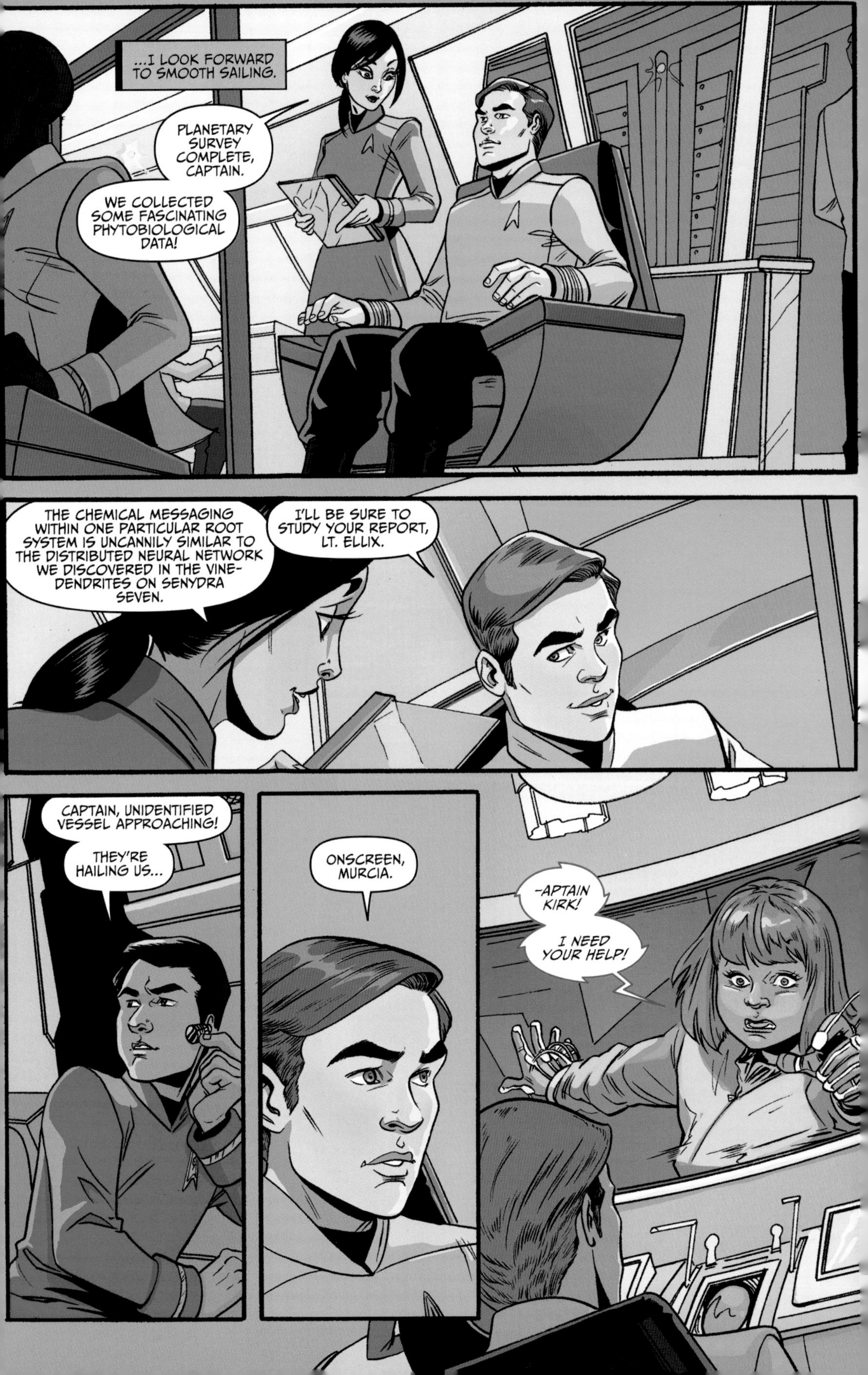
...I LOOK FORWARD TO SMOOTH SAILING.
PLANETARY SURVEY COMPLETE, CAPTAIN.
WE COLLECTED SOME FASCINATING PHYTOBIOLOGICAL DATA!
THE CHEMICAL MESSAGING WITHIN ONE PARTICULAR ROOT SYSTEM IS UNCANNILY SIMILAR TO THE DISTRIBUTED NEURAL NETWORK WE DISCOVERED IN THE VINE-DENDRITES ON SENYDRA SEVEN.
I'LL BE SURE TO STUDY YOUR REPORT, LT. ELLIX.
CAPTAIN, UNIDENTIFIED VESSEL APPROACHING!
THEY'RE HAILING US...
ONSCREEN, MURCIA.
-APTAIN KIRK!
I NEED YOUR HELP!

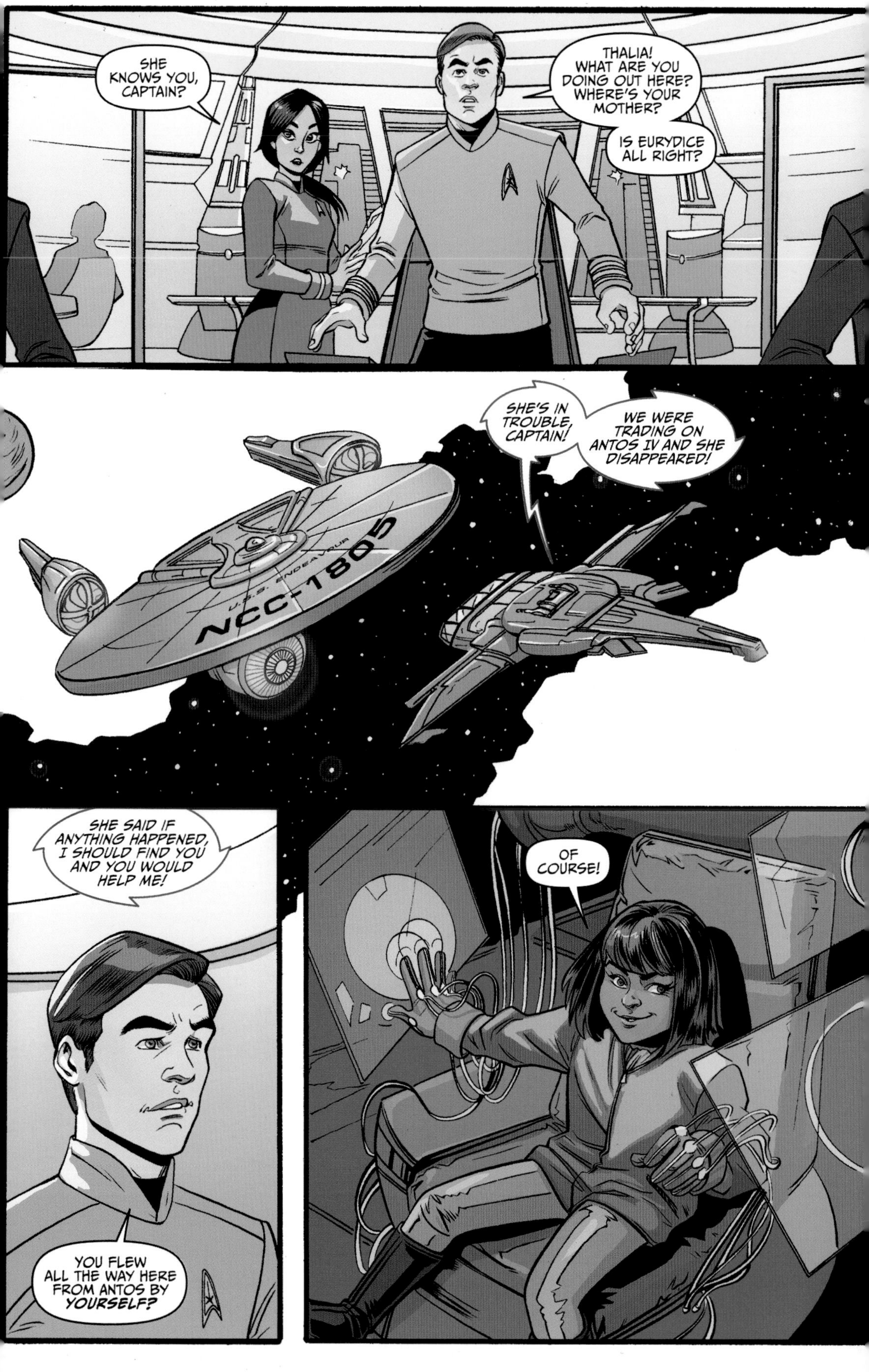
SHE KNOWS YOU, CAPTAIN?
THALIA! WHAT ARE YOU DOING OUT HERE? WHERE'S YOUR MOTHER?
IS EURYDICE ALL RIGHT?
SHE'S IN TROUBLE, CAPTAIN!
WE WERE TRADING ON ANTOS IV AND SHE DISAPPEARED!
U.S.S. ENDEAVOUR
NCC-1805
SHE SAID IF ANYTHING HAPPENED, I SHOULD FIND YOU AND YOU WOULD HELP ME!
YOU FLEW ALL THE WAY HERE FROM ANTOS BY *YOURSELF?*
OF COURSE!

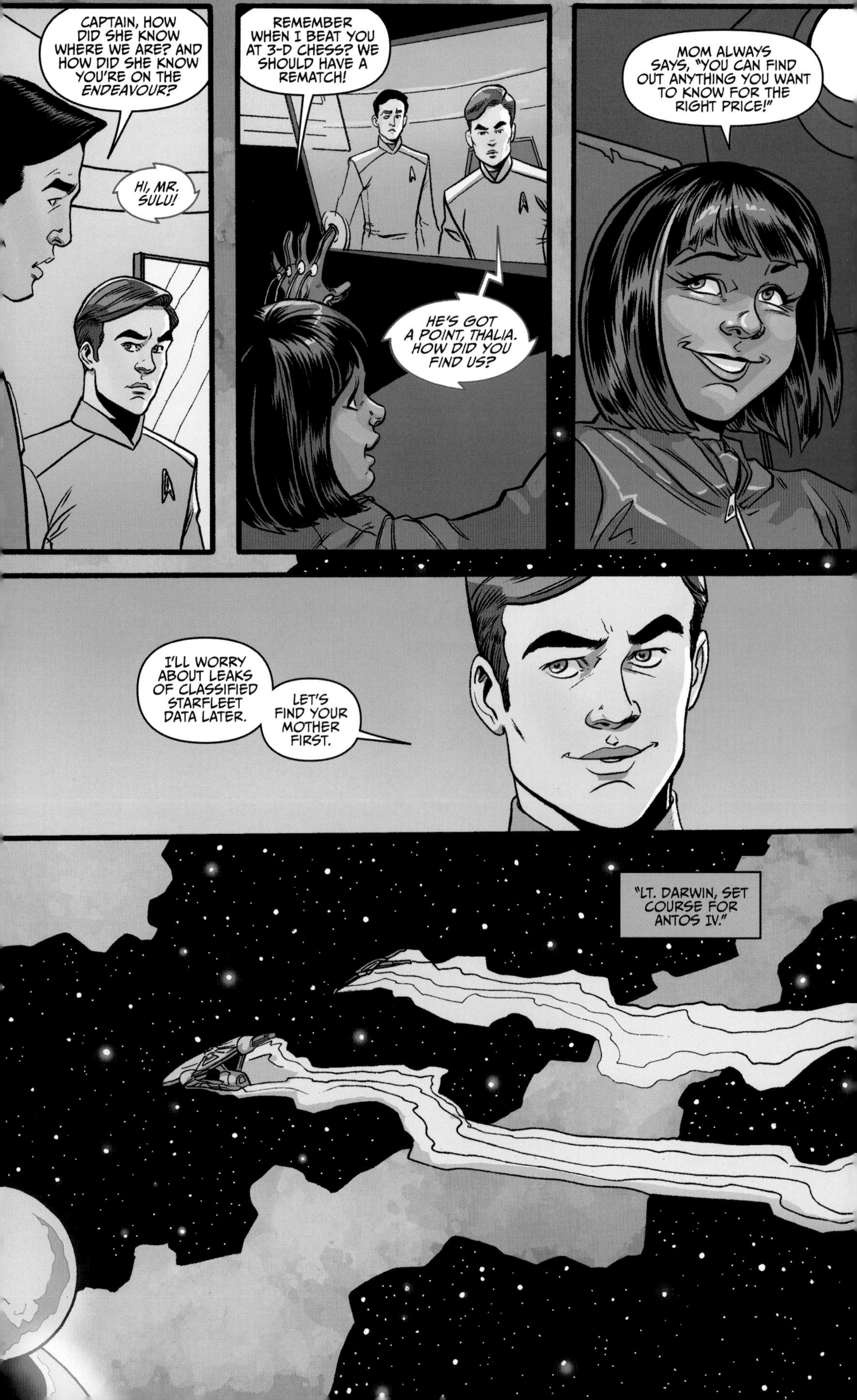

CAPTAIN, HOW DID SHE KNOW WHERE WE ARE? AND HOW DID SHE KNOW YOU'RE ON THE *ENDEAVOUR?*
HI, MR. SULU!
REMEMBER WHEN I BEAT YOU AT 3-D CHESS? WE SHOULD HAVE A REMATCH!
HE'S GOT A POINT, THALIA. HOW DID YOU FIND US?
MOM ALWAYS SAYS, "YOU CAN FIND OUT ANYTHING YOU WANT TO KNOW FOR THE RIGHT PRICE!"
I'LL WORRY ABOUT LEAKS OF CLASSIFIED STARFLEET DATA LATER.
LET'S FIND YOUR MOTHER FIRST.
"LT. DARWIN, SET COURSE FOR ANTOS IV."

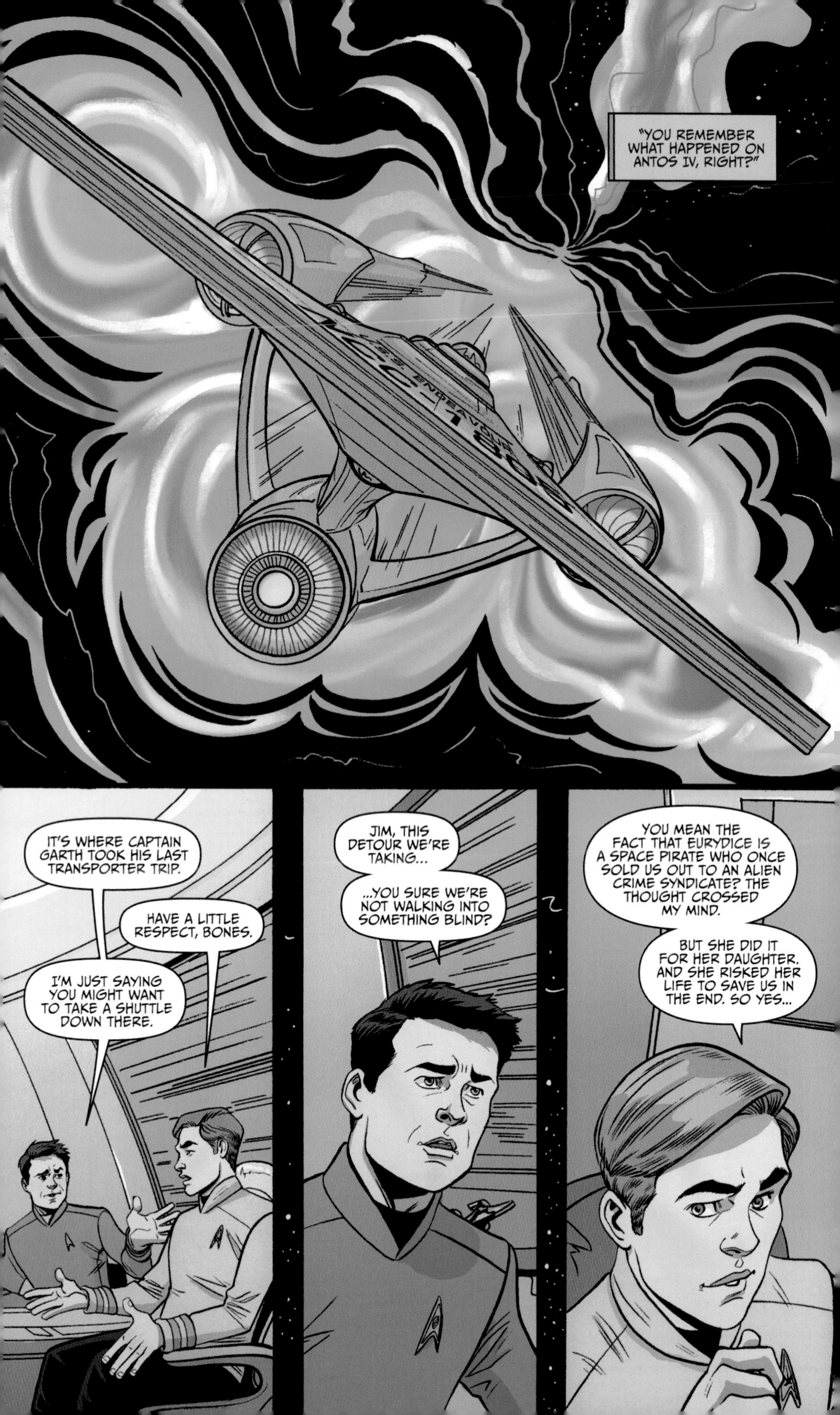
"YOU REMEMBER WHAT HAPPENED ON ANTOS IV, RIGHT?"
IT'S WHERE CAPTAIN GARTH TOOK HIS LAST TRANSPORTER TRIP.
HAVE A LITTLE RESPECT, BONES.
I'M JUST SAYING YOU MIGHT WANT TO TAKE A SHUTTLE DOWN THERE.
JIM, THIS DETOUR WE'RE TAKING...
...YOU SURE WE'RE NOT WALKING INTO SOMETHING BLIND?
YOU MEAN THE FACT THAT EURYDICE IS A SPACE PIRATE WHO ONCE SOLD US OUT TO AN ALIEN CRIME SYNDICATE? THE THOUGHT CROSSED MY MIND.
BUT SHE DID IT FOR HER DAUGHTER. AND SHE RISKED HER LIFE TO SAVE US IN THE END. SO YES...

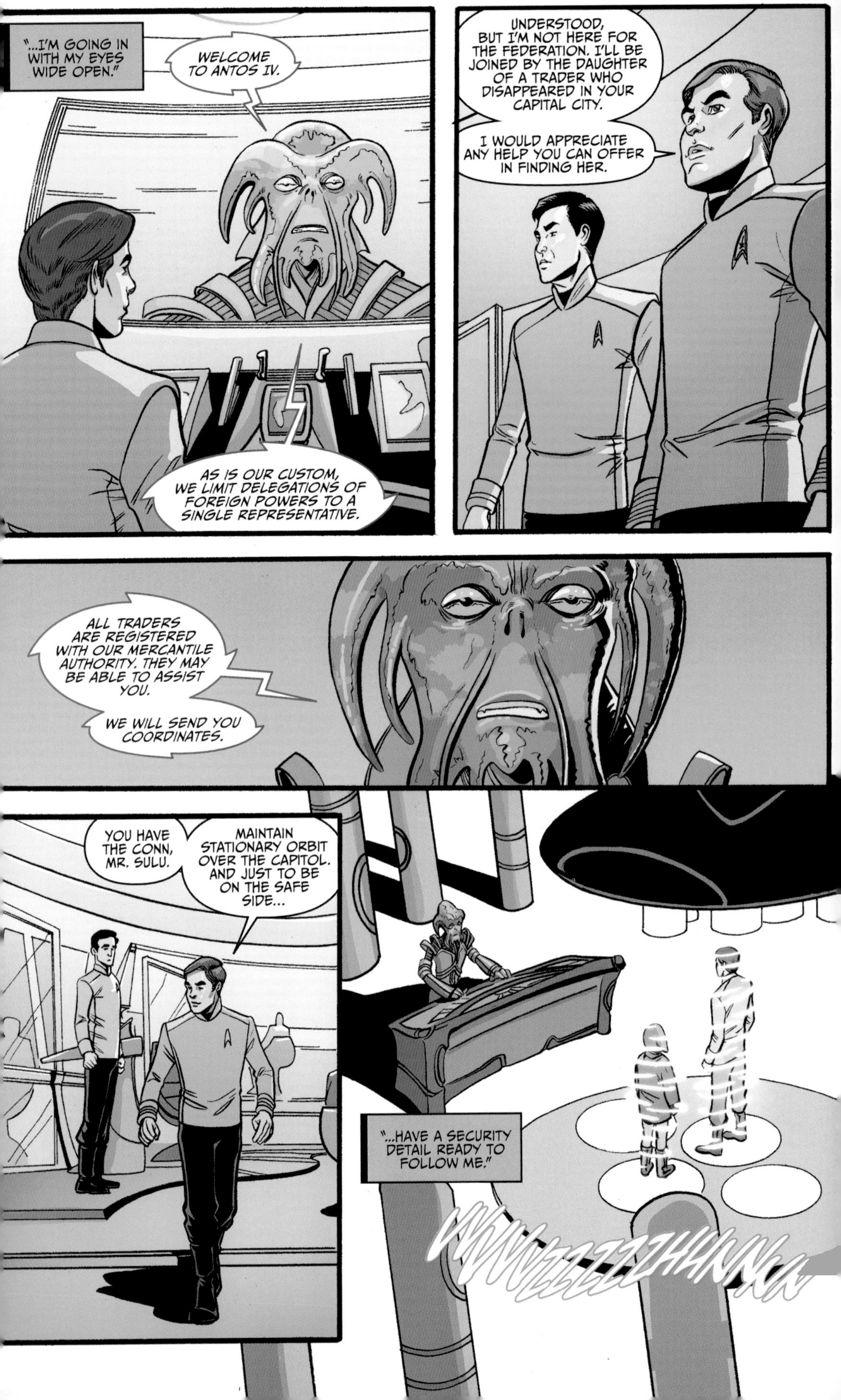
"...I'M GOING IN WITH MY EYES WIDE OPEN."
WELCOME TO ANTOS IV.
AS IS OUR CUSTOM, WE LIMIT DELEGATIONS OF FOREIGN POWERS TO A SINGLE REPRESENTATIVE.
UNDERSTOOD, BUT I'M NOT HERE FOR THE FEDERATION. I'LL BE JOINED BY THE DAUGHTER OF A TRADER WHO DISAPPEARED IN YOUR CAPITAL CITY.
I WOULD APPRECIATE ANY HELP YOU CAN OFFER IN FINDING HER.
ALL TRADERS ARE REGISTERED WITH OUR MERCANTILE AUTHORITY. THEY MAY BE ABLE TO ASSIST YOU.
WE WILL SEND YOU COORDINATES.
YOU HAVE THE CONN, MR. SULU.
MAINTAIN STATIONARY ORBIT OVER THE CAPITOL. AND JUST TO BE ON THE SAFE SIDE...
"...HAVE A SECURITY DETAIL READY TO FOLLOW ME."
VVVVVZZZZZHHNNNN

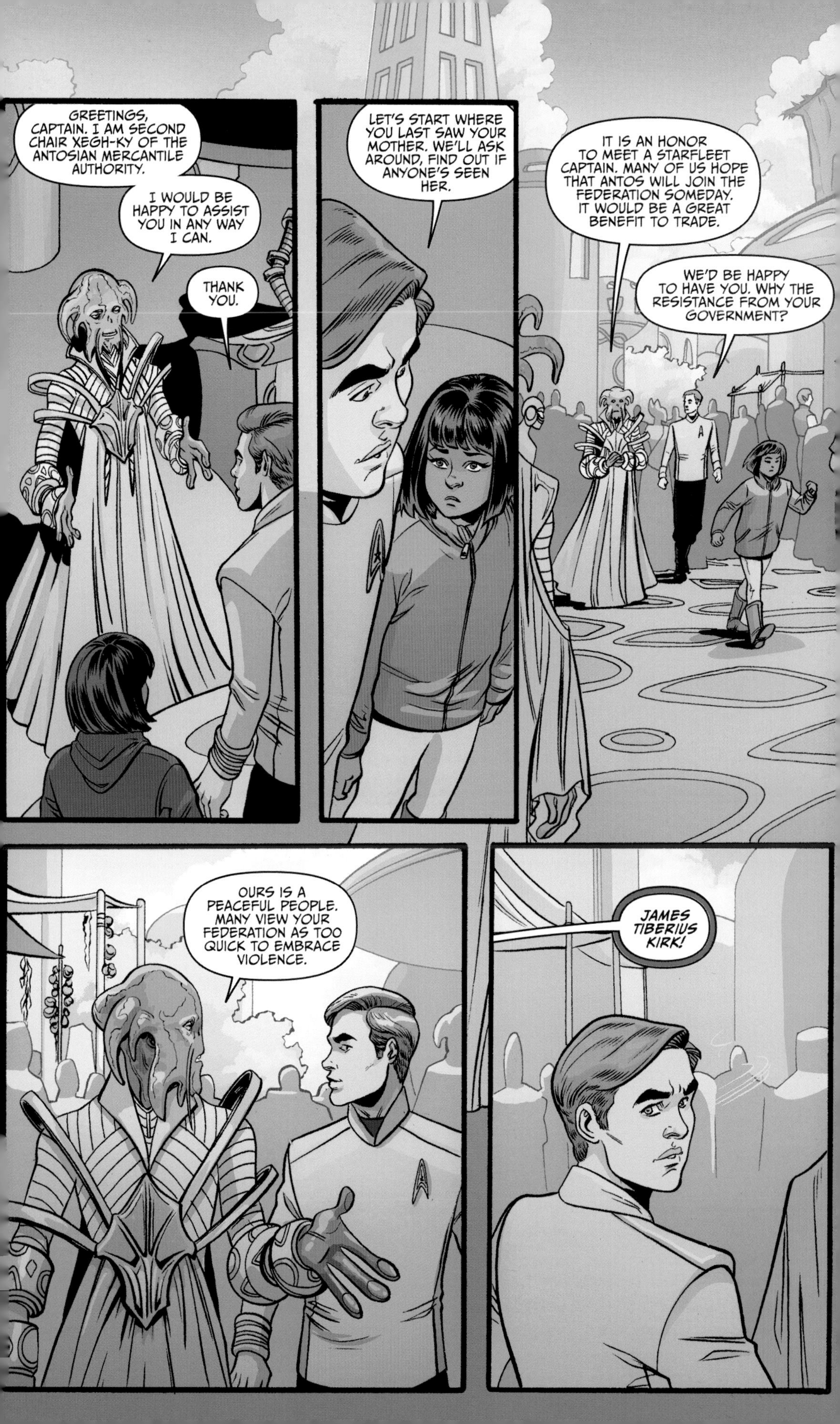
GREETINGS, CAPTAIN. I AM SECOND CHAIR XEGH-KY OF THE ANTOSIAN MERCANTILE AUTHORITY.
I WOULD BE HAPPY TO ASSIST YOU IN ANY WAY I CAN.
THANK YOU.
LET'S START WHERE YOU LAST SAW YOUR MOTHER. WE'LL ASK AROUND, FIND OUT IF ANYONE'S SEEN HER.
IT IS AN HONOR TO MEET A STARFLEET CAPTAIN. MANY OF US HOPE THAT ANTOS WILL JOIN THE FEDERATION SOMEDAY. IT WOULD BE A GREAT BENEFIT TO TRADE.
WE'D BE HAPPY TO HAVE YOU. WHY THE RESISTANCE FROM YOUR GOVERNMENT?
OURS IS A PEACEFUL PEOPLE. MANY VIEW YOUR FEDERATION AS TOO QUICK TO EMBRACE VIOLENCE.
JAMES TIBERIUS KIRK!

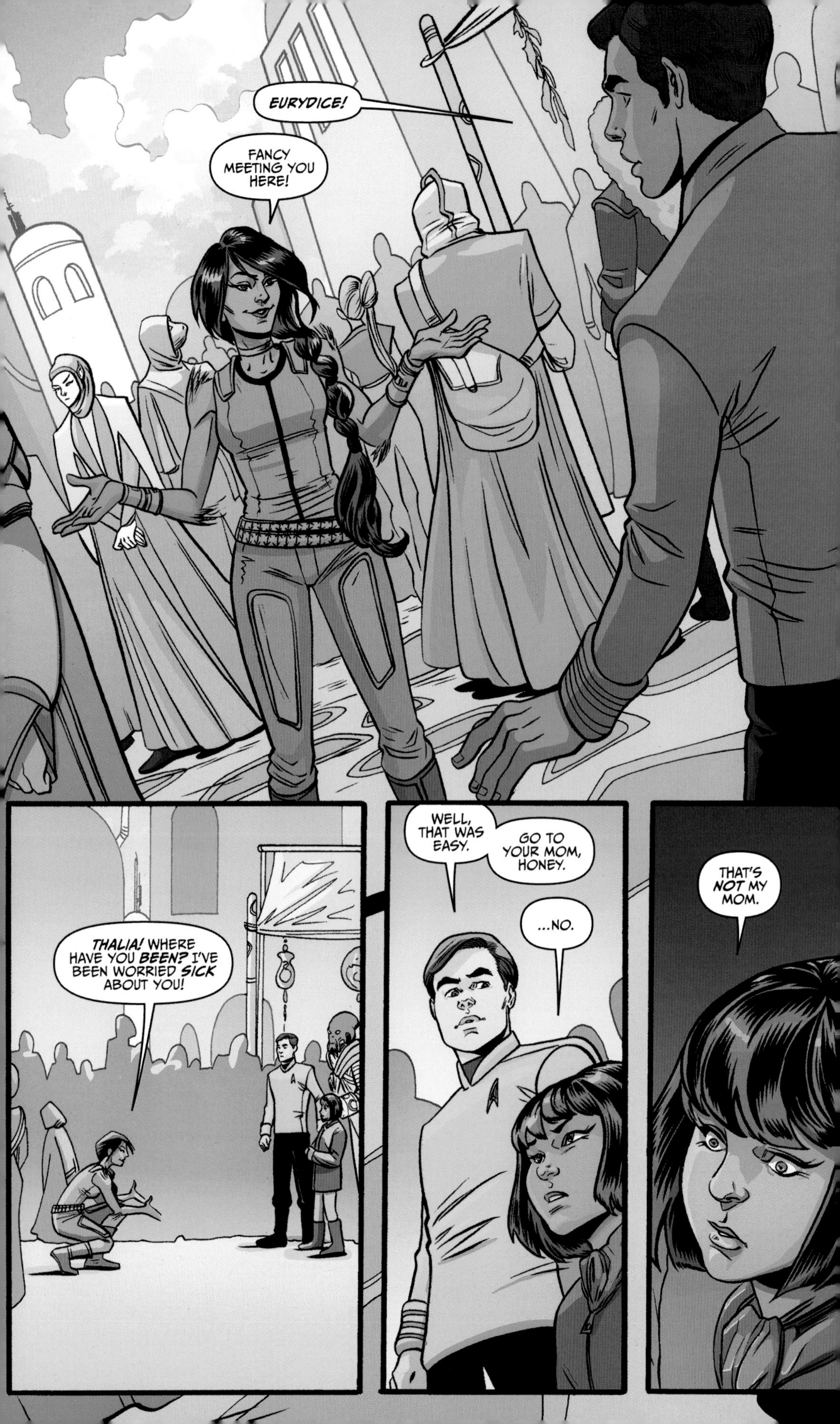
EURYDICE!
FANCY MEETING YOU HERE!
THALIA! WHERE HAVE YOU BEEN? I'VE BEEN WORRIED SICK ABOUT YOU!
WELL, THAT WAS EASY.
GO TO YOUR MOM, HONEY.
...NO.
THAT'S NOT MY MOM.

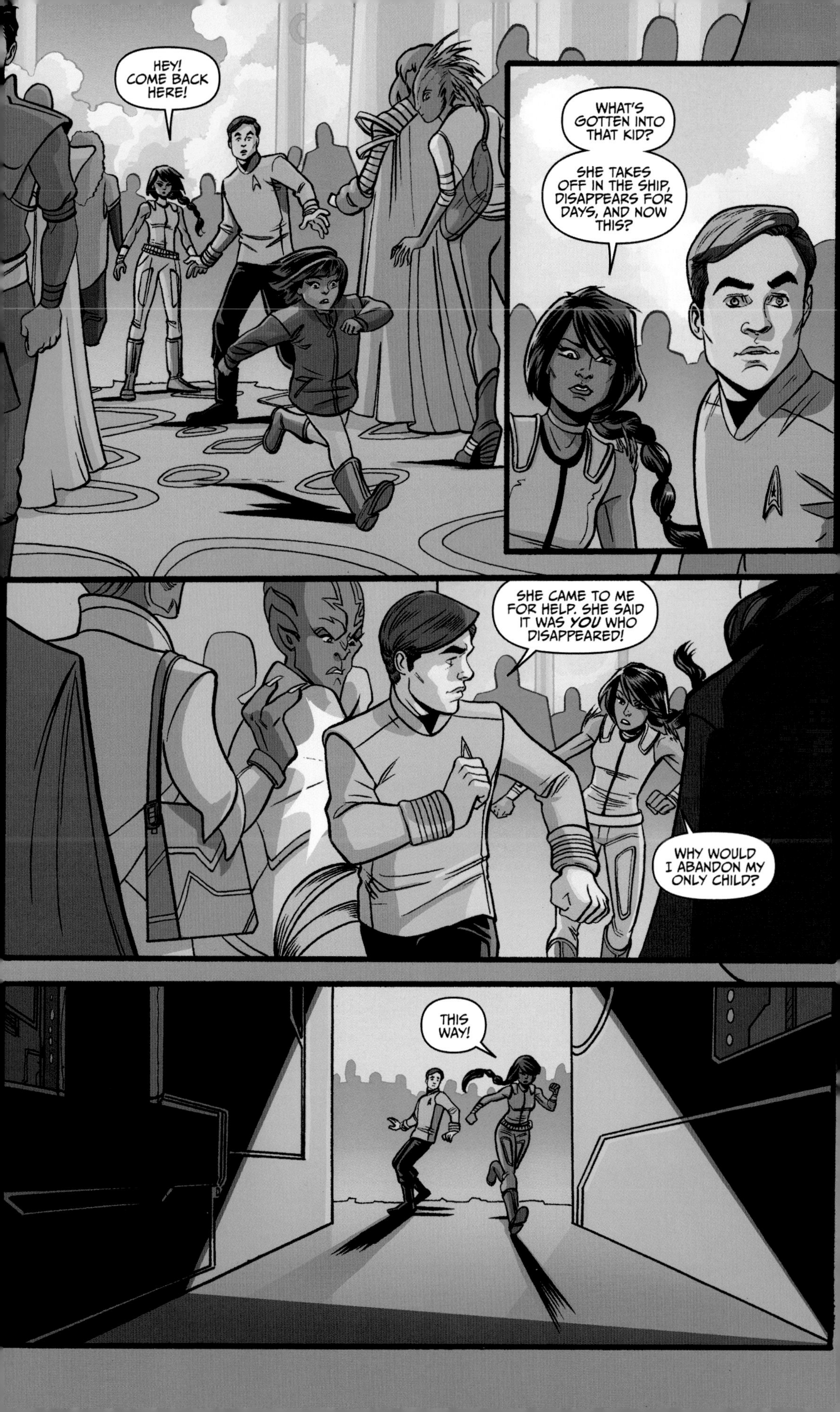

HEY! COME BACK HERE!
WHAT'S GOTTEN INTO THAT KID?
SHE TAKES OFF IN THE SHIP, DISAPPEARS FOR DAYS, AND NOW THIS?
SHE CAME TO ME FOR HELP. SHE SAID IT WAS *YOU* WHO DISAPPEARED!
WHY WOULD I ABANDON MY ONLY CHILD?
THIS WAY!

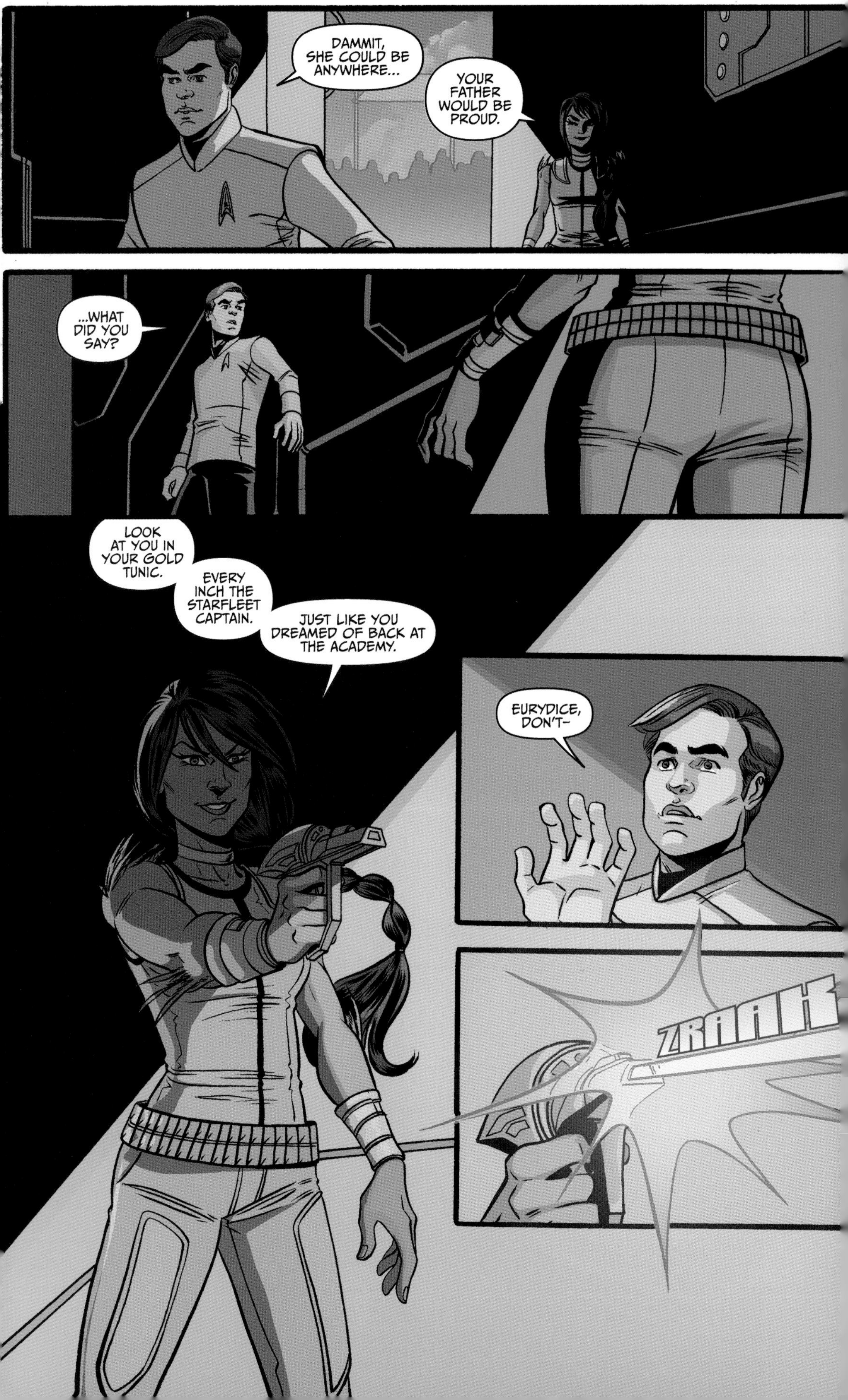
DAMMIT, SHE COULD BE ANYWHERE...
YOUR FATHER WOULD BE PROUD.
...WHAT DID YOU SAY?
LOOK AT YOU IN YOUR GOLD TUNIC.
EVERY INCH THE STARFLEET CAPTAIN.
JUST LIKE YOU DREAMED OF BACK AT THE ACADEMY.
EURYDICE, DON'T-
ZRAAK

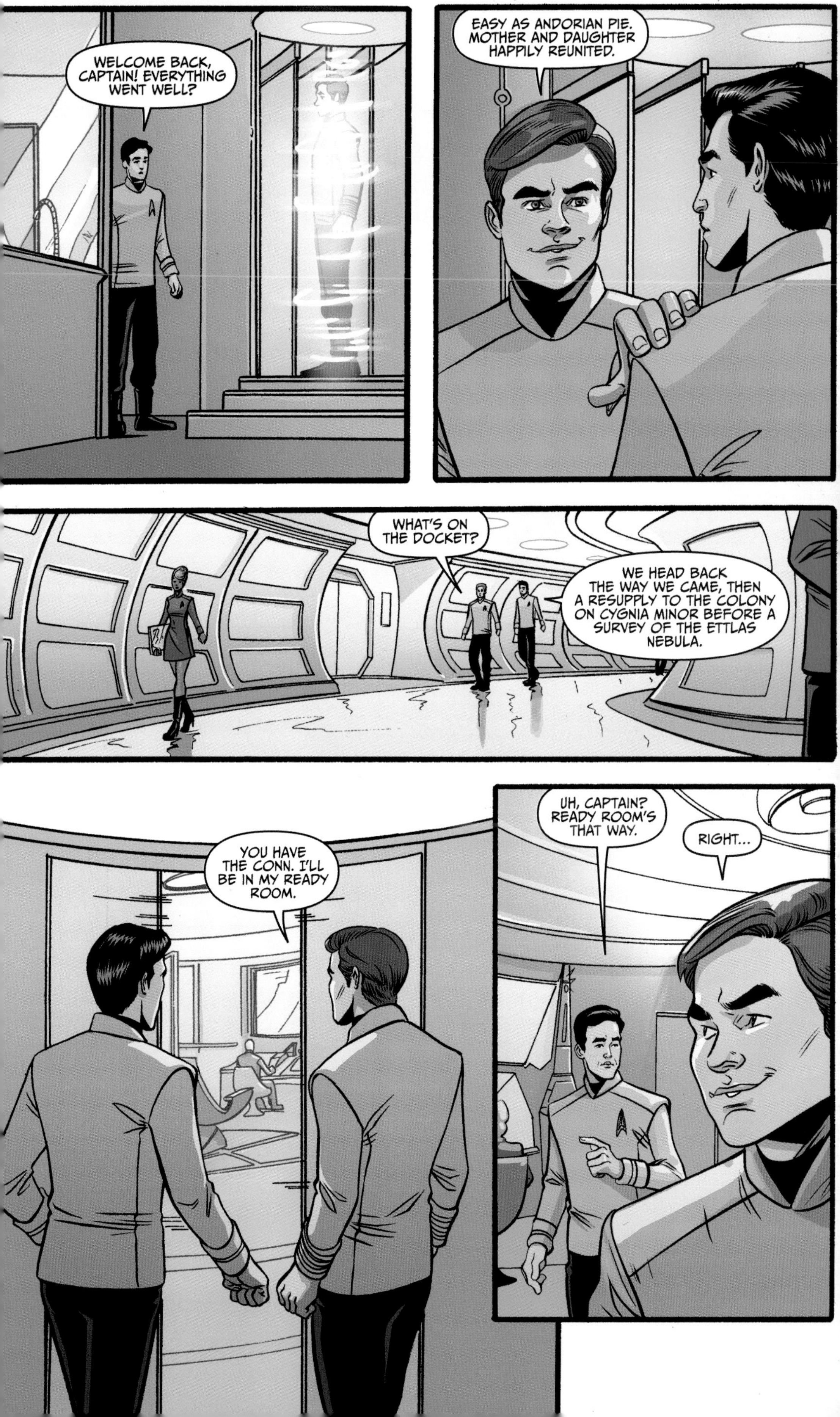
WELCOME BACK, CAPTAIN! EVERYTHING WENT WELL?
EASY AS ANDORIAN PIE. MOTHER AND DAUGHTER HAPPILY REUNITED.
WHAT'S ON THE DOCKET?
WE HEAD BACK THE WAY WE CAME, THEN A RESUPPLY TO THE COLONY ON CYGNIA MINOR BEFORE A SURVEY OF THE ETTLAS NEBULA.
YOU HAVE THE CONN. I'LL BE IN MY READY ROOM.
UH, CAPTAIN? READY ROOM'S THAT WAY.
RIGHT...

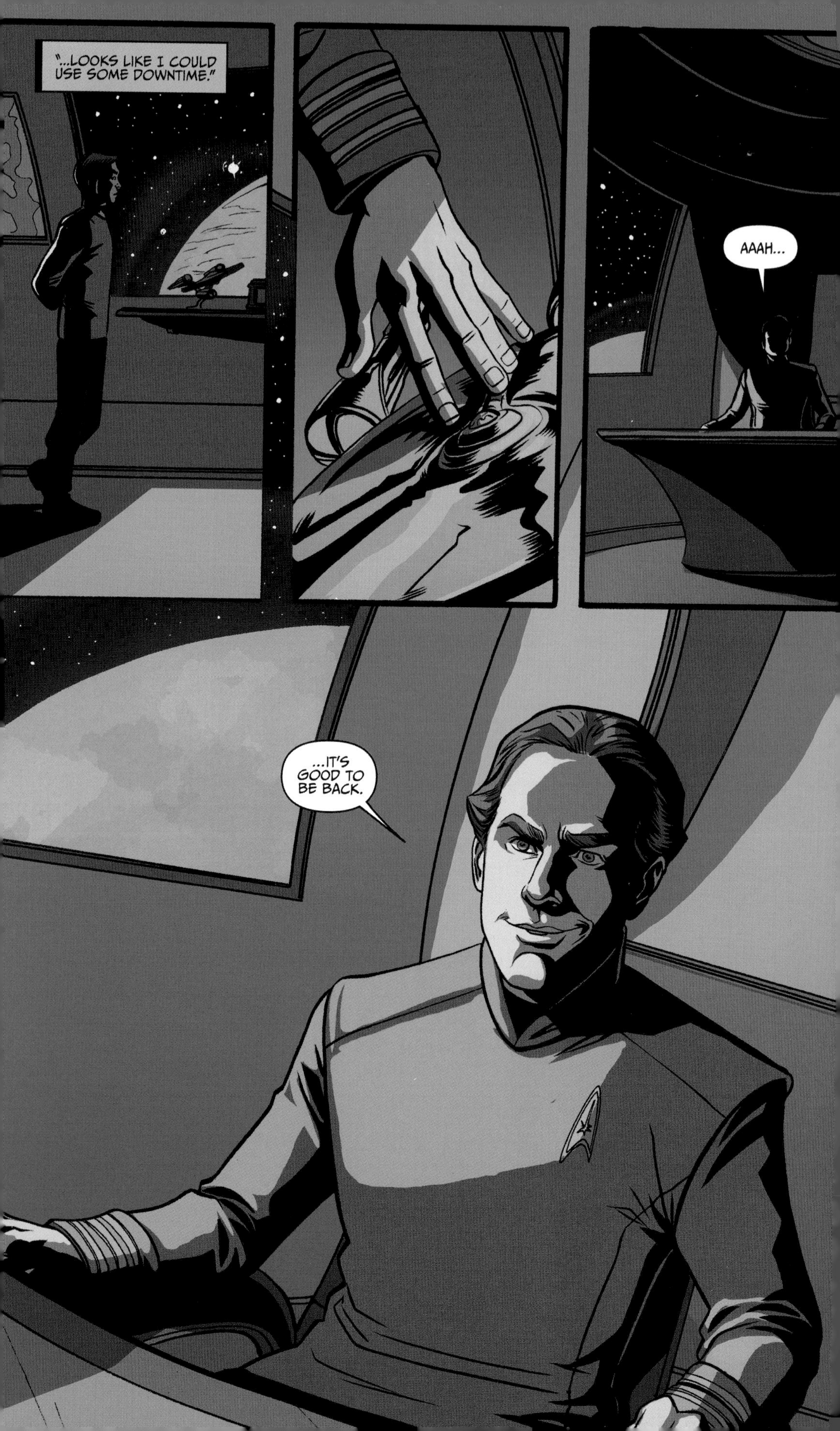
"...LOOKS LIKE I COULD USE SOME DOWNTIME."
AAAH...
...IT'S GOOD TO BE BACK.

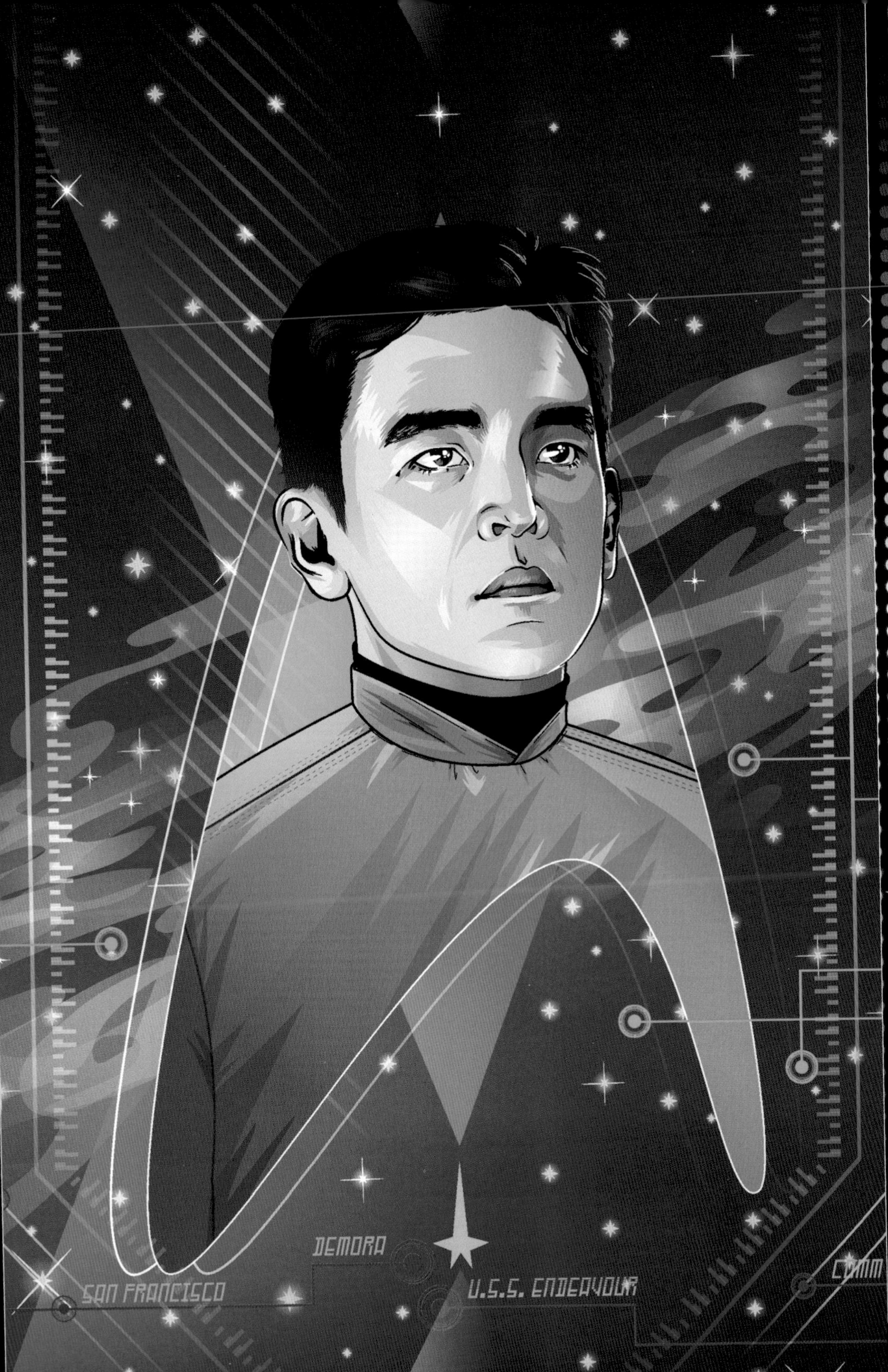
DEMORA
SAN FRANCISCO
U.S.S. ENDEAVOUR
COMM

art by

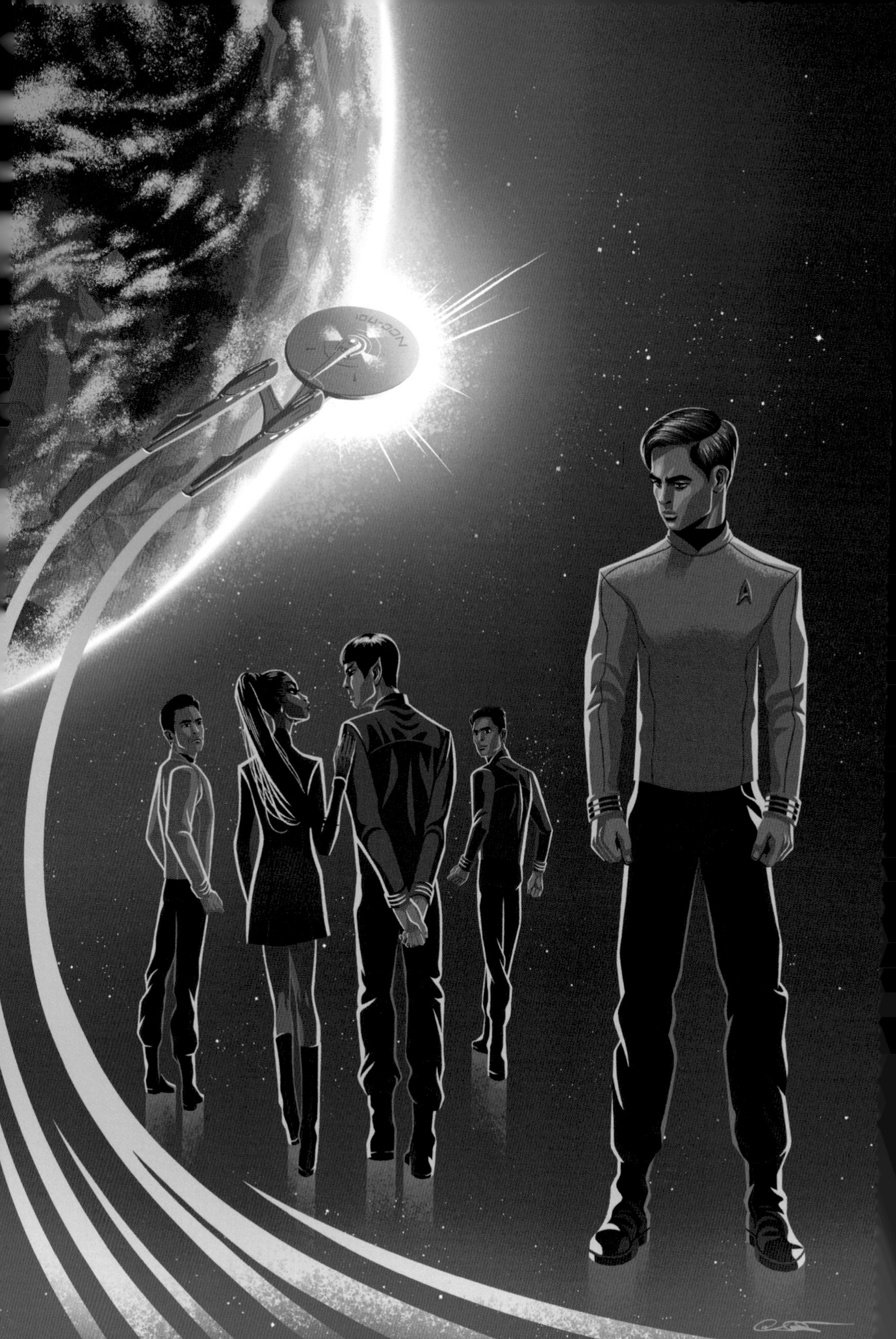

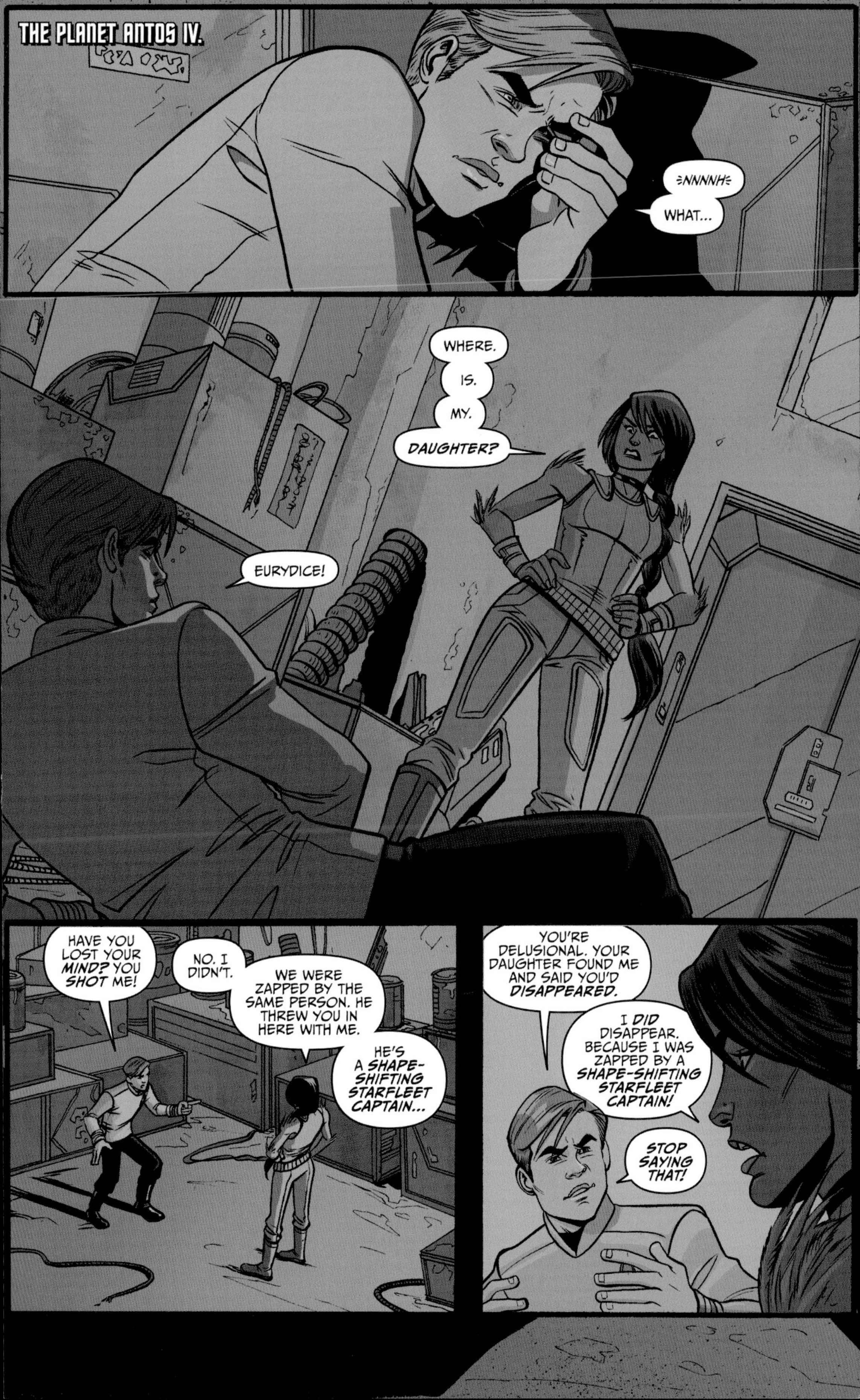
THE PLANET ANTOS IV.
NNNNH
WHAT...
WHERE.
IS.
MY.
DAUGHTER?
EURYDICE!
HAVE YOU LOST YOUR MIND? YOU SHOT ME!
NO. I DIDN'T.
WE WERE ZAPPED BY THE SAME PERSON. HE THREW YOU IN HERE WITH ME.
HE'S A SHAPE-SHIFTING STARFLEET CAPTAIN...
YOU'RE DELUSIONAL. YOUR DAUGHTER FOUND ME AND SAID YOU'D DISAPPEARED.
I DID DISAPPEAR. BECAUSE I WAS ZAPPED BY A SHAPE-SHIFTING STARFLEET CAPTAIN!
STOP SAYING THAT!

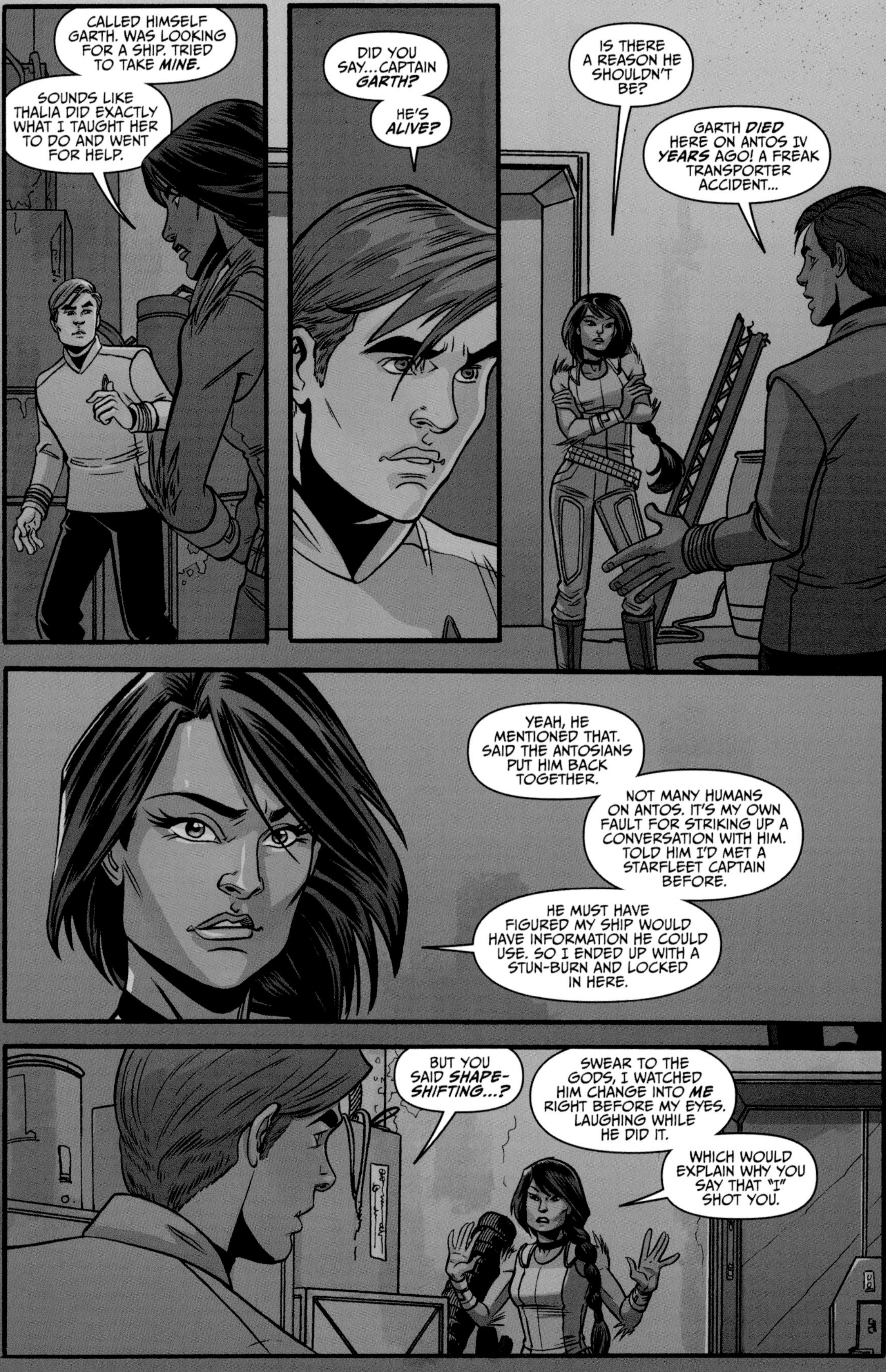
CALLED HIMSELF GARTH. WAS LOOKING FOR A SHIP. TRIED TO TAKE MINE.
SOUNDS LIKE THALIA DID EXACTLY WHAT I TAUGHT HER TO DO AND WENT FOR HELP.
DID YOU SAY...CAPTAIN GARTH?
HE'S ALIVE?
IS THERE A REASON HE SHOULDN'T BE?
GARTH DIED HERE ON ANTOS IV YEARS AGO! A FREAK TRANSPORTER ACCIDENT...
YEAH, HE MENTIONED THAT. SAID THE ANTOSIANS PUT HIM BACK TOGETHER.
NOT MANY HUMANS ON ANTOS. IT'S MY OWN FAULT FOR STRIKING UP A CONVERSATION WITH HIM. TOLD HIM I'D MET A STARFLEET CAPTAIN BEFORE.
HE MUST HAVE FIGURED MY SHIP WOULD HAVE INFORMATION HE COULD USE. SO I ENDED UP WITH A STUN-BURN AND LOCKED IN HERE.
BUT YOU SAID SHAPE-SHIFTING...?
SWEAR TO THE GODS, I WATCHED HIM CHANGE INTO ME RIGHT BEFORE MY EYES. LAUGHING WHILE HE DID IT.
WHICH WOULD EXPLAIN WHY YOU SAY THAT "I" SHOT YOU.

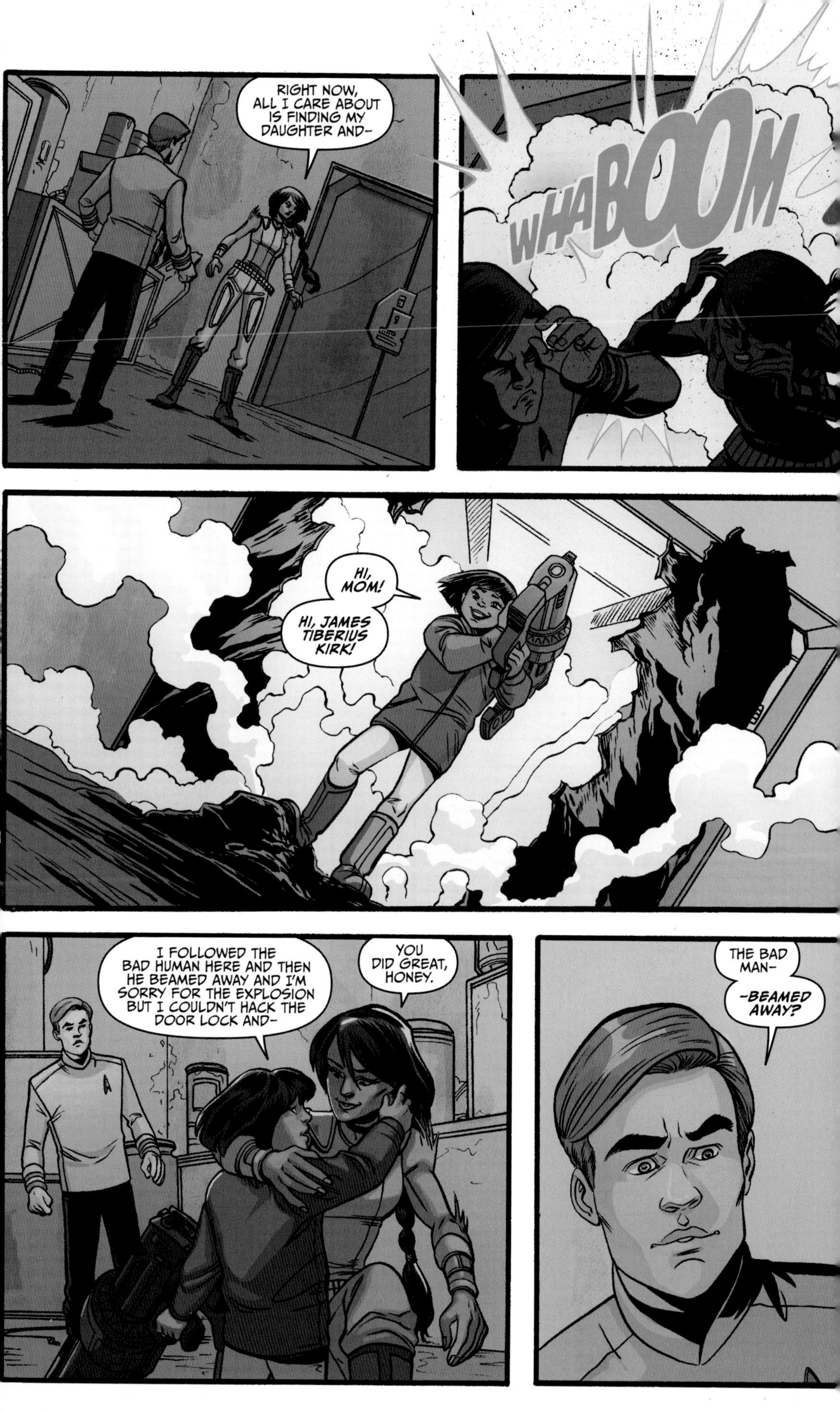
RIGHT NOW, ALL I CARE ABOUT IS FINDING MY DAUGHTER AND–
WHABOOM
HI, MOM!
HI, JAMES TIBERIUS KIRK!
I FOLLOWED THE BAD HUMAN HERE AND THEN HE BEAMED AWAY AND I'M SORRY FOR THE EXPLOSION BUT I COULDN'T HACK THE DOOR LOCK AND–
YOU DID GREAT, HONEY.
THE BAD MAN–
–BEAMED AWAY?

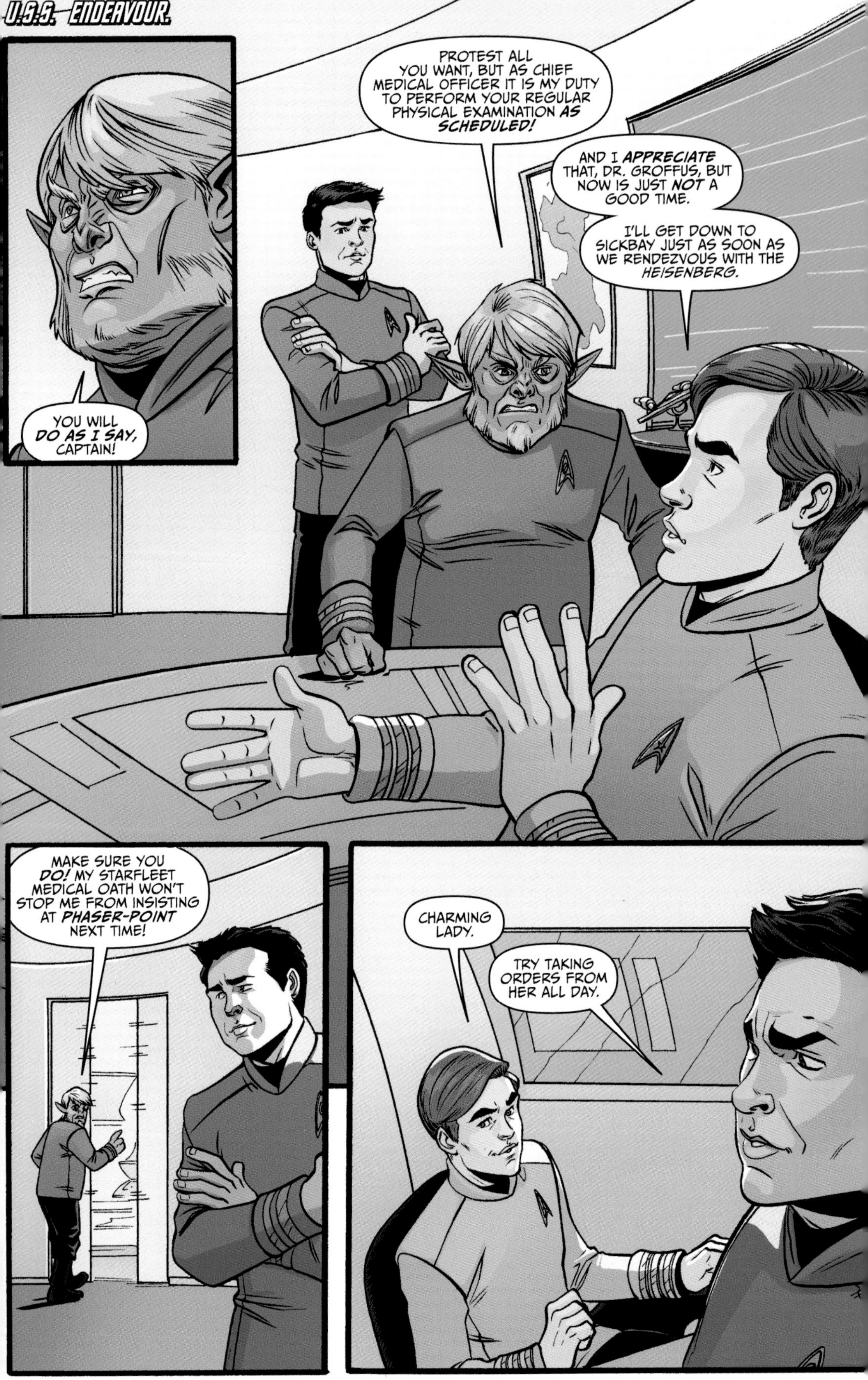
U.S.S. ENDEAVOUR.
YOU WILL DO AS I SAY, CAPTAIN!
PROTEST ALL YOU WANT, BUT AS CHIEF MEDICAL OFFICER IT IS MY DUTY TO PERFORM YOUR REGULAR PHYSICAL EXAMINATION AS SCHEDULED!
AND I APPRECIATE THAT, DR. GROFFUS, BUT NOW IS JUST NOT A GOOD TIME.
I'LL GET DOWN TO SICKBAY JUST AS SOON AS WE RENDEZVOUS WITH THE HEISENBERG.
MAKE SURE YOU DO! MY STARFLEET MEDICAL OATH WON'T STOP ME FROM INSISTING AT PHASER-POINT NEXT TIME!
CHARMING LADY.
TRY TAKING ORDERS FROM HER ALL DAY.

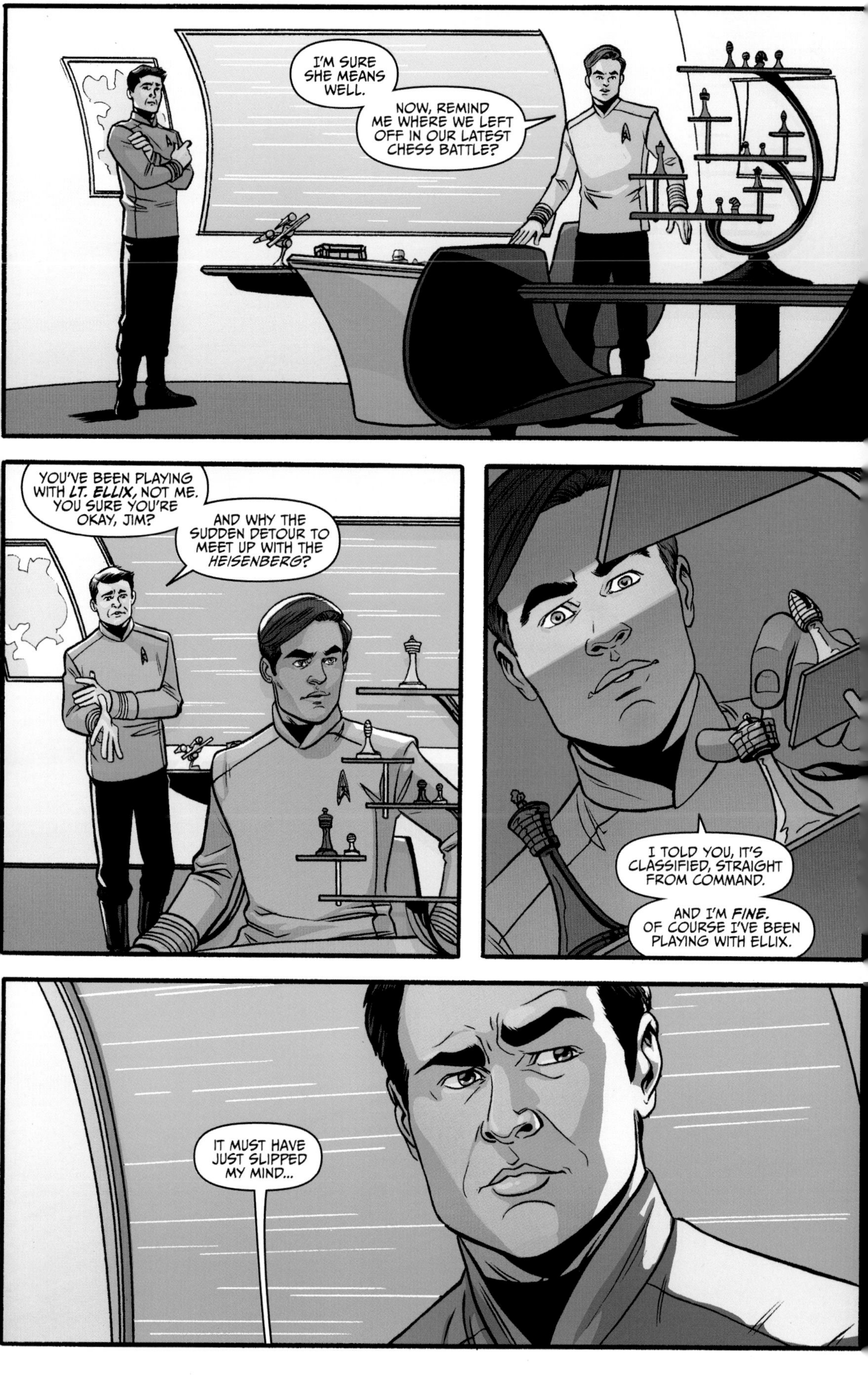
I'M SURE SHE MEANS WELL.
NOW, REMIND ME WHERE WE LEFT OFF IN OUR LATEST CHESS BATTLE?
YOU'VE BEEN PLAYING WITH *LT. ELLIX,* NOT ME. YOU SURE YOU'RE OKAY, JIM?
AND WHY THE SUDDEN DETOUR TO MEET UP WITH THE *HEISENBERG?*
I TOLD YOU, IT'S CLASSIFIED, STRAIGHT FROM COMMAND.
AND I'M ***FINE.*** OF COURSE I'VE BEEN PLAYING WITH ELLIX.
IT MUST HAVE JUST SLIPPED MY MIND...

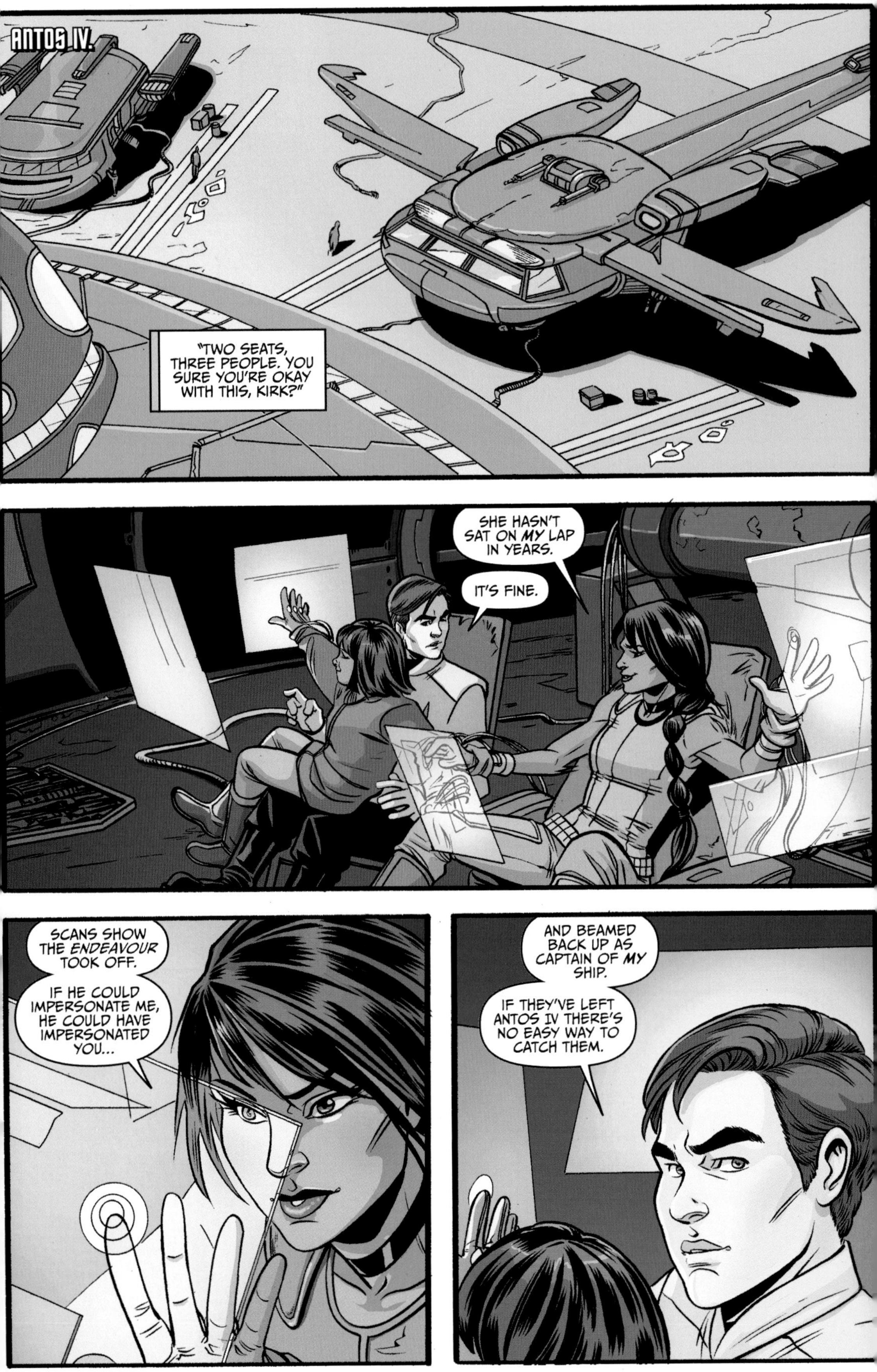
ANTOS IV.
"TWO SEATS, THREE PEOPLE. YOU SURE YOU'RE OKAY WITH THIS, KIRK?"
SHE HASN'T SAT ON *MY* LAP IN YEARS.
IT'S FINE.
SCANS SHOW THE *ENDEAVOUR* TOOK OFF.
IF HE COULD IMPERSONATE ME, HE COULD HAVE IMPERSONATED YOU...
AND BEAMED BACK UP AS CAPTAIN OF *MY* SHIP.
IF THEY'VE LEFT ANTOS IV THERE'S NO EASY WAY TO CATCH THEM.

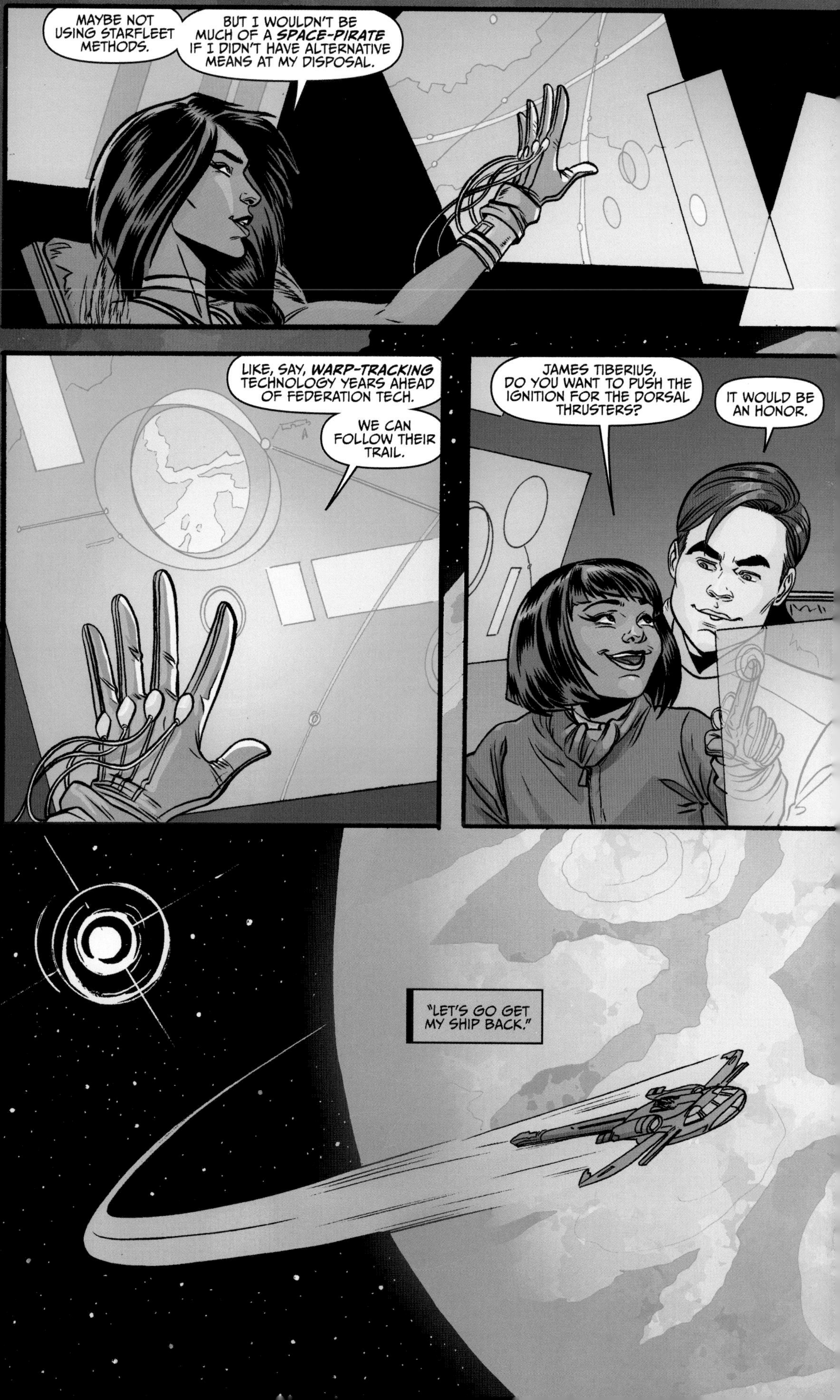
MAYBE NOT USING STARFLEET METHODS.
BUT I WOULDN'T BE MUCH OF A *SPACE-PIRATE* IF I DIDN'T HAVE ALTERNATIVE MEANS AT MY DISPOSAL.
LIKE, SAY, *WARP-TRACKING* TECHNOLOGY YEARS AHEAD OF FEDERATION TECH.
WE CAN FOLLOW THEIR TRAIL.
JAMES TIBERIUS, DO YOU WANT TO PUSH THE IGNITION FOR THE DORSAL THRUSTERS?
IT WOULD BE AN HONOR.
"LET'S GO GET MY SHIP BACK."

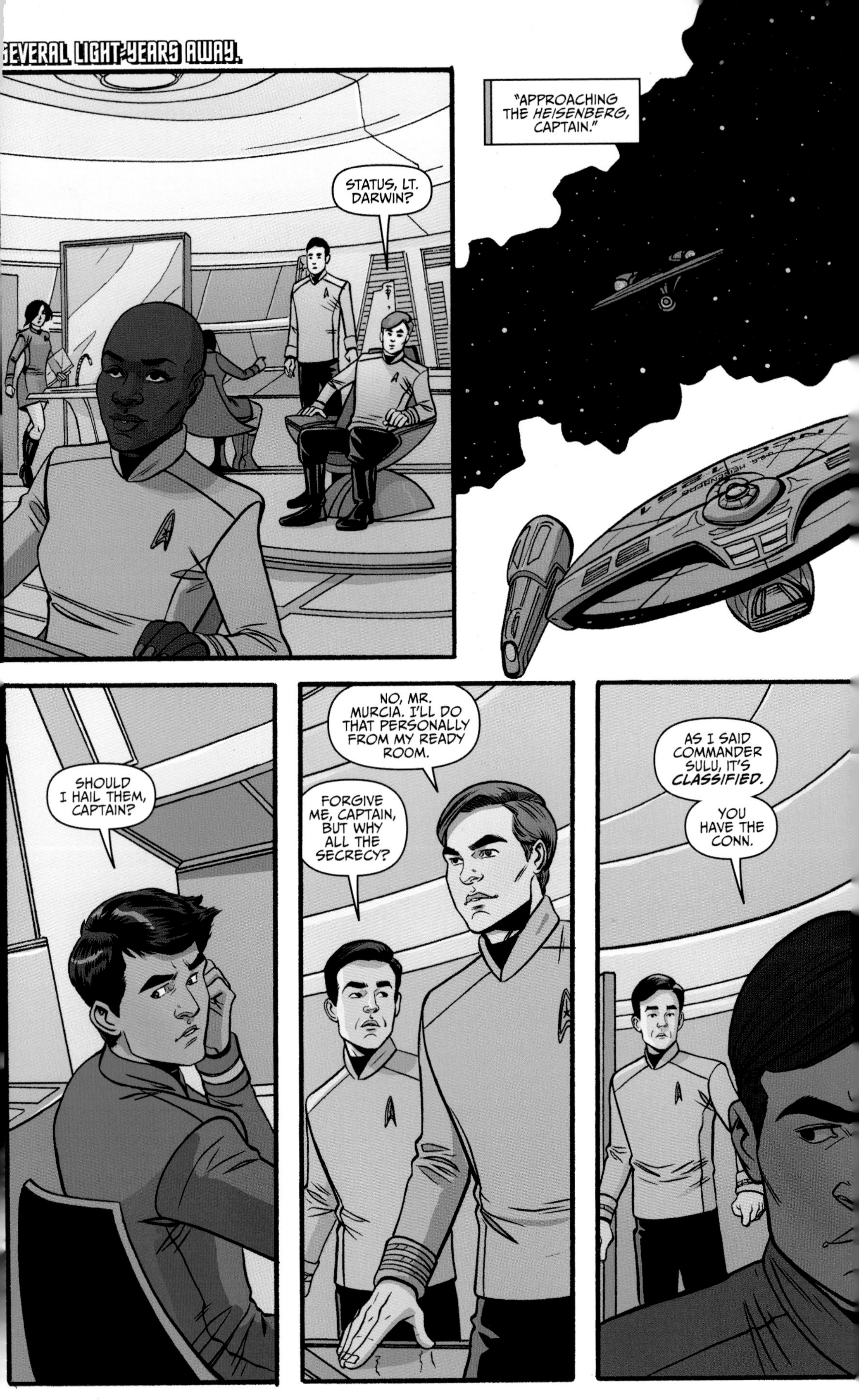
SEVERAL LIGHT-YEARS AWAY.
STATUS, LT. DARWIN?
"APPROACHING THE *HEISENBERG*, CAPTAIN."
SHOULD I HAIL THEM, CAPTAIN?
NO, MR. MURCIA. I'LL DO THAT PERSONALLY FROM MY READY ROOM.
FORGIVE ME, CAPTAIN, BUT WHY ALL THE SECRECY?
AS I SAID COMMANDER SULU, IT'S ***CLASSIFIED***.
YOU HAVE THE CONN.

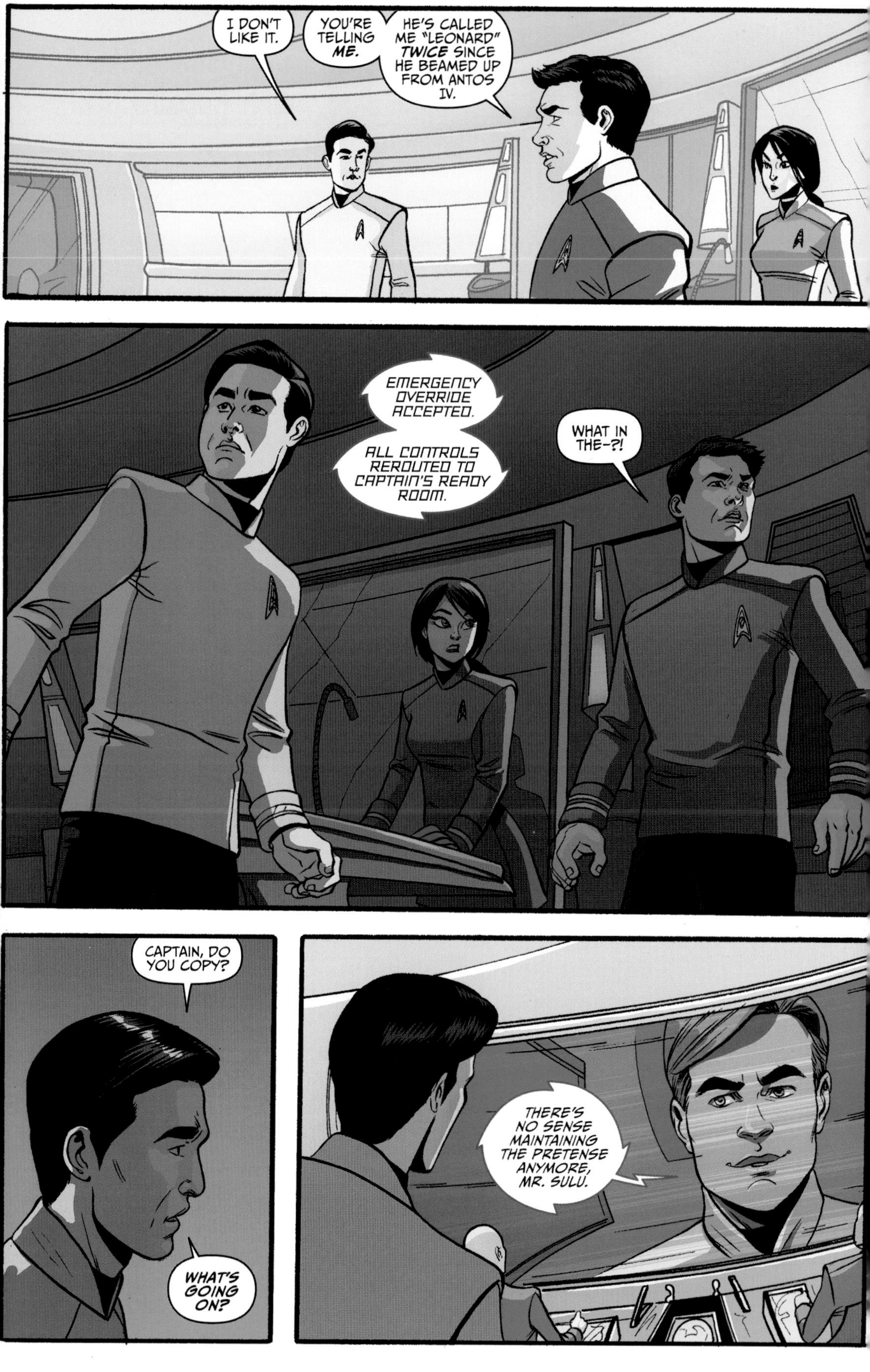
I DON'T LIKE IT.
YOU'RE TELLING ME.
HE'S CALLED ME "LEONARD" TWICE SINCE HE BEAMED UP FROM ANTOS IV.
EMERGENCY OVERRIDE ACCEPTED.
ALL CONTROLS REROUTED TO CAPTAIN'S READY ROOM.
WHAT IN THE-?!
CAPTAIN, DO YOU COPY?
WHAT'S GOING ON?
THERE'S NO SENSE MAINTAINING THE PRETENSE ANYMORE, MR. SULU.

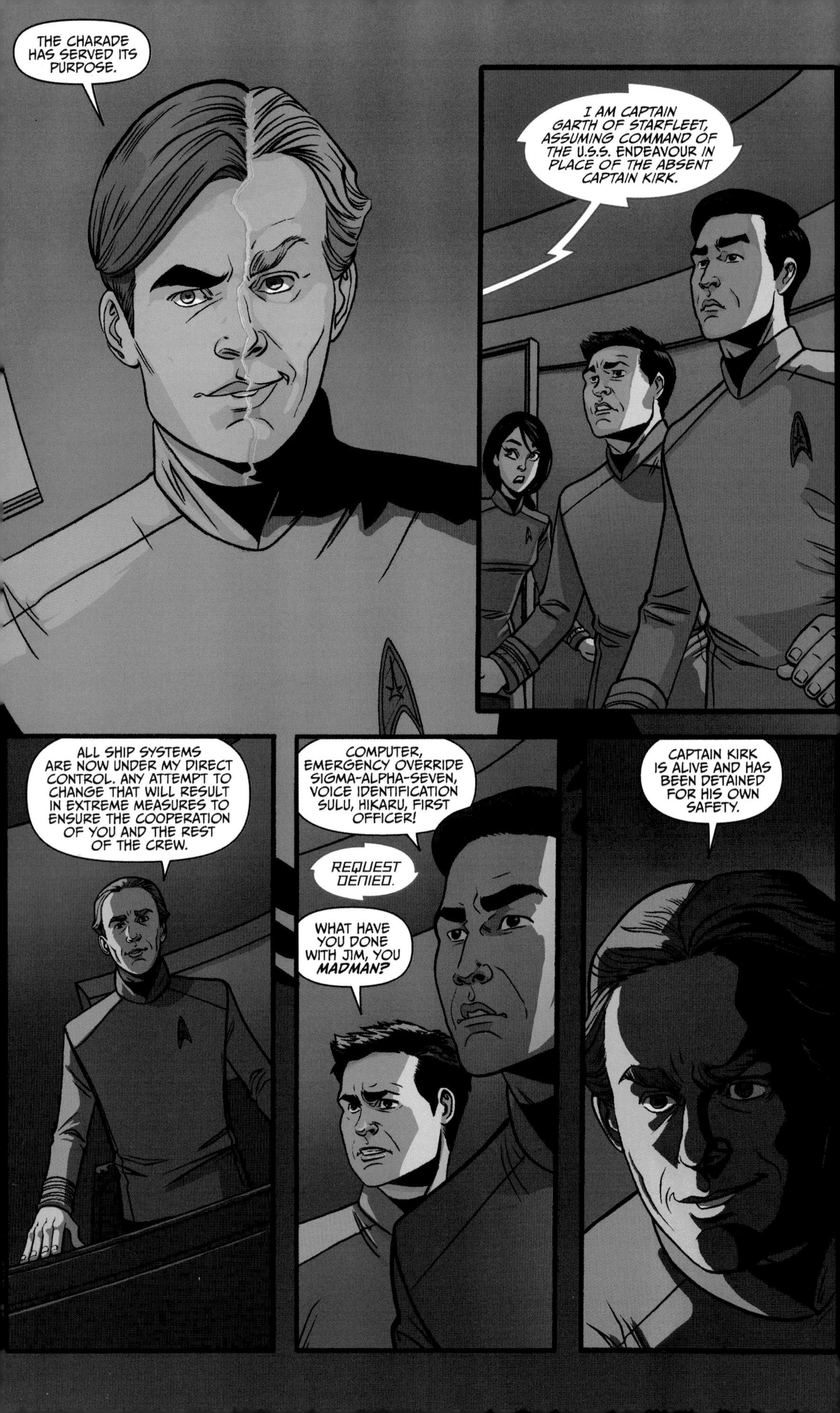
THE CHARADE HAS SERVED ITS PURPOSE.
I AM CAPTAIN GARTH OF STARFLEET, ASSUMING COMMAND OF THE U.S.S. ENDEAVOUR IN PLACE OF THE ABSENT CAPTAIN KIRK.
ALL SHIP SYSTEMS ARE NOW UNDER MY DIRECT CONTROL. ANY ATTEMPT TO CHANGE THAT WILL RESULT IN EXTREME MEASURES TO ENSURE THE COOPERATION OF YOU AND THE REST OF THE CREW.
COMPUTER, EMERGENCY OVERRIDE SIGMA-ALPHA-SEVEN, VOICE IDENTIFICATION SULU, HIKARU, FIRST OFFICER!
REQUEST DENIED.
WHAT HAVE YOU DONE WITH JIM, YOU *MADMAN?*
CAPTAIN KIRK IS ALIVE AND HAS BEEN DETAINED FOR HIS OWN SAFETY.

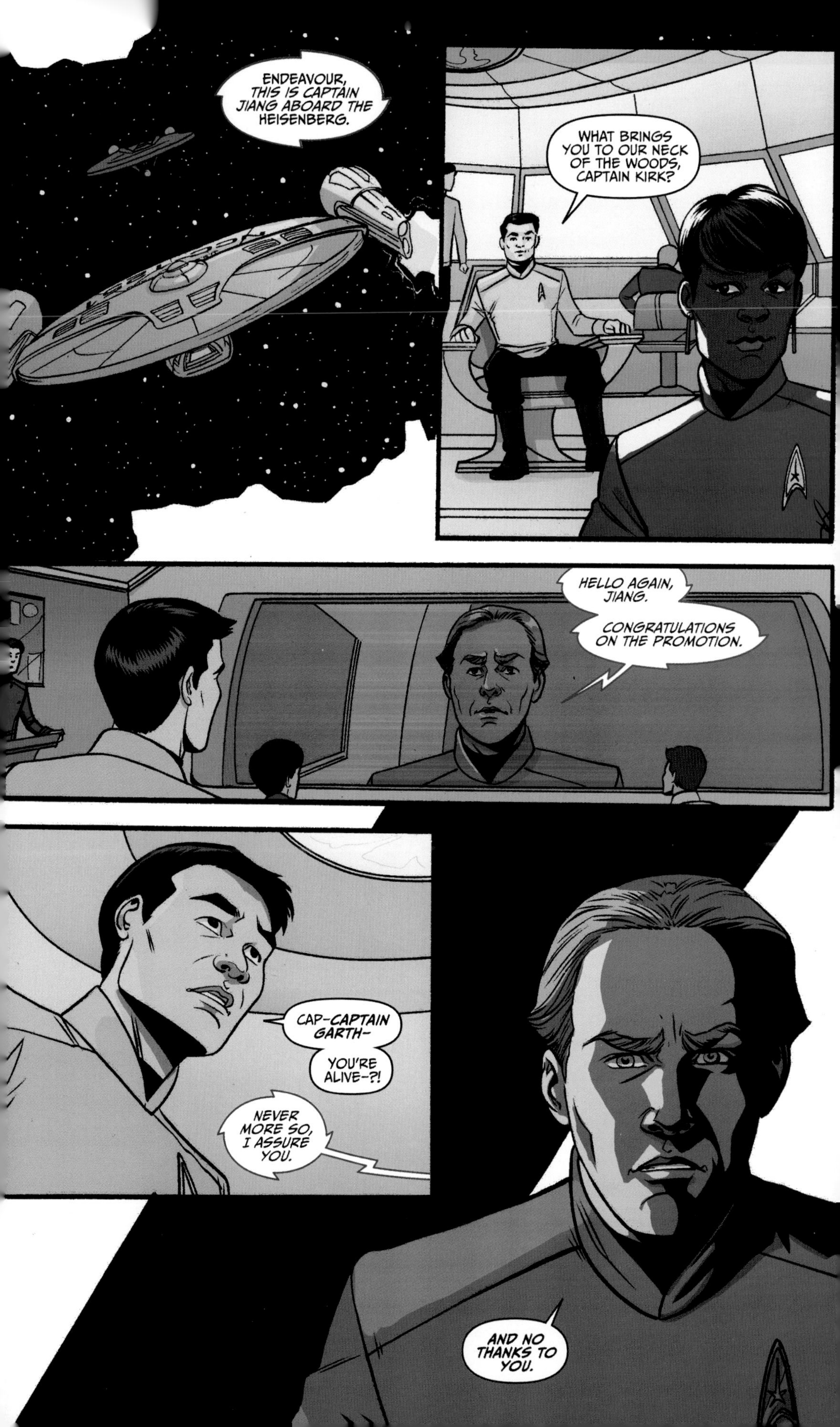
ENDEAVOUR, THIS IS CAPTAIN JIANG ABOARD THE HEISENBERG.
WHAT BRINGS YOU TO OUR NECK OF THE WOODS, CAPTAIN KIRK?
HELLO AGAIN, JIANG.
CONGRATULATIONS ON THE PROMOTION.
CAP-CAPTAIN GARTH-
YOU'RE ALIVE-?!
NEVER MORE SO, I ASSURE YOU.
AND NO THANKS TO YOU.

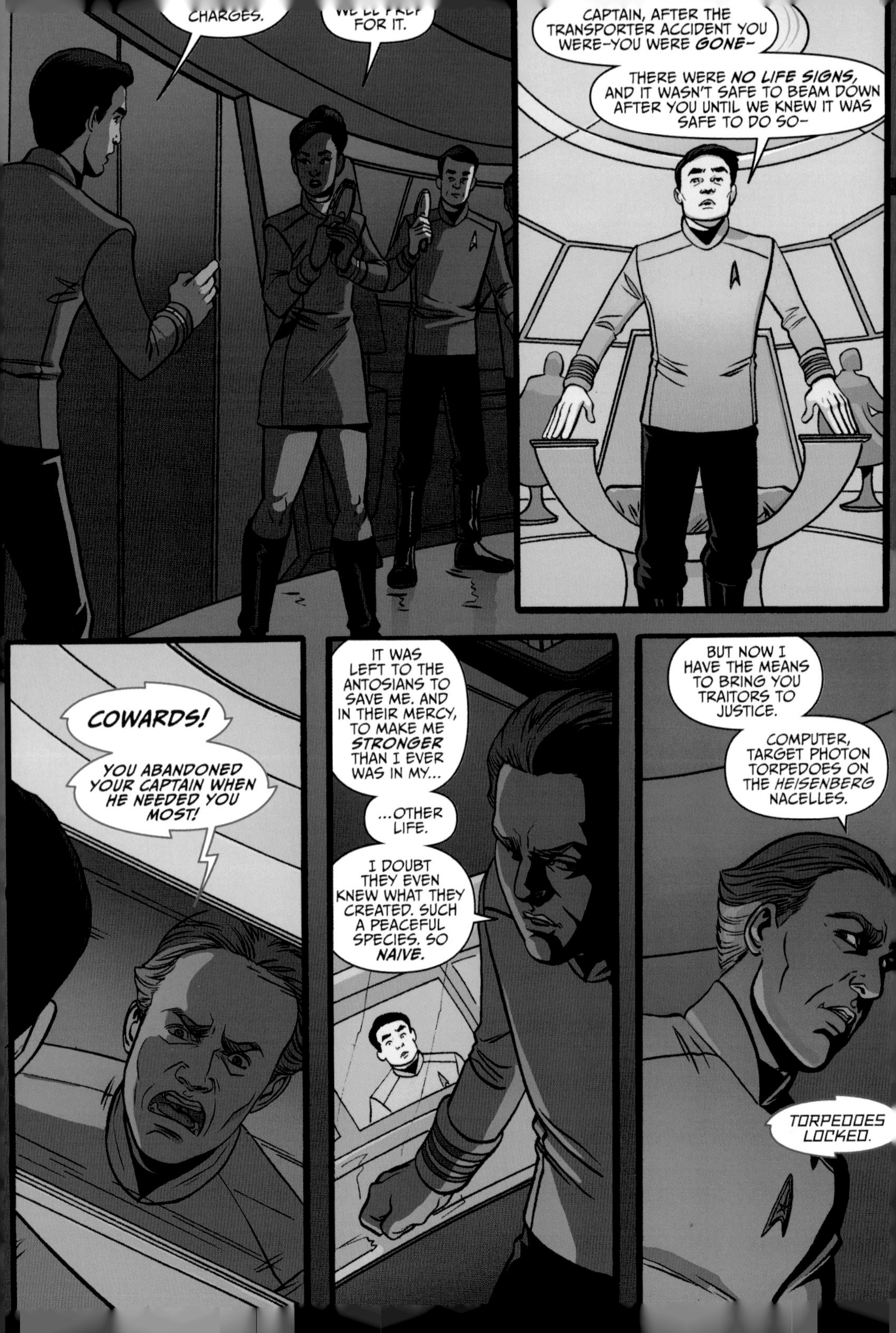
CHARGES.
FOR IT.
CAPTAIN, AFTER THE TRANSPORTER ACCIDENT YOU WERE–YOU WERE *GONE*–
THERE WERE *NO LIFE SIGNS*, AND IT WASN'T SAFE TO BEAM DOWN AFTER YOU UNTIL WE KNEW IT WAS SAFE TO DO SO–
COWARDS!
YOU ABANDONED YOUR CAPTAIN WHEN HE NEEDED YOU MOST!
IT WAS LEFT TO THE ANTOSIANS TO SAVE ME. AND IN THEIR MERCY, TO MAKE ME *STRONGER* THAN I EVER WAS IN MY...
...OTHER LIFE.
I DOUBT THEY EVEN KNEW WHAT THEY CREATED. SUCH A PEACEFUL SPECIES. SO *NAIVE.*
BUT NOW I HAVE THE MEANS TO BRING YOU TRAITORS TO JUSTICE.
COMPUTER, TARGET PHOTON TORPEDOES ON THE *HEISENBERG* NACELLES.
TORPEDOES LOCKED.

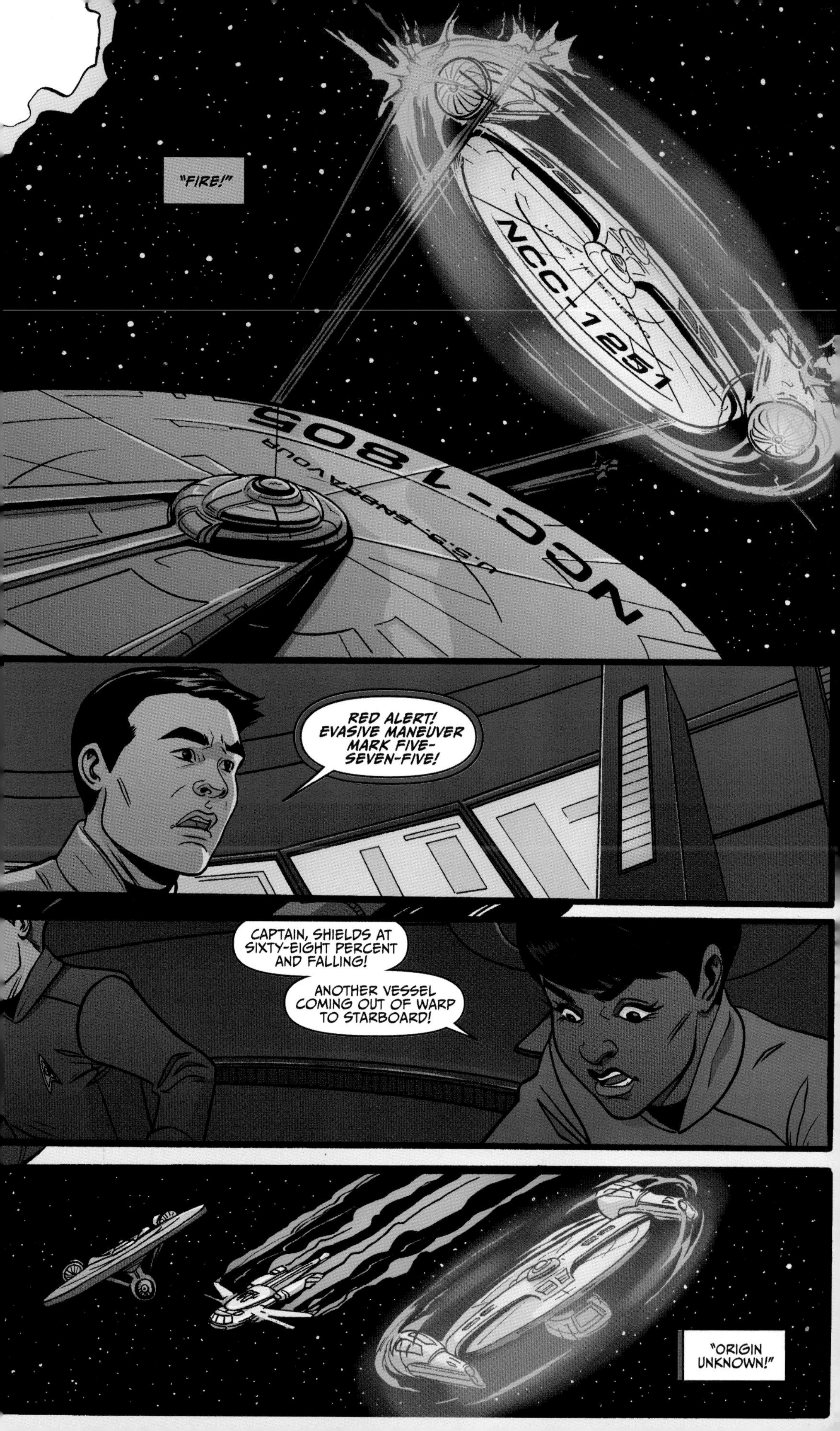
"FIRE!"
NCC-1251
U.S.S. HEISENBERG
NCC-1805
U.S.S. ENDEAVOUR
RED ALERT! EVASIVE MANEUVER MARK FIVE-SEVEN-FIVE!
CAPTAIN, SHIELDS AT SIXTY-EIGHT PERCENT AND FALLING!
ANOTHER VESSEL COMING OUT OF WARP TO STARBOARD!
"ORIGIN UNKNOWN!"

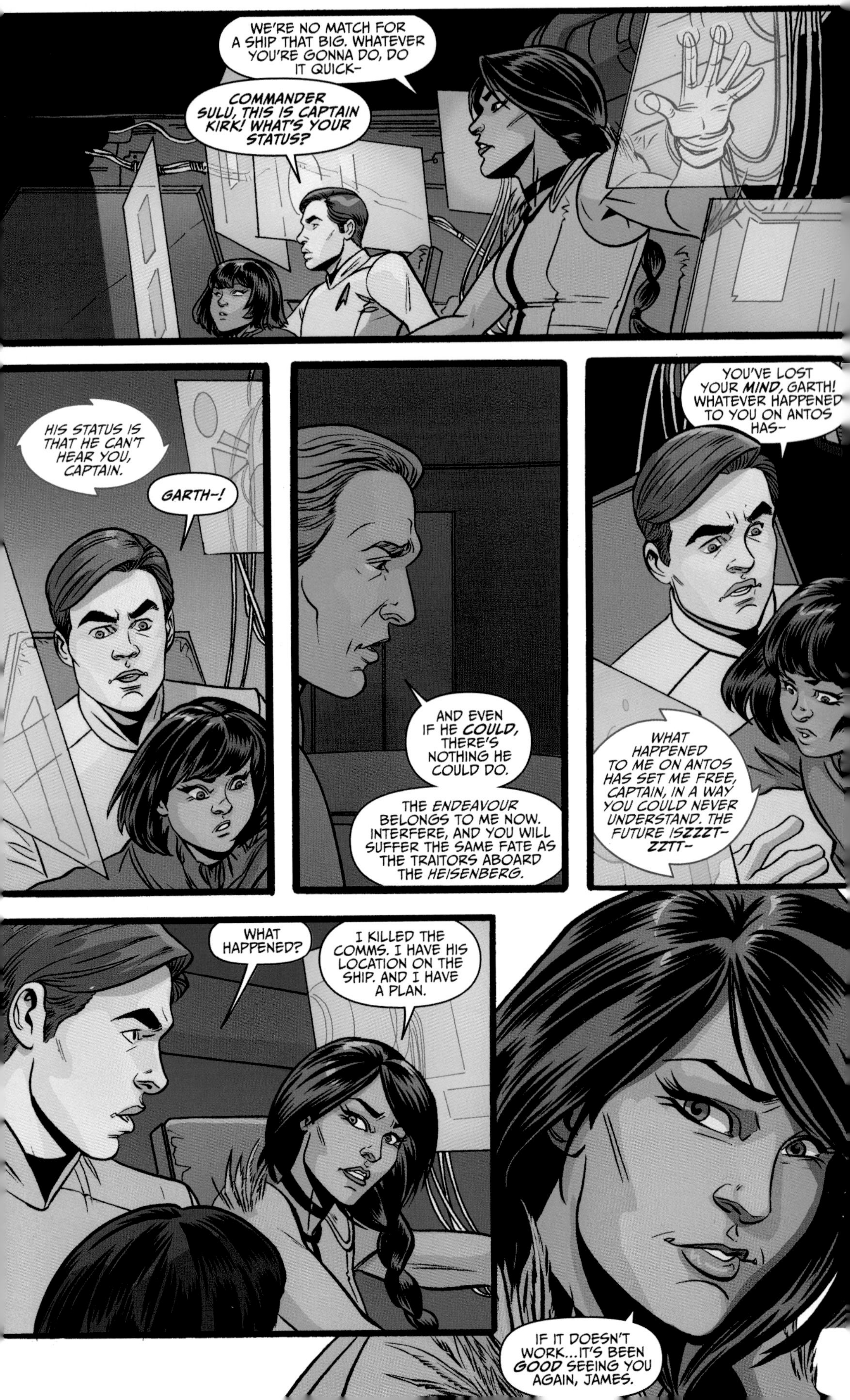

WE'RE NO MATCH FOR A SHIP THAT BIG. WHATEVER YOU'RE GONNA DO, DO IT QUICK-
COMMANDER SULU, THIS IS CAPTAIN KIRK! WHAT'S YOUR STATUS?
HIS STATUS IS THAT HE CAN'T HEAR YOU, CAPTAIN.
GARTH-!
AND EVEN IF HE COULD, THERE'S NOTHING HE COULD DO.
THE ENDEAVOUR BELONGS TO ME NOW. INTERFERE, AND YOU WILL SUFFER THE SAME FATE AS THE TRAITORS ABOARD THE HEISENBERG.
YOU'VE LOST YOUR MIND, GARTH! WHATEVER HAPPENED TO YOU ON ANTOS HAS-
WHAT HAPPENED TO ME ON ANTOS HAS SET ME FREE, CAPTAIN, IN A WAY YOU COULD NEVER UNDERSTAND. THE FUTURE ISZZZT-ZZTT-
WHAT HAPPENED?
I KILLED THE COMMS. I HAVE HIS LOCATION ON THE SHIP. AND I HAVE A PLAN.
IF IT DOESN'T WORK...IT'S BEEN GOOD SEEING YOU AGAIN, JAMES.

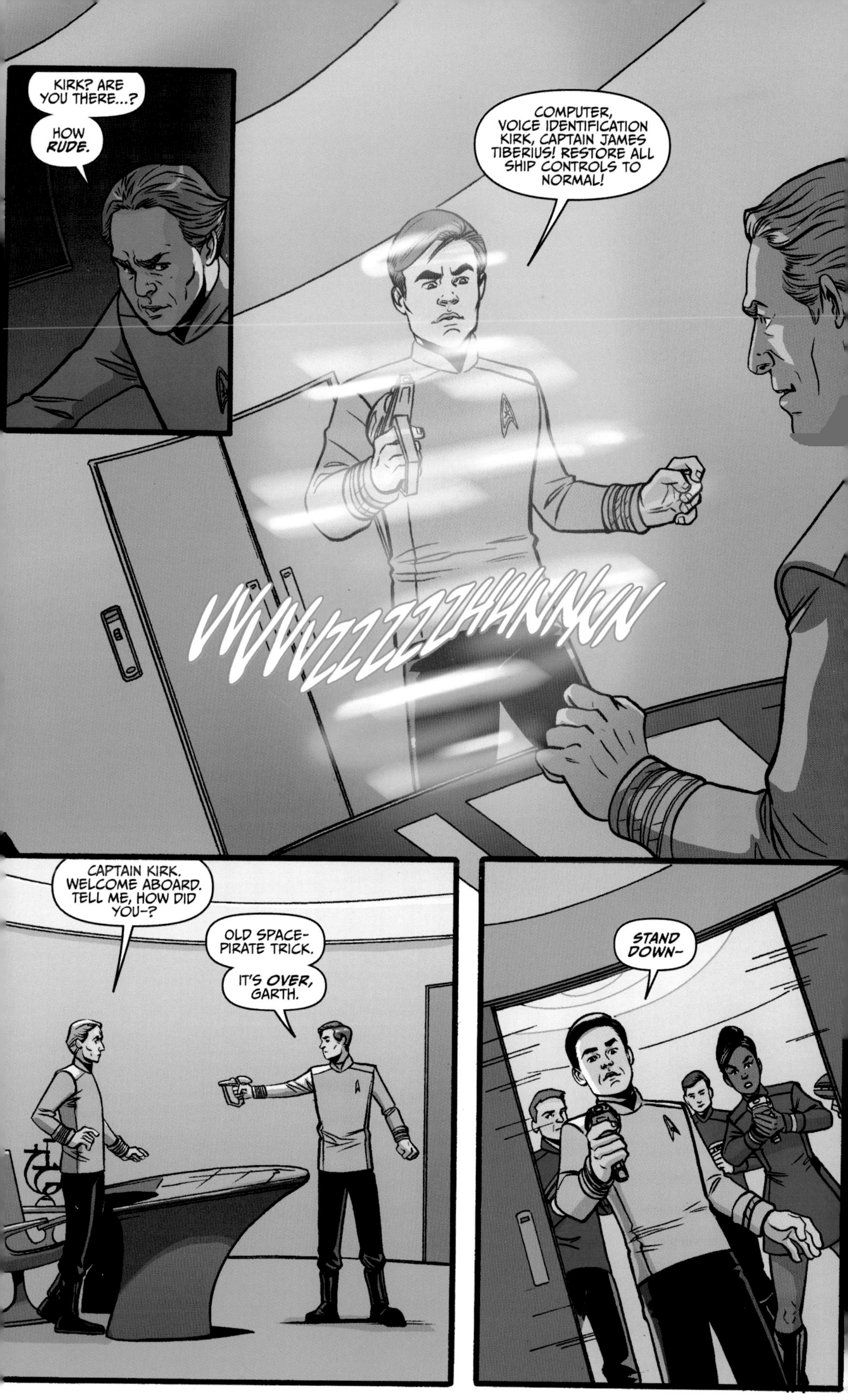
KIRK? ARE YOU THERE...?
HOW RUDE.
COMPUTER, VOICE IDENTIFICATION KIRK, CAPTAIN JAMES TIBERIUS! RESTORE ALL SHIP CONTROLS TO NORMAL!
VVVVVZZZZZZHHNNNN
CAPTAIN KIRK. WELCOME ABOARD. TELL ME, HOW DID YOU-?
OLD SPACE-PIRATE TRICK.
IT'S OVER, GARTH.
STAND DOWN-

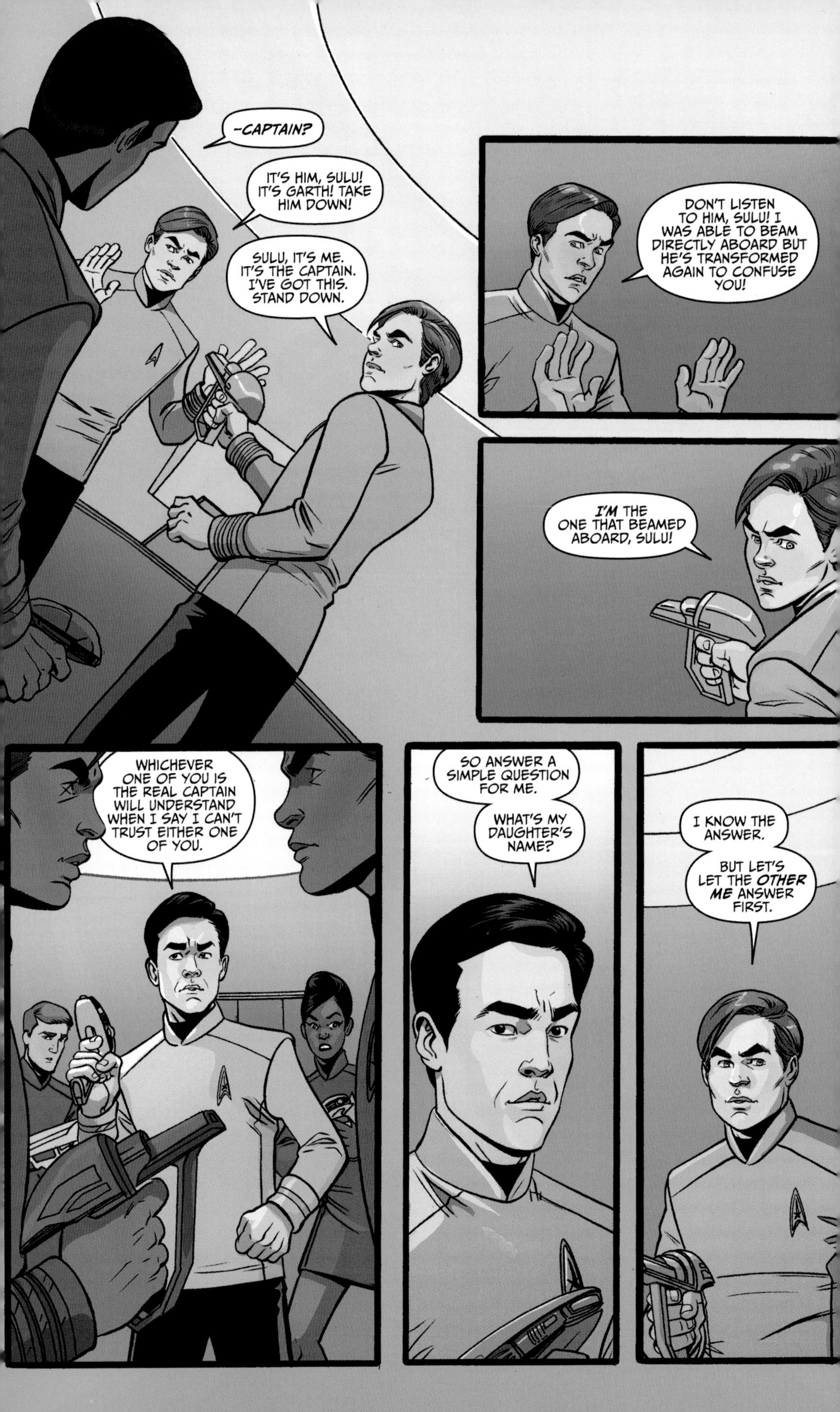
–CAPTAIN?
IT'S HIM, SULU! IT'S GARTH! TAKE HIM DOWN!
SULU, IT'S ME. IT'S THE CAPTAIN. I'VE GOT THIS. STAND DOWN.
DON'T LISTEN TO HIM, SULU! I WAS ABLE TO BEAM DIRECTLY ABOARD BUT HE'S TRANSFORMED AGAIN TO CONFUSE YOU!
I'M THE ONE THAT BEAMED ABOARD, SULU!
WHICHEVER ONE OF YOU IS THE REAL CAPTAIN WILL UNDERSTAND WHEN I SAY I CAN'T TRUST EITHER ONE OF YOU.
SO ANSWER A SIMPLE QUESTION FOR ME.
WHAT'S MY DAUGHTER'S NAME?
I KNOW THE ANSWER.
BUT LET'S LET THE *OTHER ME* ANSWER FIRST.

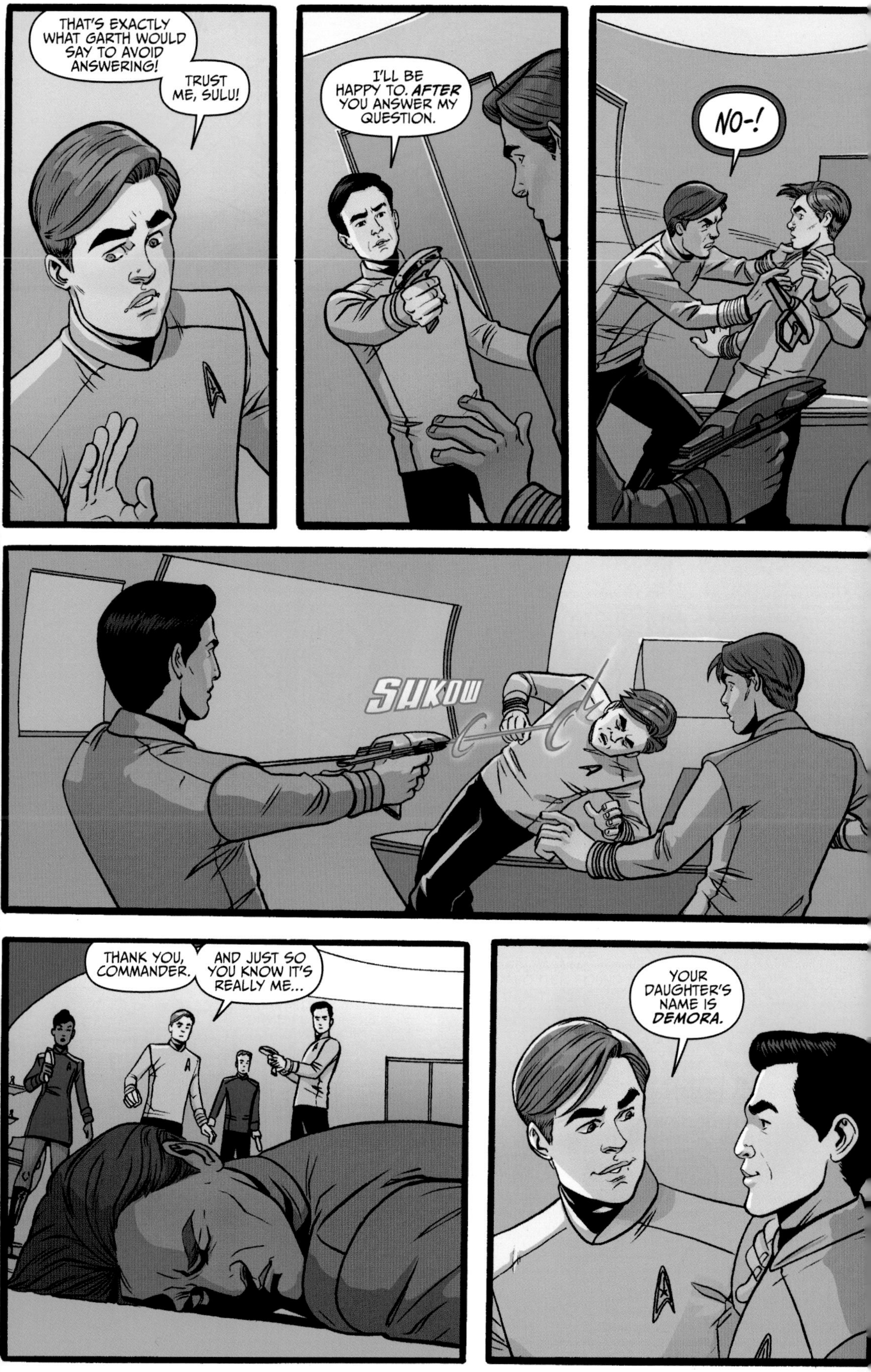
THAT'S EXACTLY WHAT GARTH WOULD SAY TO AVOID ANSWERING!
TRUST ME, SULU!
I'LL BE HAPPY TO. AFTER YOU ANSWER MY QUESTION.
NO-!
SHKOW
THANK YOU, COMMANDER.
AND JUST SO YOU KNOW IT'S REALLY ME...
YOUR DAUGHTER'S NAME IS DEMORA.

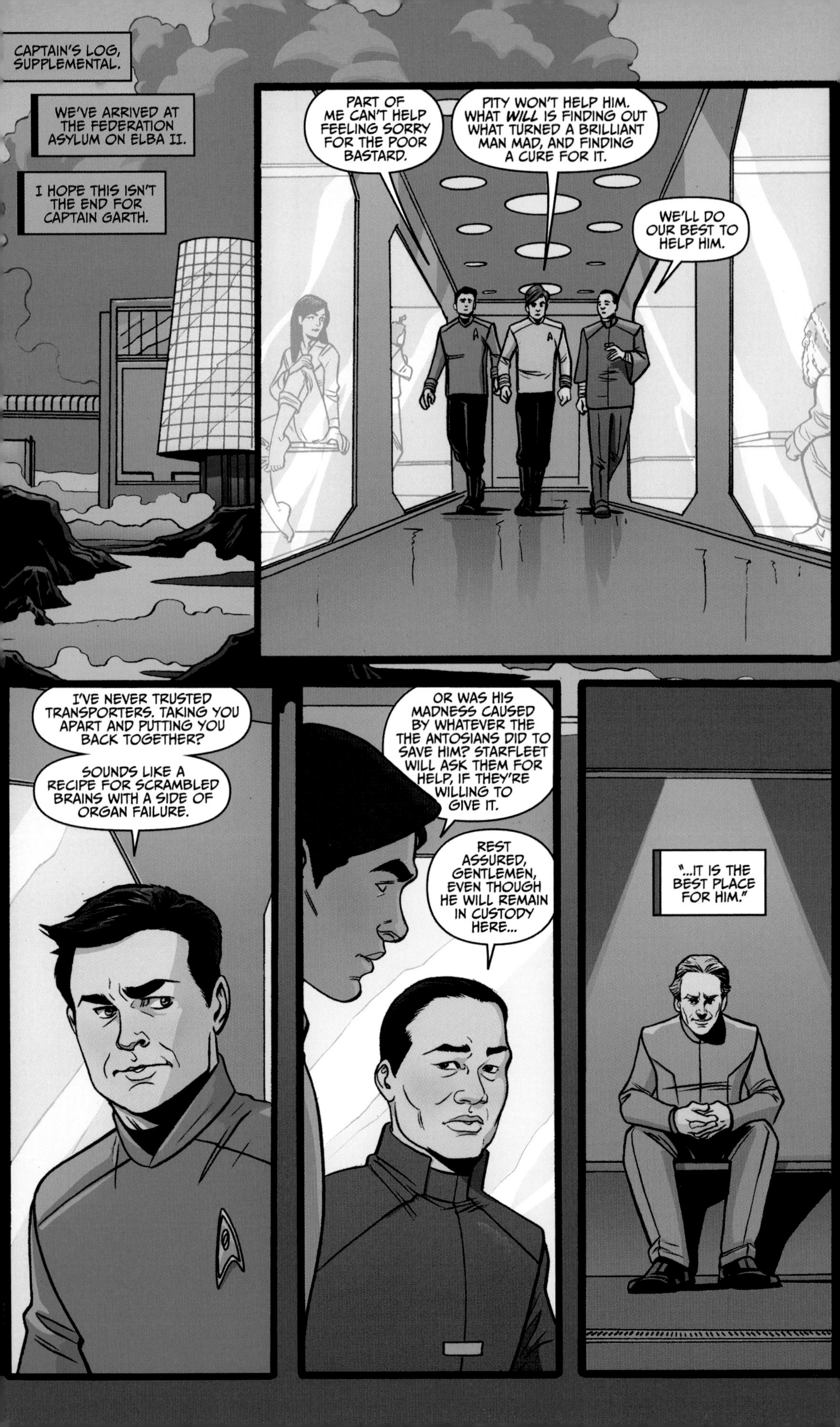
CAPTAIN'S LOG, SUPPLEMENTAL.
WE'VE ARRIVED AT THE FEDERATION ASYLUM ON ELBA II.
I HOPE THIS ISN'T THE END FOR CAPTAIN GARTH.
PART OF ME CAN'T HELP FEELING SORRY FOR THE POOR BASTARD.
PITY WON'T HELP HIM. WHAT *WILL* IS FINDING OUT WHAT TURNED A BRILLIANT MAN MAD, AND FINDING A CURE FOR IT.
WE'LL DO OUR BEST TO HELP HIM.
I'VE NEVER TRUSTED TRANSPORTERS. TAKING YOU APART AND PUTTING YOU BACK TOGETHER?
SOUNDS LIKE A RECIPE FOR SCRAMBLED BRAINS WITH A SIDE OF ORGAN FAILURE.
OR WAS HIS MADNESS CAUSED BY WHATEVER THE THE ANTOSIANS DID TO SAVE HIM? STARFLEET WILL ASK THEM FOR HELP, IF THEY'RE WILLING TO GIVE IT.
REST ASSURED, GENTLEMEN, EVEN THOUGH HE WILL REMAIN IN CUSTODY HERE...
"...IT IS THE BEST PLACE FOR HIM."

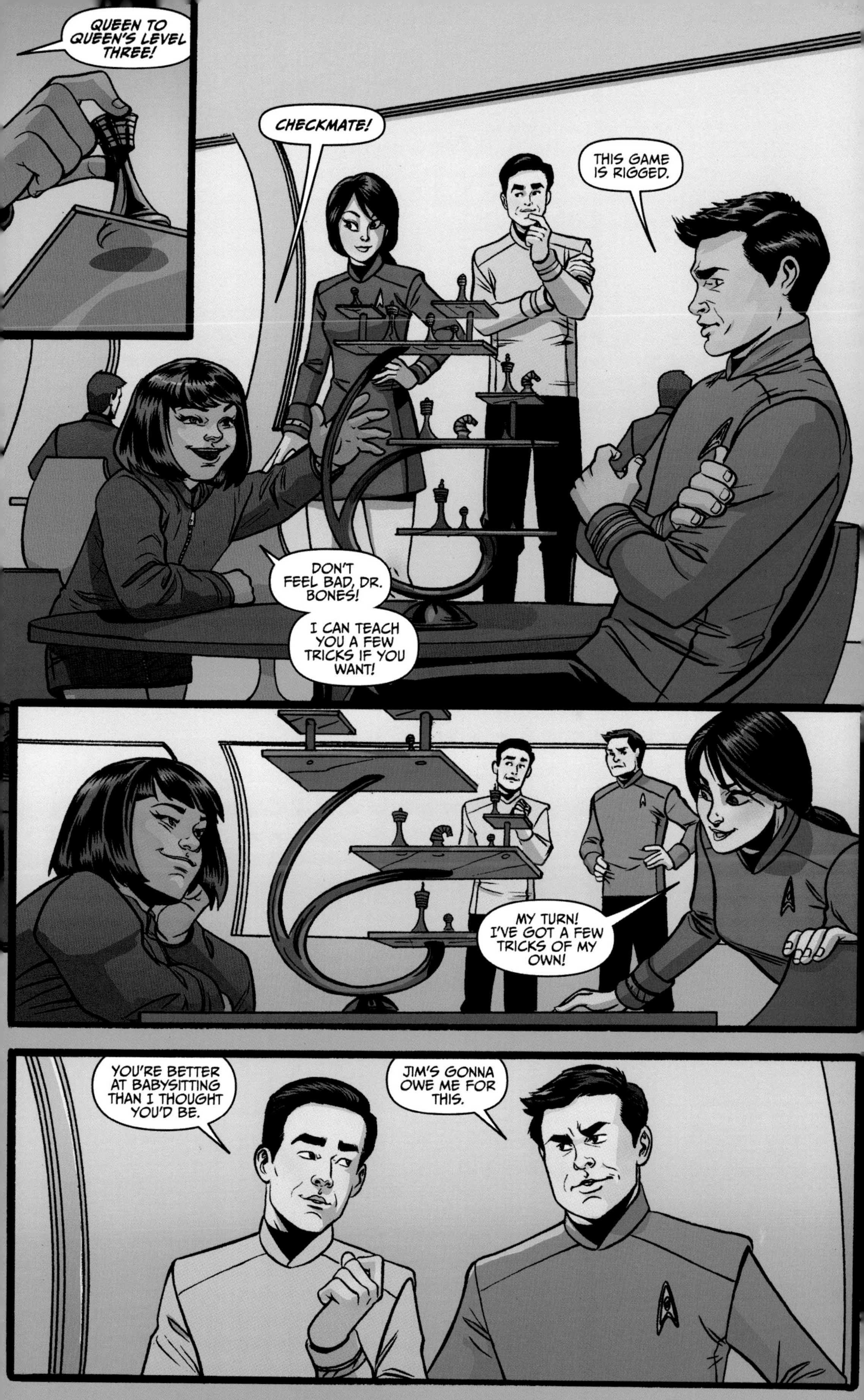
QUEEN TO QUEEN'S LEVEL THREE!
CHECKMATE!
THIS GAME IS RIGGED.
DON'T FEEL BAD, DR. BONES!
I CAN TEACH YOU A FEW TRICKS IF YOU WANT!
MY TURN! I'VE GOT A FEW TRICKS OF MY OWN!
YOU'RE BETTER AT BABYSITTING THAN I THOUGHT YOU'D BE.
JIM'S GONNA OWE ME FOR THIS.

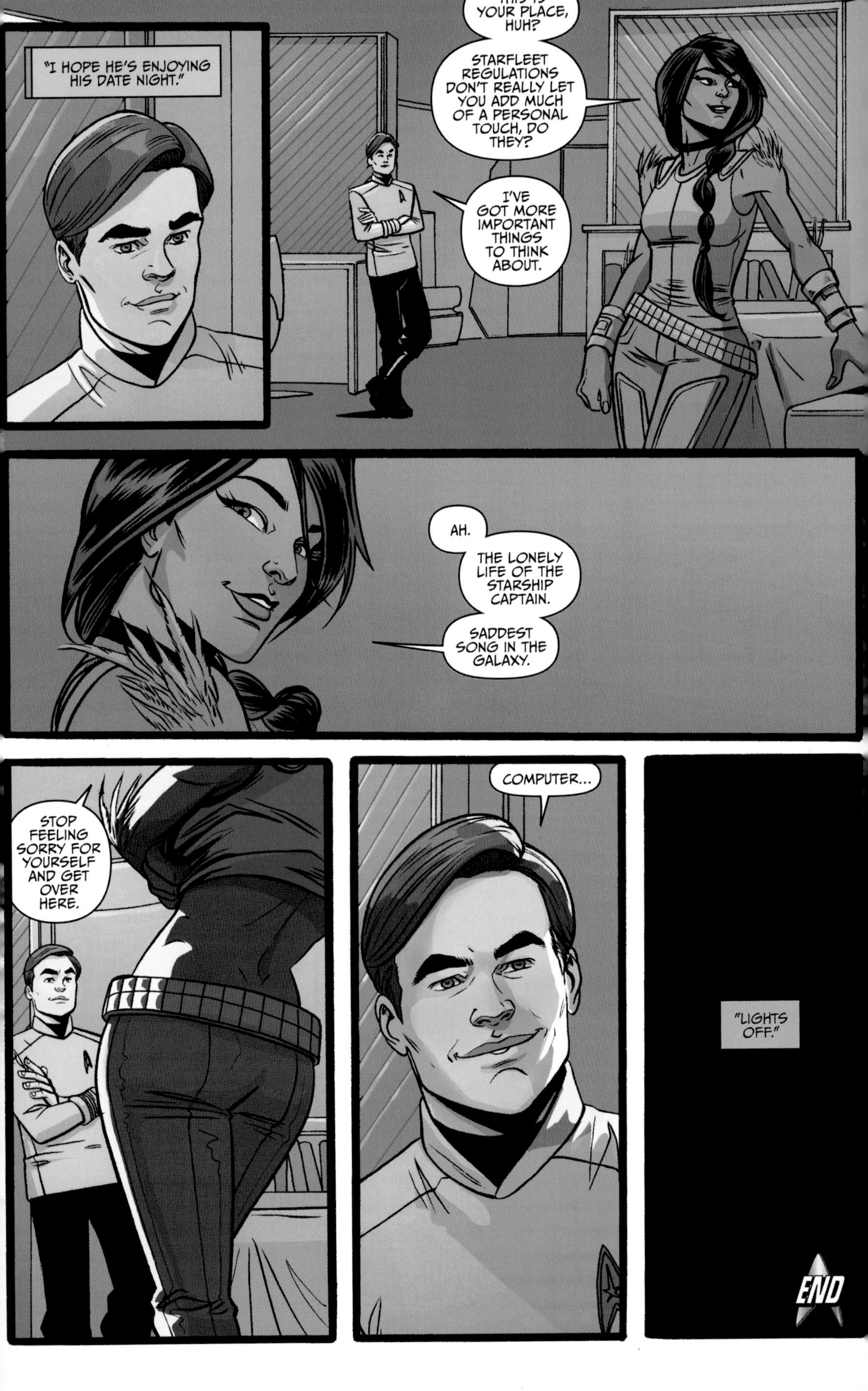
"I HOPE HE'S ENJOYING HIS DATE NIGHT."
THIS IS YOUR PLACE, HUH?
STARFLEET REGULATIONS DON'T REALLY LET YOU ADD MUCH OF A PERSONAL TOUCH, DO THEY?
I'VE GOT MORE IMPORTANT THINGS TO THINK ABOUT.
AH.
THE LONELY LIFE OF THE STARSHIP CAPTAIN.
SADDEST SONG IN THE GALAXY.
STOP FEELING SORRY FOR YOURSELF AND GET OVER HERE.
COMPUTER...
"LIGHTS OFF."
END

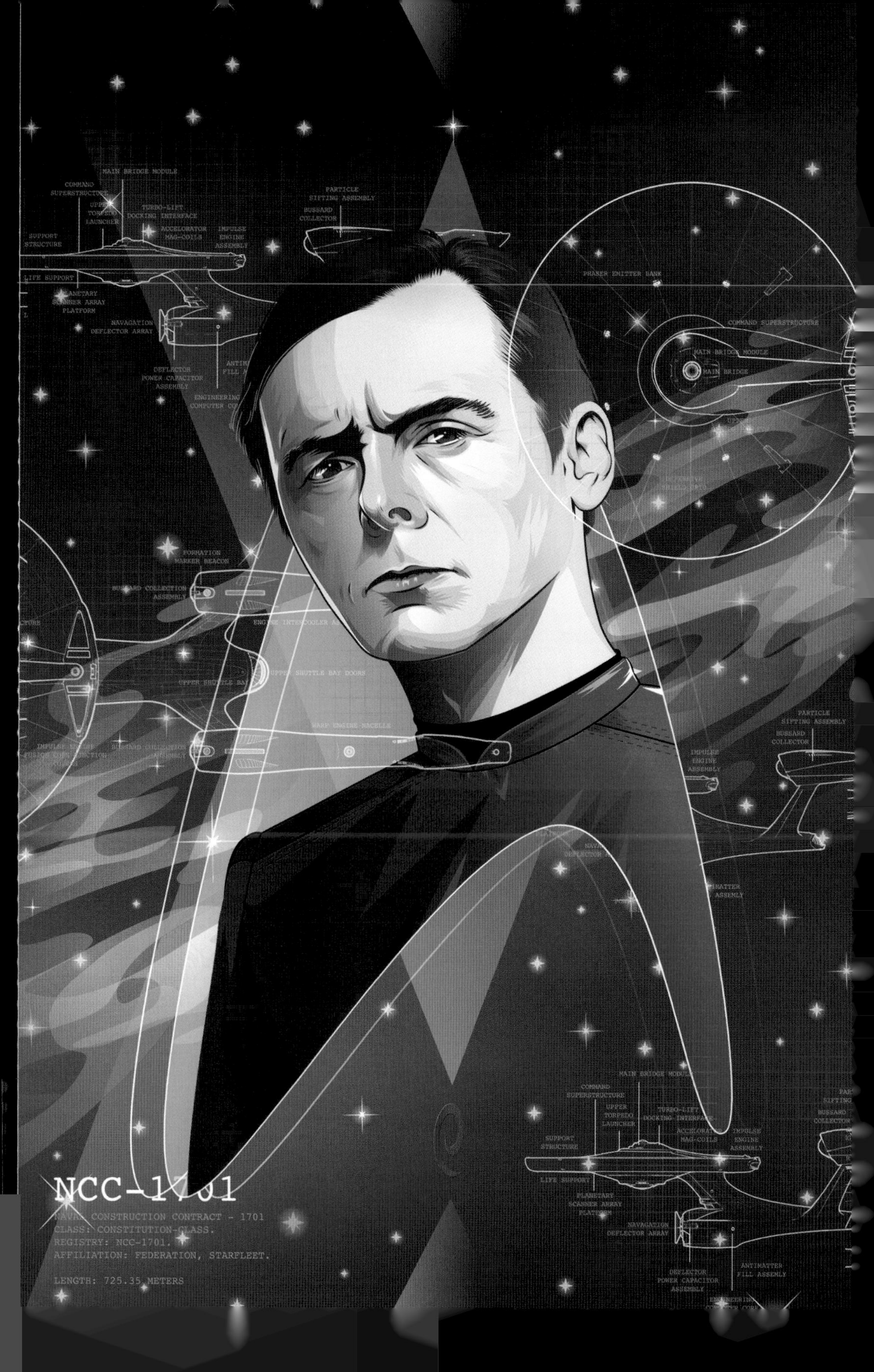
NCC-1701
NAVAL CONSTRUCTION CONTRACT - 1701
CLASS: CONSTITUTION-CLASS.
REGISTRY: NCC-1701.
AFFILIATION: FEDERATION, STARFLEET.
LENGTH: 725.35 METERS

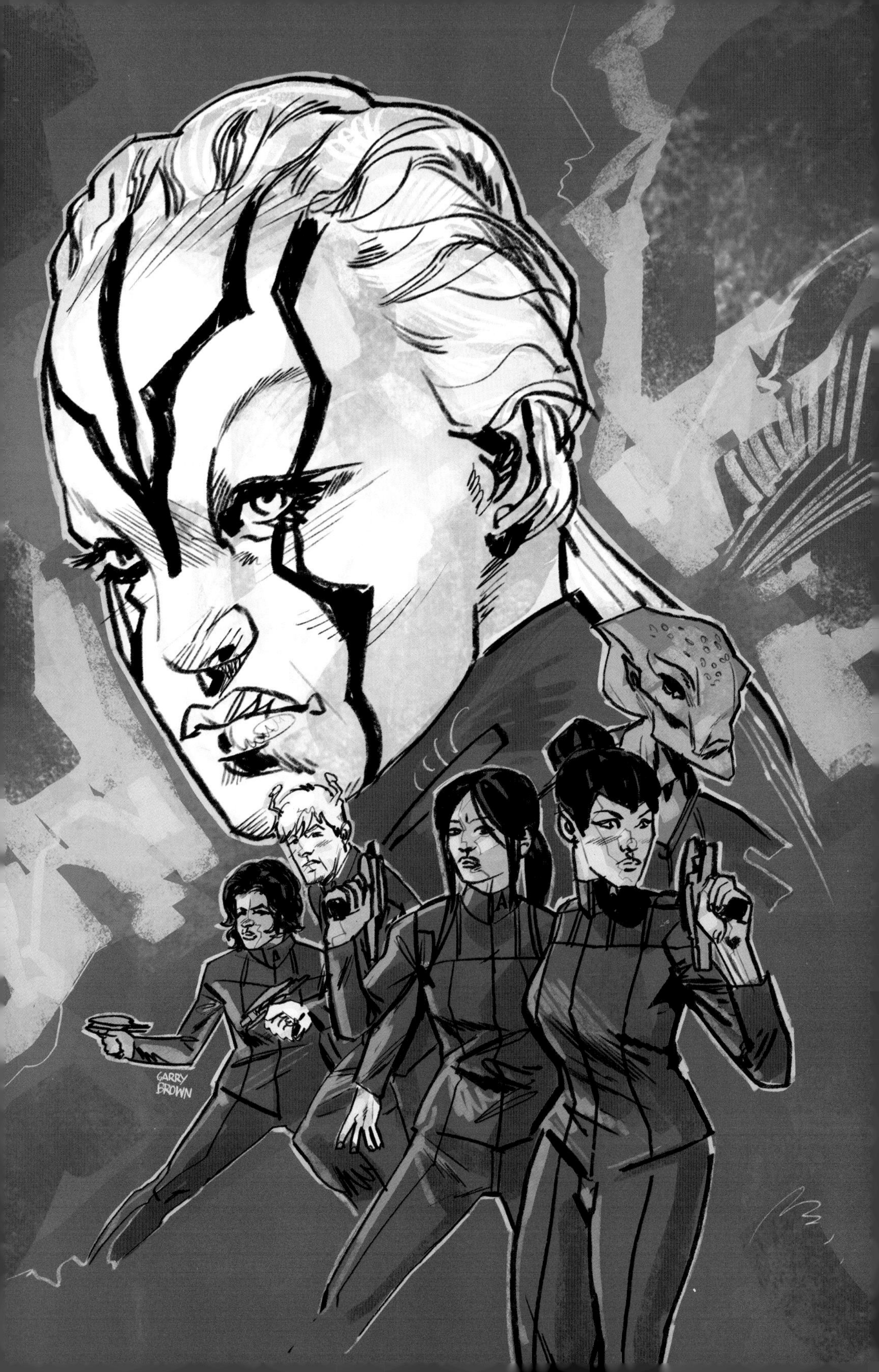
GARRY BROWN

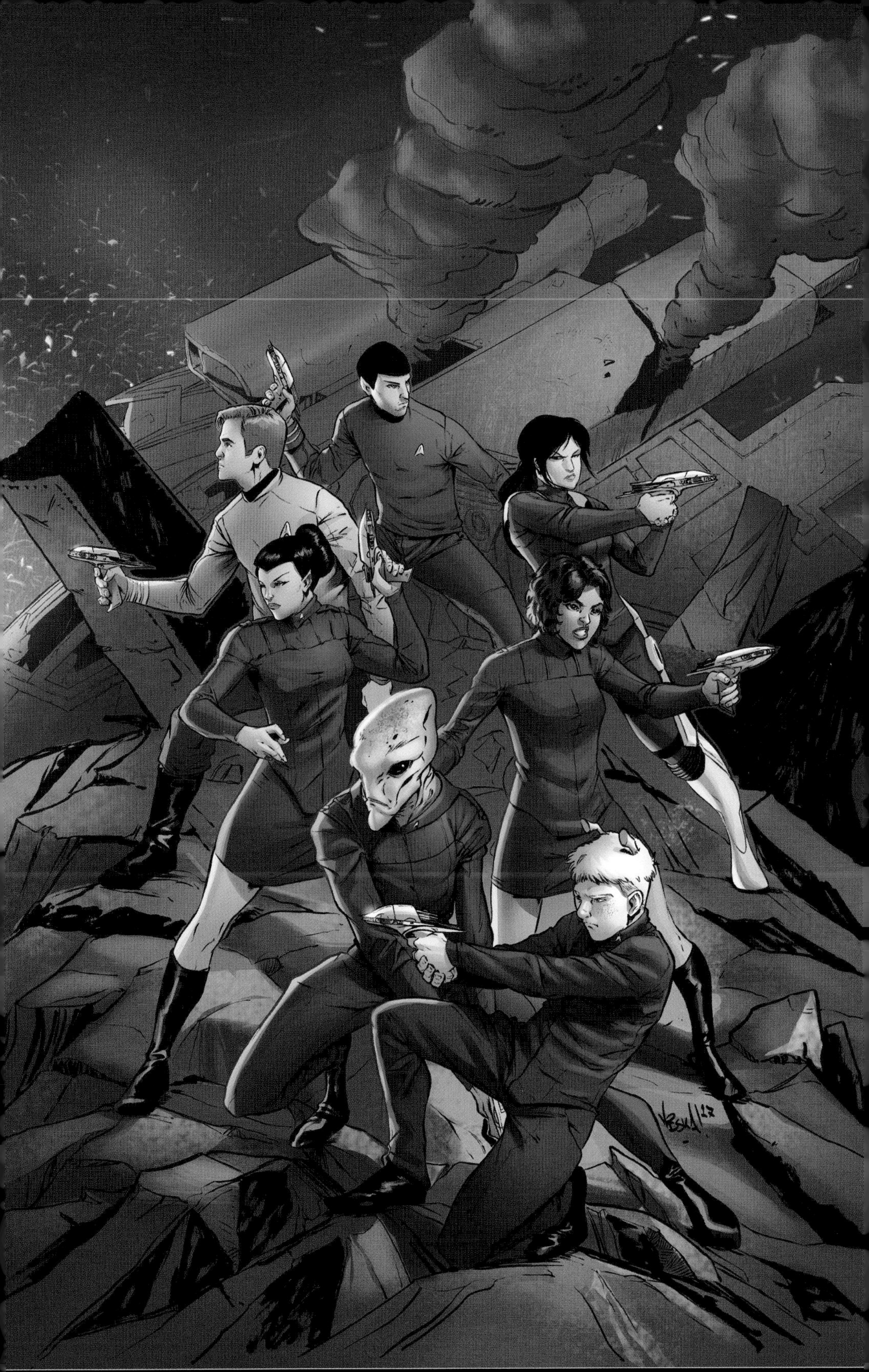

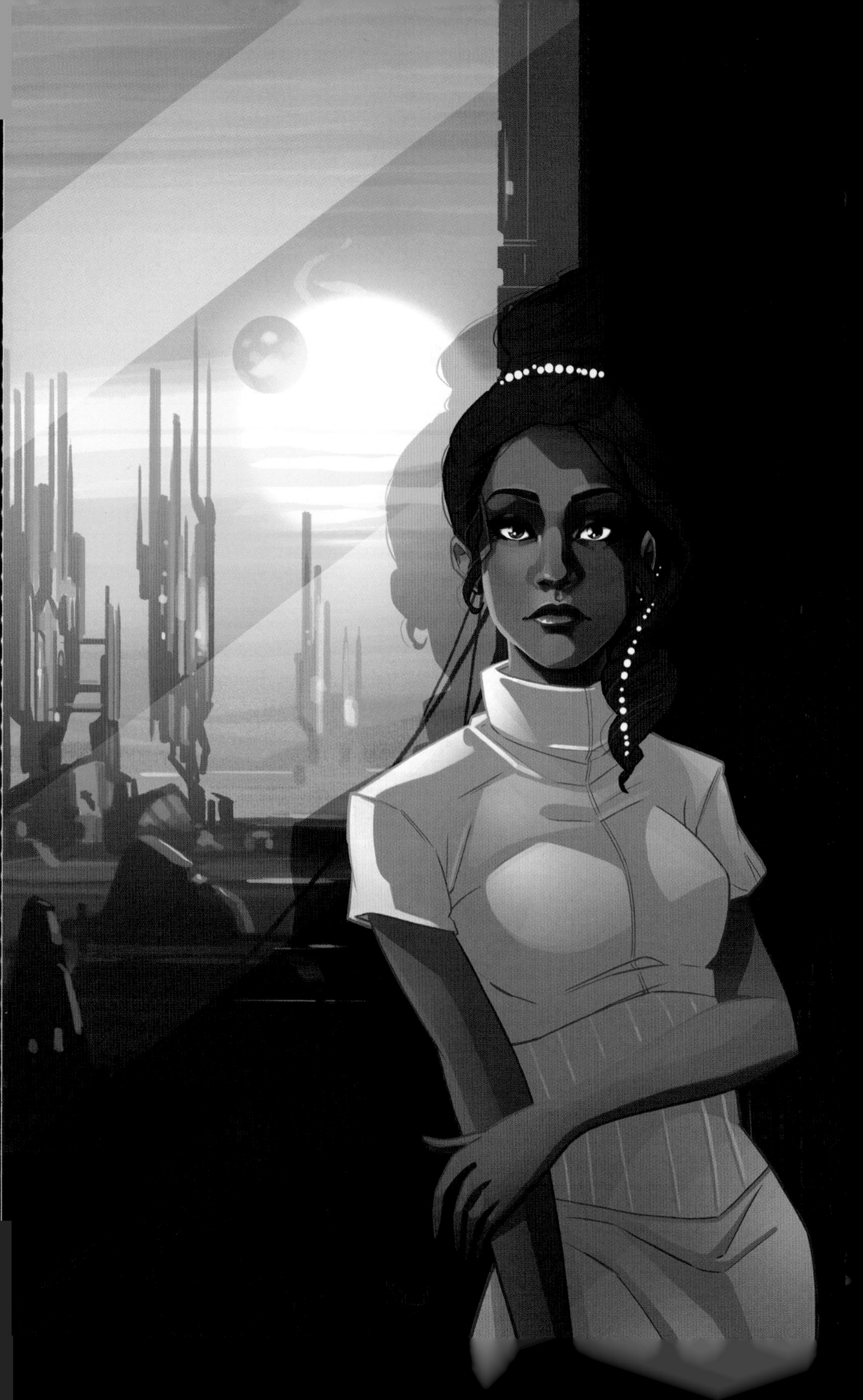

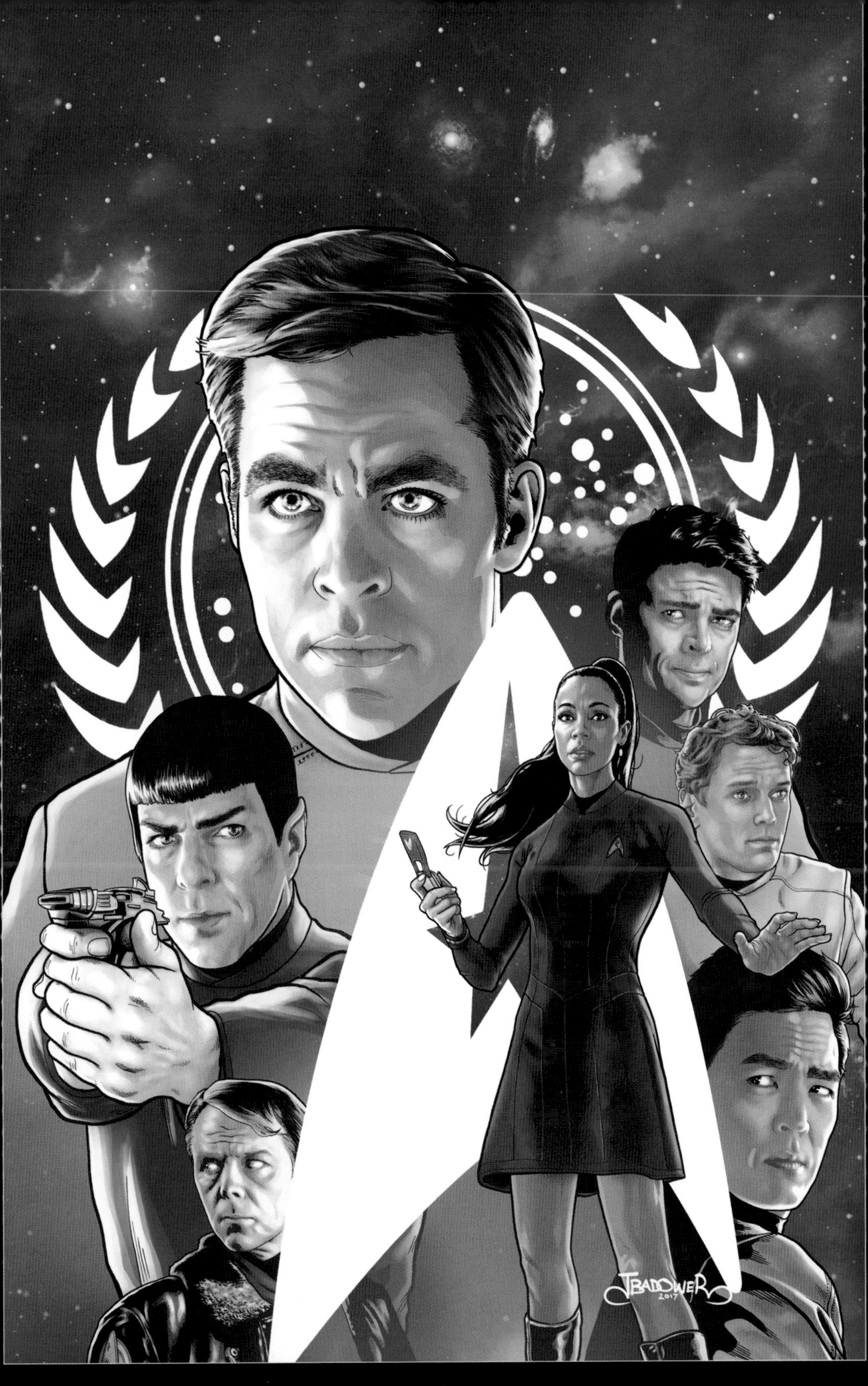
JBADOWER
2017

art by
Jason Badower

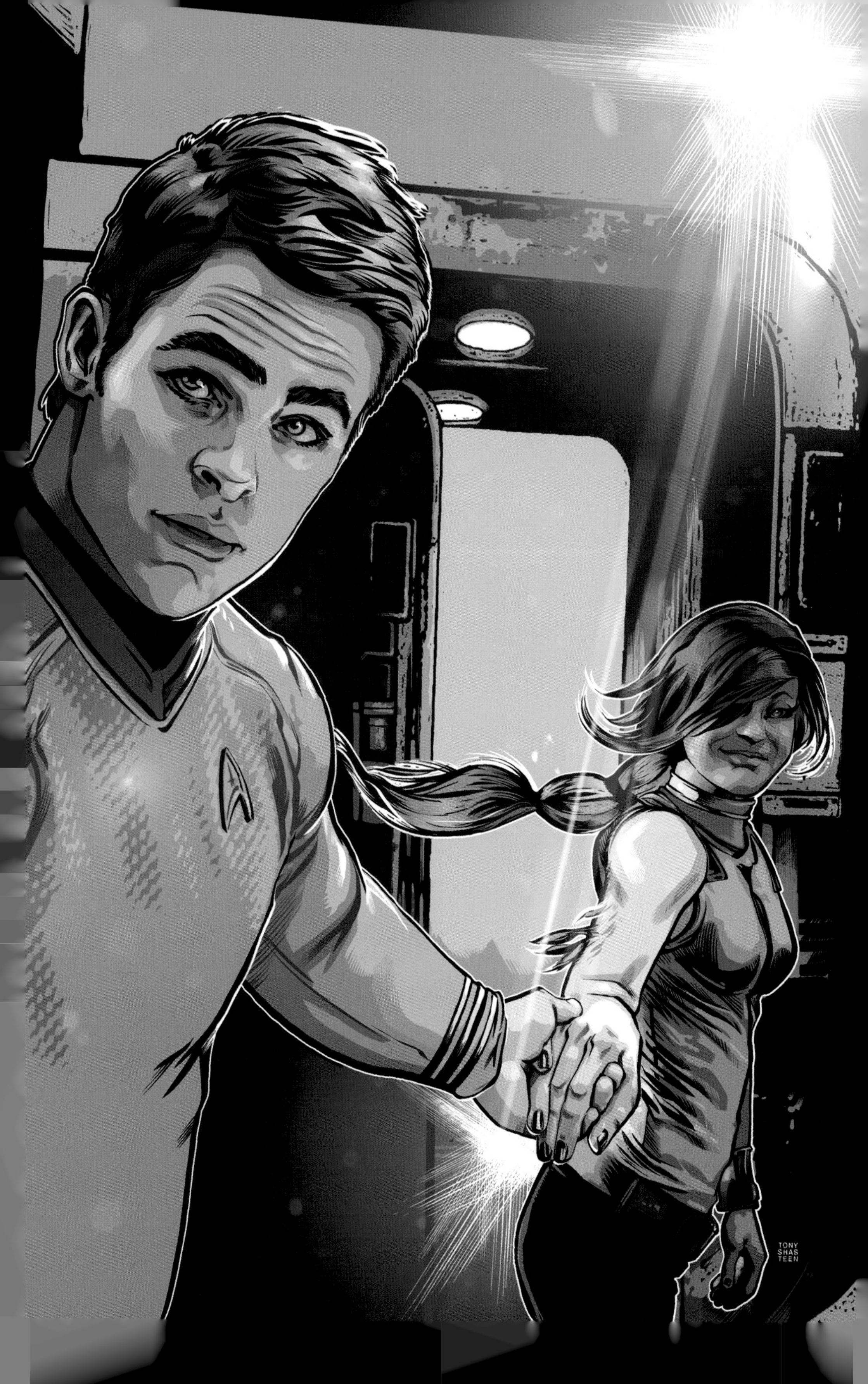
TONY
SHAS
TEEN

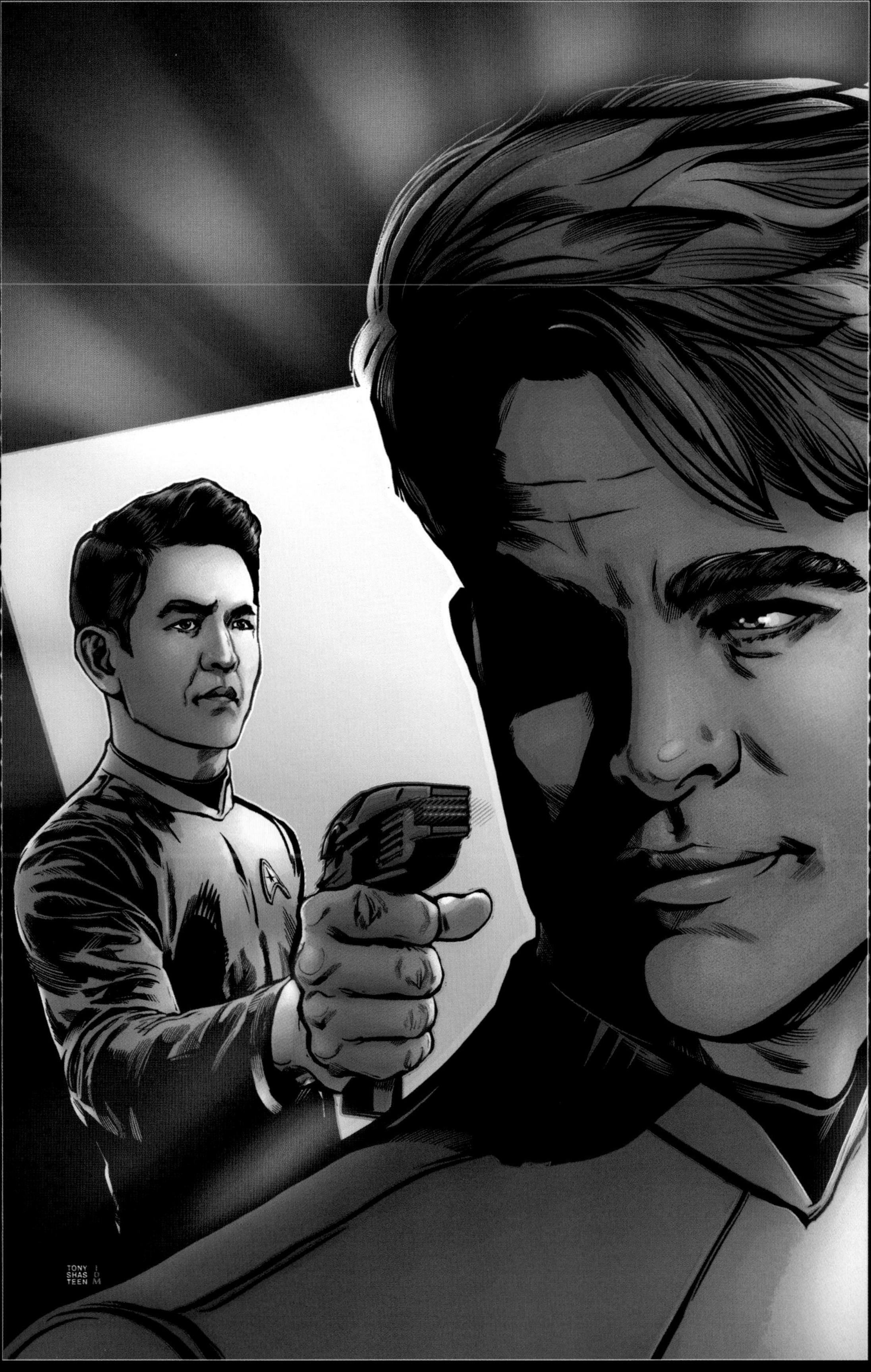
TONY SHASTEEN JDM

art by
Tony Shasteen

colors by
J.D. Mettler

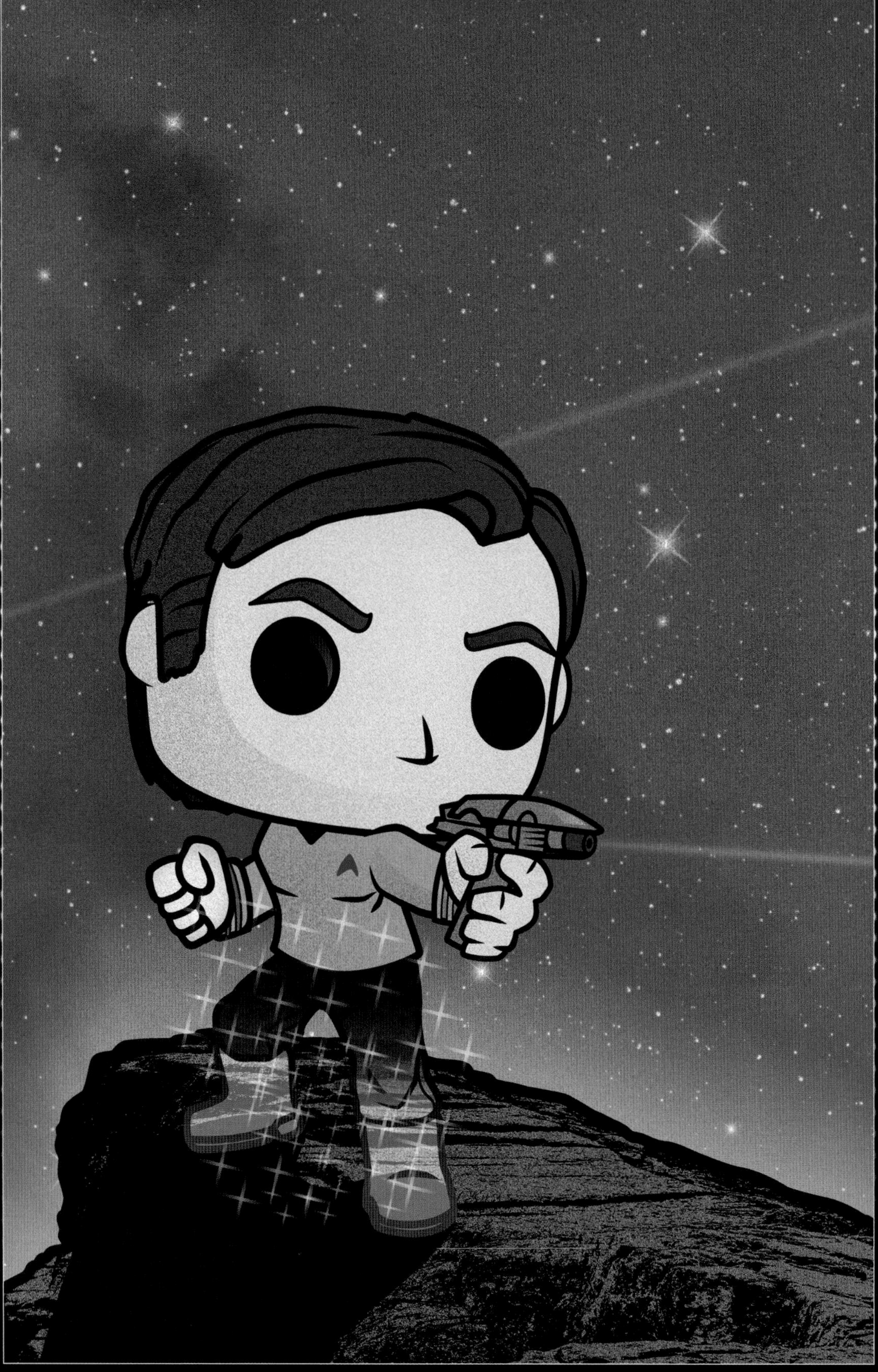

art by
Tim Gilardi

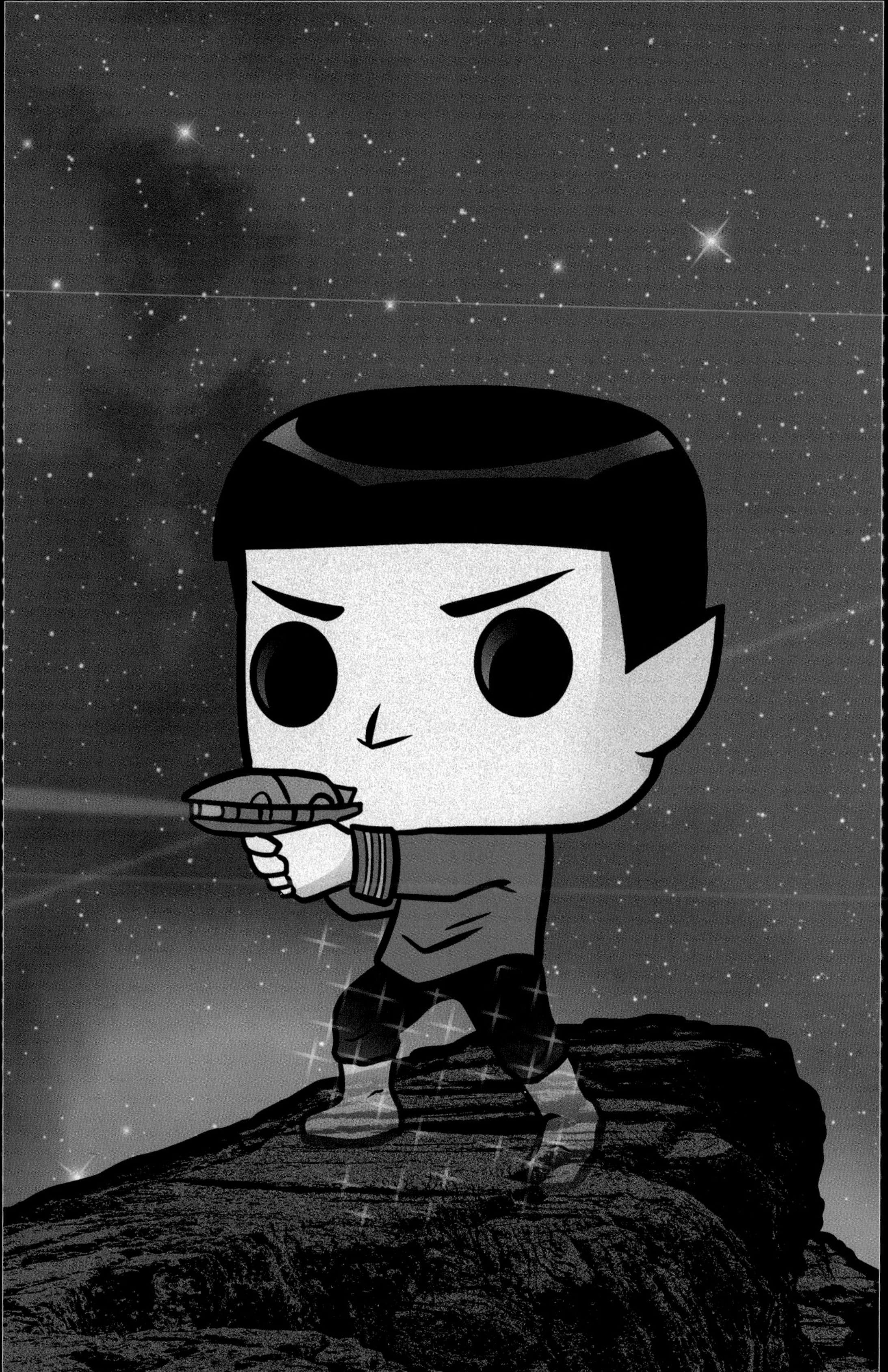

art by
Derek Charm

based on a design by
Tim Gilardi

STAR TREK

BOLDLY GO